IN A
HIGH
AND
LONELY
PLACE

IN A
HIGH
AND
LONELY
PLACE

STEVEN VOIEN

HarperCollins*Publishers*

For Lydia

Translation of Tibetan texts from *Four Lamas of Dolpo* by David Snellgrove reprinted by permission of the publisher, Cambridge, Mass.: Harvard University Press, Copyright © 1967 by David Snellgrove.

This novel was written before the author took employment with the Foreign Service.

HarperCollins books may be purchased for educational, business, or sales promotional use. For information, please call or write: Special Markets Department, HarperCollins Publishers, Inc., 10 East 53rd Street, New York, NY 10022. Telephone: (212) 207-7528; Fax (212) 207-7222.

FIRST EDITION

Designed by Cassandra J. Pappas

Library of Congress Cataloging-in-Publication Data

Voien, Steven.
In a high and lonely place/Steven Voien.
     p. cm.
      ISBN 0-06-016506-5
      I. Title.
PS3572.O327I15   1992
813'.54—dc20   91-50482

92 93 94 95 96 MAC/HC 10 9 8 7 6 5 4 3 2 1

Author's Note

Anyone familiar with the literature of the Himalayas will recognize the debt this novel owes to accounts by David Snellgrove, George Schaller, and Peter Matthiessen. The works of Corneille Jest, Guisseppi Tucci, Richard Avedon, Sakya Karna, Christopher von Furer-Haimendorf, Lynn Bennett, Fosco Maraini and Joel Ziskin also deserve mention. On a more personal note, M. Scott went the distance, Joel offered invaluable encouragement, and Lydia persevered through draft after draft.

Since this book was conceived, Rod Jackson and Darla Hillard performed a landmark field study of snow leopards in Nepal; their findings greatly increased knowledge of these elusive animals.

When any violence to the truth has been done (such as having Tibetans nod when they mean yes, rather than shaking their heads), the fault is entirely mine. For the specific liberties I have taken with animal behavior, my apologies to those in the field, for whom I have so much admiration.

This book was written before I took employment with the Foreign Service. All of the characters in this book, as well as the Lhakrinor region itself, are fictional.

High are the mountains
Shiva lives in them
This is my homeland
It is more beautiful than heaven

BHOTIYA SONG

In the place where a god lives
Lives also a demon

DOLPO PROVERB

PART 1

The *sadhu* sat straight and still, his back to the enormous banyan tree which bordered the field. Pale dust from the pre-monsoon plains covered his dark skin. Beside him lay an iron trident, symbol of his asceticism, and a little tin pot with a wire handle—his begging bowl—filled with uncooked rice. Black hair cascaded in dreadlocks over his forehead and his shoulders; a loincloth covered his narrow hips.

It was the eyes, however, that made you stop and look twice; otherworldly and staring, they seemed to study and see through you at the same moment. The eyes of a cat, Trowbridge thought. Not a holy man.

He shifted his gaze past the *sadhu* to the low stone wall, covered with thorns and red blossoms, which marked the limit of the stubbled field where they had set up temporary camp. On the other side of the wall a narrow road built by the Chinese led toward town; beyond the road a range of green hills terraced up quickly, disappearing into a low ceiling of swirling, charcoal gray clouds.

If it weren't monsoon season I'd be looking at mountains, he thought.

And if it weren't for the fact that seven different mountaineering expeditions had outfitted in Pokhara during the last two months, I wouldn't be having such a difficult time finding porters.

He watched a colorful bus, miniature at this distance, trundle down the road toward Pokhara, then turned his attention back to the argument which had been raging for well over an hour. Boxes of gear, which ought by now to have been divided into neat individual loads, lay spread in an uneven jumble around them. Dorje, the boyish Sherpa he had hired in Kathmandu to be *sirdar* for the expedition, was doing his cheerful best to negotiate reasonable rates with the dregs of the local porter population.

"Ho, Dorje," he said quietly. Dorje willingly broke off a face-to-face confrontation with a Gurung from the eastern hills, self-appointed spokesman for four of his fellow tribesmen. The Gurung had a badly infected eye; his other eye darted back and forth in an evasive and calculating fashion. Trowbridge's instincts told him that the Gurung was trouble. At the moment, however, they needed him. Aside from him and his group there were only a pair of silent Tamangs and a morose-looking Limbu, notable chiefly for his enormous ears, and for the fact that he, like most Limbus, rarely took his hand off the hilt of his curved *kukri*—the deadly chopping sword of Nepal.

"My goodness," Dorje said in English, touching his hand to his stomach. "I have troubles arguing against a man with an ugly eye like that one."

"How are we doing?"

Dorje's expression was patient, but worried. "I do not know if they really want to work. They have this objection, and that objection. Most recently, they say the monsoon is early, and that they do not like to walk in the rain."

"Tell them we'll be walking west and north. We can walk ahead of the monsoon."

If, he reminded himself, we leave tomorrow. And we can't leave tomorrow unless the permit is finally ready.

"I have explained about walking ahead of the monsoon," Dorje said. "They say that they will have to walk home in the rain."

"Without loads, that's perfectly feasible."

Dorje nodded agreement.

"How much are they asking?"

"Mountain-climbing rates."

"For the entire trip?"

Dorje nodded again, regretfully this time.

Trowbridge shook his head. "That's impossible. You've told them this is standard low-altitude porterage?"

"Many times. And I have told them you are a scholar, not a mountain-climbing man—that you do not have the money of a mountain-climbing expedition."

"Do they believe you?"

"I think so. They have looked over the gear."

Trowbridge glanced over at Jeet, the other Sherpa he had hired in Kathmandu. Jeet was huge for a Sherpa, almost as tall as Trowbridge, and impressively sturdy. One side of his face was marked by a deep scar, a pale double ridge which ran from his cheekbone nearly to his mouth and lent a somewhat intimidating air to an otherwise gentle face. Jeet stood with his arms crossed and his eyes alert, keeping an eye on the assortment of boxes and baskets.

For a moment Trowbridge wished he had hired more Sherpas in Kathmandu. They needed nine strong and reliable backs to carry this food and gear from hot and sultry Pokhara—barely two thousand feet above sea level, surrounded by green plains, low, jungly hills, and water buffalo drawing plows through terraced rice fields—on up through the Himalayan midlands and over the high passes to their destination: the remote, mountain-protected valleys of the Lhakrinor region.

Sherpas, however—justly famous for being self-sufficient, honest, and tough—commanded premium wages. A mountain tribe of Tibetan stock, they had migrated, three hundred years ago, south over the Himalayas, and now inhabited the steep slopes of Everest. Sherpas had been the original porters on the high-altitude mountain assaults; Tenzing Norgay, the most famous Sherpa, had reached the top of Everest with Hillary. These intelligent tribesmen, and tribeswomen as well, still worked the mountaineering expeditions, but more of them worked as *sirdars*—or foremen—for trekking expeditions.

"What about the other three? The two Tamangs and the Limbu."

"I think they want to work. But they will let the Gurungs bargain a long time if it means more money."

We don't have a long time, he thought, looking up at the wet, heavy sky.

He stepped forward to where the Gurung spokesman was covetously examining a *doka* filled with supplies.

"Ho, Uncle," he said quietly, speaking in Nepali. The Gurung turned and looked at him in astonishment.

"Here is the arrangement. Because of the monsoon, I will pay one and a half times normal wages. Three days' wages in advance. If this is acceptable, we leave tomorrow morning. If it is not, then *namaste*, and good luck to you. I have told my *sirdar* not to negotiate any more."

Out of the corner of his eye he saw a dour smile cross the face of the Limbu.

The leader of the Gurungs recovered from his astonishment at hearing reasonably good Nepali come out of the mouth of a Westerner, and studied him with an openly suspicious squint. Then he turned abruptly and began speaking rapid-fire Gurung at his fellow tribesmen.

"That was very good work, Trowbridge *sahib*!" Dorje said happily. "I do not know if it will make them work for us or not, but now at least they are arguing at each other, not at me."

Dorje sat down on a plump bag of rice, crossed his arms comfortably, and leaned back against a crate of cooking oil.

"Let them argue," Trowbridge told him. "And be sure to keep an eye on the gear. I'm going into town to see about the permit."

"Why," he asked patiently, "would the Indian military mission in Kathmandu concern itself with this expedition? Lhakrinor is in the extreme north of Nepal, nearly three hundred miles north of the Indian border. It has no strategic or political importance. My only purpose in going there is to study wildlife."

The Newar official, who had sent his staff to lunch for the duration of this meeting, walked to the open window and glanced out casually. Then he turned, lifted his shoulders in a graceful shrug, and placed his hands, fingertips touching, neatly before his mouth. His dark, almond-shaped eyes expressed concern, and he chose his words carefully. Above them, the fan, which had been pushing warm air sluggishly through the office, spun slowly to a halt, victim of the intermittent daily electrical brownout.

The long-delayed permit, covered with colorful seals and innumerable signatures, lay between them on the desk. Trowbridge had made no move yet to pick it up.

"First, Dr. Trowbridge, let me tell you that I am very interested in your study of high-altitude hoofed animals and their predators in Lhakrinor. And if it is true that you are also studying the possibility of creating a national park there—a rumor which a friend in the Palace relayed to me—I think this is most excellent, and have no idea why anyone would be against such an enterprise. Except perhaps the Bhotiya who live in the area."

Trowbridge said, "I think it might be preferable for that to remain a rumor. At least until it becomes clear whether the idea is feasible."

"Very wise, and very discreet. I must say that discretion is unusual for an American; Americans, in my experience, tend to be either appallingly honest, or ostentatiously secretive. Which brings us to my second point: From the moment you leave my office, you must forget what I just told you about interference on the part of India, our tremendously powerful neighbor to the south. Moreover, I advise you that if a foreign scientist—even a scientist with your reputation—suggested such a thing, he might well be deported for endangering the conduct of our foreign relations."

The slender official sat back down in his chair and studied Trowbridge to make sure he understood.

"It would be unwise," he continued after a moment, "as well as politically unethical, for India to interfere in our internal affairs. And it would be equally unwise for us to make accusations of interference on their part. India is a country on whom we are—unfortunately, and despite our best efforts—utterly dependent in an economic sense. If, for any reason, the Indians were to become annoyed with us and seal our southern border, we would starve. Few of us who live in the lowlands are hardy enough to want to walk—as you apparently do—across the mountains to the northern border. And Tibet has no food to give us even if we did."

"I understand."

"I wonder if you do. My country, Mr. Trowbridge, has been described as a tributary state by Mao Zedong, and as a part of greater India—Mahabharat—by Indian leaders. Our own leaders describe us, most accurately, as a root between two stones. For centuries we were protected by the great wall of the Himalayas to the north and the malarial swamps on our southern border. For better or worse, the draining of those swamps and the advances of modern medicine have left us vulnerable to our southern neighbor."

The official dipped his head slightly. "I do not mean to bore you with the details of our precarious political situation. But I would suggest that since you have the permit in your hand, you take it and go. Now. Before someone changes his mind. Or before someone decides to whisper that perhaps you are not a scientist, but an agent of—"

He paused, and then continued, "—an organization the name of which sounds like our word for tea."

Chiya. This is all I need, Trowbridge thought grimly. There was no easier way to ruin a scientist who worked in developing countries than by spreading a rumor that he worked for the CIA.

A weary smile crossed the official's intelligent, sympathetic face. "If *I* had been the one who wanted to block your permit, that is what I would have done. Fortunately, I am on your side. But the last thing I will tell you is this: If there were not people in my government unhappy with Indian interference in our affairs, then you would never have received this piece of paper."

Silently, almost imperceptibly, the fan had started up again. Trowbridge felt the stratas of warm humid air shift lazily. Outside a motor scooter with no muffler roared past; in the ensuing silence he heard laughter, and a horse neighing plaintively.

He nodded and stood up, slipping the bright document into his shirt pocket, buttoning the pocket carefully.

"Thank you for your help," he said simply.

The Newar official nodded graciously, then looked up at the fan above his head with a frown. It was slowing to a halt, making a tiny, frustrated, buzzing noise. He reached down behind his desk, pulled out an ornate, ivory-tipped cane, raised it above his head, and gave the fan a deft spin in the proper direction. Trowbridge reached the door as the fan came back to life.

"Mr. Trowbridge," the official called out. He stopped in the doorway and looked back.

The official was staring up at the ceiling, holding the cane in the air, its tip quite close to the turning blades.

"Walk quickly," he said. "And carefully. And take care when you pass through Jorkhang."

Trowbridge waved off the brightly colored taxi and walked along the lake, giving himself time to think. Boats with curved prows were moored at the water's edge; women squatted beside the greenish water, washing clothes, beating them, spreading them on flat rocks. Tiny stalls, hardly larger than phone booths, offered books, postcards, candy, and rolls of toilet paper—the luxuries demanded by tourists, most of whom had fled the approaching monsoon. On the far side of the lake, behind a small pavilion perched atop a knoll, a green slope rose steeply into cloud. Ahead of him was a cluster of lakeside houses made of pale orange brick, decorated with red poinsettia bushes.

After seven weeks of frustrating delays, of being shuffled from office to office both here and in Kathmandu, he'd finally been given the permit. His main feeling was an overwhelming sense of relief; it didn't make any difference why it had been held up, really, as long as he had the thing.

But interference on the part of the Indian military mission in Kathmandu? Why would they care? Lhakrinor, the region he planned to study, lay in the far north of the country, hundreds of miles from Nepal's southern border with India. The more he thought about it the less it made any sense. And yet this official had seemed not only to believe what he was saying, but to think he was taking a fair amount of personal risk to say it at all.

He shrugged it off. There was nothing he could do about it now except get moving. Do the footwork. It was all footwork until he reached the high valleys and began making observations and compiling data.

He turned into the bank, a balconied, cinder-block structure surrounded by a wrought iron fence, and began exchanging traveler's checks for bundles of dirty bank notes. In the hills, where people looked suspiciously on large notes, small bills were essential. It was only recently that the hill tribes would take paper currency at all. The earliest scientific and mountaineering expeditions in Nepal had been trailed by extra porters carrying baskets heavy with coins.

He stuffed the bills into his canvas pack, slung it over his shoulder, and walked through the tropical heat, beneath the heavy swirl of premonsoon cloud, toward where the expedition was camped, resisting the temptation to stop in one of the cool, darkened tea shops for a final beer. He expected to be out for five months this trip; it was time to start getting into shape.

Rain spattered lightly against the tent, waking him from an uneasy sleep. He lay a moment, listening, head pillowed on the pack full of bills, then pulled on shorts and tennis shoes and walked through the jumble of gear and supplies. Dorje, supposedly on guard, had fallen asleep with his head on his hand; his face looked much younger than it did when he felt the responsibility of being *sirdar*. Jeet was snoring loudly from their tent. In the sky to the southeast, lightning flickered softly.

He turned his back on the gathering deluge and faced north, into a pure, tangible darkness, a darkness in which he could almost feel the massive presence of the mountains, looming like a vast reef in a dark ocean.

If the porters showed up in the morning, they would be trekking into the foothills of those mountains shortly after lunch, threading their way northwest beneath Annapurna and Dhaulagiri, two of the giants of the range. With luck, three weeks later he would have penetrated the high valleys of Lhakrinor, leaving behind the hot lowlands, the crowded dwellings, the tourists, and the bureaucratic entanglements. He would be up roaming among the high mountains where he was happiest.

Once again he wished Norbu had shown up, and wondered what had gone wrong. It was hard to imagine making an expedition in Nepal without him. On the other hand, Norbu, while always useful, was not always reliable; it wouldn't be the first time he had failed to turn up when expected.

He looked at his watch, wondering how long Dorje had been asleep. It didn't make any difference; nothing seemed to be missing, and the sun would be up within an hour. Once they were out of Pokhara they would no longer have to take turns standing guard. Taking a certain amusement in the fact that Dorje's name meant "Thunderbolt," and making a mental note that his *sirdar*, while a hard worker during the daylight, was still a nineteen-year-old who needed to sleep, he woke him and sent him sheepishly to his tent. Then he sat with his back to the comforting, rounded strength of the massive banyan tree.

Rain gusted in occasionally under the branches, cooling his face. At first light he woke Jeet and crawled back into his tent for another hour of sleep.

The gloomy Limbu showed up first: barefoot, scrawny but hardy-looking, and dressed in a torn T-shirt and a pair of impossibly baggy shorts. His expression was as dour as it had been yesterday, and his ears, shining in the gloomy morning light, were the most notable Trowbridge had ever seen on a human being. After walking in with his hand on his *kukri*, the Limbu declared that he agreed to work on Trowbridge's terms. Dorje paid him two days' wages, and he went to sit under the banyan tree.

One, Trowbridge thought.

The pair of Tamangs trickled in shortly afterward, accepted their wages, asked shyly for something extra with which to rent a rainproof tent, and promptly disappeared back toward town, leaving a small bundle of what were apparently mutual possessions.

Three.

An hour later, there was still no sign of the Gurungs. The sun cast occasional celestial shafts of light through a sky which was active with heavy dark clouds. The air was oppressively hot. Dorje, whose responsibility it was to have found porters for the expedition, was trying hard not to look miserable. The Tamangs had returned, and were practicing setting up their tent, crawling in and out of it, laughing good-naturedly. The Limbu sat stolidly beneath the banyan tree as if it were all the same to him. And of course it was—from this moment on he would be paid whether they walked or not.

When the Gurungs finally arrived, they came in a tight, sullen-looking knot. Trowbridge was angry that they were late, relieved that they had shown up at all. The leader marched up to Dorje and thrust his bad eye into Dorje's face.

"We will work for you," he announced in Nepali. Dorje nodded and started to speak.

"—at two times normal wages, not one and a half," the Gurung finished.

Dorje choked.

"—and we require ten days' wages in advance."

Finding his voice, Dorje began berating the Gurung for bad faith.

Trowbridge resisted the impulse to hurl something in the direction of the Gurung's head, and glanced at the Limbu, who wore an expression of disapproval. For the Gurungs to have shown up this morning meant they agreed to the terms; to have gone back on that agreement was clearly not, in the Limbu's opinion, proper behavior.

We may have at least one good porter, he thought.

He turned his attention back to the argument raging between Dorje and the Gurung. The other Gurungs hollered encouragement at their leader—who seemed to be enjoying his role—and jeered at Dorje. In any other circumstances Dorje would have told the Gurungs to jump from a high bridge, but the Gurungs were all that was available, and everyone knew it. Trowbridge, hating his helpless position, and the fact that the expedition was in danger of sinking into the mud of this rice field, began doing some despairing arithmetic to see what double wages would do to the expedition budget.

Behind him a voice cut through the argument.

"*Namaste*, Aite," the voice said calmly.

Trowbridge turned to see who had spoken, and felt a rush of surprise and relief. Norbu stood looking coolly past him at the Gurung, whom he appeared to know, and who looked back with a certain apprehension.

"You intended to work for this expedition, Aite," Norbu said, making it more a statement than a question. "I wonder how that is possible, when you have not finished your work for another? I am told you took a week's wages from a group of Japanese climbers and disappeared the first night."

The Gurung muttered something inaudible.

"You are right," Norbu said easily. "I am not a policeman. As you are not a porter. Perhaps you and these men should leave and find other work. I know there are many hides to be tanned at the butcher in Khairani."

The Gurung looked up with sudden fury. Among both Hindu and Buddhist, tanners were outcasts, the lowest strata of society. The Gurung spit on the ground, turned, and thrust his way through his followers, who grouped dispiritedly behind him and trailed away.

Trowbridge, looking his friend up and down with a smile, said, "I was beginning to think I would have to make an expedition in Nepal without you."

Norbu hesitated, then shook his head happily.

"Never," he said. "But I am sorry to be late. It is raining between here and Kathmandu. The bridges are washed away."

He motioned to the disappearing Gurungs, his smile disappearing.

"You would not have gotten far with those porters. Even if you paid them what they asked."

"There are no other porters in Pokhara," Dorje said a little stiffly.

He had come up to join them, and stood openly considering Norbu. "I have looked carefully, and asked many questions. I have gone to all the trekking agencies as well."

"Dorje," Trowbridge said quickly, "this is Norbu, who traveled with me five years ago in Manang, and two years ago in the Solu Khumbu. He is an expert tracker, and will help me with my research once we reach Lhakrinor."

To Trowbridge's relief, Norbu didn't contradict him; three months ago when he'd agreed to join Trowbridge in Pokhara he'd mentioned offhandedly that he might not go all the way to Lhakrinor.

"Norbu, Dorje is *sirdar* for this expedition, and a good one. He has already found us three excellent porters."

"I have heard of your reputation in Kathmandu," Norbu said graciously.

"I have not heard of yours," Dorje said coolly.

There was an uncomfortable silence. Then Dorje, who was too open and cheerful to maintain a severe face for long, relented somewhat. "But if Trowbridge *sahib* recommends you, then I recommend you also."

"Good," Trowbridge said. "That settles that. Now we have work to do."

Norbu looked at the sky appraisingly.

"Tonight," he said, "or tomorrow, the rain will begin."

"We need porters," Trowbridge said.

Norbu nodded. "Give me two hours," he said.

In spite of the imminent rain—or perhaps because of it—the market-place was swarming with activity. Traders from Manang, wearing expensive Japanese wristwatches and the confident, watchful, innocent air of smugglers, mingled with townspeople, a smattering of late tourists, and orange-robed Buddhist monks. The monks, Tibetan refugees, fingered their prayer beads as they moved through the crowd, open-faced and smiling, their hair cropped short. Trowbridge noticed a party of Limbus, all wearing *kukris*, and all with ears that stuck out from the sides of their heads—though none so prominently as those of their gloomy porter, who was, at the moment, looking doubtfully at a pair of bright green tennis shoes which he was trying on under the darting eye of an Indian trader. Behind him a solid, swaggering Khampa bandit, also a Tibetan refugee, bits of knotted red yarn wound into his hair, was arguing loudly over the price of a rug he was trying to sell to a dealer.

Trowbridge's attention was distracted by a low, chuffing cough and a jingling of bells. Shuffling slowly through the marketplace on its hind legs, standing a foot or more above the heads of the crowd, came a large black bear. After a startled moment Trowbridge spotted the bear's owner, a barefoot lowlander wearing baggy trousers. The bear was being led by a chain through its mutilated nostrils. Not far from Trowbridge the bear's keeper stopped and began scanning the square for a suitable performance site. He jerked hard on the chain, eliciting a nasal, peculiarly bear-like moan of protest.

The sound took Trowbridge back to the wild bears he had studied in the mountains of Siberia; they'd made a similar noise when frustrated at getting grubs from a rotten log. But there was a deeper, more anguished note in this moan, and it was not hard to see why. The bear's teeth were smashed to stumps; its fur was patchy, and it looked miserable and beaten in the heat.

The keeper began playing a crude wooden flute. The bear—a female, perhaps three years old—began an awkward dance, shuffling in a circle, forelegs held high in a grotesque parody of human movement. A crowd began to gather. Shoving his way toward the front, apparently enjoying the spectacle, came a fleshy, powerful-looking Indian hunter, a *shikari*, with a rifle slung over his back, a filthy turban atop his head, and high-top canvas shoes stained the lurid red of betel juice. The *shikari* stooped, picked up a piece of rotten fruit and threw it at the bear, laughing as the animal jerked its muzzle away instinctively.

Trowbridge observed a fury go through himself when the chain cut into the bear's swollen nostrils, but willed himself to coldness. There was nothing he could do about this. He was a field biologist, a scientist who made studies, and on occasion, recommendations. The rest was up to the politicians and the policemen.

The bear's small moist eyes were dark, nearly closed. It waved its large paws above the heads of the crowd, arms encircling an invisible partner.

Norbu appeared at Trowbridge's side. "May we see one in the mountains," he said, a look of sudden sadness on his expressive face. "One that is free."

Trowbridge studied his friend. This handsome Nepali, the best tracker he had ever known, had for years made his living as an itinerant hunter. The irony that Norbu's profession had been to slaughter precisely the same animals Trowbridge made a profession of studying had occurred to them both, but Trowbridge didn't hold it against him, and Norbu had never apologized, nor expressed regret. There was even a way in which this shared, diametrically opposed history bound them together.

"Would it be difficult," he asked carefully, "to capture a bear like this?"

Norbu watched the bear a moment longer before he spoke.

"Here is how a hunter would do it," he said. "You begin by finding a mother with cubs, and observing her habits. In this you must be careful, because she is very determined to protect them. You must wait, and watch, and not shoot the mother until just after the cubs are weaned, when they are still small enough to control and train. With an iron bar, you smash the cubs' teeth. Then you heat the bar and put it through their noses, and thread a chain through the wounds, and teach them that if they do not dance, they do not eat."

He paused and looked at Trowbridge. "This is how it is done. I could have done it many times if I had wished to."

Trowbridge said nothing.

"As a hunter, David, I liberated many souls from their animal bodies. That was my *karma*, and will be my *karma* when my own soul is liberated. Death is not a thing to fear or be ashamed of. But I never sold an animal into slavery."

They watched the bear slump down onto all fours, sides heaving, its performance ended. The keeper collected coins from the crowd, and then, with an impatient flick of the chain, led the bear past a bicycle-drawn rickshaw and around a corner.

Trowbridge took a deep breath. "May we see one in the mountains," he agreed.

He looked over at Dorje and their somewhat motley collection of porters, who were nearly done making their final purchases.

Less than two hours after walking away from the encampment, Norbu had returned with three more porters. Trowbridge's elation at seeing the four approaching figures had been tempered somewhat when they actually walked into camp. The first porter, a retired Gurkha soldier, had marched up to Trowbridge, saluted, and informed him that he was a member of "the First Battalion of the Seventh Duke of Edinburgh's Own Gurkha Rifles, recently retired, name of Chandra Shamsher, sir," then had turned on his heel and gone to sit on a crate near the fig tree.

"Recently retired?" Trowbridge asked quietly of Norbu.

"Perhaps some time ago," Norbu acknowledged.

"Will he stay with us? He must have a fairly good pension from the British government."

The Gurkhas, a warlike hill tribe to the east, had once ruled all of Nepal. They were famous as soldiers, and had been recruited for decades—along with other tribes like Mangars and Gurungs—by both the British and Indian governments to form elite fighting regiments; Gurkha regiments, most recently, had fought in the Falklands. Once retired, they generally returned to their home villages, where their experience—and their pensions—gave them positions of status and influence.

Norbu nodded. "His granddaughter is getting married in the fall. He says he wants extra money so he can give her a more generous dowry and wedding feast. Also, he says that after the life of a soldier he is bored in his village."

The second porter was a Rai, one of the ancient races of Nepal. He had rounded, nearly Oriental features, and wore a great number of protective talismans around his neck. Bobbing his head vigorously when Trowbridge asked if he would stay with the expedition at least as far as the Serpo La—the first of two major passes they would have to cross—he stepped back, whirling a small prayer wheel with nervous movements.

The third porter was an extremely filthy young woman of medium height, with an awkward build, and a slender face and limbs which contrasted incongruously with her stocky trunk. She looked to be about twenty years old, but between the dirt, her eyes-down restraint, and a ratty stocking cap pulled down over her forehead, it was difficult to get a good look at her.

On both his previous expeditions Trowbridge had hired female porters, and they had been excellent. But they had also been Bhotiya—tough, mountain-dwelling Buddhists—with open, smiling faces, sturdy legs, and independent attitudes.

He watched this porter trying on tennis shoes at the marketplace stall, tying the laces with careful movements of her fingers. Norbu saw him studying her doubtfully.

"I hope," he said, following Trowbridge's gaze with amusement, "that when the rain begins and the dirt washes away there will be something left beneath."

"She's a Newar?" Trowbridge said, more as a statement than a question. Beneath the dirt there was evidence of the graceful features of these valley-dwellers of Nepal. Slender, comfort-loving, and artistic, Newars cultivated bright poinsettia flowers outside their houses, consulted their astrologers before making any important move, and dominated the upper classes and the government.

Norbu shrugged. "I think so, but she does not say much. All she would tell me is that she wants to work, and wants to go to the mountains."

That was curious in itself. Most lowland Nepalis—especially porters—had no intrinsic love for the mountains. Mountains were lonely, treacherous places filled with demons, bad weather, and steep slopes where it was difficult to raise crops.

"She'll never carry a full load."

"She agreed to two-thirds normal wages for carrying two-thirds the normal load."

The porter stood up, stepped gingerly forward and backward, and looked down with evident satisfaction at her new footwear.

"Have you ever even *heard* of a Newar porter?" he asked Norbu. "Especially a female?"

"I have known many good porters who were women," Norbu said. "But I will confess, never a Newar."

Trowbridge tagged this porter mentally as their first dropout, and hoped they would be able to find a replacement in one of the villages they passed through.

The purchasing of shoes was nearly finished. Dorje negotiated patiently with the shoe merchant to get a fair price, inspecting the shoes carefully. Indian traders had a reputation not only for pomposity, but for dishonesty. Trowbridge's attention was caught by the *shikari* hunter who had thrown fruit at the bear; he was loitering on the far side of the square, spitting betel juice into the street, staring insolently, for no evident reason, at Dorje and the female porter.

Norbu touched Trowbridge on the arm, motioning to the north with a satisfied expression. The dense gray of the monsoon cloud cover had swirled momentarily apart, revealing the sheer face of one of Nepal's sacred mountains.

Machapuchare lay barely a day's walk to the north, but soared four miles in altitude above this muddy lowland town. Its nearly perfect triangle of a peak was so steep it seemed to arch backward; its sheer face, a harsh vision of black rock and white snow, gleamed in the shifting monsoon light. Because it was considered a holy mountain, no climber had ever actually set foot on its peak; the only mountaineering expedition to climb it had planted a flag a few yards short of its highest point.

He stared at the mountain, pleased, as he always was when he saw it, that it had never been violated. He felt a certain amount of professional admiration, but no affinity, for the mountaineers who crawled tortuously to the top of sterile inaccessible peaks, risking their lives—and their fingers and toes—for the empty and short-lived victory of standing atop them.

"David *sahib*!" Dorje said, coming up to them. "We are nearly finished buying the shoes."

Dorje was clearly pleased that his organizational duties were nearly fulfilled, that the expedition would soon be out and walking. "I will be happy to get over the mountains and into Lhakrinor," he continued, "although I cannot believe any place could be as beautiful as my home in the Solu Khumbu."

Dorje looked at Norbu in friendly curiosity. "What part of Nepal are you from?"

Norbu shrugged, as if to communicate that he was indifferent to where a person came from, and said, "From the mountains to the west." Then, realizing that this response bordered on rudeness, he added, "Near Mount Saipal." For a Nepali, Norbu was uncommonly reluctant to discuss his childhood or his family; in the past Trowbridge had heard him tell people dismissively that he came "from nowhere."

Sudden shouting erupted from the stall of the shoe merchant. Their female porter had drawn herself up to her full height, and was pointing an accusing finger at the Indian, who had been standing with his back to her, tying up the pair of tennis shoes in paper.

"Aiee," Dorje said disgustedly, running back to see what was going on. Chandra, their retired Gurkha, stepped in, supporting his fellow porter's contention that the merchant had substituted inferior shoes for those which had been agreed upon. The merchant stood · wrathfully amid the dirty canvas of his stall, waving the package of shoes in one hand and the money in the other, refusing to let them have either until there was an apology. The dignity of all Indians in all parts of the world, he maintained in a shrill voice, had been insulted.

Trowbridge noticed the *shikari* hunter shoving his way purposefully through the crowd. A Tibetan girl was thrown to her knees; her tray of candy and gum was upset into the muddy street, and she began yelling vigorous, obscene protest at the rudeness. The *shikari* spit a gout of red betel juice into the street, ignoring her, and moved steadily toward the shoe merchant's stall.

Others in the square got out of the *shikari's* way.

Ahead of him, Dorje had stepped between the shoe merchant and the two porters in an attempt to calm the situation. "There is no need for argument," Dorje said rationally to the shoe merchant. "We will simply look at the shoes."

The *shikari* shouldered the shoe merchant aside, sending him sprawling into a pile of his own merchandise. The merchant opened his mouth to protest, took a closer look at the threatening individual who had come to his assistance, and said nothing.

With a stare that was simultaneously indifferent and menacing, the *shikari* turned his attention to Dorje. Trowbridge quickened his pace through the crowd.

"Excuse me, sir," Dorje said firmly, "but this is not your affair."

In a movement which suggested long experience, the *shikari* slipped the rifle from his shoulder, reversed it neatly, and swung the butt up into Dorje's jaw. There was an audible click of wood on bone; Dorje staggered and fell backward into the street.

"Are you out of your mind?" Trowbridge said angrily, breaking through the crowd.

With no change of expression, the *shikari* swung to face Trowbridge, reversed the rifle, and placed its barrel against Trowbridge's throat.

Around them, slowly, the yelling and bartering died down. Trowbridge took a deep breath, forcing his mind to work logically. This *shikari*, out of some idiotic sense of loyalty to a fellow Indian, had overreacted. In a moment he would realize the fact and put down the rifle.

The rifle, however, was not lowered. And as Trowbridge studied the oily, sweating face, the flat dark eyes set closely together, he felt a sudden doubt, and a tingling flush of fear.

In the lengthening silence, Chandra asked—a reassuring steadiness in his voice for which Trowbridge felt grateful—"Trowbridge *sahib*, shall I bring a policeman?"

Without taking his eyes off Trowbridge, the *shikari* said, "That is a good idea, Gurkha pig. Why don't you run crying to a policeman?"

After a moment's hesitation, Chandra slipped away through the silent crowd. As he did so the *shikari*, with a slow, deliberate movement, tightened his finger on the trigger. The rifle of a professional hunter would have a fairly light action; Trowbridge felt an overpowering sense of disbelief, and a clear preference not to die. If this fellow really intended to kill him, Chandra would never be back in time.

The *shikari* seemed to be searching his face for signs of fear. There was no hint in his eyes of anger; he seemed, in fact, to be enjoying himself.

Trowbridge felt a bead of sweat go into his eyes, and blinked at the salty sting. The seconds passed with an agonizing slowness as the *shikari* continued to study him. Then, with another fractional and deliberate movement of his finger, he tightened the trigger further.

"This way, policeman sir! Quickly!"

Trowbridge looked past the *shikari* uncomprehendingly. It was Norbu's voice he was hearing, not Chandra's.

A brief look of satisfaction crossed the *shikari's* face and he turned in the direction of the voice. As the rifle barrel came away from Trowbridge's throat, Norbu sprang against the *shikari's* legs, toppling him over backward. Trowbridge dived awkwardly forward, grabbing for the rifle, and found himself lying atop a motionless figure. His nostrils were filled with a sweet-acrid smell of sweat, long-unwashed clothing, and patchouli. There was no need to wrestle the weapon away; the *shikari's* skull had slammed hard into a paving stone.

"Quickly," Norbu said, springing to his feet, scanning the

square. "We must get him out of sight."

Norbu took the *shikari's* legs; Trowbridge gripped him under the shoulders, and they carried him behind the shoe merchant's stall. Norbu bent briefly to be certain the man was still breathing. Then they tied his feet together and his hands behind his back, jammed a scrap of cloth into his mouth, and covered him with a filthy piece of canvas. The shoe merchant was nowhere to be seen.

Trowbridge, with fingers which showed an annoying tendency to tremble, worked the action of the *shikari's* rifle, emptying it of bullets and stuffing them into his bag.

Norbu went to Dorje, still sitting in the square, and spoke rapidly, in a low voice, in his ear. Dorje took a deep, shuddering breath, then nodded, pressing the back of his hand to his chin.

"Is it broken?" Trowbridge inquired urgently. Norbu was methodically smearing some of the blood from Dorje's shirt onto the knuckles of his right hand.

The Newar porter, kneeling beside Dorje, shook her head. "The skin is broken," she said. "But his jaw is not broken."

Trowbridge looked at her in brief surprise; her English was clear and precise. Then he heard a hubbub at the edge of the square, and stood up.

Chandra and a policeman were pushing their way through the crowd; Chandra was breathlessly attempting to explain the circumstances of the assault. The policeman spotted Dorje sitting on the ground, and began demanding, in Nepali, to be told what had happened.

Norbu stepped forward, swaying a little, a sheepish look on his face, rubbing his fist.

"Eeesh," he said regretfully. "It was me. And I wish I had not done it. I think my hand is broken."

Norbu looked down with regret at his bloody fist, flexing it painfully. His left knee buckled slightly beneath him, and he wavered, eyes crossing slightly as he concentrated on keeping his balance.

The policeman considered Norbu sternly. Then he looked at Dorje. "Is this true? Is this drunken fellow the one who hit you?"

Dorje nodded miserably, wincing as he tried to speak.

"He is trying to tell you that we are cousins," Norbu offered helpfully. "With your permission, we will settle this at home, in the Solu Khumbu."

Dorje mumbled something inaudible.

"What are you saying?" inquired the policeman sharply.

"He will owe me a healthy young yak for this!" Dorje blurted out. "I will speak to his uncle!"

Blood flowed between Dorje's fingers.

"Please stop speaking, there is no need," the policeman said uncomfortably. Then he looked at Norbu skeptically. "A pair of Sherpas fighting? I have never heard of such a thing. Who began this fight?"

Norbu pondered the question, a guilty look on his face. Then he grinned foolishly.

"*Rakshi* began this fight!" he said, making a cup out of his fingers. "Not me. *Rakshi*! I hope I do not offend a Hindu like yourself, sir, but my religion does not prohibit the drinking of *rakshi*."

The policeman addressed himself to the square at large.

"Are they speaking truthfully? Is this what happened?"

In the ensuing silence, Trowbridge felt the fate of his expedition balance precariously. A trial, even an inquiry, would delay him in Pokhara for weeks. Chandra, fortunately, had given up trying to explain what had happened, and was standing with a perplexed look on his face.

The Tibetan girl who had been knocked down by the *shikari* stepped forward and began speaking rapidly, assuring the policeman that it had been a simple argument between relatives. That the drunken one—Norbu—had started it, and no real harm had been done. Other voices around the square began to offer agreement. The policeman studied the faces around him skeptically, then addressed himself in English to Trowbridge.

"These are men you have hired?"

"Yes."

"May I see your papers, please?"

Trowbridge produced his passport and the travel permit. The policeman read carefully, and looked impressed.

"A doctoral scientist," he said. "And you have a long distance to go. I do not wish to slow you. I will take this one to jail," he motioned to Norbu, "and this one as well," motioning to Dorje, "and you may carry on. We are a peaceful people in Nepal—we do not appreciate violence in public. And may I suggest you hurry, sir, because soon it will be raining."

"Excuse me, but if you take my two best men, I will not be able to leave. And as you said, it will soon be raining."

The policeman frowned, studying the permit once again. "If these are your two best men, I should probably take the rest to jail as well!"

He returned the permit. "All right, then. I do not wish to make problems for your expedition because two foolish Sherpa cousins have hit each other. You may go. And you," he said sternly, turning to Chandra, who still wore a confused look on his face. "You are the one I should take to jail! I was worried that something serious might be occurring. Speaking of rifles and murder, when it was only a simple fist fight!"

Chandra's mouth opened and he began to protest.

"Thank you very much," Trowbridge interrupted.

The policeman nodded in a dignified fashion, straightened his jacket, and sent a final withering look in Chandra's direction before moving away through the crowd.

"How long do you want me to keep him here?" the Khampa asked with a wolfish grin, his hand resting lightly on the slender silver dagger in his belt. "With the proper encouragement, it could be a long time. Even forever."

The bandit, whose homeland was the vast Tibetan steppes north of the Himalayas, fingered his dagger lovingly, and looked down at the *shikari*, whose head lay between the bandit's felt boots. He did not seem to be intimidated by the pure, glittering malevolence which shone in the *shikari's* eyes. Trowbridge, however, felt a chill go down his spine.

"Two hours," Norbu said. "Long enough for us to leave Pokhara."

The Khampa shrugged and grinned, feigning a look of disappointment. Trowbridge pulled out money and counted several notes into the Khampa's hand.

"Ah," the Khampa said. "This appears to be . . . I would say . . . perhaps encouragement enough for one hour."

He looked up, a Tibetan love of barter in his face.

Trowbridge looked at him severely. "You are a thief."

"I am!" the Khampa replied cheerfully. "But an honest one. So I will tell you that this is perhaps somewhat more than an hour's worth of encouragement—but certainly not two hours. No, never two hours."

Trowbridge gave him a few more *rupiya*, which the Khampa pocketed with a grin. As he did so, he glanced down at his charge.

"Ah, look," he said, "our friend is trying to say something. Perhaps his manners have improved."

Before Trowbridge could stop him the Khampa reached down and removed the gag which stopped the *shikari's* mouth. The *shikari* made no attempt to shout; he took a deep breath and said, staring directly at Trowbridge, "My name is Naraka. Remember it."

"He is boring," the Khampa said, shoving the dirty piece of cloth back into the *shikari's* mouth. The Tibetan girl who had argued their case to the policeman hovered nearby, glaring at the *shikari*, brushing the mud from her long skirt.

Norbu regarded the *shikari* thoughtfully a moment, then turned to the Tibetan girl and whispered in her ear. She laughed, took the coins he handed her, and disappeared.

As they left the stall the Khampa called out softly after them: "Thank you, brothers. And do you know something? I would have guarded this pleasant fellow for *nothing*."

The Khampa laughed, then spat beside himself in the street, glanced at the sun, and settled himself comfortably to watch his charge.

"What did you give the girl money for?" Trowbridge asked as they moved through the narrow afternoon streets.

"Lemonade," Norbu said.

"Lemonade?"

"Lemonade is excellent on a hot day."

Nepali lemonade was made from real lemons, sweetened to an impossible stickiness with sugar, and sold from large glass jars in the marketplace.

"I thought you preferred *rakshi*."

Norbu laughed. "The lemonade is not for me. It is for our friend who, no doubt, feels hot and thirsty after causing so much trouble. The Tibetan girl has gone to purchase an entire jar of lemonade. She will pour it over him while he relaxes so that he will feel refreshed. And she will pour some into the breech of his rifle so that he does not take life so seriously when he is set free."

Trowbridge stopped abruptly.

"What is it?" Norbu asked.

"The shoes."

Norbu began swearing eloquently in Tibetan.

The porters could walk barefoot for the greater part of the journey—in fact, most preferred walking barefoot, for comfort, and to save the wear on the shoes, which were a luxury. But shoes were not a luxury on the passes. Without tennis shoes and wool socks, the porters' feet would freeze in the snowfields.

"We have to go back," Trowbridge said reluctantly. "We have to have the shoes."

Norbu looked uneasy. "Perhaps in Narula," he said. "There are Thakali merchants there who may—"

Wordlessly, the Newar held up a large bundle wrapped in paper.

Trowbridge looked at her. Then he looked at Norbu. A grin was beginning to crack Norbu's face.

"The shoes?" Trowbridge said.

The Newar nodded. "The shoes which were agreed upon."

4

The outskirts of Pokhara—away from the beauty of the lake, and the lively prosperity of the marketplace—were no travel poster. Tiny one-room hovels made of cinder block, scrap wood, and corrugated aluminum clung to each other hopelessly; their roofs, patched with cardboard and plastic, were held in place with stones. People were everywhere, sitting half-visible inside the darkened interiors of their dwellings, squatting beside piles of broken concrete and greasy-looking weeds, talking indifferently, staring at nothing.

"Eeesh," Norbu said, catching up with Trowbridge, shaking his head.

"Do you think we can get up into the hills before dark?"

"A little ways," Norbu replied. "Sarangkot is possible, if we walk seriously. But it will be dark when we arrive."

"Let's try," Trowbridge said, looking at the sky, which churned with heavy dark clouds. The heat was still intense, the humidity more so. The air itself seem to sweat in a varnished afternoon light.

Ahead of them Pokhara died out at the edge of a wide, dry riverbed. Beyond the riverbed the dirt road turned to the north, skirting a barren hillside. He looked back impatiently at the porters, and considered asking Dorje to have them pick up the pace. But Dorje, determinedly bringing up the rear, a white bandage looped beneath his jaw, had them moving as well as could be expected. They were still short-handed, so the loads were heavy; Jeet was carrying close to eighty pounds. Trowbridge shifted his own pack, moving the bite of the straps from one part of his shoulders to another, and willed the expedition to speed.

These porters were probably as rag-tag a bunch as he had ever worked with, but at least, with the exception of the Newar, they were Buddhist, not Moslem or Hindu. Buddhist Nepalis, especially Sherpas, were justly famous as the best porters on earth, not merely for their strong backs and legs and willing personalities, but for their relaxed eating habits. They would happily eat anything the *sahibs* would eat— be it fresh, canned, or dehydrated, brought along with the expedition or purchased in tea houses or private homes along the way. This relaxed attitude was partly a result of the less exacting nature of Buddhism, and partly a practical accommodation to a nomadic way of life. The Buddhists of the hills and mountains had learned to move with grace and confidence in unfamiliar environments, to survive and prosper by cheerfully making do with what was available. Most Buddhists would not butcher an animal—that onerous job was reserved for a certain low class of specialists—but few had qualms about eating meat. Orthodox Moslems and Hindus, on the other hand, were difficult to provide for in the wilderness. They not only required special dishes, foods, and even cooking oils, but needed hours to set up and prepare for the meals, which included, for the Hindus, purification rituals and sacrifices to the gods. Meat, for the Moslems, had to be *halal*, ritually slaughtered by slitting the animal's throat. Expeditions had been torn apart before because an impatient *sahib* had tried to rush his porters, or been unable to fulfill their exacting dietary requirements.

"An hour before the road ends?" he asked Norbu.

"Two," Norbu said.

Trowbridge frowned.

Norbu said, "I do not think our *shikari* friend will go to the police."

"I don't either. Still, I'll be happier when we're beyond the road."

They walked in silence for a while. Then Norbu grinned suddenly. "You were very impressive, David. Leaping onto him like a wolf onto a frightened goat."

"More like a frightened goat leaping onto a wolf," he said wryly. "I was concerned about the rifle."

"Understandably so," Norbu said. "That was a very good rifle, by the way."

"I noticed."

"David, there is something strange about what happened. Do you remember how this fellow did not try to stop Chandra from going for a policeman? You would almost think that he *wanted* to have problems with the authorities."

Trowbridge considered this. The Newar official had told him that someone in the Indian military mission had tried to block his getting the permit for this expedition. Was it too farfetched to think that someone had paid this Indian hunter to provoke the incident deliberately?

That's preposterous, he told himself. You're a biologist, not a spy. No one—aside from yourself—cares about the Lhakrinor region.

"Perhaps he simply lost his temper," Norbu continued. "You looked him in the face, David. Was he angry?"

"No. He looked pleased. As if things were going exactly as he intended."

He looked back toward town. The dirt road behind them was empty. To the south, dark columns of rain moved slowly through a vastness of sky.

"Perhaps he only wanted to frighten you," Norbu shrugged.

"If that's the case," Trowbridge said, "he got what he wanted."

Two hours later, they left the stony riverbed and began climbing a series of steep switchbacks. The narrow trail crisscrossed steadily upward for a thousand feet before leveling off onto a wide, rambling ridge which ran to the northwest. This ridge would carry them for thirty miles—through the green rumpled foothills beneath the Annapurna range—to Narula, perched precariously on one high wall of the dark gorge of the Kali Gandaki. After leaving Narula their journey would take them steadily higher over a series of intermediate passes, until, two weeks after leaving Pokhara, they crossed the formidable snowfields of the Serpo La and breached the Himalayas. Once over the Serpo La the better part of their trek would be over, and they would be safely beyond the reach of the monsoon. In the shadow of the Himalayas the land would be drier, and the villages would be populated by Bhotiya, a mountain people primarily Tibetan in culture and racial stock. At that point they would begin a shorter, week-long climb, a trek which would culminate in a crossing of the Krimshi La, the final pass this side of Lhakrinor.

Houses and small farms began dotting the side of the track; goats bleated plaintively; water buffalo, in the dying evening light, were being escorted in from the fields. The rank odors of the town had been replaced by the musty, pleasant smell of wet fields and the strong healthy tang of animal dung. Trowbridge smelled wood smoke and cooking food. His heart, which had pounded hard up the switchbacks, slowed to a pleasant rhythm. His blood sang cheerfully in his ears and his mood improved.

They were away from Pokhara, and walking. He was still concerned about the checkpoints they would have to pass through, but at least they'd left civilization behind. He felt instinctively inside his shirt for the permit, reassuring himself that it was safely in its plastic wrapping. Then he looked back at the strung-out expedition, feeling happy, as he always did when he finally began a journey.

A hundred yards behind, Dorje's white bandage bobbed brightly in the deepening twilight as the first rains of the monsoon gusted across the track.

5

In the early light he stepped down from the wood-plank porch of the lodge where they'd spent their first night, and looked to the north. The Annapurna range—eight peaks, each more than twenty thousand feet in height—raised the horizon into a shining white wall. These were among the highest mountains on earth, and among the cruelest; and yet at this distance, in the softening morning light, they looked deceptively accessible, uncharacteristically gentled and orange as the sun rose.

The morning air here was already cooler than that of humid, lakeside Pokhara. He looked to the south, back down into a thick, dark haze. One day ahead of the monsoon, they were poised on a border between two worlds. From here on they would be thrown onto their own resources, beyond roads or electricity. Everything civilized and complicated would be left behind.

He noticed a jagged fragment of mirror hung by a nail on a porch post, leaned down, and looked into it. His own features looked back at him from the smudged surface of the glass: sandy brown hair, a slightly crooked nose, blue eyes with perhaps one or two more lines around them than someone in his mid-thirties ought to have. A face other people seemed to think was handsome. He rubbed the beginnings of his beard, which he knew from experience would grow in unevenly and give him a rather scruffy look. It was not a face with which he was dissatisfied, but neither was it a face he would miss—which was good, since he might not get another glimpse of it for months.

The trail led them through terraced rice fields, up steeply rolling ridges where low green trees closed in around them, then into open rice fields once again, which they crossed by balancing on thin, smooth, earthen dikes. The air warmed quickly and grew steadily more humid, as if it were inhaling moisture from the monsoon behind them. Trowbridge felt his thin shirt sticking to his shoulders. Farmers rode crude wooden plows behind teams of yoked oxen, turning over the warm mud. In a field of pale wheat stubble, a woman dressed entirely in scarlet stopped for a moment to watch them pass. In this well-traveled area, the existence of the expedition was not a novelty—only its appearance so late in the year.

"How is the chin?" Trowbridge asked Dorje, dropping back a few steps and falling in beside him. Before they left Pokhara, Trowbridge had washed the cut quickly with soap and water, applying a butterfly bandage to draw the edges of the wound together. Dorje had submitted gratefully to the attention, firmly believing, like most Nepalis, that all Westerners were accomplished doctors.

"I feel just fine," Dorje assured him. "Better already."

He made Dorje stop, and looked closely at the bandage.

"When did it bleed?"

Dorje shrugged. "A little, yesterday, when we climbed up the hill. But today is better. Anyway, if we still have problems later, you can give me some medicine."

"Medicine won't heal it," Trowbridge told him bluntly. "The wound has to knit."

Dorje looked disappointed. Trowbridge decided not to change the bandage until this evening, fearing to reopen the wound while Dorje was walking in the heat. He cursed himself for not including something in the medical kit with which to stitch up cuts. As long as Dorje was carrying a heavy load, and walking uphill, the wound would stay open; it would be better if he could rest, or at the very least walk without a pack for a day or two.

But there wasn't time for that, not with the monsoon on their heels.

A few feet behind them, Chandra and the Limbu walked together in a comfortable silence. The old Gurkha wore sunglasses, khaki shorts, and a tattered, military green T-shirt over his ample trunk. Like Dorje, Norbu, and the young Newar woman, he carried his load in a nylon backpack, a leftover piece of equipment from some mountaineering expedition. The other porters carried their loads in the traditional Nepali *doka*, a deep, cone-shaped basket, with straps over the shoulders for stability, and a tumpline around the forehead which provided a good part of the hoist. The tumpline required a bent back, a head-forward stride, and tremendously strong neck muscles, which most Nepalis began developing as children. On his last trip to Nepal, Trowbridge had tried carrying a lightly loaded *doka*; the hour's experiment had cost him a week of neck pain.

"Dorje," Chandra called out conversationally, "when the bandage comes off, you will have a fine scar. Not so fine as Jeet's, but fine nevertheless."

Dorje looked pleased at the idea of having a scar.

"When you return to your village in the Solu Khumbu," Chandra continued, "you can tell them that your chin performed bravely in battle, and did great damage to its enemy! I am certain there is at least a small nick in the stock of that rifle. The poor *shikari's* weapon will never be the same."

Jeet, walking a few steps behind, called out mildly, "Dorje stepped between you and that rifle, Chandra. He took a blow that might have struck you instead."

Chandra's eyes glinted with amusement, and he snapped his right hand into an exaggerated British salute.

"That is true! The action of a true commander! Left-tenant Dorje, I pledge you a soldier's loyalty—following only that, of course, which I give to King Birendra, and Elizabeth, the English Queen."

"You, of course, looked very much like a soldier yesterday," the Limbu said to Chandra in Nepali. "Trying to give your report to the policeman, then standing like a five-year-old boy with his mouth open."

"You are right—I made a great fool of myself." Chandra shifted his pack with a groan. "But it is not the first time. I am many times a fool. Not least for carrying this heavy load, when I could be home in my own village, sleeping in the shade."

"I am with you there," the Limbu agreed, adjusting the tumpline of his *doka*.

Chandra's expression grew severe. "I do not sympathize with that *shikari* fellow," he said. "Six weeks in jail might improve his temper."

I doubt it, thought Trowbridge, remembering the face.

"I confess," Chandra continued, "that I do not sympathize with most Indians. I am very glad I was taken into a British regiment of Gurkhas, and not into an Indian regiment. I was much happier in Brunei and Hong Kong than I would have been in Rajasthan, standing between Sikhs and Hindus whose main spiritual ambition in life is to kill one other."

"In fairness," Dorje said, "they have many problems and difficulties in India. One must understand and make allowances. India is a complicated country with many religions."

"*Nepal* is a complicated country," Chandra pointed out, "with many religions. And yet I do not strike people with a rifle when I disagree on the price of a pair of shoes!"

"The *shikari* has not enough self-control," Dorje said. "For this he will lose *sonam*. It will be more difficult—" Dorje touched his chin gingerly "—for him to be born as a human being in his next life. And that is difficult enough already."

"What if he had broken your jaw?" Chandra asked. "Would you still be so forgiving?"

"Then it would have been an even greater loss of *sonam*," Dorje said stubbornly. "I wish him no more punishment than what he is already bound to suffer in his next life."

Sonam, for the Sherpas, was one's personal stock of religious merit, the quantity which determined one's fate in future incarnations. Proper behavior increased one's stock of *sonam*; wrong, or hurtful, deeds reduced it. Eventually, the accumulation of enough *sonam* would allow one to be set free from the obligations of reincarnation, and thus from suffering and illusion.

And in the meantime, thought Trowbridge, it was a practical and admirable way of looking at things. The concept of *sonam* relieved one of the burden of judgment. There was no need to concern oneself deeply over a member of the community who transgressed the law, since the price of such actions would be exacted—inevitably—in a future existence. An increase in one's personal stock of *sonam* could be brought about by making peace, helping those in need, or forgiving an offender; *sonam* could be lost by making children cry, or even by picking a flower.

"This Naraka fellow showed you what he thinks of your *sonam*," Chandra snorted, adding, for Trowbridge's benefit, "this is why Sherpas make good *sirdars*, Trowbridge *sahib*, but not good soldiers. They do not know how to bear a grudge!"

Chandra looked up at the hazy blue sky, through which distinct, gray-and-white clouds raced quickly, wiped the sweat from his forehead, sighed deeply, and adjusted the straps of his pack. The Limbu stared forward, a piece of dirty cloth beneath the broad band of the tumpline above his eyes, never varying his step.

"Ho," Dorje said simply, looking up at the high ridge ahead of them. "Some work now."

The trail steepened steadily beneath their feet; high above them was evidence of a village.

"Naudanda?" Trowbridge asked him, and Dorje nodded.

Naudanda, a spread-out collection of houses, scattered down both sides of a twisting, spiny ridge. A stiff half-hour climb through narrow wheat fields had carried them to the top of the ridge, where they found Norbu's blue pack leaning against a rock before one of the lodges. It was nearly noon, late for the first meal of the day; the porters, who breakfasted lightly, had been nearly five hours on the trail. The two Tamangs and the Rai had begun to grumble that no more *dal-bhat* would be available.

But it had been a good morning's walk, and he felt pleased. With luck, another five hours this afternoon would bring them to Biretanti before dark.

Norbu, who could outwalk anyone Trowbridge had ever known, was comfortably ensconced in the dark interior of the lodge, speaking with the young hostess, who, by the look of the vermilion mark in the part of her hair, was married. Outside, the porters eased their loads onto the porch, sliding out from beneath them one by one and crowd-

ing noisily into the lodge. The young Newar woman, rather to his surprise, had kept up with the others.

Dorje announced triumphantly, "By hard walking, we have
escaped the *tsugas!*"

Tsugas were the leeches which came out when the monsoon began
in earnest.

"I am not so sure," the Limbu said gloomily. "I do not think the
monsoon is finished with us so easily."

The hostess reluctantly withdrew her attention from Norbu, and
began dishing up nine plates of *dal-bhat*. The first plate was offered to
Norbu, who shook his head and pointed to Trowbridge. Trowbridge,
in turn, pointed to Dorje.

"Our *sirdar* is injured," Trowbridge said, speaking Nepali to the
hostess. "He needs strength."

Dorje shook his head, gesturing somewhat self-importantly
toward the porters.

"I will be the first to eat," Chandra said. "With so much politeness
we could starve to death!"

Chandra carried his plate to the corner and settled onto a bamboo
mat, making a place beside himself for the Limbu. The two Tamangs,
Jeet, the Rai, and the Newar all waited their turn as the hostess
scooped twin ladlefuls of white rice from an enormous, blackened pot
onto shiny aluminum plates. Over the rice was ladled a full measure of
dal—a pale, greenish-yellow gruel made from lentils, the staple of the
Nepali diet. On his earlier expeditions, Trowbridge had discovered
that one could subsist, with reasonably good health and strength, on a
diet of nothing but this rice and lentil combination. It was even fairly
tasty.

At least for the first few weeks, he remembered, accepting his
plate.

After the meal he removed his boots and hung his socks to dry
near the fire, then sat sipping tea. Chandra lay snoring on his side, taking rest, like an experienced soldier, when he could find it. The
Tamangs sat smoking, staring at nothing; the Newar had flung herself
down onto a sack of rice, and Norbu had gone outside. Standing just
inside the door, the Limbu studied the sky. The light which silhouetted
his stooped, disheveled figure was cooler and thinner than when they
had first arrived. A cloud, no doubt, passing before the sun. Trowbridge felt a moment's urgency, wondered if he should rouse the

porters now, then realized he had to give them an hour's rest if he were to ask them to make it to Biretanti this evening. He lay back on the bamboo mat with his hands behind his head, and closed his eyes, tracing their progress, with satisfaction, on the map he carried in his head.

He woke with a sense that something was wrong. The interior of the hut was virtually dark. For a disbelieving moment he wondered if they'd slept away the afternoon. Then he checked his watch. It was only two o'clock—he'd been sleeping less than forty-five minutes. He got to his feet quickly and went outside.

A moist breeze flowed like a cool sluice of water across the ridge. The sky was low and black, and the northern horizon had disappeared, buried entirely in thick, menacing clouds. To the south, obscuring the trail on which they had arrived, massive rain curtains shifted in a slow, ponderous dance. He woke the others, and they set out hurriedly as the first sprinkles of rain came down. Jeet drew a long knife from inside his shirt and began cutting neat covers for the *dokas* from a roll of sheet plastic, handing them out to the porters, who slipped in behind one another, fastening them over the open tops of each other's loads with bits of string. Soon it was pouring. The huge drops pelted them hard, drumming on the plastic, drumming on Trowbridge's poncho, inside of which he was soon—even though he was wearing only shorts and a T-shirt—warm and sweating.

The trail was clear at first, and not too steep, although increasingly muddy. After a couple of hours it began to incline, and grow narrow and wandering. Low trees closed in around them; the sky grew even darker in the late afternoon. Somewhere ahead of them, invisible in a high mass of lowering gray clouds, was the ridge which separated this valley from the valley of the Modi Khola, and Biretanti, their destination.

No one spoke. There was only a vast washing noise, water rushing down through trees, over stones and roots, saturating the increasingly dark landscape about them. Trowbridge was the first to slip, going forward heavily onto his right knee, feeling the weight of the pack swing down a split second later to force the knee, a second time, onto the rock it had already located in the mud. He pushed himself upright, with hands which sank fist-deep into the mud, and climbed again, ignoring the pain. He began hearing the other porters slip as well. They went down without exclamation, splashed to their feet, and continued—all except Chandra, who swore in a profuse and multilingual patois.

After a final steep stretch they crested the ridge in an eerie twilight. The last rays of the sun broke, for a few spectacular moments, through the clouds; for a brief period the rain relented. The shivering bodies of the porters seemed luminous in the evening light. Norbu and Dorje counted heads, making sure no one had gotten lost along the way. Then, one by one, as the rain began again and the light died, they began their descent, picking their way down into darkness.

The only virtue of trekking when it's pitch black out, Trowbridge thought grimly, grabbing a tree branch as his feet went out from under him on a steep part of the trail, is that you cannot see the *tsugas* crawling into your clothes.

It had been dark almost three hours when he decided, reluctantly, that they were lost. He, the Limbu, Chandra, the Newar, and the two Tamangs had ended up together; the others were somewhere ahead of—or perhaps behind—their soaked, depleted little group. None of them were familiar with the area; even if they had been, Trowbridge doubted they could have made sense of the path, which led this way and that, rushing like a small stream through a tangled forest in which there were strange, slippery rustlings, in which the eyes of ghostly insects hung ominously in the trees. The Limbu looked grim; Chandra and the two Tamangs exhausted. No one, however, complained, or suggested stopping; no one wanted to pitch tents on ground which was swarming with *tsugas*.

Finally the light of a flashlight winked ahead in the darkness. Chandra hailed it hoarsely. The light waved slightly, bobbing as it came toward them. Then Norbu materialized out of the darkness like a confident ghost.

Gratefully they followed him across a swaying suspension bridge—above the swollen roar of the Modi Khola—into the town of Biretanti, where he led them to the shelter of a comfortable lodge.

Dorje, Jeet, and the Rai were already inside; Dorje, sitting by the fire, looked pale and weak. His shirt front was pink, and the back of his hand, pressed to his chin, was scarlet. "Bleeding a little," he said apologetically to Trowbridge.

While the porters stripped off their outer clothes and hung them around the warm, fire-lit room, Trowbridge removed Dorje's blood-soaked bandage. There was no infection, which was miraculous. But the wound was as wide open as it had been when Trowbridge first dressed it.

The Limbu placed himself close to the fire, sighed deeply, and began scraping the leeches off his legs with the sharp blade of his *kukri*. Fresh blood streamed down his legs as he worked; speaking to no one in particular, he commented stoically, "Monsoon legs."

Sheared off at the neck, the swollen black leeches plopped down onto the hard dirt floor. The Limbu flicked them into the fire with his free hand, where their blood-filled bodies crackled in the flames.

6

"My least favorite," Trowbridge said, methodically applying salt to the dark, irregular pattern of leeches on his right ankle, "are the ones that attach between your toes."

He preferred salt to the *kukri*; it took longer, but the leeches backed out by themselves, so there was less chance of infection.

"They like it where the skin is thin," Norbu commented, hunched over beside him. He'd been studying the map for several minutes. "There is a decision to make tomorrow, David."

Trowbridge stopped working on his leg and looked at the map. Their intention had been to turn south here, toward Kusma, then north again to Narula. This was the shortest route, with the smallest change in elevation. But going south meant they would be marching directly back into the monsoon.

The alternative, which Norbu was tracing with his finger, was to go north—a much steeper route—to the hilltop town of Ghorepani, then cross the Kali Gandaki and follow it down to Narula, hoping to arrive before the monsoon did.

"It may be raining to the north as well," Trowbridge said.

"But we are certain it is raining to the south."

Trowbridge sighed, and looked at their plucky *sirdar*, who was snoring beside the fire. Blood was already staining his newly changed bandage.

"Dorje's lost a lot of blood," Trowbridge said. "If we go by the northern route—which means a good deal of climbing—he'll lose more."

He shook his head in frustration. "If only I had something to sew up the wound with."

He looked into his pack, which was lying beside him. The first aid kit was there, beside his journal, a heap of damp clothing, two cameras—each in its own plastic bag—and the small kit that held his toiletry articles. Sunscreen, a razor, toothbrush . . .

Something occurred to him.

Norbu was saying, "There is another problem with the northern route. If we go that way, there is only one bridge over the Kali Gandaki. If it is washed out—"

"Then we're stuck."

Norbu nodded.

Trowbridge glanced over at the Newar porter, who sat alone in near darkness against a low stack of firewood. The other porters were already fast asleep. Beside her, on the packed dirt of the floor, lay the *kukri*, its curved blade stained a dull scarlet. Trowbridge had the strong impression that shaving leeches off her legs was not something to which she was accustomed.

"Do you think this one will carry a load in the morning?" he asked quietly.

Norbu shrugged. "She walked very well today."

"Dorje is too weak to carry a load tomorrow. If she refuses . . ."

He stopped, considering the prospect of being unable to leave this wretched, rainy little village, barely out of the lowlands.

Norbu regarded him seriously a moment. Then his face lit up with the sudden grin which overwhelmed him at the most unlikely times.

"David," he said, "do not worry so much! It is not your fault that it is raining! The porters will carry as much as they are able to, and no more. They will walk as fast as they are inclined. Beyond that, we are pilgrims living out our *karma*. Obstacles are placed in our path as a test of faith."

"And to see how badly we want to get from here to there."

Norbu laughed softly. Then he sighed, and his expression changed. "Aiee," he said, with disgust, looking down at his ankles in the yellow firelight. "I am ready to be in the high mountains, where it is dry, and cold, and clean."

"If it's raining in the morning, we go north," Trowbridge said, studying the blood-soaked bandage on Dorje's chin. "We'll take our chances that the bridge will still be there—I've had enough of walking in the mud."

"And Dorje's chin?"

"I have an idea for Dorje's chin."

Near the open doorway, in the thin light of dawn, Jeet and Norbu redistributed Dorje's load. Rain drummed intermittently on the roof. By the fire, the hostess sat watching intently. Dorje lay on his back, calmly staring at the ceiling, arms crossed on his chest. The expression on his face was not stoicism, more a conscious acceptance—an alert willingness to live in this moment, to accept the sensation of pain as the ultimate reality, and as no reality at all.

Trowbridge wished he could say the same for himself; there was a doubtful feeling in his stomach at this first attempt at surgery.

"Almost got it," Trowbridge said, pulling the needle carefully through for the last time, tightening the stitch slowly. He tied the knot, clipped away the excess with the scissors on his Swiss knife, then dabbed Dorje's chin once again with alcohol.

The wound was not pretty, but it was closed. Six white knots in a somewhat irregular row; six stitches, taken in waxed dental floss, with a needle from the sewing kit.

"Yes?" Dorje asked.

"Yes."

Dorje sat up, flexing his jaw tentatively. He winced at the unaccustomed tightness, putting his fingers to his chin. Then he smiled gratefully.

"I cannot see it," he said. "But I am sure it is very good work."

"I wouldn't know," Trowbridge said dryly. "I've never done this before. You're walking with half a load today, by the way."

Dorje protested mightily until Trowbridge made it a direct order. Then he looked downcast, as if he'd been stripped of his authority. It wasn't until an argument broke out among the porters—the two Tamangs complaining they'd been given more extra weight than the Rai, and the Rai complaining the Newar had been given less extra weight than any of them—that Dorje, wading in to mediate the argument, became animated once again.

Eventually they were all assembled on the porch. Trowbridge had hoped the rain might abate by the time they were ready to leave, but it was pouring again. The drops made millions of tiny, momentary explosions in the mud of the trail before them.

No one stepped off the porch, and no one spoke. Eventually one of the Tamangs sat down quietly on his load, looking out meditatively at the rain. Chandra lit a cigarette, cupping the flame before his face, drawing the smoke deeply into his lungs. Even Dorje and Norbu had reluctant expressions on their faces.

"The bridge," the Limbu said, interrupting the silence with gloomy certainty. "I am sure it will be washed away. And, *sahib*, respectfully—you will not be able to repair it with your white string."

Without a word, and without looking at anyone else, the Newar porter got up from where she had been sitting, pulled her stocking cap down over her ears, shouldered her load, stepped down off the porch into the rain, and struck out up the trail.

Trowbridge looked at Norbu, eyebrows raised.

"My goodness," Norbu said, as the other porters, shamed by her action, stepped off the porch and followed her north.

The long, steady ascent took them up endless flagstone steps set in open forests of tall rhododendron. The bright red flowers stood out in gorgeous, nearly phosphorescent contrast to the charcoal gray sky; rain gusted in around them, stopped precipitously, then gusted in again. Long strands of dark moss hung from the branches of sixty-foot trees, dripping darkly, reaching toward the ground. A pair of pale monkeys, langurs, scattered through the treetops; Trowbridge stopped a moment, pleased to see wild creatures in an open forest. In the heavily populated areas through which they had been traveling, there had been only domestic animals.

At sunset they reached Ghorepani, a rumpled little village on a rounded hilltop. When the rain stopped they were rewarded with a view of the high-shouldered bulk of Annapurna South, its dark lower slopes dusted with snow.

Trowbridge spread out his sleeping bag on a bunk in the dim interior of the sleeping area, then stepped out onto the terrace. The Newar porter was standing alone beside a rhododendron tree on a rise behind the lodge, gazing at Annapurna's pristine white mass, which filled a good deal of the northern sky. Trowbridge studied her curiously. It was generally Tibetans and Sherpas who felt this kind of innocent awe, this mystic communion with mountains, not valley-dwelling, comfort-loving Newars.

With a start, the porter noticed she was being observed. Usually she kept her eyes lowered, as a Nepali woman from the lowlands would be trained to do, but when she did look at someone directly—as she was looking at Trowbridge now—there was often a flash of independence, something close to willfulness, in her expression. She held his gaze for a moment, then looked down quickly and walked off through the trees.

Trowbridge ducked back into the warm and smoky interior of the lodge. "Norbu," he said, "what's our Newar porter's name?"

Norbu seemed mildly surprised. "I never asked. I have only called her *Bahini*."

Bahini, in Nepali, meant "younger sister," and was a common, and polite, form of address.

Jeet looked up from what he had been doing; every night, with blunt, fluid fingers, he carved tiny Tibetan characters onto a wooden printing block no larger than his hand.

"Her name is Nima," Jeet said.

"Isn't that usually a boy's name?"

Dorje nodded. "Usually it is. But she told us that is what she wishes to be called."

On a promontory a hundred feet above the swollen river, Trowbridge paused. Upstream, in a constant, hellish roaring, white water exploded from the mouth of a narrow defile, smashing over enormous black boulders before smoothing into a wider—but still wickedly rapid—course.

Trowbridge was relieved. The bridge beneath him, a slender, rickety structure, was still in place. Another day, perhaps less, and the water would tear it away. Like many bridges in Nepal, it was built to last a season, and would be rebuilt after the monsoon abated and the level of the river dropped.

The Kali Gandaki, one of the great rivers of Asia, was one of only a handful of watercourses which had succeeded in breaching the ramparts of the Himalayas as they thrust themselves upward fifty million years ago. Originating in the Tibetan plateau, the river sliced a deep, shadowy canyon—the deepest in the world, five times the depth of the Grand Canyon—between Annapurna on the east and forbidding

Dhaulagiri on the west. During the monsoon, thunderstorms funneled violently northward from the lowlands; the rest of the year a fierce afternoon wind blew nearly every day between canyon walls which were endlessly high and dark.

Because the Kali Gandaki transversed the Himalayas, it was a vital conduit for trade and travel. Prosperous Thakali communities dotted its lower and middle reaches, and the trails were good. Trowbridge's original intention had been to follow the Kali Gandaki north to Jomosom, in the Mustang region, then head west, passing through Dolpo into Lhakrinor. But the Nepali government was reluctant to issue permits for Mustang—a border area even more sensitive than Lhakrinor—because it had been the badlands hideout of the renegade Tibetan army for years after the Chinese invaded Tibet in 1950.

The truth was, most of Nepal's northern border was sensitive. As a tiny country lodged precariously between two aggressive colossi—or, as the official in Pokhara had described it, as a root between two stones—Nepal occupied an impossibly vulnerable position. Yet the country had managed never to relinquish its sovereignty, despite being invaded, on various occasions over the centuries, by the Chinese, Indians, and British. Nepal's survival in the last few decades was explicable only because any move against it on India's part would be viewed in Beijing as an attack on China, with the reverse holding true for Delhi.

Trowbridge had a good deal of sympathy for the delicate position of the plucky Nepalis. And he was infinitely grateful to be a long way from the political intrigues of Delhi, Kathmandu, and Beijing.

He looked more closely at the bridge beneath him. Branches and vines, crudely worked together, made up its superstructure; water rushed hungrily beneath its crude planking with only inches to spare. On the near side of the river, he saw a man leading a small, tough-looking mountain pony out onto the beach by the near side of the bridge.

We could use a pony like that, he thought admiringly, looking back up at the steep, twisting trail that he and the pony before him had descended. He started down, placing his feet carefully on the sandy, eroded trail. When he came out onto the beach the man was beating the pony.

7

The rushing of the river made speech difficult; three times Dorje remonstrated loudly with the owner of the pony, and each time the owner half-turned irritably, cupping his hand to his ear to hear better. Finally he turned in a rage, threatening Dorje with the stick with which he'd been beating his animal.

Dorje turned on his heel, and crunched back across the sand to where they were standing.

"I can do nothing," Dorje said. "He owns the pony. And the pony refuses to cross the bridge."

"Of course the pony refuses to cross the bridge," Trowbridge said, coldly furious. "No animal would cross that thing. Especially no hoofed animal."

"This fellow is not in his proper mind," Norbu said.

"Also," Chandra said succinctly, "he is drunk."

The pony, a shaggy, barrel-chested creature, was tied to the bridge cable so it could not back away from the blows delivered to its neck and withers. Head up, eyes wide, it swung its head desperately between every blow. The Rai, looking nervous, said something unintelligible, fingering a silver amulet. Trowbridge looked at Chandra, who understood his language.

"He says that we must not interfere. That the fellow is possessed by the demon spirits of the river."

As they stood on the little beach in the deep, shadowy cleft of the Kali Gandaki, with white water bursting violently from a narrow outlet upstream and the noise reverberating like thunder from the canyon walls, it did seem as if they'd stumbled into a place where demons and spirits, relics of an earlier, grimmer age, might still hold sway.

"There are enough of us to take the stick away," Dorje suggested.

"Then what?" Norbu said. "Do we take the pony too, and meet the police at Narula? They will return the pony to its owner for a worse beating. And we will go to jail."

Trowbridge tried to decide if their already strained budget could support the purchase of a pack animal, then realized they could never get it across the river if they bought it.

Jeet and Nima had emerged onto the beach, and were shrugging

their loads off quickly as they watched the beating. Nima spoke quickly to Jeet, then jogged across the sand and stepped between the pony
and the stick. The pony's shocked owner, arm upraised, regarded her
in disbelief.

"A brave gesture," Chandra said. "And one, like most brave ges-
tures, that will earn her a broken head."

"Jeet is there," Dorje said.

Nima spoke to the pony owner, gesturing urgently at the bridge.
The owner shouted at her, then threatened her with the stick as he'd
threatened Dorje. She stood her ground, making no move to defend
herself. A moment later a slashing blow landed across her arm and
shoulder. The stick rose again; this time Jeet's massive arms closed
around the owner from behind, imprisoning him. The stick dropped to
the sand.

Stepping past Jeet and the pony owner, Nima stroked the animal's
neck with one hand and held the other hand palm-up below its flaring
nostrils, speaking to the pony as if they were old friends. Trowbridge
watched in fascination, recognizing an instinctive ability with animals.

She was not only instinctive, he realized, but practiced; she must
have worked with horses before. She was calming the terrified animal
before their eyes, speaking to it, leaning into it comfortably, letting it
grow accustomed to her weight and feel, and finally untying it from
the cable of the bridge.

"Now what?" Chandra asked.

Nima was studying the river. She drew a rag from inside her
clothes and wrapped it around the pony's head with a smooth movement, covering its eyes. Jeet still had a firm grip on the pony's owner,
who was no longer struggling; he watched curiously, his expression an
unpleasant combination of suspicion and cunning.

The pony submitted, doubtfully at first, to the blindfold. Then it
threw its head back and snorted, struggling. Once again Nima calmed
it before leading it forward across the sand toward the bridge.

"Never," Chandra said flatly.

Trowbridge watched in disbelief as Nima persuaded the blindfold-
ed animal to place a hesitant hoof onto the first rickety board. Backing
a step farther onto the bridge, she guided the second foreleg toward a
safe purchase on the thin planking. Then she grasped the first hoof,
and guided it lightly forward again.

What about the back legs? Trowbridge wondered. She can't help
with those.

The pony, however, seemed to learn its footing as it went, memorizing the placement of the planking. In several places, guided by Nima's sure hands, it stepped over gaps beneath which dark water flung by. They watched, spellbound, as Nima and the pony picked their way slowly to the center of the bridge. Here, at the farthest distance from its moorings, the rickety construction swayed slightly beneath their movements. The pony's front legs stiffened and its hindquarters bunched nervously.

The pony was a second away from panicking, Trowbridge realized. If it shied sideways it would pitch through the twisted bark strips which formed the sides of the bridge—and if Nima tried to help she would almost certainly go in as well. The canyon walls were high and steep, the current deadly; even a strong swimmer would never survive.

Trowbridge, from the shore, willed the pony to stillness. Nima rose with perfect balance, stroking the pony's neck, leaning into it as she had on the beach, speaking to it in the same practiced fashion. The slightest movement now would send both of them into the water. For almost a full minute the pair stood utterly still. Then Trowbridge saw a relaxation in the pony's stance, a resumption of trust. Slowly, painstakingly, Nima led the pony the rest of the way across the bridge onto the little beach on the far side.

I don't believe it, Trowbridge thought wonderingly.

Nima drew the blindfold from the pony's eyes. Examining its new surroundings calmly, the pony raised its nose and sniffed the air, glanced at the bridge without evident recognition, then spotted a patch of grass a few feet from the canyon's edge, ambled in that direction, and began tearing contentedly at its dinner.

From the far side of the river Nima turned and looked back, triumph on her face. Trowbridge glanced at Dorje, who was shaking his head happily, then looked to see the pony driver's reaction. Jeet, once Nima and the pony had reached the safety of the far side, had dropped the man unceremoniously onto the sand, turned on his heel, and walked back toward his *doka*.

Curiously, the pony driver behaved as if nothing out of the ordinary had happened. He stood up, brushed himself off, and slung a small bag of belongings over his shoulder. Then, ignoring Trowbridge and the others, he began to pick his somewhat drunken course across the bridge. The water had risen noticeably while they'd been standing on the beach.

"We're on the wrong side of the river," Trowbridge said. "Is every-one here?"

"All but the Tamangs," Dorje said. "They should not be far behind. I will wait for them."

Trowbridge shook his head. "Let's wait on the far side. I don't trust this river."

They went one at a time, at first, to minimize the swaying, then two at a time as the water began fussing at the bridge's lowest point. The water level was rising quickly, and each crossing took several min-utes. Trowbridge, gripping the slippery cable above his head to keep his balance, marveled once again that the pony had been persuaded across. It would have been impossible, even now; white water foamed up through the planking, and the bridge had begun to shudder steadi-ly against the downstream flow.

Eventually they stood together in a small group on the far side.

"If the Tamangs do not hurry," Norbu said, "we will lose them."

"We can't afford to lose them," Trowbridge said, studying the trail. "Or what they carry."

"David *sahib*," Dorje said. "The owner of the pony wishes to know if we want to hire him and his animal."

Trowbridge turned incredulously to look at the owner, who stood with his arms crossed a few feet away, hatchet-faced and filthy in his dark rags, staring sullenly out at the river.

"After what happened, he wants us to hire him?"

Dorje nodded. "He has seen the size of the packs we are carrying. He knows we could use the help."

"Tell him we'll buy the pony. If the price is reasonable."

Dorje relayed the message in Nepali. The pony driver unleashed a flood of rapid, slurred speech, the gist of which was that the pony was his livelihood and he could never sell it—although in the event that he were to sell it, he could never part with it for less than, say, twelve thousand *rupiya*.

"That's absurd," Trowbridge said. He turned his back on the pony driver and looked across the river once again, watching the water rise, waiting for the Tamangs.

By the time the two slow-moving porters trickled out onto the far beach the bridge was bucking heavily into the fast-moving chop. Planking and strips of twisted bark were being worked loose, slipping and pitching into the river.

"It's breaking up," Trowbridge said. "They have to hurry."

Dorje climbed onto the near end of the bridge and gestured at the Tamangs—who could hear nothing in the constant roar of the river—to hurry across.

Looking like frightened children, the Tamangs stepped reluctantly onto the first planks at the far end. When they felt the bridge move beneath them, they lost their nerve and backed away. One of them lifted his arms apologetically. Before Trowbridge could prevent it, Dorje and Jeet started back across. They moved steadily toward the far side, carefully negotiating the center of the bridge, which had tilted, by now, almost entirely over onto its side, forcing them to walk a tightrope on the cable meant originally to be a hand rail.

When they reached the far shore, Dorje and Jeet slipped into the *dokas* of the relieved Tamangs, who looked more than happy to give up their loads. Jeet started back across immediately. Dorje paused long enough to give instructions to the two frightened porters, gesturing encouragingly at Jeet as he crossed the bridge—suggesting, no doubt, that if Jeet could do it with a full load, they could do it unburdened. The Tamangs stood with their heads down, listening. Dorje started back across, stopping once to beckon them to follow. Trowbridge watched with his heart in his throat as Dorje made his way, a few yards behind Jeet, toward the lowest point of the bridge, where a heavy plume of water was skating upward off the planking. Only Jeet's upper body had been visible as he negotiated this constant explosion of water; as Dorje moved slowly through it, all but the top of his head disappeared.

When Dorje reached the beach he was soaked from head to foot.

"Cold water," he declared, his teeth chattering and his fingers blue. Slipping out of the *doka*, he turned, agilely remounting the near end of the bridge, and beckoned urgently to the two Tamangs.

"They will not do it," the Limbu said quietly.

"I would not," Chandra said, standing at his shoulder. "It has grown much worse."

The Tamangs were clearly in an agony of frightened indecision. A few moments later the decision was made for them; the bridge came apart before their eyes.

The two halves swung downstream, still anchored, at either end, to opposite shores. Writhing against the current, spinning, breaking up, losing bits of twisted construction, the two sections eventually trailed like a pair of scarecrow arms along either shoreline, leaving the Tamangs standing hopelessly on the far side.

Trowbridge looked over at the pony driver, who remained at the water's edge, staring out at the wild, now-unbridged river. His expression of sullenness had been replaced by a rather wide-eyed look; he had to be considering that if it were not for Nima he could easily have been stuck with his pony on the wrong side of the river. A moment later something else occurred to him, and he shot an unpleasant look of triumph in Trowbridge's direction.

It didn't take a mathematician to figure out that without the Tamangs they had at least two more loads than porters.

8

On the morning they left Narula the day dawned hot and clear. As the expedition moved in silence down a narrow street at the far end of the village, a voice came from inside a narrow doorway.

"Checkpoint."

Trowbridge slipped out of his pack and stepped inside, waiting patiently as his permit was scrutinized.

"Lhakrinor!" the soldier said, obviously impressed. "I have never traveled there. But I am told it is a very cold place, and very poor. Why do you want to go to Lhakrinor?"

"Research," Trowbridge said. "I'm a scientist."

Trowbridge heard movement behind him and turned, slightly startled. A lean figure stood in the doorway, backlit, with features that could not be discerned in the shadow.

"The land of Lhakrinor is fit only for yaks, demons, and crows. Not for human beings. Above all, not for the faithful."

Trowbridge and the soldier stared at this apparition.

"Excuse me?" the soldier said.

The figure stepped out of the shadows into the light beside the soldier's desk.

"And perhaps not fit for scientists," the newcomer added with a mild, humorous look. "Or poor pilgrims either."

He extended a hand to Trowbridge, looking him in the eyes in a friendly manner. Trowbridge, responding automatically, shook his hand, then realized he was dealing with a Westernized Asian; Nepalis did not, as a matter of course, shake hands.

"And you are . . . " Trowbridge said.

"You are the scientist, are you not? In that case I must be the poor pilgrim."

The man, smiling openly now, was Indian; Trowbridge could tell by the straight narrow nose, the formal inflection with which he spoke English.

"I apologize for speaking in riddles. My name is Krishna Sanwal. I am from Uttar Pradesh, where I have given up the life of a university professor. An anthropologist, to be precise. I have said good-bye to my family so that I may visit the holiest of all mountains before I die."

"Kailas," Trowbridge said.

"Yes."

"You have permits to cross the border into Tibet?"

The Indian nodded.

"Those are not easy permits to obtain."

Krishna dipped his head modestly. "I found support in government quarters for my pilgrimage. Many government employees, both in Nepal and India, would like to do as I am doing."

"And in China?"

Krishna spread his hands in a small gesture of explanation. "Relations are improving between India and China."

"But there are shorter routes to Kailas," the young soldier said. "You can cross directly from India, avoiding Nepal altogether."

"This is true. However, when one makes a journey of the spirit, the shorter way may not be the most direct."

Trowbridge felt a certain wariness. If this fellow really intended to travel by foot to western Nepal before crossing into Tibet—an absurdly lengthy route to get to his destination—then they would be traveling, at least for a time, in the same direction. He had no real desire for company which could only complicate, not aid, his expedition.

"And you, sir, must be the famous biologist, Dr. David Trowbridge."

Trowbridge studied him in open surprise. Krishna had pronounced his name as a fact, not a question.

"How do you know that?" he asked bluntly.

"Well, to begin with, you are clearly not a frivolous mountaineer—you travel without Western companions, and lack the proper equipment for ascending peaks. And you cannot be a simple tourist, or you would have read in your guidebook that traveling in Nepal during the monsoon is . . . well, problematical."

"Problematical," Trowbridge repeated, smiling in spite of himself.

Krishna's eyes crinkled with pleasure when he saw that Trowbridge was amused.

"Finally," he said with a disarming shrug, "when I passed through Pokhara, I heard your name spoken. So the truth comes out—I am not as clever as I tried to make you think."

"Sometimes I wish I were less well-known."

"You could give up your profession, as I have done, and become a pilgrim."

Trowbridge looked at Krishna closely, trying to figure out his tone of voice.

"I'm a pilgrim of sorts already," he said.

"I had not thought of that," Krishna admitted. "Yes, that is true, you are a pilgrim already. We are similar in more ways than I had realized."

"Here is your permit," the soldier said, passing it across the rickety wooden table. Trowbridge checked that the carefully stamped authorization to continue was in the proper place, and slipped it back into his pocket. Krishna's eyes followed the permit as it disappeared.

"You have some very high passes to cross to go to Lhakrinor," the soldier told him. "I suggest you carry firewood, because the passes are barren. The next checkpoint is at Chitragong. Keep a close eye on your possessions in Chitragong, there are many thieves there. What else can I tell you? Ah yes, there was another scientist who went toward Lhakrinor. This was many weeks ago. Perhaps you will see him on the trail."

"Do you know his name?"

The soldier shook his head apologetically. "He was British, I think."

Trowbridge thanked him and turned to his new acquaintance.

"Well," he said, "I wish you the best of luck. And now I think I must see about my porters."

"Of course," Krishna said politely. "The best of luck to you also."

Trowbridge was relieved he had not asked to join the expedition.

His pack landed on the uneven stone porch of the lodge with a flat "whump." He sat beside it, wiping the sweat from his forehead, taking deep gulps of the cool clean air, wondering if he would be able to carry a full load at higher elevations when the air grew thin.

"I have never heard of a *sahib* who carried his own load," he had overheard the Limbu say admiringly to Dorje earlier in the afternoon.

"It is very impressive," Dorje had agreed. "Still, it is a reflection on my abilities as *sirdar* that he must do so."

Dorje and Norbu had tried to hire more porters in Narula, but none had been available.

Farther up the trail two more houses—the grouping qualified as a village on his map—nestled into the blue slope of the mountain. The houses had a distinctly alpine look, with slate rooftops and sturdy, hand-hewn wooden sides.

"*Namaste*," he said when the hostess, a solid, good-looking woman with strong features and large gold earrings, stepped out of the lodge.

"*Namaste*," she replied easily.

"*Chiya*," he requested.

It was not necessary, in most situations, to say "please" in Nepal; respect was indicated by one's tone of voice.

The hostess stepped inside the dark lodge and returned moments later with a glass filled with fragrant, steaming, sugary tea. Handing him the hot glass, she squatted comfortably at the edge of the porch and lit a clay pipe, serenely considering the long green valley below.

This vantage afforded a clear view back down the trail they had followed this morning from Narula. Norbu, as usual, had disappeared somewhere ahead to scout the way, and to arrange for lodging and food. Below, working up through the sloping conifer forest, came the rest of the expedition. In the middle of the straggling line was Nima, followed closely by the pony. On the pony's back was the matched pair of *dokas* which had been carried, until two days ago, by the Tamangs. Piled atop the *dokas* were a number of miscellaneous items, none overly clean; the pony driver had insisted on loading his few personal possessions onto the pony instead of carrying them himself. At the moment he was dragging along somewhere out of sight at the far end of the expedition. Only the fact that the pony—his meal ticket—moved along at a steady pace prevented him from spending the entire day in the tea houses, drinking *rakshi* with the sizable advance he had demanded.

No matter, Trowbridge thought. The loads are moving.

He squinted into the blue, sunny sky. In the air was a faint hint of coolness, foreshadowing the mountain passes to come. He blew on the tea and felt warm tendrils of steam curl around his face. His breathing had returned to normal. He felt pleased at the quick recovery time; he was definitely getting back into shape.

He finished the glass of tea, and looked over at the hostess. She stood easily, took the glass from his hand, then lifted it slightly, eyebrows raised, with the courteousness characteristic to hill people: Did he wish another glass? He nodded, and she disappeared into the hut.

Once again, he looked back down the trail. A full half mile behind the rest of the expedition, the pony driver had come into view. Farther back, rounding the huge mass of rock which marked the mouth of the valley, came another figure. Trowbridge looked more closely, then dug his binoculars out of his pack. Focusing carefully, he made out the second figure. It was Krishna Sanwal, the Indian pilgrim.

For the first time that night they made camp instead of staying in a lodge. Smoke from the cook fires lifted into the evening clarity. There was an invigorating chill in the air; sweaters appeared from the bottom of various packs and *dokas*. Jeet served up cucumbers in yogurt, fried bananas, and *tsampa*, a doughy paste made of barley flour mixed with tea. Afterward, while the others washed the dishes, the pony driver disappeared down the trail in the direction of the nearest lodge. No one was unhappy to see him take his sullen expression and go.

Sitting closer to the fire as the sky grew dark, Chandra and the others discussed a recent scandal involving the *kumari*—the Living Goddess, sometimes known as the Virgin Goddess, of Nepal.

"She has run away from her husband," the Rai said, clutching his silver amulets nervously as if the very statement might incur bad luck. The Rai lived in a strange, multitudinous shadow-world, a world populated by as many spirits, it seemed, as human beings; he was often seen mumbling prayers and moving his fingers in the air in some strange pattern meaningful only to him.

"I had heard of that," the Limbu said. "She has not come back?"

"She has not come back—and they say she *will* not. Even as a girl she was rumored to be strong-minded and proud. She has disappeared, and no one knows where she is."

Kumari. Trowbridge thought back to what he knew about the isolated, fairy-tale existence of the Living Goddess of Kathmandu. Several candidates were chosen, at the age of three or four, for their exceptional beauty and physical flawlessness. The girls were then examined against a long list of perfections. Once a candidate was deemed to be a perfect physical vessel, she was tested for fearlessness, the final quality that would indicate she was, in the eyes of the goddess, the right young girl among thousands to be her living incarnation. The young candidate was thrust alone, in the middle of the night, into a darkened temple where masked priests attempted to shock her into a show of fear. If the girl retained her composure, she was elevated to the status of *kumari*; the power of the goddess entered her body, and for the next few years of her life she lived in a luxurious Kathmandu palace, a child goddess to whom even the king of Nepal bowed his head.

Trowbridge remembered catching a brief glimpse of the most recent *kumari* five years ago, on his way through Kathmandu before leaving for a survey of bharal and wolves in the Manang area. He'd been passing through Durbar Square when she had made her daily appearance at the intricately carved upstairs window of her palace. He remembered clearly the intent, curious stare, the graceful features, the full, child-like lips and slightly flared nostrils. She had been wearing a gorgeously colored garment and an ornate, jeweled headdress; on her forehead had been painted a third eye, shining like a scarlet flame.

The girl could not have been more than thirteen years old then. He remembered being impressed by her breathtaking beauty and her apparent poise, and he remembered wondering if she ever felt trapped in this peculiar form of existence.

Perhaps not, since she had hardly known any other.

The reign of the Living Goddess ended abruptly when she manifested some physical imperfection, or at first menstruation. At this point she left the palace and the *kumari* tradition grew somewhat darker. It was common belief that bad luck accrued to the man who married a *kumari*; because of this superstition, a number of ex-*kumaris* had ended up marrying beneath their caste, had never married at all—a fate looked upon with extreme pity in this society—or ended up as prostitutes. After several scandals, the government had begun providing the young women with a pension which made it easier to attract a husband and resume something like a normal life.

According to the Rai, however, the most recent *kumari* had not taken kindly to an arranged marriage in a small village in eastern Nepal.

"They say that her husband has petitioned the government to receive her pension," said the Rai, poking at the fire with a stick. "He claims he needs the money to continue searching for her. He will die soon, of course. Any man foolish enough to marry a *kumari* will have bad luck—and the husband of a *kumari* who runs away will, no doubt, have even worse luck."

"Well," Chandra said, "I wonder. Let us examine the case: This fellow marries a beautiful young virgin, and lives with her for a year—long enough for any man to get tired of his wife, even if she *is* young and beautiful. Then, most conveniently, she runs away. And if she is not found, the poor fellow may be forced to accept her pension from the government! Yes, that is certainly terrible luck. In my case, I had to be a soldier thirty years to get my pension. And I promise you, no one provided me with young virgins!"

"You are sacrilegious," the Rai told him soberly.

"And you are afraid of ghosts," Chandra replied, taking no offense.

"I am," the Rai agreed fervently. "As any man should be."

The Limbu regarded both Chandra and the Rai with a dour, skeptical expression, and said, "Whether or not the husband experiences bad luck, it remains a scandal. It is not proper that she has run away."

"She is a free person," Jeet said unexpectedly, his face impassive in the firelight as he looked up from his carving. "Why not let her do as she likes?"

Nima glanced at Jeet with approval.

"She is not a free person," the Rai said firmly. "She is the *kumari*."

"She *was* the kumari," Jeet said.

"Some of the power of the goddess remains within these girls," the Rai insisted, "even after they leave the Palace."

There was a lengthy silence in which the group studied the fire.

"Well," Chandra said finally, "if she did not like this first husband, we must simply find her one she likes better."

He reached into the fire, picked up a smoldering stick by its unburnt end, and pointed it at Dorje with a grin.

"I have already found a wife," Dorje shook his head. "She is waiting for me in the Solu Khumbu. We are to be married next year."

"But think of the pension, Dorje! And I hear she is a real beauty, this one!"

"From the sound of it, she would be too much for him," Norbu said.

The other porters laughed. Dorje only shook his head, fingering the healing cut on his chin, smiling sheepishly.

9

Trowbridge emerged from the depths of a cool green forest into newly turned fields. Steam rose from a fresh mound of water buffalo dung beside the trail; a rooster crowed somewhere ahead. A few minutes later he walked into one of the most pleasant villages he had yet encountered. Children played before open doorways; red peppers hung drying on a rough wooden rack; grain, spread out beneath, dried on bamboo mats. An old man in a white turban sat cross-legged, weaving pale green bamboo strips beside his cone-shaped, red clay house. Chickens scratched in the neatly kept yards; from inside the houses came sounds of conversation, laughter, and the smell of cooking food.

The higher they went, Trowbridge thought, the more cheerful the people seemed to become. He remembered the awful silence which characterized so many poor Indian villages, the overpowering sense of a population desperate, starving and hopeless. Most Nepalis, by contrast, seemed to have a genuine sense of well-being, even if they were poor.

Half a mile beyond the village, walking again through the cool, welcome shadows of the forest, Trowbridge came across a slope of ring-barked trees. The government, because of Nepal's severe erosion problem—probably the worst in the world—had placed restrictions on the cutting of live trees, be it for timber, firewood, or to clear land for cultivation. Villagers got around this by slashing a deep cut around the tree's base; the tree then died, and could be cut down without legal repercussions. Once the trees were felled, the steep slope was cultivated; the soil, which had taken millions of years to create, supported a single crop and washed away in the next year's monsoon, leaving a rocky wasteland. Close to a third of Nepal's mid-Himalayan forests had already disappeared in this fashion.

The wild animals, of course, already hard-pressed by the expanding population, disappeared with the soil.

He rounded a turn in the trail and stopped. Before him stretched a wide, sloping gash in the forest, a slash-and-burn field. Next year, the ring-barked stand of trees he had just seen would look like this; the following year, it would be a barren slope.

In the corner of the field stood a temporary-looking shack. Beside the shack the remains of a fire smoldered. A stream choked with red clay ran down through the open, unterraced land. The pleasant feeling he'd had while passing through the village disappeared. He paused beside the stream, watching it drain the hillside of life. This soil would filter down through the foothills of the Himalayas into the jungled swamp of the Terai, then into the vast brown Gangetic plain; finally it would flood out into the Indian Ocean, making an ocher cloud in the water which extended out four hundred miles.

The Himalayas, the greatest mountains on the face of the earth, were being washed away into the Bay of Bengal.

He was startled by someone at his shoulder.

"They call Nepal the Switzerland of Asia," Krishna said. "But in Switzerland they do not destroy their own livelihood. They manage their mountains and forests carefully."

The noise of the water had covered the sound of the Indian's footsteps. Trowbridge was annoyed at being caught unaware twice in twenty-four hours.

"You keep a brisk pace," he said coldly.

"Ah!" Krishna said, with an apologetic look. "I have startled you once again! I offer my humble apologies."

"That's all right," Trowbridge said, jumping the stream and striding on. "I would imagine holy men are supposed to tread lightly."

Krishna laughed softly and leaped over the stream, keeping pace with him easily. The trail passed through the ugly gash in the hillside and entered the forest once again.

"I do not think I am very holy yet," Krishna said.

"That makes two of us."

"Do you mind if I walk with you? It is not every day I have the chance to share the company of a scholar and an educated man. Perhaps, at the next village, I might buy you lunch."

Trowbridge glanced at Krishna, who was smiling in serene pleasure at the joke. Lunch in the next village, of course, would be *dalbhat*—there was little else available—and would cost about twelve cents.

"For a holy man—and a university professor—you have a sense of humor. What university did you say you taught at?"

"The University of Fatehpur," Krishna said. "Not such a famous place, I'm afraid."

"And now you are on your way to Kailas."

"Yes," Krishna said. "And may I ask—because I have been a long, solitary time on this journey already, and am a curious fellow by nature—in which area of Lhakrinor you plan to be studying animals?"

"That will be up to the animals," Trowbridge said dryly.

"Yes, of course. Then, may I ask you a more personal question: Why do you care so much about animals, Dr. Trowbridge?"

There was a silence disturbed only by the fall of their own footsteps on the soft forest floor. Krishna, he realized, was admirably fit; his breathing was inaudible, even though the trail was uphill and he was carrying, like Trowbridge, a sizable pack. Krishna had the slight, rounded belly many Indian men acquired at an early age, but his limbs were lean and strong, nearly ascetic looking.

"It's not just the animals," he said. "Although when I watch a species vanish from the earth—when I walk through this forest, in total silence, and know that it was once filled with the presence of deer and panda and brown bear—it feels as if some kind of rare and beautiful light has disappeared forever. But it's also the land itself. That field we just passed through will wash away within the year. Multiply that by two or three generations of Nepalis…"

He shrugged. "These people are destroying their own birthright. It's happening everywhere, of course, but the Himalayas, in particular, are dying. Few people realize it, or are willing to do anything about it. The thing is, even if you *only* cared about the people, and had no interest in the land or the animals, you would have to see that people cannot survive on bare rock. Not if—"

He stopped, mildly embarrassed. "Sorry," he said. "Any minute you'll expect me to ask for a donation."

Krishna shook his head seriously. "What you say is true. And yet I wonder, on a more personal level, if you find the adventure of what you do to be an appealing thing. The exploration, and the conquering of wild places."

"That's part of it," Trowbridge admitted. "I seem to be happiest when I'm moving."

"Then that is something else we have in common," Krishna said. "Ah!" He stopped and pointed. "Perhaps I have found some wildlife in your silent forest. Look there! In that tree top. Is it a monkey?"

Trowbridge looked where he was pointing. The top of a tall tree was shaking vigorously. A branch cracked free and crashed down to the forest floor.

"It's a human being," Trowbridge said. "Cutting firewood."

* * *

"You are right, you know," Krishna said. "They are children."

He and Trowbridge sat in the shade on the lodge porch, eating *dal-bhat* and drinking tea. Krishna had performed lengthy ritual ablutions, washing himself and praying before he was ready to eat. Trowbridge had been glad once again that his porters were either Buddhists or non-orthodox Hindus.

" 'Children'?"

Krishna, with a dismissive movement of his hand, indicated Jeet, Dorje, and the others, who were taking an after-lunch nap in the shade of a fig tree. The tree had a white stone ring around its base, notice that the villagers had agreed among themselves not to cut it down.

"I don't think I said they were children."

"They *are* children," Krishna said. "The erosion we saw today is clogging rivers throughout India. The port of Calcutta now has navigational hazards because the Nepalis cut down all their forests, and do not replant the slopes. These people utterly lack discipline."

Trowbridge watched a little girl with plump brown legs emerge from the door of the lodge and toddle toward the stone steps. Reaching the steps, she turned around and climbed down, careful and serious, negotiating them one at a time. Her hair was tied up in a dark spray atop her head; in the warm weather her outfit consisted of tiny gold earrings and a pair of high-topped, pink plastic shoes.

He said, "I suppose you're aware that India buys a good deal of the wood that's cut for timber from the Nepali hills."

"Further evidence that India would do a better job of managing the situation! It is a great shame, in fact, that the British did not conquer Nepal when they had the chance. They tried, you know. Unfortunately there was no cure for malaria at the time, and the British soldiers died in droves—wiped out by mosquitoes, of all things—in the southern swamps of the Terai. It would have been better for all concerned if they had been more persistent. It is perfectly evident to any scholar that all of Nepal's culture flows from India—that only a historical accident kept Nepal from being included in Greater India: Mahabharat."

"Gracious," Trowbridge said. "An Indian wishing the British had conquered more of the Indian subcontinent."

Krishna failed to acknowledge the irony.

"I have a great admiration for the British," Krishna said. "The British of the last century, of course. In this century they have fumbled things rather badly. A country whose sphere of influence shrinks has failed its destiny."

"Are you suggesting India take over Nepal? I have a feeling the Nepalis would prefer you didn't do that. This country is also called the Switzerland of Asia because it's managed to maintain its independence for centuries—even surrounded, as it is, by larger, warlike countries."

Krishna smiled serenely, and looked up at the sky. "India is not a warlike country, Mr. Trowbridge—we would not invade poor little Nepal. Although if we wanted to, of course," he could not resist adding, "they would not be able to stop us."

Trowbridge stood up, brushed himself off, looked at the sun, and checked his watch. The porters, without having to be told, had begun to rouse themselves. Krishna also stood and began preparing for departure. He obviously intended to continue walking with them.

The Limbu stepped across the track and up onto the porch. Standing gloomily, a cup of tea in his hand, he stared down the trail the way they had come.

"Cheer up," Trowbridge told him, following his gaze. "I think we've finally outwalked the monsoon."

It hadn't rained for three days now. With luck, in two more they would reach Chitragong, the settlement which the soldier had warned them was filled with thieves. At Chitragong they would replenish supplies and begin their first serious climb, a two-day ascent of the main Himalayan range that would culminate in the crossing of the Serpo La pass. Once over the Serpo La, they would be nearly three-quarters of the way to Lhakrinor.

As if reading his mind, the Limbu said, "I will believe that when we have crossed over the Serpo La, *sahib*. Not before."

10

The path turned up and away from the Gangkara Khola, following a high ridge above a narrow green valley. The river, far below, was a ribbon of dark blue. Among daisies, wild strawberries, and rhododendron, in a clearing surrounded by oak and bamboo, Norbu found panda sign. The red panda, a smaller relative of the better-known giant panda, looked more like a raccoon than a bear; the animal was increasingly rare, less because it was hunted than because of the ongoing deforestation of its habitat. To come across traces of its continued existence was a pleasure.

"Two days," Norbu said, squatting, examining the crushed vegetation, the scat, and the tracks carefully. "Maybe three."

He looked up and grinned. "Shall we take a trophy?"

Norbu would trail a loping predator for hours, or lie motionless all day, in intense heat or cold, waiting for the approach of some grazing wild goat. It had not been a difficult transition for him to go from finding and killing animals to finding and studying them. But the idea of gathering up animal shit, saving it in labeled plastic bags, and carrying it as if it were something precious for hundreds of miles, he found endlessly comical.

Trowbridge shook his head. "No trophies until we're in Lhakrinor."

They straightened up and swung back onto the trail, both of them pleased to have found signs of life in the increasingly beautiful forest. For the first time, Trowbridge allowed himself the luxury of looking forward to being in Lhakrinor—to having a base camp, striking out into the mountains away from the established trails, roaming the high country with little more than a spotting scope and a canteen.

"You look like a novice monk who has skipped his lessons," Norbu said, laughing at him.

"I feel like one," he said, studying the snow line, barely a thousand meters above the trail. Now was the time to enjoy walking. The passes beyond Chitragong would be deep in year-round snow.

In the late afternoon he moved alone through the forest at a steady, effortless pace, without pain or weariness. His legs felt lean and infinitely strong; his body, light as air, experienced neither heat nor cold as the trail passed through sun and shadows. This was the purest, loneliest joy he knew—the simple act of walking through a wild part of the world where there was no sign of another human being.

The trail narrowed through a stand of gnarled oak trees. He turned sideways, easing his pack between the double trunk of the largest tree. Then he stopped, staring in disbelief at what he saw in the sunlit clearing beyond. An overweight, middle-aged man—a freckled Westerner, with a floppy hat and a sunburned face—sat leaning comfortably against a log, reading what looked like a newspaper.

Without looking up, the man began lecturing him.

"It's about bloody time you got here, you laggard—do you always let your man Norbu do the trailblazing? Lunch was on the light side today, and I'm awfully hungry, so I hope you've got more to eat in your pack than I have in mine."

"Mallory?" Trowbridge said incredulously.

"Have a look at these *thankas*, will you? They're absolutely gorgeous. They're not the originals, of course—it would be unethical to take those from the monasteries. But by virtue of my own outstanding abilities I was able to get access to the wood blocks and print my own copies. They're really quite remarkable. You should have a look, and not stand there gawking at me as if we didn't know one another."

"Mallory! I'd heard there was an English scientist working up here, but I had no idea it was you!"

Trowbridge dumped his pack and sat down on the log next to his friend. "Jesus, this means you're the scientist who had permits to get into Lhakrinor. This is wonderful, you can tell me what to expect—I'm on my way there myself."

"Lhakrinor, is it?"

"Yes."

"'Fraid not, old fellow."

"What are you talking about?"

Mallory folded the block-printed piece of parchment he had been studying, smoothed it carefully, and set it down on the grass.

"I had the permits, all right. But I was turned back, regardless, at Jorkhang. I never even got close to Lhakrinor. Of course I was terribly disappointed, but I ended up going to Jumla and doing quite well there. Trowbridge, do you realize what I've got here? Copies of Bon-po *thankas* from the twelfth and thirteenth centuries—*thankas* no one else even believed existed! This will bring my jealous colleagues to commit academic suicide. They'll hang themselves from the rafters of the faculty lounge—it'll be absolutely marvelous!"

"Why wouldn't they let you into Lhakrinor? Was there something wrong with your permit?"

"The permit was immaculate—I'm not an amateur in this country, you know that. They turned me back anyway. But I'll tell you all about it later. I'm starving! What have you got in that pack you're carrying? My lord, it's huge—have you given up hiring porters and become one yourself?"

Mallory eyed his pack covetously.

"I have some cold *chapatis*," Trowbridge said. "And peanut butter."

Mallory's eyes lit up at the mention of peanut butter.

"I've been living on noodles and *dal-bhat* for eight weeks. Do you hear what I'm saying? *Eight weeks!*"

"The peanut butter is in the front pouch of the pack."

"You're a wonderful man, Trowbridge. In spite of what everyone says about you. A wonderful, wonderful man."

"So, what is it this time?" Mallory asked, sniffing interestedly at the smoky dinner smells wafting through the air. "Adding to your reputation as the world's foremost expert on snow leopard?"

The quiet clearing had been transformed into a cheerfully busy campsite. Mallory's six porters and two Sherpas had set up camp beside Trowbridge's expedition; three separate cook fires winked peacefully between the colorful nylon balloons of the tents. Dorje and Jeet were talking animatedly with Mallory's Sherpas, with whom Jeet had worked on a recent expedition to Lhotse. The only individuals not participating in the general mingle were the owner of the pony, who sat sullenly waiting for dinner with his back against a tree, Krishna, who was off by himself, carefully laying out what Trowbridge noticed to be a good-quality, military-issue sleeping bag, and Nima, who—as she did every evening—was grooming the pony. Trowbridge found it amusing that she rubbed every speck of dirt and sweat from its coat with a square of rough burlap, but failed to wash her own face.

Trowbridge nodded. "That's part of it. I'd like to know how many snow leopard are up there, how many the habitat can support. If I can get a good look at even one leopard it'll make the walk worthwhile all by itself. And I've rigged up a new trip-wire for the camera which might get me some close-ups."

Mallory said, "You'll be the first naturalist they've ever let into Lhakrinor, won't you?"

"Yes. So there's more to this trip than just snow leopard. I'll be conducting a generalized, high-altitude predator/prey study. Primarily snow leopard, wolf, bharal. Also Himalayan tahr—another species of goat antelope—although it sounds as if the Lhakrinor population has mostly died out."

"Sounds like a sizable project."

Mallory let the obvious question—what was the point of such a comprehensive study—hang politely in the air.

"There's some talk about making a national park out of a substantial portion of Lhakrinor," Trowbridge explained. "The government has asked me to do a feasibility study. I also heard a rumor—and I'd appreciate it if you'd keep your mouth shut about all this—of a shou sighting near the Tibetan border."

"Shou? Isn't that a deer-like sort of thing? And aren't they extinct?"

Trowbridge nodded. "Sub-species of red deer. The last confirmed sighting was years ago in Bhutan, and most biologists have written them off. But Lhakrinor is some of the least accessible and least-studied terrain in the world. Very little information gets out of there—either from the Tibetan side or the Nepali side. It's not impossible that a small enclave of shou has survived. If so, I'd like to find them."

"My, that would be a feather in the old professional cap, eh?" Mallory grinned at him knowingly. "And exactly your style, eh? Turn the scholarly world on its head?"

Trowbridge shook his head. "Mallory, you're utterly corrupt."

"And you, my friend, are hopelessly pure. Do you know what Wapner said about you when I saw him last spring at a conference in Miami? He said you'd 'gone feral,' which I thought was rather amusing, and probably the first sign of intelligent life ever manifested by old Wapner. He's absolutely right, you know. You're the only person I know who thrives on hardship, poor diet, and general high-altitude deprivation. I do it because I have to. But you actually seem to like it."

"One thing I don't thrive on is solitude—it's good to see you. Although I can't say I'm thrilled about your having been turned back at Jorkhang. What happened, exactly?"

Mallory shrugged. "It's quite simple. The policeman chap there is a hard-nosed son of a bitch. For some reason he's made it a personal crusade not to let any outsiders into the area. My permits were in per-

fect order, and he knew it. Claimed he couldn't guarantee my safety—
said there were Khampa bandits working this side of the border. That's
never stopped anyone with a permit from traveling near the border
before, of course. I'll most certainly lodge a complaint when I get back
to Kathmandu, but a bloody lot of good it will do me then."

"What about slipping past the check post at night?"

"It's a possibility. I didn't try, because I'd already been denied
entry, and this fellow made it clear I'd be clapped in jail if I were
caught. You'd have a better chance, since you haven't been officially
turned back."

Out of the corner of his eye Trowbridge noticed Krishna sitting
down unobtrusively nearby.

"Let's think about this," Mallory continued. "There's another
check post at Bragamo, a day's walk before you reach Jorkhang. If you
stop in there—thus giving the appearance of acting in good faith—
then sort of lose your way and miss Jorkhang, you might pull it off.
Skipping one checkpoint would be a plausible accident; skipping both
would have a rather calculated look to it."

"Mallory," he said abruptly. "Let's walk. There's something I want
to show you."

"In the woods?" Mallory looked at him as if he were crazy. "I'm
quite comfortable here, actually."

"Mallory."

Mallory sighed, heaved himself to his feet, and shambled after
Trowbridge into the woods. They walked a few moments in silence,
then Trowbridge stopped.

"What's this all about?" Mallory asked him.

Trowbridge shrugged apologetically. "It's probably nothing. But
Krishna, the Indian who's attached himself to the expedition—I had
the strongest feeling he was listening to us as we talked."

"So what? We weren't saying anything particularly interesting.
He's just eavesdropping, like most people do when they're bored.
Unless, of course, you suspect he's been sent by your colleagues to fer-
ret out trade secrets. You're getting paranoid in your old age, David."

"No doubt. Still, I'd rather he didn't know the exact details of what
I'm doing."

"Well, I guess that's reasonable," Mallory said. "We'll stay off the
subject when he's in earshot."

They stood in darkening, greenish, tree-filtered light, looking back
at the firelit clearing. Above them, through a sieve of tree tops, stars

were emerging in a deep blue sky. The trickle of a nearby stream insinuated itself into the evening silence.

"Extraordinary how *outside* of things one can feel simply by walking fifty meters into the woods," Mallory mused. "Makes you feel rather less human. More like one of your animals."

He looked at Trowbridge, the whites of his eyes bright in the surrounding darkness. "What else do you know about this fellow?"

"Not much. Says he's a religious pilgrim, a former anthropology professor. Have you heard of him? Krishna Sanwal, University of Fatehpur."

"No, but I wouldn't have unless he'd done something particularly outstanding."

"He's on his way to Kailas."

"Kailas? Through Nepal? Well, that's certainly the long way round. He could have gone directly to the border from Delhi and saved himself six hundred miles. On the other hand, who knows what makes sense to a religious fanatic—or worse, to a university professor? Now, is there anything else you'd like to discuss before we go back and eat? I'm famished."

Trowbridge shook his head.

"Who's this fellow Norbu?" Mallory asked as they stumbled back toward the clearing. "Seems like a capable chap."

"I worked with him in Manang five years ago, and in the Solu Khumbu two years ago. Has a tendency to come and go as he pleases, but he's the best instinctive tracker I've ever seen."

"Is he from Lhakrinor?"

"No," Trowbridge said, mildly surprised. "He's from somewhere in the west. Near Mount Saipal, I think."

"Really," Mallory said. "I thought that might have been why you hired him. His features are rather longer and straighter than most western Nepalis—quite like the people you'll meet in Lhakrinor, if you're allowed in. Tenzing!" Mallory called, as they stepped into the clearing. "What's for dinner?"

Tenzing, Mallory's Sherpa cook, grinned wickedly. "Very sorry, Mallory *sahib*, food is all gone."

Mallory turned to Trowbridge. "You see how they treat me," he said. "It's a wonder I haven't wasted away entirely."

They dined on quantities of roast potatoes, cucumbers in oil with fresh herbs, and omelets made with onions and the soft, sweet white cheese of water buffalo. Afterward, to Mallory's immense delight, Trowbridge broke out a small bottle of rum. They sat watching the various fires burn down into beds of nervous, scarlet coals.

"I'm awfully pleased to lighten your pack by this much," Mallory said, lifting the rum bottle contentedly. "You've got a hell of a trek ahead of you getting over the Serpo La. Deep snow—your pony may not make it—and no shelter. The day we crossed was fine, but I'd hate to get caught up there in a storm. You're not really going to carry this pack over the Serpo La, are you?"

"Unless we can find another porter or two in Chitragong. Anyway, the Krimshi La, the last pass into Lhakrinor, is supposed to be worse."

"So I hear. Well, you're one *sahib* they won't call an *aalu* behind his back."

Trowbridge laughed. *Sahibs*, in Nepal, were often referred to as *aalu*—potatoes—for being soft and white.

"Chitragong's a hell of a place," Mallory continued. "Mostly Tibetan refugees, with the usual theft and poverty of any refugee camp. You may find some inhabitants of Lhakrinor there to talk to, though—they do some salt trading in Chitragong. Might learn something about the condition of the passes."

Mallory took a swig from the bottle of rum, then sat thoughtfully for a moment.

"If you do set up this park in Lhakrinor, I suppose you'll have to move the people off the land?"

"Probably, yes."

Mallory sighed. "Now I see why you want to keep this thing under wraps. Resettlement is damned controversial stuff, even when it's justified. Let me know ahead of time, so I can come collect the local manuscripts. Ah, David, we should have been born a hundred years ago, when the world was new and scientists were innocent bystanders."

They sat in silence a while. The fires had burned down; he and Mallory were the last ones in camp still awake. The black sky above them was filled with incandescent white stars, points of white light which seemed to be falling away from the earth at a great rate.

The morning dawned clear and fine and he was sad to see Mallory go.

"The bridge north of Narula is washed out," he told Mallory, gripping his hand as they stood in the sun-drenched clearing. "Take the southern route."

Mallory nodded. "I'll think of you up here in a couple of days, when I'm knee-deep in leeches. But I know there's a hot bath in my future, and nothing's going to stop me from having it. Listen, I'll be back in Kathmandu for some follow-up work in October—will you be out of the mountains by then?"

"With luck."

"Then good luck. If I can't visit Lhakrinor myself I'd like to be the first to hear about it."

They shook hands once more, then Mallory turned and followed his expedition down the trail, turning once to wave merrily before disappearing into the forest.

11

Trowbridge paused on a promontory, the first time he'd allowed himself to stop in nearly four hours of hard uphill walking. The delicate, pale green ferns which had illuminated the oak forest at lower elevations had disappeared, replaced by shadowy stalactites of hanging moss. He braced his pack against a rock outcropping, slipped out of the straps, and let it slide to the ground. A cool breeze brushed his sweat-soaked shoulders as he checked the altimeter.

Ten thousand feet. According to his map, the Sunakuri Ridge was another thousand feet up.

He looked at his watch. Dorje, quite a ways back down the trail, would have called a halt by now to prepare the mid-morning meal. Trowbridge decided to push on to the ridge by himself. He shouldered the pack once again, feeling its straps bite deeply into his shoulders, and moved out.

The trail passed a small *chorten*—a mound of flat stones carved with *Om Mani Padme Hum*, the omnipresent prayer of the Buddhist faith; the prayer translated, roughly, to "Oh thou of the Jewelled Lotus," and sounded, to Western ears, like "Oh money penny hum."

Soon oak and hemlock gave way to fir and birch. As he climbed higher he felt himself walk beyond the loneliness he'd felt after saying good-bye to Mallory. He hadn't been the only one; the entire expedition had been a bit subdued this morning. Mallory and his people may have been footsore, exhausted, and short of supplies, but they were going *down*—down to family and friends, down to the thousand simplicities and comforts of civilization.

An hour later, he reached Sunakuri Ridge. In an open space of grass, filled with blue primula and swept by a chilly insistent wind, he lay down beneath his goose-down parka in the bright thin sunlight, head pillowed on his pack, and slept.

Sunset lit up the vast lower reaches of Annapurna and Dhaulagiri, and shone in splinters, as if through broken glass, on the shifting clouds which obscured their peaks. The Kali Gandaki, far behind them now, was a wedge-shaped shadow between the two great mountains. The expedition had reached a point quite close to Dhaulagiri, the sixth-highest mountain in the world; tomorrow afternoon, at the refugee settlement of Chitragong, they would turn its giant corner and move to the northwest. Four days of steady climbing later, with luck, they would crest the Serpo La and be over the main Himalayan range.

Dinner was prepared in relative silence. Jeet studied the bubbling rice impassively as the pair of cook fires crackled. The pony, tethered off to the edge of the open space, tore hungrily at the grass which feathered palely around its hoofs. Under Nima's attention, it was looking healthier; she'd named it "Seto," after a fat, comical, Kathmandu demigod. Krishna sat cross-legged in the last light, reading from a thin, leather-bound book whose pages fluttered slightly in the evening breeze.

Trowbridge walked back along the trail to fill his canteen at a spring. He passed through a grove of low, stunted trees, then stopped a moment, standing on the edge of a sheer cliff, watching a mist drift slowly above the broad valley which led toward Chitragong. Turning, he found Chandra waiting a few paces behind him.

"Trowbridge *sahib*," Chandra said, staring straight ahead, shoulders squared back. "I have some information. But I am not sure I should trouble you with it. It may be of no consequence."

"Tell me," Trowbridge said. "Of course."

Reassured by Trowbridge's tone, Chandra continued. "The Indian fellow traveling with us. I do not believe him when he says he was a professor at a university."

"Why?"

"Well, I do not know how a university professor behaves. But I know how a soldier behaves. Even when he is not in uniform."

"A soldier?"

"It is not my place to instruct you in any subject, Trowbridge *sahib*. But I was a Gurkha soldier for thirty years. I had much opportunity to study my commanding officers. This man," he gestured back toward the campsite, "would like to be giving the orders. I can see it in his eyes. In the way he watches—as if he were not watching—what is going on around him."

"Most people, in most situations, would like to be giving the orders."

"But most people are not *used* to it. This fellow is used to it. Also, did you notice his sleeping bag?"

Trowbridge nodded. "I did. But that hardly identifies him as a soldier. He might well have purchased it surplus."

"That is true. But he could not have gotten the possession which he carries wrapped in his extra shirt from military surplus."

"What's that?"

"A nine-millimeter Browning. The pistol issued to officers in the Indian military."

Trowbridge felt a quiet current of anger.

"How do you know?"

"All men must relieve themselves. I took the liberty of investigating his things this morning while he was off behind some rocks. My friend the Limbu stood watch. If I had found nothing, I would have said nothing. As it is . . ."

Chandra shrugged.

Trowbridge was silent a moment. "Chandra," he said finally, "if you're right, and Krishna Sanwal is a soldier, why would he lie about it?"

"We are sensitive, in Nepal, about Indian soldiers. India is a large country, and we are a small one, and we share a border. For many years India had military observers on our northern border with Tibet. The Nepali government, as a matter of pride, insisted they leave. But many Nepalis now feel it would have been better to let them stay. Better to have soldiers in uniform than spies out of uniform."

"But why would an Indian soldier—or an Indian spy—be traveling with us?"

Chandra faltered, then chose his words carefully. "I do not wish to give offense. But perhaps you would be able to answer that question better than I. Trowbridge *sahib*, I am a Nepali—in my head, in my heart. I do not like Indian soldiers in my country pretending to be someone else. But I would also be unhappy if I were carrying a load on an expedition working secretly for another government."

In the silence, the wind ruffled softly across the top of the ridge.

"Chandra," he said to the troubled Gurkha, "I'm a biologist. I work for no government. But I have no real means of convincing you other than giving you my word."

Chandra was silent a moment.

"I accept your word," he said finally. "I have watched you also. You are an impatient man, but not a bad one. You are not a hidden man like the Indian."

Chandra made to leave, then turned. "I am happy that I am able to believe you," he said, before disappearing into the grove of trees.

Trowbridge filled his canteen, then waited a few minutes so that he and Chandra would not return to the clearing too closely on one another's heels.

He would confront Krishna in the morning, he decided, and ask him to leave the expedition.

12

"Yes, I was a soldier," Krishna admitted readily. "Before I became a professor, I spent ten years in the army—although I would have thought all traces of that life had been erased. Perhaps having been a soldier is like having an accent; no matter how fluent one becomes in a new language, some trace of the old always gives you away.

"But I am not a soldier now, Mr. Trowbridge."

They stood on the bank of a narrow river, watching Nima perform another miracle, coaxing Seto—who moved in delicate, patient steps—over a log bridge. An oyster-colored mist hung above the grass on the far side; beyond the bridge a broad valley filled with juniper and blue pine led toward Chitragong.

"I am surprised that you would notice it in me," Krishna said. "But perhaps I shouldn't be—a biologist is trained to study animal behavior, is he not? Or were you helped by one of your porters? Chandra Shamsher, perhaps. An old soldier, that one."

Trowbridge shrugged. He saw no reason to conceal it.

"Look, I know nothing about you, and I'm not accusing you of anything. But I have a responsibility to this expedition, and I don't want it endangered by any kind of controversy. I think it's time to pursue our separate ways."

He had decided not to bring up the issue of the gun. There was no point, really; he just wanted to get rid of the man.

Krishna tipped his head slowly. "I will separate from your group at Chitragong. Unless you would prefer—"

"Chitragong will be fine," Trowbridge said.

The expedition stayed close together as they neared the settlement of refugee Tibetans, mindful of the warnings they'd heard about banditry in the area. Slash-and-burn buckwheat fields appeared with increasing frequency; the river became choked and silty, and an occasional tumbledown hut appeared. After climbing a final hill, they paused, looking down on Chitragong. The sprawling encampment was larger than he expected; dwellings crowded close upon each other; tiny lanes twisted between tents, *chang* stalls, and wooden huts; herds of ponies were tethered in the few open spaces. Smoke lifted into the air from a multitude of fires, making a blue haze above the settlement. Trowbridge was not altogether pleased at this abrupt plunge back into civilization.

"Do you think we can complete our business and get out before dark?" he asked Norbu, as he watched Krishna, who had politely taken his leave, angle down the slope toward town.

Norbu shrugged. "Finding porters will be the problem. This is planting season. They may not want to leave the fields."

"See what you can do."

Norbu nodded and set off down the hillside toward the bazaar.

Dorje was conferring with the pony driver, who had been more than usually sullen all morning—in preparation, Trowbridge was certain, to announce a demand for higher wages. His quarrelsome tone indicated he was slightly drunk; he must have located some *rakshi* at one of the farmhouses.

Dorje approached Trowbridge with a sigh.

"He says he is losing money to stay with us. That there will be a great deal of work for his pony and himself in Chitragong. He will not stay with us unless we advance him a week's wages."

"Maybe if I took a stick and hit him several times on the head," Chandra suggested, "he might become more reasonable."

"Tell him we'll advance him two days' wages. No more."

"He will argue," Dorje said simply.

"If he argues, remind him that his is not the only pony in Chitragong. He has a good thing going, and he knows it. Chandra," he beckoned, "you know this town. Where can we set up camp for a couple of hours?"

"Only a couple of hours?" Dorje said. "Do you wish to go on tonight, David *sahib*?"

Trowbridge nodded. "We can finish our business, and get a two-hour jump on tomorrow's walk."

Trowbridge concluded the purchase of a pair of aluminum pots and turned to look for Dorje, who was buying lentils from a Nepali merchant. The merchant looked to be from one of the northern border areas; he wore long turquoise earrings and a necklace of turquoise and pale red stones. His hair was wrapped in a high topknot; his eyes were skeptical and tough, and his copper skin was burned dark, indicating he was a veteran of many yak caravans over the high passes.

He and Dorje, after lengthy negotiations, had agreed upon a price. The deal closed, Dorje mentioned that he was *sirdar* of an expedition heading north, and asked the merchant about the condition of the passes between Chitragong and Lhakrinor. The passes, he was told, were open at the moment. Only a freak storm would close them before winter. Dorje nodded and began counting out the money. The merchant fingered his scraggly black moustache, studied Dorje with a mischievous expression, then glanced at several friends who lounged nearby, drinking *chang* from wooden cups.

"And why are you going to Lhakrinor, the poorest, coldest, highest place in existence?" the merchant asked him. "Did your mother have trouble finding you a bride in the Solu Khumbu?"

Dorje's youthful face had gotten him into trouble once again.

He looked up and flushed. "For scientific study. That is why we are going."

One of the merchant's friends laughed hugely. "The witch of Narling will eat this one alive!"

"Who is the witch of Narling?" Dorje asked.

The merchant grinned. "You will find out soon enough. But I will tell you this: She is a Bon-po witch, and not a young one. Once a year she requires the services, for a single evening, of a strong young Bhotiya like yourself. For the occasion she transforms herself into a beautiful girl. When you wake up in the morning, expecting a sleepy young beauty to make your porridge, you find instead, crouched by the fire, a mumbling hag who has cast a spell on you so you cannot move. After you have realized your mistake, she cooks you over a fire, piece by piece, and eats you alive."

"There are heaps of bones on the slope beneath her hut," one of the friends added. "I have seen them myself. They are bleached white. She has built her bed with those bones—and every year the bed gets higher."

Dorje, a plausible look of bravado on his face, said, "Oh, yes, I believe everything you are saying."

He shouldered the heavy bag of lentils, turned to go, then stopped. "When I reach Narling," he said carelessly to the merchant, "I will pay a visit to this witch. It will be the first thing I do. If you tell me your name, I will give her your regards."

The grain merchant's look of amusement disappeared, and he looked distinctly uneasy.

"There is no need for that," he said seriously. "Just remember that you have been warned."

Leaving the bazaar, they heard, for the first time, *Om Mani Padme Hum*. The deep chanting resonated from the interior of a Buddhist temple, and was accompanied by a jarring, dissonant clash of cymbals, horns and drums. Dorje stopped a moment and listened. Then he looked around at the high surrounding slopes of the valley. The geography and vegetation, Trowbridge realized, were similar to Dorje's home district, the Solu Khumbu region on the slopes of Everest.

"I am glad we are in the mountains where I can hear Buddhist chanting once again," Dorje said. "But it makes me sick for home, a little."

He adjusted the heavy load of lentils, sturdily refusing Trowbridge's offer to take a turn carrying it.

"You have seen Chomolungma, David *sahib*, have you not?"

Trowbridge nodded. Chomolungma—"Mother Goddess of Snows" —was the Sherpa name for Everest.

"It is the most beautiful mountain in the world," Dorje said. "It will always be my good fortune to have been born there."

* * *

When he and Dorje rejoined the expedition on the outskirts of Chitragong, they expected it to be nearly ready to move out. Instead, it was in utter disarray. The pony driver, when no one was looking, had slipped away with Seto—and two days' advance wages—and disappeared into the maze-like encampment. Norbu, returning with two new porters, had learned that the pony driver was gone and plunged back immediately into the bazaar to try and find him. Shortly afterward it was discovered that Nima had also disappeared.

Finally, in the general confusion, the two new porters had decided they were more interested in tending to their buckwheat crop after all, and had wandered off.

Grimly, Trowbridge sent Dorje back to the bazaar to help find the pony driver, and, if possible, more porters. He forbade the others to go anywhere—not wishing to lose any more of his expedition—and added up the pluses and minuses of the afternoon's work. They'd added two full loads of supplies to what needed to be carried, and lost the pony and perhaps Nima as well. Unless Norbu and Dorje found more porters, they were grounded.

The sun had just touched the tips of the mountains to the south, and Trowbridge had just decided they would be forced to spend the night in Chitragong, when Norbu appeared with three porters: a tough, professional-looking Gurung, and a less substantial pair of Mangars. Behind him, trotting steadily across the airfield, came Dorje.

"I have seen him," Dorje said, gasping for breath.

"The pony driver?"

Dorje shook his head and tilted his head back, indicating the scar on his chin.

"The one who did this to me," he said. "Naraka, the *shikari* hunter from Pokhara."

"Are you sure?"

Dorje nodded. "I saw his face clearly."

"Did he see you?"

"I do not think so. He was in a *chang* stall arguing with a Khampa bandit. A man whose rifle barrel was painted red."

"A Gorchok," Norbu said quietly.

"Do you know this man?" Trowbridge asked.

"Not this man specifically," Norbu said. "But I know of the Gorchok, the Khampa tribe which paints its rifle barrels red. They are originally from Tibet, and were among the last to be forced by the Chinese over the border. Most of the other Khampas have gotten used to living in Nepal—but this group remains bitter about the loss of its homeland, and is among the worst for banditry and killing here in Nepal. They also cross the border from Lhakrinor to attack the Chinese."

"Why would an Indian hunter be arguing with a bandit from Tibet?" Dorje wondered.

"I don't know," Trowbridge said, "and I don't really care. But I have no desire to run into this Naraka again. We need to get moving."

Dorje and Jeet supervised the division of loads. Jeet was preparing to break Nima's load down into three portions when she returned to camp, her face stubborn and unhappy, and shouldered her pack.

As dusk fell, they followed a clearly marked trail up the south-facing, sparsely forested slope of the valley. From the interior of an occasional hut came muted sounds of dinner, of conversation and children playing. Soon the inhabited areas ended and it was all silence and near darkness. Moving single-file, they passed a long *mani* wall, a waist-high construction covered with hundreds of flat, carefully carved prayer stones. The stones caught the last light and gave it back, glowing with an energy that seemed to come from within. Above the stones, eight prayer flags rose on tall slender poles. Two sounds existed in the universe: the scuff of their feet on soil and stones, and the flags, snapping crisply in the evening breeze.

Forty miles away, above the eastern end of the valley, the rounded crest of Annapurna South hung in the sky like an enormous, rising planet. There was no moon, and as darkness descended, it grew cold.

Three hours later Trowbridge decided he could ask no more of the expedition. By lantern light they set up camp in a sandy riverbed, lashing the tent-lines to stones. Jeet lit a fire and began cooking for those who weren't too tired to wait for supper. Chandra, looking exhausted, declared that while he may have been middle-aged when he woke up this morning, he was now, unquestionably, an old man.

Norbu was standing in darkness a little ways up the trail. Trowbridge walked up to join him, shining the flashlight on his altimeter.

"Wet feet tomorrow," Norbu said.

"You smell it too?"

Norbu nodded. "Snow."

They were silent a moment. Then Norbu said, "It is strange to see this Naraka again."

"Would a *shikari* from the lowlands come all the way out here to hunt?"

"It is possible. There are still a few musk deer in the mountains to the west." He looked up at the night sky. "This has been a strange expedition from the beginning. Perhaps we were not meant to go to Lhakrinor."

Trowbridge recalled, with a stab of uneasiness, Norbu's comment three months ago that he might not accompany the expedition all the way to Lhakrinor.

Before he could say anything, Dorje appeared out of the darkness.

"David *sahib*, I am sorry, but we have another problem."

"I didn't think there were any left," Trowbridge said.

"Nima has disappeared," Dorje said. "I think she went back to find the pony."

In the white light of dawn Trowbridge was wakened by a hard clopping on the stones of the riverbed, then a soft crushing through the sand beside his tent. He sat up and put his head out into the chilly air.

Nima was tethering the pony in a grassy area next to the camp.

"Nima," he called quietly. "What happened?"

Without looking at him, she said in an exhausted voice, "I found the pony driver face down in a *chang* stall. I woke him up and he sold me the pony."

Trowbridge, still half-asleep, endeavored to make sense of this. How could Nima possibly have had the money to buy the pony?

Nima turned to him. "It is all right. We made the agreement, and I gave him the money, in front of witnesses."

"How much?"

"Six thousand rupiya."

"*Six thousand rupiya?*"

"It is a fair price." She held his gaze briefly, then lowered her eyes. He was struck, once again, by the contrast between her slender limbs and her strangely thick waist.

She said, "If you rehire Seto at two-thirds what you were paying before, he will carry the same amount, and you will be better off."

"Nima," Trowbridge said, "I'm glad to have you and the pony back. But I need to know where you got that kind of money."

This time when she looked up there was a flicker of defiance in her eyes.

"It was given to me by my mother. When I left my home."

She turned back to check the tether of the pony. "And now, if you do not mind, *sahib*, I think I will rest some."

13

The sky was overcast and dark, the knee-deep snow a filthy, mushy gray, and tough going. To the northeast, through intermittent clouds, Dhaulagiri—a hard, vast wall of ice and rock—loomed in occasional, menacing glimpses. In the thin, chilly air the porters struggled for breath as they humped their loads toward the top of the pass. Trowbridge reached it first, dumped his heavy pack, and was lying atop a low rock, scanning the surrounding slopes for blue sheep, when Dorje caught up to him.

"Nima could have carried her load," Dorje said, breathing hard as he reached the top. "It is what she is paid to do."

"Nima walked all night."

Trowbridge didn't take his eyes from the bare slopes. Visibility, because of the low cloud cover, was poor; still, they were into blue sheep country, and he was excited at the possibility of a sighting.

"I will be very happy, David *sahib*," Dorje complained, "when you are not carrying a load any more—even a light load. As *sirdar*, I feel bad to see you carry lentils and cooking gear."

Dorje waited for a response, then asked curiously, "Do you see any sheep?"

"Not yet," Trowbridge said.

Early that morning, unable to go back to sleep after Nima's return, he'd slipped out of camp and climbed a nearby ridge, hoping for a blue sheep sighting, or at least to find telltale shreds of wool on the brush. He'd seen no sign of blue sheep, but on his way down a small-ish, agile form had leaped into an opening in the brush a few feet before him. The slender beast had sniffed the air alertly, apparently unaware of his presence. Trowbridge, holding his breath, had recognized it instantly: a Himalayan weasel. A moment later, with a fluid whip of its mahogany-colored body, the weasel was gone.

It felt like a good omen. Trowbridge had been pleasantly reminded that soon—assuming they managed to slip past the checkpoint at Jorkhang—he would be able to stop being an expedition manager and start being a field biologist.

Norbu joined them at the top of the pass, blowing vigorously, stamping his feet. "Seto is having difficulties in this snow," he announced.

Dorje turned and looked back down the way they had come. "It is no surprise. Will he make it?"

Norbu nodded. "He will make this *col*. But the Serpo La..." He shrugged. Then he called out, in a studiously mocking tone, to Trowbridge, "Well, Doctor Trowbridge, do you see any bharal?"

"Not yet," Trowbridge said.

"Then please point your binoculars at this."

Trowbridge sat up, climbed down off the rock, and looked at what Norbu held in his hand. In the stiff twigs of a sprig of cotoneaster were tiny strands of fleece. The strands were bone-white for most of their length, but at the tips they became darker, almost blue.

Trowbridge took the sprig of cotoneaster, studied it, then looked up, pleased, at Norbu, who was grinning happily.

"Blue sheep?" Dorje asked.

"Blue sheep," Trowbridge said.

They spent the night in a Gurung village, deep in a shadowy gorge between mountain passes, driving their tent pegs into the hard dirt roof of one of the Pueblo-like dwellings. On the following day Nima resumed carrying her own load. This allowed Trowbridge—to Dorje's delight—to begin walking with only a light pack, and he quickly left the rest of the expedition behind. After several hours of steady hiking, he chose a promising gully which led up and away from the trail. Scrambling up an awkward series of boulders, he emerged onto a high, clear place.

Ahead of him stretched a cobbled line of peaks, connected by a narrow ridge which rose and fell precipitously. He stopped, placed his boots carefully into a slight niche, and leaned back against the rock behind him. The sun was warm on his face, but the breeze belied that warmth, and the rock at his back radiated cold.

He shifted the smooth pebble in his mouth—a pebble which helped keep his mouth from feeling dry—and studied the slope across from him. It looked more promising than any he'd yet seen. At its upper perimeter the soil ended in a high cliff slashed with tiny, grass-covered ledges. Picking out natural landmarks, he developed a grid and moved the binoculars up and down, side to side. Suddenly, something was there. Emerging from a stand of pale birch came first one grazing animal, then two more.

Blue sheep? No, the coats were shaggy and long, almost a chocolate brown, swaying as they moved. The short horns swept sharply back and down to narrow tips. Himalayan tahr. The elegant shape of the head was unmistakable; the alert, prominent eyes, high in the forehead, gave an impression of sharp attention, in contrast to blue sheep, whose eyes looked sleepy, almost sensual.

Three more tahr emerged from the small stand of trees, and the small herd—four adult females and two yearlings—grazed slowly and peacefully out into the open stretch of meadow. There would be a bachelor herd somewhere in the area, but it was far too early in the season for them to be mingling. He made a few notes, then flipped to the back of his notebook and began sketching.

This was more for his own amusement—and because he was suddenly content, for the first time today—than for any scientific reason. Tahr, one of the oldest and most primitive of the goat antelopes, had been fully studied; there were no controversies over its classification or behavior as there were over bharal. Finishing the sketch, he closed the notebook, looked down to where the expedition had pulled up and was making camp, then glanced at the afternoon sun. Tomorrow they would be up into the snow fields. The following day, with luck, they would cross the Serpo La and arrive at Bragamo. From there on it would be populated areas until they reached the Krimshi La, and Lhakrinor. This might be his last chance to spot blue sheep for a full week.

He began climbing again, slipping and sliding across a broad slope of gravel-like scree, following a barren ridge until he reached the snow line, where he concealed himself in a stand of gnarled cedars. He was pleased at the wildness of the country; there was no sign of human encroachment anywhere. Working systematically, he scanned the slopes.

Nothing. He looked back down the way he had come. Perhaps he ought to have been content with sighting the tahr.

Movement. A glint, something deep in the ravine beside the river. He aimed his spotting scope, focused carefully, and exclaimed in surprise.

It was a young woman of slender build, standing with her back to him, removing the last of her clothes. He scanned the area around her, but she appeared to be alone. He moved the scope back and watched her place a final article of clothing on a neat pile beside the shallow, sun-warmed stretch of water, then wade out slowly until the water rose above her knees. She leaned down, splashing water onto her legs, then squatted, washing herself thoroughly, paying special attention to her armpits and crotch. Finally she bent her head forward to wash her close-cropped dark hair.

Trowbridge took note of the fact that he had no right to watch like this, but he was too charmed and curious to lower the scope.

Even in this shallow stretch of river, the water was too cold for a lengthy bath. As the woman waded toward the beach he studied her face closely.

"I don't believe it," he said quietly.

Standing on the beach, she shook the water vigorously from her hair, then brushed the drops with her hands from her shoulders and legs. Her breasts were small and lovely, dark at the tips; her body was slender, but with a tough ripple of muscles in her back and thighs. She reached into her bundle of things, attached gold hoops to her ears, and turned her face toward the sun. For several minutes she sat like this, clearly luxuriating in the warmth, and in the sensation of being naked and clean.

Eventually, as the sun disappeared behind a mountain to the west, she stood and removed the earrings with obvious reluctance. Then, with practiced movements, she wound a length of quilted fabric around her waist, thickening her body from below her breasts to the graceful curve of her hips. She dressed quickly in baggy, filthy, nondescript clothing—the clothing she'd worn every day of the trek—and pulled on her stocking cap. Finally, she searched around the river bank until she found some acceptable muck, and smeared it on her face before disappearing in the direction of camp.

The flicker of a pair of cook fires lit up the clearing. The trees around them were solid and calm; water slipped in near silence along a riverbed filled with small stones and pine needles. It was hard to imagine that tomorrow they would leave this fairy-tale atmosphere and strike up into deep snow.

"She has to be from one of the better Nepali families to have that kind of money," Trowbridge said quietly, squatting beside the fire sipping tea. "And there's something else, something that struck me only yesterday. She has a hint of an American accent. She may have had more than one teacher, but the most recent was certainly someone from my country."

"A well-bred Newar," Norbu mused, "with an American accent,

and enough money to spend six thousand *rupiya* on a pony—working as a porter for thirty *rupiya* a day."

"Curiouser and curiouser," Trowbridge said.

Beyond the crackle of the fires, and the murmur of conversations, Trowbridge could hear, far in the distance, the sound of avalanches sliding down the slopes of invisible mountains.

14

Dorje peered into the mist, which ghosted in eerie tendrils around them, and said, "It's getting thicker."

The visible world had disappeared; they walked in a small gray room through a gray universe. In the clammy mist sounds were strangely muffled, arriving from the wrong directions; the scuff of a boot, the clank of a cooking pot, the clop of Seto's hoofs seemed to come from some other expedition moving along parallel to theirs. The porters, Trowbridge noticed, had bunched quite closely together.

Norbu, in the lead, stopped suddenly, peering into the fog ahead of them. In the mist something loomed like a dark, misshapen pillar.

"Just a rock," Norbu said.

A second shape rose out of the gray indistinctness, and then a third. Soon the valley was filled with the strange formations, which seemed to crowd increasingly close to the trail.

"It almost looks like they are waiting for us," Dorje said.

Norbu grinned. "Like *ro-lang*," he said.

Trowbridge looked at Norbu curiously.

"A *ro-lang* is a walking corpse," Norbu explained.

"If you are struck by lightning," Dorje said, "you become a *ro-lang*. Your body stands upright and walks, even though its eyes are closed. No one can stop you from walking or make you change direction."

The Rai hissed unhappily. "It is better not to speak of such things in a place like this."

An hour farther on, the valley stopped its gradual descent and sloped suddenly upward. They scrambled up into brilliant sunshine and stood on an icy ridge in the exhilarating light. Ahead of them, toward Lhakrinor and Tibet, the sky was a deep shade of blue, nearly black, as if they were looking directly into outer space. To the south, behind the valley from which they had emerged, there were clouds moving through the sky, great dark masses casting ominous shadows across the snowfields and peaks around them. The clouds had not been there at daybreak when they entered the valley.

"A storm is coming," the Limbu said simply.

Norbu nodded agreement. "I am afraid the monsoon is not finished with us yet. First *tsugas*, now snow."

Above the snow line the going became increasingly difficult for the pony, which plunged awkwardly, struggling for breath, through the deep mushy snow. Nima and Seto trailed in well after the others at each halt; at lunch on the second day, they did not arrive until the others had eaten and were nearly ready to continue. Nima squatted next to Seto, ready, without complaint, to move out again.

Trowbridge offered her a steaming cup of tea, but she shook her head.

"You have to drink," he said, "or you'll get dehydrated and lose your strength."

She brushed back the rag which covered her eyes to protect her from snow blindness.

" 'Dehydrated,' " she said. "I had forgotten this word."

She took the tea. "Thank you," she said, cupping her hand to its warmth.

He reached out and stroked Seto's nose. "Where did you learn to work with horses?" he asked.

"In Kathmandu," she said simply. He waited a moment, but she volunteered nothing more.

Trowbridge and Norbu reached the top of one of the interminable preliminary passes and stopped to confer. The altimeter indicated fourteen thousand feet. Another fifteen hundred feet and they would crest the Serpo La. It was noon, and dazzling sunshine blazed around them—even with goggles, the glare hurt the eyes—but the sky was extraordinarily active. Tremendous columns of black cloud marched this way and that, as if rushing toward some cataclysm for which they were late. To the southeast, in the direction of the monsoon, a solid darkness was rising in the sky.

"The storm will catch us," Norbu said. "We are moving too slowly."

"We'll get over, nonetheless. We have to."

"And when we are over?"

"We'll stop at the checkpoint, like we're supposed to, at Bragamo."

"Then slip past Jorkhang at night?"

Trowbridge nodded.

An hour later, in rapidly worsening weather, he stood by the side of the trail, watching the last of his porters file by. After a few more moments Dorje clumped into view.

"Where are Nima and Seto?" Trowbridge asked.

"They were right behind me," Dorje said, peering behind himself with a guilty look. "They cannot be far."

Trowbridge dropped his pack and set off down the trail. Several hundred yards back he found Nima trying desperately to coax the pony to its feet. The frightened animal had collapsed back on its haunches, nose raised high in the air, chest heaving convulsively. It was simply incapable, at this altitude, of drawing enough oxygen into its lungs to support the extreme effort of plunging through deep snow.

"It cannot breathe," Dorje said unhappily, materializing with Norbu behind him.

The four of them pushed and pulled on the pony, but it was no good. Trowbridge stepped back, telling himself that he should never have allowed Nima to bring an animal up here in the first place.

"There's something we can try," he said reluctantly, "although I'm not sure it will do enough good. It worked once when I was on a high pass in the Altai Mountains. The pony won't like it, though. You won't like it."

"What is it?" Nima asked.

"I would need Norbu's knife."

Nima looked at the pony for a long moment, then looked back at Trowbridge.

"We will go back," she said.

"It is too far," Norbu said. "The pony will freeze. And you will freeze with it."

There was a long silence. Then Nima nodded, almost imperceptibly. Norbu pulled the knife from inside his clothes and slipped it out of its sheath, handing it to Trowbridge. The dull metal shone obscurely in the snowy light.

"Hold his head," Trowbridge said.

Norbu and Dorje moved to either side of the pony. Nima wrapped her arms around its neck. Trowbridge stepped forward, inserted the knife into one of the pony's nostrils, and lifted in a hard, quick movement. The pony screamed, flinging its head backward. Blood sprayed onto the snow; Nima was thrown to her knees.

"Hold him," Trowbridge said evenly. "We have to do the other one as well."

"No!" Nima cried.

"Nima," Norbu said, "it must be done."

She struggled to her feet, tears freezing on her cheeks. "I brought Seto up here," she said bitterly. "I will do it."

Trowbridge looked at her. "Are you sure?"

Nima nodded, and took the knife from his hand.

The wind blew thick drifts of snow across the track, obscuring the trail. Dorje and Jeet worked together in the lead, testing the snow surface for hidden crevasses. Their pace had slowed to a crawl. On either side of them, snowfields stretched anonymously into the lowering, snow-thickened light. The porters labored slowly behind, stopping when Dorje and Jeet were forced to cast about for the trail, dully following the heels in front of them when the expedition moved forward again. Stopping was a relief for aching muscles and straining lungs, but it allowed the cold to penetrate.

Trowbridge stepped off the trail and pulled out his altimeter. Nearly sixteen thousand feet. They had to be close. He brushed the snow off, put the altimeter away, and watched the Mangars file uncomplainingly past. Their naked toes were bluish against the snow. Behind them came Seto, gulping quantities of thin air through torn and scarlet nostrils.

Trowbridge heard his name called from the head of the expedition. He clumped forward, followed by Norbu, and joined Dorje and Jeet. Dorje lifted his hands helplessly. "It is impossible to tell where the trail is," he said.

They stood in the falling snow, peering in the direction the trail had been taking.

"That's it, then," Trowbridge said reluctantly. "We make camp here. I don't want anybody walking into a crevasse, or off a cliff."

Camping in the snowfields was not an appealing prospect. The storm, they all knew, might last two or three days, and the Gurungs and Mangars had no shelter. Without firewood, they wouldn't even be able to melt snow to drink.

Jeet, furrowing his brow suddenly, said, "Listen."

At first, Trowbridge heard nothing. Then, faintly up ahead, he could hear it: cloth whipping furiously in the wind. They hurried onward, following the sound, which led them into a narrow defile between sharp black rocks. The sound grew louder, and then, materializing in the gloom ahead of them, they saw a cairn of head-high stones.

The stones were topped by a pair of prayer flags. They had reached the Serpo La. Gratefully, each member of the expedition placed a stone on the cairn and hurried on, down into a yawning, snow-driven darkness on the north side of the Himalayas.

15

In the hot, dry canyon beyond Bragamo white butterflies floated above layers of eroded stone the color of pale brick. It was hard to believe that the snowfields of the Serpo La were only a day's walk behind them. But they had beaten the monsoon, finally, and found shelter in the great rain shadow of the Himalayas. The afternoon clouds to which they were accustomed were absent; the sky was clear and dry. Far beneath them, in the deepest notch of the canyon, flowed the Shabki River, its water heavy with soil, moving like a muscular dark cord along its twisting course. Above them a tributary to the Shabki flung itself in a series of miniature cascades down from an anonymous snowy peak.

For the first time in a week the porters were wearing short pants; the warm weather had them expansive, and enjoying themselves. Trowbridge, in shirt sleeves, stopped by the side of the trail a moment, allowing the warmth to penetrate his bones. Then he looked back at the pair of young soldiers who had been attached to the expedition in

Bragamo with explicit instructions to escort them to Jorkhang—almost as if the Bragamo police chief had known that Trowbridge had intended to bypass the Jorkhang checkpoint.

If it weren't for the fact that he had a military escort, he thought, and for the fact that he was about to meet the police chief who had refused to allow Mallory into Lhakrinor, things would be going just fine.

"The region is politically sensitive."

From behind his desk the police chief regarded Trowbridge with a stony expression. The interview was not going well. Considering what had happened this morning, it was no surprise.

Trowbridge and Norbu had been walking toward Jorkhang from where the expedition had camped outside of town. Out of the vegetation to their right, with a great shaking of brush, a hunter had emerged; slung over his shoulders, its tiny, delicate hoofs dangling, was an immature musk deer. Blood trickled down onto the hunter's baggy green jump suit.

The hunter flung the deer into the dust, knelt, and inspected the valuable musk pod in its belly. Sitting back, he grunted in satisfaction, ignoring Trowbridge and Norbu—who had stopped in the trail only a few feet away—as if they did not exist.

"That animal is protected by order of the King," Trowbridge had told him coldly. "You've broken the law."

Norbu had added, "We are on our way to see the police chief. We will report what you have done."

The hunter had turned a hard expression upon Trowbridge, regarding him with flat dark eyes. Then he'd laughed suddenly, pulled a knife from his belt, slashed the musk pod from the deer's belly, and looked at them once more contemptuously before walking rapidly up the trail.

When they'd reached the office, a clerk had insisted that Norbu wait outside. Trowbridge had been shown in, and received an unpleasant shock. The police chief, regarding him with an unfriendly expression from behind his desk, had changed into a wrinkled khaki uniform. But he hadn't bothered to wash the bloodstains from his neck, and his rifle leaned against the wall in the corner.

Neither Trowbridge, nor the police chief, acknowledged the morning's encounter. There was no point. And yet it had not helped their cause, to say the least.

"I realize the region is politically sensitive," Trowbridge said. "But our intention is to have a minimum of contact with the people of Lhakrinor. And we'll stay far away from the border."

"Nowhere in Lhakrinor is far from the border. There is no reason to discuss it further."

Indifferently, the police chief added, "You are welcome to make a study of animals in this area."

Outside, in a sandy field filled with chips of bluish slate, a noisy volleyball game was going on. Dorje, Jeet, Nima, the Mangars, and the two soldiers who had escorted them from Bragamo were taking an animated part. Trowbridge, looking out the window, made an effort to control his temper, and failed.

"If the animals in this area are slaughtered by the police whose job it is to protect them, I wonder if I would find any."

The police chief fixed him with an ugly stare. "I have another idea, then. There are a great number of rats and lice in my jail. Perhaps you would like to study this sort of wildlife for a few days."

Trowbridge heard a door open and close behind him.

"Is there a problem?"

The voice was mild; the elegantly accented English sounded both familiar and out of place. Trowbridge turned. It was a Newar from the lowlands: slender, well-dressed, and obviously a long way from home. An intelligent smile played across his face as he leaned against the rough-hewn wood of the door frame. Trowbridge looked back at the police chief, whose expression had undergone a bizarre change. He was showing his teeth. It was the first smile Trowbridge had seen cross his blunt features; the transformation was neither pleasant nor convincing.

"Vikram!" the police chief greeted the Newar, making a pretense at pleasure. "How good to see you. But surely you do not wish to take up your official duties so soon after your arrival. You must be tired."

"Not too tired to take an interest in district affairs."

This high-caste Newar, fresh from the capital, would be an appointed official. From the expression on the police chief's face, he must represent some kind of threat to his power.

He might also represent Trowbridge's only chance of being allowed into Lhakrinor.

Vikram stepped forward, limping slightly on bandaged feet, and shook hands with Trowbridge. "Good morning, Mr. . . ."

"Trowbridge."

"I understand you have just come over the Serpo La."

Trowbridge nodded.

"I came over the Serpo La myself several days ago, with a fair amount of difficulty—including some frostbite, I'm afraid. And I had rather better weather than you. I trust that you and the members of your expedition are well?"

"Just fine," Trowbridge said cautiously.

Vikram turned to the police chief. "Phuntsok, this is the gentleman I told you we might have the good fortune to meet. Mr. Trowbridge is a well-known scientist. Isn't it wonderful that we are now in a position to help him?"

Before the police chief could answer, Vikram added, "It is my impression that Mr. Trowbridge's permits are in order. Is that right?"

"Yes," the police chief said reluctantly.

"Then I wonder where the problem lies?"

"The problem, Vikram, is that bandits have been attacking villages near the border. I cannot guarantee the safety of a scientist. Naturally, as you have only just arrived, you could not possibly know how dangerous the situation is."

Vikram took no offense at this barely disguised suggestion that he didn't know what he was talking about. Instead he said, in an agreeable tone of voice, "You are right, Phuntsok, it is a dangerous world. Even for a poor animal which is legally protected by a direct order from the King! I am told, for example, that someone shot a musk deer today and left its carcass lying in the trail. I assume you will be investigating this matter?"

Vikram was still smiling, but his eyes moved briefly to the bloodstains on the police chief's neck. Trowbridge felt his estimation of the man rising rapidly.

"No doubt it was bandits," Vikram continued mildly. "But that is another issue for another day. Frankly, I believe Mr. Trowbridge can take responsibility for his own safety. By traveling this far, he has already shown himself to be quite resourceful. And we must consider, Phuntsok, that his permit was approved in Kathmandu! Individuals of a higher rank than either you or I took these questions under careful consideration."

"Vikram," the police chief said, barely controlling his annoyance, "this is not technically your business."

"Not technically, no. But it is something about which I could communicate my concern to Kathmandu."

An ill-disguised note of triumph crept into Phuntsok's voice. "I think that would be wise, Vikram. And while you wait for a response, I would prefer that Mr. Trowbridge remain here, for his own safety."

A response could take weeks, Trowbridge thought with a sinking heart. If not months.

"Actually, Phuntsok, he won't have to wait at all," Vikram said. "I will simply use the radio."

"Radio?" Phuntsok said, with a look as if he had swallowed something unpleasant.

"Absolutely. One of the items I brought from Kathmandu was a transceiver. A very powerful one, with its own generator. In fact I have just come from setting it up in my office. You will be pleased to know, Phuntsok, that it is working excellently. From this day forward we will be able to consult Kathmandu when making important decisions. No longer will the heavy burden of responsibility rest on your shoulders alone! A wonderful thing, a radio. Ah! I am afraid we are boring Mr. Trowbridge with these bureaucratic details. Surely he wishes to be on his way. Shall we call Kathmandu first, Phuntsok, or shall we simply let him carry on?"

There was a long silence. The police chief looked first at Trowbridge, then at Vikram, with an expression that bordered on open animosity. Finally he leaned forward, scribbled the necessary authorization into Trowbridge's permit, shoved it forward across the desk, and swiveled around in his chair, turning his back—and his bloodstained neck—on his visitors.

"I am in your debt. And I'm afraid you've created an enemy for my sake."

Vikram waved a hand gracefully in the air. "Not at all, Mr. Trowbridge. Phuntsok and I were bound to disagree sooner or later."

"He's an easy man to disagree with. I was about to argue my way into jail."

Vikram smiled. "I rather enjoyed what Phuntsok said about the rats and lice in his jail—I did not know he had a sense of humor! And he was not exaggerating, by the way. I have inspected the local facilities."

"Why is he so adamant about keeping outsiders out of Lhakrinor? He turned back a colleague of mine only a couple of months ago."

Vikram shrugged. "For some time Phuntsok has been, shall we say, somewhat arbitrary about whom he allows into Lhakrinor. It may be that he simply dislikes outsiders intruding into what he regards as his personal kingdom. Or perhaps there is more to it than that."

They stood on the edge of an open field, watching the volleyball game. Trowbridge realized that Vikram had led him, with apparent casualness, to a place where they were in full view of those who were playing and watching, but out of earshot of anyone who might choose to listen.

"Mr. Trowbridge," Vikram said. "You owe me nothing for the help I have given you. Your permits are in order, your project is a worthy one, and you have every right to proceed without interference to Lhakrinor. I hope, however, that you might do us a small favor during the course of your studies there."

Trowbridge considered this a moment.

"Who is 'us'?"

"The Nepali government."

This wasn't particularly enlightening; the "government" could mean anything from immigration to intelligence, and Vikram didn't seem inclined to be more specific.

"What's the favor?"

Vikram shrugged. "Simply to keep your eyes open when you are in Lhakrinor. And to let me know if you see anything unusual."

Trowbridge's first instinct was to refuse flatly. He was a scientist; there would be no profit in him getting involved in what was probably some internal dispute within the Nepali government. On the other hand, this "favor" was clearly important to Vikram—and he had the feeling that Vikram, for all his genial manner, was capable of withdrawing his assistance as quickly as he'd extended it.

"Look, I hate to be rude, but if you're asking for my help, maybe you ought to tell me what's going on."

"To be honest," Vikram said, "I do not know. Probably little of consequence."

Trowbridge said nothing. Vikram glanced at him, seemed to realize this was a less-than-satisfactory answer, and looked back at the volleyball game.

"Have you, by any chance," he said, "run into an Indian citizen during the course of your expedition?"

"Yes. Someone named Krishna Sanwal."

"What do you know about him?"

"Not much. He told me that he was on a pilgrimage to Kailas, by way of Nepal, and that he was a former professor. Later on he admitted he'd once been a soldier."

"Very good," Vikram said, looking mildly impressed. He paused for a moment, then went on. "Now I will share with you what I know about Krishna Sanwal. He passed through here last fall on his way to Lhakrinor. At that time he claimed—as you say he is claiming now—that he was a religious pilgrim. His professed destination, however, was not Kailas, but rather Torma Mountain."

Torma Mountain was a holy site for Buddhists, a sacred mountain whose symmetrical peak dominated the eastern portion of Lhakrinor. Near its base lay Trang, an ancient monastery complex where Trowbridge planned to set up his first base camp.

"What caught our attention last fall," Vikram went on, "was that he carried more in the way of worldly possessions than might be expected of a religious pilgrim. We learned, through one of his porters, that his baggage included what might have been at least one—and possibly two—radio transceivers, as well as a generator and batteries. There is nothing inherently illegal, of course, about carrying radios on a pilgrimage, but it was an unusual enough detail to warrant a bit of research on our part."

Vikram shifted his weight slightly, glanced down at his bandaged, frostbitten feet with a wince, and continued. "We discovered—as you seem also to have done, with rather less effort—that he had been a member of the Indian military. That he had not been retired, precisely, but detached in some way just over a year ago from his regular duties as a lieutenant colonel in the Air Force. Not terribly high-ranking, this fellow, but evidently both well-connected and a bit of a loose cannon."

Vikram shrugged. "It's really not much to have learned. But it was enough that we preferred he didn't travel again in this part of the country."

"How did he get a permit to come back?"

"He didn't. Whatever permit he's traveling on is evidently forged. This is actually rather convenient; he may be nothing more than an eccentric religious fanatic, but when he passes through Jorkhang I plan to arrest him for false documents, and then I plan to ask him whether his activities last year in Lhakrinor were, as he states, of a purely religious nature. I'm hoping that you, Mr. Trowbridge, will keep your eyes open in Lhakrinor for anything that might answer the same question."

Trowbridge considered this reluctantly. "I'll be honest with you. If whatever he was doing is important enough to bring someone like you to a place as remote as Jorkhang, I'm not sure I want to be involved."

Vikram shook his head dismissively. "Krishna Sanwal is only one of a number of matters that have brought me here, Mr. Trowbridge. Frankly, I wouldn't take this little favor too seriously. Simply keep your eyes open. Many strange things happen, in many parts of the world; very few of them prove to be of any significance."

Something occurred to Trowbridge. "Did you know that my permit was held up for some time in Pokhara," he asked, "and that supposedly the Indians had something to do with it?"

Vikram paused a moment before responding. "No, I did not know that. But I doubt it has anything to do with our discussion today."

Trowbridge had the distinct impression that Vikram wasn't taking this piece of information as lightly as he wanted to let on.

"One more thing, then: Just how, exactly, am I supposed to contact you if I *do* see something out of the ordinary?"

"Simply stop by and see me on your way back out of Lhakrinor. Your permit is good until October, I believe?"

Trowbridge nodded.

"Or," Vikram added with a smile, "perhaps one of those famous radios will turn up. Fifteen two-fifty megahertz is a good frequency for reaching me."

Amid much yelling and shouting, the volleyball game was still going on. The Sherpas and Mangars played with gleeful abandon, diving wildly for impossible saves, yelling happily at the top of their lungs when they made a point. As Trowbridge watched, Nima dived for a ball near the sidelines. Getting a fist beneath it, she flipped it to Dorje, who lofted it up and over the net for a point. Nima paid for the effort by running her face into the thick rope stretched across the stony ground to mark the boundaries. She sat up spitting sand, her lip bleeding. For the Sherpas—as was the case with almost any mishap short of serious injury—her accident was the cause for loud and general laughter.

Nima stared at them furiously, looking utterly offended. Then her expression changed and she began laughing. Dorje extended a hand to her. She got to her feet, wiped the blood from her lip, and rejoined the game.

"It is a shame she will have to turn back at the final pass," Norbu said.

"There's no way to get a pony over the Krimshi La?" Trowbridge asked.

Norbu shook his head. "Never—the final descent must be made with ropes. And I do not think she will leave the pony behind."

"It's too bad. We'll miss the extra provisions Seto could have carried in."

"There is another route which a pony might be able to travel. You have to cross three separate passes—but none is as steep."

"Would it take longer?"

"Much longer. It would take a week at least."

Trowbridge considered this, then shook his head.

"There isn't time. Not if I'm going to get this study completed and get out by October."

16

The narrow path leading north from Jorkhang had been carved directly out of the dark stone of the mountain; the high steps were smooth, rounded with centuries of use, and steep, and Trowbridge was soon breathing hard from the effort of the climb. He was glad for the physical exertion; it helped take his mind off this morning's talk with Vikram.

He appreciated what Vikram had done for him, but he was far from happy with the favor that had been asked in return. The joy of his work had always been to get away from precisely this sort of thing—away from the politics, the bureaucrats, the thousand entanglements and complications of the civilized world.

Now it seemed the complications were following him up the mountain.

They made camp in a rare wide place in the trail, spreading sleeping bags, not bothering to set up the tents. In the twilight, an occasional rock skittered past them.

"Many rocks falling here," Dorje said, cheerfully squatting on the edge of a thousand-foot precipice. He sipped noisily from a mug of tea, looking down. A hundred yards below, a hawk soared on air currents near the sheer face. In the bottom of the canyon, white water shone in the twilight.

"No falling Sherpas, I hope," Trowbridge said, sitting a bit farther from the edge.

"Sherpas never fall," Dorje assured him.

"I'd heard that falling is one of the common causes of death in Nepal."

"Well, yes," Dorje admitted, "but that is *children*. You see, in this way only Sherpa children with good balance grow up. Very practical arrangement."

Dorje stood and stretched lazily, a significant portion of his tennis shoes hanging out over the edge of the cliff. At that moment, moving with perfect balance down the trail, came a Tibetan couple. Both carried packs and wore a great deal of turquoise around their necks. While the man struck up a conversation with Dorje, his wife squatted and began rubbing yak butter from a small silver pot into her sleek black hair, smiling shyly at the expedition. Trowbridge, listening carefully to the oddly accented Tibetan, understood most of what was said. Apparently an avalanche had come down in a high valley along their route; two porters had been buried beneath the falling rock.

He noticed that Nima also seemed to be listening attentively. Could it be that she spoke not only Nepali and English, but Tibetan as well?

The man and his wife filed peacefully down the trail into darkness, and Dorje watched them go, fingering a turquoise amulet which he wore around his neck. He looked troubled.

"Avalanche," he said.

"Do not worry, Dorje," Jeet told him. "Your turquoise will protect you from any avalanche."

"I am not worried for myself," Dorje said. "I am thinking of my older brother."

"Does he not wear turquoise?" Chandra asked.

"He was buried in an avalanche. On Manaslu, with a mountain-climbing expedition. I do not know if he was wearing turquoise that day or not."

"When?" Trowbridge asked.

"One month before we left Pokhara."

"I'm sorry."

Dorje turned to him earnestly. "David *sahib*, there is no need to be sorry. Only to hope that after his spirit flew from beneath the rocks it was able to resist earthly temptation and achieve enlightenment, or at least to be reborn in a human body." He was silent a moment. "Sometimes I do not feel hopeful about this. There was no lama to sit beside him and read to him from the Bardo Thodol."

He took a deep breath, then went and sat on his sleeping bag. "Tonight, I am thinking about my brother," he announced.

Sitting cross-legged on his sleeping bag, his back to the stone of the mountain, he closed his eyes, meditating, his body perfectly still.

17

The avalanche gave off a deep, peculiarly resonant sound, as if a vast chorus were singing within the earth. Hard resounding cracks traced the downward path of stones the size of grapefruit; clattering noises rose from a multitude of smaller stones, each following its own tricky path down the slope. Beneath these individual sounds was a vast hissing, as a river of sand sifted downward.

The avalanche had brought down the entire side of the mountain—at least to the extent that the mountain, which stretched upward out of sight, could be seen. After obliterating the trail, the scree had pushed on down into the river which marked the center of this pocket valley, damming it, creating a small lake on the upriver side. On the far side of the avalanche, beside the lake, a group of Gurung traders sat patiently beside their loads, waiting for this dangerous obstacle to become less active before they risked a crossing. As if to reinforce their fears, there came a sudden increase in the noise level, a washing, showery sound like a wave gathering strength and breaking. Stones cascaded in a secondary slide down over the surface of the main avalanche; dust rose in an irregular cloud as the sound receded.

"Goodness," Dorje said, shading his eyes, peering upward toward the invisible origins of the rock fall. "I have never seen an avalanche so large."

Trowbridge was studying a barely discernible line which threaded across the enormous gray bulge in the mountainside, evidence of the successful passage of those hardy souls who had been willing to attempt it. From one side of the avalanche to the other, the distance was perhaps a hundred and fifty yards.

"Do we cross?" he asked Dorje.

He thought it was feasible, but wanted Dorje to volunteer agreement on his own.

"Oh, I think yes," Dorje said without hesitation. "We might wait a week for the rocks to stop coming down."

On the far side, two of the Gurung traders decided to make the crossing. One of them began jogging slowly across, his *doka* bouncing awkwardly on his back. More than once he slipped to his knees in the loose rock; each time he rose and scrambled doggedly onward, keeping a wary eye on the uphill slope as he made for a fishtail-shaped rock which protruded up through the rubble. It was a poor enough sort of shelter, but it was all that was available. Trowbridge estimated that before the avalanche came down the rock must have loomed thirty or forty feet above the trail; now it extended up only three or four feet.

The Gurung ducked beneath this rock with obvious relief, pausing a moment to catch his breath before slogging on across. He reached safety dusty and pale, hobbling from a bruised shin.

The second Gurung started across. Almost immediately, a quick shower of small stones chased him back to his starting point. The first one waved vigorously until he gathered his courage and set out again, crossing the slide without incident. When he stumbled down out of the scree down onto firmer footing, his friend met him excitedly. They threw down their *dokas*, chattering animatedly, acting out various moments of danger, laughing, pointing back at the way they'd come.

"See?" Dorje said. "It is easy."

There was no trace of last night's sadness in Dorje's face, no sign of fear or hesitation.

"Let's hope so," Trowbridge said. "We'll go one at a time."

"I would like to go first, David *sahib*," Dorje said. "I am the *sirdar*."

Trowbridge nodded agreement. Dorje gave rapid instructions to the porters, telling them to dump their loads and run if necessary. Then he conferred with Nima, agreeing that Seto ought to be able to negotiate the scree slope without too much difficulty. Before setting out, Dorje pressed something into Trowbridge's hand. It was a piece of turquoise in an intricate, blackened-silver setting.

"This is good luck," Dorje said.

"Keep it," Trowbridge said. "I have my own luck."

Dorje reached inside his shirt and brought out a turquoise necklace. "I have this already," he said earnestly. "Now is your chance to learn something from a Sherpa. You cannot always make your own luck, David *sahib*. Please take it."

Trowbridge accepted the turquoise and slipped it into his pocket. Dorje turned and started across the slope, moving awkwardly in the loose stone. Midway across, in the shelter of the rock, he turned in a crouch and smiled broadly. Then he set out again, looking increasingly small as he negotiated the bleak gray scree. Watching his progress, Trowbridge felt an increasing tension, but Dorje reached the far side of the slope without difficulty. Waving with exultation, he yelled encouragement; the sound was inaudible above the hiss and clatter of stone.

Nima began leading Seto across. Lifting its hoofs high, tossing its head as if it found the deep sand and stones in which it was forced to walk merely distasteful, the pony moved steadily behind her. Trowbridge marveled once again at its nimble toughness. Nima passed the center rock without stopping or looking back.

One by one, the Mangars and the Gurung crossed without incident, followed by the Rai, the Limbu, Norbu, and finally Jeet.

Chandra was halfway to the rock shelter when a stone the size of a suitcase came bounding down the slope toward him. Hearing the heavy sound, he flung himself face down onto the trail, hands covering his head. Trowbridge watched in disbelief as the stone caromed, in erratic trajectories, closer and closer to where Chandra lay. Cupping his hands, he yelled a last-second warning. Without looking up, Chandra flung his heavy body to the right. The stone crashed, in a shower of dust and pebbles, into the place where he had been lying a split second before, then bounded down the slope, catapulting with a tremendous splash into the lake. Chandra scrambled to his feet and hurried across, turning to wave, wide-eyed and exultant, when he reached safety.

Trowbridge glanced upward, toward the invisible place where the mountain was belching out its innards, and set out. The footing was worse than he'd expected. His feet sank deep into sand, then slipped bruisingly off half-buried rocks. He moved steadily—if awkwardly—across, keeping an eye on the uphill slope, blinking against the dust.

As he neared the fishtail rock, he heard a faint, sustained washing noise above him, then a cascade of little stones. There was a vibration in his feet. He glanced upward, saw the first small stones whirl into view, and ducked into the protection of the rock.

Moments later sand and rock began pouring by him on either side in a clattery, frightening roar. Coughing in the rising dust, he pulled out his shirt tail and breathed through the cloth, squinting as the flow around the rock grew heavier. Stones hurtled above his head now; sand was beginning to pour in on top of him.

If this went on too much longer he would be buried alive.

Another threat penetrated his consciousness: a deep, ominous thrumming. Something large was coming down the slope. He felt it rumble closer and wondered if this was the moment and place in which he would die. A sickening impact shook the fishtail rock. He felt a tremendous wrenching, a grinding of stone on stone; the vibrations shimmered through his bones with the thrill of annihilation. The dusty light filtering into his shelter was blocked for a long second, as if a cloud had passed before the sun. Buried in darkness, he felt a strange moment of loneliness and elation: elation at what he had done in this life, at the places he had been and seen; loneliness that somehow it had been his fate to move largely in solitude.

With a massive groaning, the boulder heaved its bulk over his shelter, landing in the scree a few feet below where he lay, then lumbered down the slope. Light returned. He spat sand from his mouth, and breathed again. The sand was trickling in more slowly now. The noise diminished; he heard himself gasping for breath.

An eerie silence settled in, broken only by the occasional clatter of a single falling stone. Then shouting, as if at a great distance. Dorje's voice. Jeet's, and Nima's. He glanced cautiously around the edge of the fishtail rock that had saved his life, saw that nothing moved on the uphill slope, then stood up and waved.

Dorje and most of the others were exhilarated that evening, filled with energy and slightly jumpy after the experience with the avalanche. There was a good deal of laughter at Chandra's having flopped down, arms over his head, precisely in the downward path of a large rock. Jeet observed with quiet amusement that it was a wonder he had survived thirty years as a soldier with such a poor instinct for choosing shelter.

They were set up in a flat place above a stream. Beyond Trowbridge's tent, which glowed a welcoming, artificial blue in the twilight, and beyond the pair of small cook fires flaring brightly, the walls of a narrow gorge formed a V-shaped notch in which the lowering sun had lit a fiery blaze. The evening air on his face was cool; he felt good, curiously calm, blessed somehow by the nearness of his escape.

He filled his plate with more *dal-bhat*, and went and sat next to Dorje.

"I have something of yours," he said. When he fished in his pocket, however, he found only sand.

"It's gone," he said. "I'm sorry."

"Do not be sorry," Dorje said. "Perhaps its store of good luck was used up in protecting you. Now it has returned to the earth to gather its powers once again."

Dorje set down his plate and motioned to the north, in the direction they would be taking tomorrow. With reasonable luck they would reach Lhakrinor in five days. When he spoke, he sounded pleased and proud.

"David *sahib*, we have crossed rivers and passes, and escaped the monsoon and two police chiefs. We have even crossed an avalanche. I have a feeling, now, that nothing more can go wrong."

Trowbridge nodded, realizing that for the first time in days he felt a similar optimism. The problems the expedition had experienced seemed suddenly to be trivial, and a long way behind them.

"I wanted to be a monk from the time I was a little boy," Jeet said, staring into the dying coals as his fingers moved unconsciously over the tiny Tibetan characters of the wooden carving he held before him.

"But my father quarreled with his brother—my uncle—who was a lama. He would not let me go to the monastery to study, fearing I would fall under my uncle's influence and turn against him. They did not reconcile until after I was a grown man, and working for mountain-climbing expeditions. By then I felt I was too old to learn the things that I had missed—that it would be shameful to have ten-year-old boys knowing so much more than I."

Jeet saw something on the wooden block that bothered him; with a careful movement of his small knife, and a puff of breath to blow away the tiny wood chip, he corrected the problem.

"Still, the desire to learn had not gone away. And so, three years ago, I began going to Rongbuk Monastery half of each year to work for a lama and to learn what I could. Part of each day, when I am there, I cook for the monks and lamas, and I make these carvings. The rest of the time I sit with the young boys learning the holy texts."

"And you are not embarrassed to sit with these young boys?" Chandra asked.

"No. At the end of this trip I may go to live there permanently."

"What does it say, Jeet?"

Trowbridge gestured at the wooden tablet; Jeet held it up in the firelight, as if to be sure what Trowbridge was asking. When Trowbridge nodded, Jeet said, "The characters explain the sacred teachings. Teachings which help us to lead a proper life and journey toward enlightenment. This block speaks about Outlook, Meditative Practice, and Conduct. When it is finished, I will begin another which speaks of the Three Jewels and the Four Topics of Inspection. And if I have enough time before I return to the monastery at Rongbuk, I will carve one which contains the Six Perfections—"

"Each of which is divided into a further six."

It was Norbu who had spoken.

Jeet looked at him in brief surprise, then said, "Yes, that is right. Then there are the Nineteen Commitments, the Fourfold Purity, the Four Initiations, and the Three Structural Ways."

"And soon, of course, you will learn the Three Modes and the Three Phenomena. Then, most difficult of all, the Coarser and Subtler forms of the Unifying Process."

Jeet looked at Norbu in amazement.

"How do you know these things?"

Norbu shook his head and grinned, as if embarrassed at having shown off in this fashion. "When it comes to matters of spiritual understanding, who can tell with certainty? Perhaps I was a lama in a former lifetime."

Jeet studied him gravely, then persisted. "Truly, how do you know these things? Even the simplest of the teachings you mentioned requires months of study."

Norbu shrugged, and his face grew more serious. "My father was a lama. One of the Red-Hat sect, who are allowed to marry. He wished me to become a lama as well, which is how I learned the teachings. Unfortunately, I did not wish to become a lama. I wished to become a hunter. My father found himself preaching against the killing of animals while his own son roamed the hills with a bow and arrow. It was the source of much conflict between us."

"Did you show signs of having a lama's soul as a child?" Dorje asked.

"My father wished to believe so, but in fact I did not. When I was still an infant he placed a holy relic among my toys, hoping that I would choose this sacred item and thus demonstrate signs of imminent lama-hood. I chose a carved wooden yak instead."

The others laughed, but Jeet's face remained sober. "No father should force his son to be other than what he wishes to be."

"No," Norbu said slowly. "No father should force his son to be other than what he wishes to be. But there are times when I wish I could tell him that I forgive him for trying."

"He is dead?" Jeet asked.

Norbu nodded, staring into the fire. "He was killed by a Khampa bandit. A Gorchok, with a red-barreled rifle."

No one spoke. Norbu continued, "And my mother died when I was very young. By now, both of them have long since been reborn into another life, somewhere on the face of the earth. I, who was the youngest of the family, am now the oldest, and the only one who still walks in this lifetime."

"Perhaps you will meet them one day," Jeet said, "and not know them, but treat them well just the same."

18

"Here is Nuth, where we will be tomorrow," Dorje said, smoothing the map carefully with his fingertips. "After Nuth there is only one more village before the Krimshi La."

"Choko," Trowbridge said, identifying the village on the map by firelight. It was still light outside, but the interior of the hut in which they were staying was shrouded in permanent gloom.

Dorje said, "The Mangars and Gurung will go no farther than Choko. They are tough, but they are not equipped for a pass like the Krimshi La."

"We have to find new porters in Nuth, then," Trowbridge said.

"The people of Nuth will not work as porters," Norbu said. "We may find porters in Choko, but they are quarrelsome and greedy, and they know they are the last village before crossing the pass."

Norbu continued to display a detailed knowledge of the area. Dorje had asked him once if he had actually come this far on a former trip. Norbu's reply had been vague, and Trowbridge didn't really care; one way or another, his knowledge was proving invaluable.

Trowbridge said, "What about this other way into Lhakrinor you mentioned? There's nothing shown on the map."

"That is because it is long and difficult. It would take us eight days, perhaps nine. Three separate passes must be climbed—although none is as difficult as the Krimshi La."

"And if we go over the Krimshi La, as planned?"

"Three days."

"That's the route, then," Trowbridge said. "I can't justify the extra time and walking. We just have to hope we can get extra porters in Choko to replace Nima and the pony."

"Seto and I could go the long way and meet you there."

Nima stood in the doorway.

Trowbridge looked up at her, noticing, as he did so, that she was going to less elaborate lengths to downplay her attractiveness. The stocking cap was gone, and with it some of the dirt on her face.

"It's a long, hard journey," he said. "Too dangerous for a porter traveling alone."

Cautiously, Dorje said, "The pony can carry as much food as two porters, David *sahib*. Perhaps Jeet and Chandra could go with her..."

Trowbridge considered this. The three of them would be able to travel safely, and because the passes were lower they would be able to carry heavier loads. He was in a hurry to get himself and Norbu into Lhakrinor to start the study, but there was no reason all of their provisions had to arrive at the same time.

"There is something else," Nima said. "I could be of help to your study of animals. If you tell me what to look for, I will watch carefully for animals in which you are interested, and ask questions of the people I meet along the way."

This was not a bad idea at all. An informal survey of the snow leopard, bharal, and wolf populations in the approaches to Lhakrinor could prove extremely useful. Predators, in particular, ranged widely; the sighting of even a single animal would help establish range boundaries.

"You should know," he said, "that there are three separate passes to cross on the route you'd be taking. According to Norbu, none are as bad as the Krimshi La, but you'll be carrying heavy loads, so it'll be difficult going. Once you join us in Lhakrinor, it'll be a matter of dropping off the food you've brought, resting for a day or two, and leaving again."

"Only Norbu and I will remain with David *sahib* for the summer," Dorje explained.

"I understand these things. If I can be of use, I still wish to go to Lhakrinor."

He studied her a moment. "Why?"

The question seemed to take her by surprise.

"I am a porter," she said.

Sensing that this was not an entirely sufficient explanation, she continued, "I have been happy with the expedition. And in truth, I have no place else to go."

Trowbridge rummaged through his pack, pulling out a notebook and pen. He looked up, motioning her to come closer, then began sketching swiftly. She looked over his shoulder as an animal came to life on the pad.

"A goat!" she said.

"In point of fact, there's some disagreement over whether it's a goat or a sheep. What's important is that you recognize it when you see it. The villagers will know it as *na*, the Tibetan name. Westerners call it blue sheep, or bharal."

"Bharal," she repeated.

"Here's what a bharal hoof print looks like."

He sketched rapidly. "And this," he said, flipping the pad, starting a fresh sketch, "is what a snow leopard pug looks like."

"Pug?"

"Paw print. With a snow leopard you're not likely to see anything more."

"David is one of only three people to have photographed the snow leopard," Norbu said with a flash of pride.

Nima said, "I will watch, above all, for a snow leopard. What is the best way to see one?"

Norbu said, "Since you will be on a well-traveled trail with a noisy pony, the best way to see a snow leopard will be to close your eyes."

"Close my eyes?"

Norbu grinned. "Close your eyes, and go to sleep—then dream a snow leopard."

Nima regarded Norbu steadily, then looked at Trowbridge.

"I will dream a snow leopard if I have to," she said. "But I would prefer to see one living in freedom, in the mountains."

They reached Nuth—a pleasant village of twelve well-kept houses, each with its own neatly fenced garden in back—just after noon the next day, and decided to spend the night there before splitting into two groups. Behind the village, buckwheat fields sloped gently upward toward a ring of high white peaks. A half mile to the west soared a great shining waterfall; above it, invisible from this vantage point, was Dre-Mo Lake and the village of Choko—their final stop before crossing the Krimshi La.

They found lodging in the house of a woman whose husband and sons were away on a trading trip. She served them *momos*, fried ravioli filled with cheese and fried potatoes, and a tasty, sour beer brewed from barley. Afterward, a man who had been hoeing in the field behind his house showed up with a gift of dark, sweet honey; they smeared it with yak butter on freshly made *chapatis*. In the early afternoon, while Dorje and Jeet purchased what food was available, the rest of the expedition fell asleep contentedly, some lying in the sun before the house, others inside on bamboo pallets.

Feeling restless, Trowbridge grabbed his spotting scope and tripod and set off up the switchback trail which led toward the top of the ridge, two thousand feet above Nuth. This high earthen barrier was a natural dam, holding back the waters of Dre-Mo Lake. If this natural dam ever failed, he realized, the sweet and peaceful village of Nuth would be washed away in an instant.

As he climbed, the roar of the falls grew steadily louder. A spine of rock lifted between the trail and the down-rushing water, and the sound diminished. Near the top, wanting a view, he scrambled up a rock face toward the sound. As his head came level with the top of the rock, the tremendous roaring enveloped him with a dizzying rush. The torrent was only a few feet away. Its weight seemed extraordinary as it slid, in an immense, smooth, undisturbed coil, over the lip of the falls, exploding six hundred feet below, at the bottom of a slender chute, in rising clouds of vapor. Tall blue pines, lifting up from the banks below, looked like saplings. The Nuth valley was laid out neatly like a child's diorama in a shoe box.

Looking up at where the water first began its downward slide, he saw that he was not alone. Nima was perched on another precarious rock not twenty feet away, looking out at the valley. He yelled a greeting, then realized the sound of the water was so loud he might as well be on another planet. He pulled out his scope, arranged the tripod, and began scanning the western slopes beyond the waterfall for signs of wildlife.

A few minutes later, finding nothing, he lowered his scope and glanced upward once more. The rock was empty. Had she seen him? He slid back down to the trail, glanced at the sun, and kept climbing.

After topping a rise, the land gentled downward through a low, silent, conifer forest to Dre-Mo Lake. The water was a dark cobalt in the late afternoon light, its surface scored by a light breeze. He worked his way around the lake and up the northeastern slope, climbing until the entire basin was in view.

Above him, in the trees, he heard a shout of excitement. Someone calling his name. It could only be Nima. He hurried up the trail and found her pointing at a high slope, several hundred yards above them. At the base of a sheer cliff, in the last light of the day, was movement. Quickly he set his spotting scope on its tripod legs, jamming them into the dirt, and focused.

"Blue sheep?" she asked.

"Blue sheep," he confirmed, counting rapidly.

Twenty-three animals: fourteen adult females and nine healthy-looking young. After noting their characteristics quickly, he passed the scope to Nima and began writing on the pad he kept in his shirt pocket.

"They are beautiful," she said.

It was a joy to be gathering information again; a joy to see a herd which was apparently healthy, with healthy young, on a range which was in reasonably good shape.

"But their horns are not nearly as large as in the drawing you made."

"These are females; the males' horns are much larger. Enormous, in fact, given the size of the animal—up to fifteen centimeters across the base, and eighty-five centimeters measured along the curve. How did you know I was down there?"

"I saw you coming up through the trees."

The herd, following the leader, was grazing around a spur which extended down from the base of the cliff. Nima watched them until they disappeared, then raised her eyes from the scope.

"Already I have found you bharal," she said in a satisfied voice.

Below them the lake glittered turquoise and gold in the last few minutes of daylight. White birch trees shone along the lake shore, interspersed with little meadows of bright green grass. On the far side of the lake, marked by a pair of fat entrance *chortens*, was the village of Choko—their final stop before the assault on the Krimshi La. Beyond its two-story, fortress-like houses a sheer wall of brown rock lifted from the water—marked, he noted, by an impossible-looking trail.

"Is that why you came up here?" he asked. "To look for bharal?"

"Yes. Also, since I am taking a different way into Lhakrinor, to see the lake. Ever since I was a little girl I have heard of Dre-Mo Lake."

"Dre-Mo means demoness, doesn't it?"

She nodded. "There was once a village where the lake is now. A *Bon-po* village, but the people were peaceful and good. Then a Buddhist saint came to the region. A *Bon-po* demoness, fleeing him, passed through this valley. She gave the villagers a beautiful turquoise, making them promise not to tell that she had come this way. But the Buddha's magic was stronger, and he caused the turquoise to be turned to dung. Believing they had been tricked, the villagers betrayed her passage. In revenge she flooded the valley and drowned the village. It is said that if you look down through the water, on a day when the sun is not too bright and not too dim, you can still see the village on the bottom of the lake."

He studied her a moment, then looked back out at the lake.

"What are you running from," he asked.

"From the life I led before."

She gestured toward the lake. Her face was happy, in a strange, solitary way.

"This place is as beautiful as I thought it might be. It would be a place to rest."

"To rest?"

She was silent a moment. Then she said, "I had a Western friend in the village I lived in—an American like you, a Peace Corps worker— and he told me of an expression of yours: 'No rest for the wicked.' "

"Yes?"

"Well," she said. "It is because I am wicked."

"I find that hard to believe."

"I'm afraid it is true," she said. "And I am fleeing, like the demoness in the story."

The last sunlight raced up the sheer rock walls across the lake; the lake looked infinitely dark, and cold. Suddenly, there was little more to say. In gathering darkness, and in a rather uncomfortable silence, they descended toward Nuth.

19

"Look there!" Dorje called softly, pointing to the river which flowed fifty yards away.

Moving in an unhurried fashion along the river bank, through irregular patches of sun and shadow, was a young moon bear. Negotiating a fallen tree, it paused—perhaps smelling the pony—and stood upright, regarding the expedition a long moment with small, dark, unafraid eyes. The bear's fur shone a lustrous purple-black against the mossy green tree trunk; the crescent of white on its chest, from which it took its name, was as unmistakable as its large rounded ears. After a few moments it resumed its calm progress, disappearing into a thicket.

Nearly three weeks of walking through the Himalayas, and this was the first bear they'd seen. He looked at Norbu.

"That makes up for the one in chains, in Pokhara."

Norbu shook his head, eyes crinkling with pleasure. "It does not make up for it. But it is a good thing to see, nonetheless."

"It is a very good omen," Dorje said. "For Nima and Jeet and Chandra, and for us as well."

They stood at a fork in the trail just outside Nuth. One path led to the west, the other began the series of switchbacks up toward Choko. The morning sun had just cleared the mountains. A good smell came from the warming earth and grass.

"Watch for bandits," Trowbridge said.

"One eye for bandits," Nima agreed. "And the other for snow leopard."

"And *my* two eyes for a comfortable place to sleep, and something to eat," Chandra said practically. "Trowbridge *sahib*, we will walk quickly, say our prayers, and see you in Trang, beneath Torma Mountain."

Chandra drew his bulky body up straight and saluted as Nima turned away. Dorje and Jeet looked at each other, nodding with the calm acceptance of Sherpas. Then the three of them, followed by the pony—loaded heavily with grain and potatoes they'd purchased in Nuth—disappeared up the trail.

* * *

By the time they crested the ridge, Dre-Mo Lake was a cheerful, late-morning blue. Yaks, the first they'd seen, grazed in a meadow near the water: shaggy, humpbacked and heavy-headed, they were big as buffaloes, with tails like soft brooms and wide-eyed faces as innocent as those on stuffed toys. Deceptively innocent, Trowbridge remembered; they were in fact the balkiest, most stubborn and cantankerous creatures he'd ever encountered.

Banked in the shadows of occasional boulders in the meadow, as they walked along the blue sparkling lake, was snow: silent, cool, and gray. The Krimshi La was not far ahead now. They crossed a pair of ornate bridges over streams which rushed foaming into the lake, then reached a long, waist-high prayer wall covered with flat stones. The stones were a dark slate color; carved on them was *Om Matre Muye Sale Du*, a change from the Buddhist invocation *Om Mani Padme Hum* to which they'd grown accustomed. They stopped a moment to study the unfamiliar, flowing text.

"Bon-po," Trowbridge said.

Dorje nodded. "Before the birth of Buddha, Bon-po was the religion of these mountains. When Buddhism came here, the Bon-po were overwhelmed with the new ideas, and so they imitated the ways of the Buddha—but backwards."

Fingering his protective amulets, the Rai said, "It is against the true *dharma*."

Dorje shrugged. "In both religions, the five parts of a *chorten* are air, fire, water, earth, and spirit."

A *chorten* was a place of worship, and often housed sacred relics, or the remains of the holy masters.

"For myself," Dorje continued, "I do not care if they walk around the prayer wall in the wrong direction."

Choko was filled with laughing children chasing one another between high stone houses, white-toothed Tibetan dogs on chains, and noisy, sharp-eyed, curious adults who wore long *chubas* and plaited their black hair Tibetan style, in double pigtails. The villagers tipped their heads to one side while thinking, and all talked at once. Great doubt was expressed as to the possibility of hiring porters to go over the Krimshi La. It was unlikely that the pass could be crossed this early. No one had done it yet. Had anyone done it yet? No, it was generally agreed that no one had done it yet, and an attempt carried great risk, which would require—if such a thing as a May crossing of the pass were even possible—great compensation.

Dorje waded into the negotiations with his customary enthusiasm, but it was not until the following morning that seven skinny and rather disreputable-looking villagers began to prepare their high-altitude clothing and boots. Even this process took several hours, so that it was not until after lunch that the expedition seemed to be ready to set out.

Dorje took a short break from the haggling to pay off the existing porters, who came to take their leave. Trowbridge was sorry to see them go, particularly when he looked over their argumentative replacements. The Limbu tugged on one of his great ears, and wished him good luck in avoiding bandits; the Rai echoed these sentiments in reference to demons. The Gurung dipped his head with gruff, serious looks; then the Mangars, nodding shyly, grinning in embarrassment, shook his hand with gentle fingers. Moving quickly without loads, the group disappeared back toward Nuth. Trowbridge turned with a sigh, listened for a moment to the argument before him—which had increased to an astounding volume—and thoroughly lost his temper. Yelling furiously in English, he assigned the loads at random—earning himself some deadly looks from his new porters—and they set out around Dre-Mo Lake.

The trail led them up onto the face of the high black cliff on the far side of the lake. Soon it became little more than a ledge, and then, in places, fell away altogether. To bridge these gaps, slender birch branches had been jammed into crevices so they stuck straight out; the sticks had then been covered with flat, heavy stones, forming a kind of narrow sidewalk against the cliff face. Trowbridge was accustomed to dicey trails and dangerous heights, but this was decidedly unnerving. Dorje, in the lead, tested each stone carefully before putting his full weight on it, since it was impossible to tell if the branches beneath were rotten.

Eventually the ledge reemerged from the cliff face, and they moved at a better pace until dusk. They made camp on the lake's northern shore, where the Dre-Mo River—in a winding labyrinth of gravel-bottomed streams, bogs, and pine-needle muck—meandered down from the snowy slopes.

20

The leader of the Choko porters ignored Dorje, carefully rolling a cigarette with blackened fingers. He lit the cigarette, breathed deeply, then stared up the long white slope. At its top—maybe three miles of walking, two thousand feet of altitude—a narrow notch was evident against a cobalt sky. Snow plumes trailed around the top of the pass like a ring of white flags.

The porter squinted in the direction of Dorje's feet.

"No," he said, in heavily-accented Nepali. "We will go no farther. The snow is too deep."

"The snow is *not* too deep," Dorje said.

There was a long silence. The porter drew deeply on his cigarette, flung it away, and grimaced. Then he shrugged, and looked back down the slope toward the trail which led toward Choko. Dorje opened his mouth to speak.

"Let them go," Trowbridge said.

The porters were already dropping their loads into the snow and turning to descend the slope. Like a band of blackened scarecrows, they trooped down toward the mouth of the narrow gorge which would lead them back toward Dre-Mo Lake.

"They've been worse than nothing, anyway," Trowbridge said. "Ever since we left the lake and started climbing."

The seven heavy *dokas* lay at awkward angles in the snow. It was very quiet. A breeze moved across the intensely white surface of the snowfield, pushing tiny crystals past their boots with a little sighing sound. Trowbridge looked back up at the pass. The distance was not far, but the physical effort, at this altitude and in the deep snow, would be enormous. His muscles were quivering already from the exertion required to climb this high.

"If we strap my pack to one of the *dokas*," Trowbridge said, "then we can ferry this stuff up in only three trips. We might as well get started."

He and Dorje shrugged out of their packs and slipped into a *doka* each, grunting as they hoisted the heavy loads.

"We should stay to the left," Dorje said wearily, studying the way to the pass. "The sun has not been on that side. The snow is firmer there. Easier to walk in."

Dorje stopped. Norbu was staring up the long slope, as if hypnotized by the gap which would allow them into Lhakrinor. A moment later he became aware that he was being watched. Without a word, he tore himself away from the view and hefted the nearest *doka*. His expression was impossible to read; his eyes, behind his goggles, invisible.

Trowbridge tugged the glove off his right hand, holding it in his teeth while he finished the knot. Then, crawling on his belly across the sharp, ragged ice, he pushed the *doka* toward the edge. The glove, sodden with blood from an ice cut on his palm, froze stiff in a matter of seconds; he decided to leave it off in hopes the cut would stop bleeding.

He and Norbu were lying on their bellies, battered by a savage wind that made it dangerous to stand. Around them, seemingly near enough to touch, high white peaks pierced the cloudless sky. The atmosphere was so thin as to be nearly black.

They had reached the rugged, narrow gateway of the Krimshi La. Stretched out before them in splendid, staggering clarity lay Lhakrinor: dark ravines trickling among a chaos of bright jagged peaks, vast brown hillsides rolling toward a horizon which was Tibet.

After almost three weeks of walking, they had finally made it, something that ought to have been cause for celebration. At the moment, however, Trowbridge was concerned primarily with the mechanics of getting the loads down over the vertical drop on the far side of the pass, and with the fact that the sun was dropping almost as rapidly as the temperature. Dorje had already descended and was receiving the loads.

"One more after this one!" he yelled over the precipice.

Bracing his feet in the snow, he let the final *doka*—only Norbu's pack remained—bump awkwardly over the edge, lowering it out of sight for what seemed like an eternity.

"I have it!"

Dorje's voice, battered by the wind, floated up as if from miles away. Trowbridge grasped the piton which he had driven into the ice, crawled to the jagged edge, and looked over. Fifty feet below, at the bottom of a wall of ice as steep as a breaking wave, Dorje crouched over the *doka*. A moment later he stood and let the *doka* slide away from him. Like an unmanned sled, it flung smoothly half a mile down the steep snowy slope to join the others—in a ragged bunch, like a herd of dark animals—each at the end of its own long track.

Dorje looked up and waved. Trowbridge waved back, and began making the line fast to the *piton*.

"Pass me your pack!" he yelled. Norbu, a few feet away, had been passing him the *dokas* one by one. "We'll leave the piton and rope in place. Maybe they'll still be here when we leave."

"I cannot!"

Trowbridge edged closer, so that their faces were near one another, and lifted his goggles.

"What?" he yelled. "Do you want to go first?"

Norbu shook his head. "I cannot go further!"

"What are you talking about?"

"I am not able to go into Lhakrinor."

"Why not? This is crazy! Can't we discuss it on the slope down there?"

The wind slashed at them with violent force; Dorje was waving urgently at them to descend so they could get the loads to a lower elevation before the sinking sun made it necessary to make camp.

"I cannot enter Lhakrinor."

"Why the hell not?"

"I made a vow."

"What kind of vow?"

Norbu was silent a moment. When he spoke, his voice was defiant.

"Lhakrinor is my home!"

"*What?*"

"I grew up here. I lived here until I was seventeen. Then . . . bad things happened. I decided never to return."

The wind, howling with sudden vehemence, threatened to blow them both over the edge. Trowbridge clutched at the piton with one hand and grabbed at Norbu with the other. Norbu, in his misery, seemed almost indifferent to the danger.

"I am sorry. But for me, Lhakrinor is a place of memories worse than demons."

Trowbridge looked out at the savagely intricate maze of valleys, the stern, bleak landscape where he would be spending his summer.

"*I need your help.*"

"You have Dorje. Jeet and the others will show up soon."

"Dorje is a *sirdar*, not a tracker. He can't help me with the study. The others are no better. I need you."

Conflicting emotions struggled on Norbu's face, but he shook his head.

"I cannot. I am more sorry for this than anything I have done in my life. But I cannot."

"Christ," Trowbridge said, suddenly furious. "You could have told me sooner!"

"I tried to—"

"One offhand comment in Pokhara? Three months ago?"

He looked away from Norbu's stricken face at the glittering slopes which surrounded them, and took a deep breath. The only thing clear in his mind was that he was about to enter Lhakrinor—with or without Norbu—and begin the study. It was time to go to work.

"I have to get down to Dorje," he said. "And you need to get back down to some shelter."

"David—" Norbu started miserably.

"You could have told me," Trowbridge said bitterly, and turned toward the precipice. Norbu, in an instinctive, desperate effort to make some last contact, reached out to touch Trowbridge's arm. Trowbridge, however, had pivoted his body around the piton, and taken the rope in his hands. Without looking back, he began letting himself down the ice cliff on the far side.

PART 2

21

A soft washing noise: shallow water rushing over gravel and small stones.

Then a cracking: frozen door hinges, and footsteps. A crackle of dry twigs, Dorje starting a fire.

Morning.

He drifted upward, away from the icebound cliff on which he'd been hanging in a dream, and opened his eyes.

Above him, the familiar, translucent blue of his nylon tent. He tipped his head back and looked out. Across the river the dark slopes of Torma Mountain, patchy with snow, slumbered like nighttime landscapes. He felt a controlled, steady excitement. In a little while he would be up there compiling data.

He sat up, gave a solid elbow to the heavy, warm body beside him, reached for his pants and down jacket, and pulled them into his sleeping bag. A pair of long-lashed, golden-slitted eyes opened, regarding him with a detachment that was nearly sublime. Trowbridge stared back at the gorgeous—if otherworldly—eyes in amusement. Sharing the warmth was a good arrangement for them both, although it had not been his idea.

"Rise and shine," he told the white goat. "You'll miss the seven-thirty bus."

After a moment's deliberation, the goat, which had been snuggled against him, rose stiffly to its feet. Its ears brushed with a shooshing noise against the nylon as it left the tent.

Still inside his sleeping bag, Trowbridge pulled on his by-now-warm clothes. Then he unzipped the bag, pushed his wool-stockinged feet into boots which had an interior temperature ten degrees below freezing, and crawled out of the tent. The morning was cold, and splendidly clear. His breath stood out in distinct white clouds. He made his way, stiffly in the icy boots, toward a nearby stone hut.

A hundred yards away an old woman—the only inhabitant of Trang, at the moment, other than him, Dorje, and the white goat—emerged from her tiny home and began making her way up the slope, where she would spend the day gathering yak chips for fuel.

He ducked inside the hut, an outbuilding of the Trang monastery complex, the only structure which had not been locked upon their arrival. Dorje was crouched by the fire tending a pot of bubbling oatmeal.

"Everyone sleep well?" Dorje asked cheerfully, handing Trowbridge a mug of steaming tea.

Trowbridge sipped the tea gratefully, feeling its warmth spread through his body.

"I do not understand why you do not wait until the sun is on the slopes to go watch your animals," Dorje said. "In three hours it will be very pleasant outside."

"In three hours most of the morning activity will be over. Can't learn much about an animal by watching it take a nap."

"I would not learn much about an animal if it walked up to me and told me who its parents were and what it ate for dinner. It is too bad Norbu is not here to help you."

"Speak to the old woman this morning?"

Dorje nodded. "She finally agreed to sell me turnips and potatoes—we will have a nice stew for dinner. But she still believes we are bandits. She said, 'I know that you are *gyami* bandits, and you probably plan to kill me. But I am old and I do not care, so it will give you no satisfaction.'"

"*Gyami?*"

"*Gyami* means 'a foreign man who comes from afar.' I hope, David *sahib*, that we do not have to spend too long here. She is not very good company."

"Better her than a witch who devours young men. Yesterday on the mountain I spotted Narling. It stands out on the canyon wall like a red flame."

Dorje shivered and held his hands close to the fire, as if seeking reassurance in the warmth and flickering light.

Trowbridge said, "Did you ask the old woman about the lama?"

"She says he is in solitary meditation in the lamasery across the river—the place is called Gelingdo—and is not to be disturbed."

"For how long?"

"Two years completed, and three more to finish. She says it is a very short time. A very hasty meditation. In the old days, she says, lamas were more devout, and would meditate in solitude for ten years at least. Things have not improved in Lhakrinor, she said."

"The terrain certainly hasn't."

"Do you think that is why there are no other people here at Trang?"

"Possibly. I'd like to hear what she has to say about it."

"I will speak to her again," Dorje said. "I must do my share to help with the study. Although, in truth, I would prefer talking to your goat."

Trowbridge methodically checked the contents of his daypack: spotting scope, tripod, plastic sample bags, notebooks and pen, *chapatis* with peanut butter—frozen solid, at the moment—canteen, also frozen solid, binoculars, emergency blanket, matches. Everything was there.

"When do you think we will move to Jaramar, David *sahib*?"

"In two or three weeks, probably. As soon as I've studied this area thoroughly."

"And Jaramar is a real village, is it not? With people living in it?"

"So I'm told."

Dorje nodded, pleased at this prospect, as he handed him a bowl of porridge. Trowbridge ate quickly, swallowed a second cup of tea, bade Dorje farewell, and stepped out into the morning.

He climbed steadily up the slope behind the monastery. The air against his face was icy and exhilarating; his skin, inside his clothes, felt pleasantly warm. Partway up the slope he spotted the old woman, a small persistent presence on a barren slope. She straightened, observed him for an impassive moment, then returned to work, placing the dried chips into a yak-hair bag.

An hour of stiff climbing carried him to a high ridge. There he paused for a moment's rest, his breath still clouding the air, and surveyed his new home.

Beneath him, marked by the spot of blue which was his tent, was Trang, an ocher-yellow complex of buildings set on a bluff above a shallow river. According to the old woman, Trang was abandoned for most of the year; only a yearly religious festival, held every spring, brought the place to life. South of the monastery a trail led back toward the Krimshi La, the pass by which he and Dorje had entered Lhakrinor a week ago. From this height and distance, the Krimshi La was a misty nick in the wall of mountains which separated Lhakrinor from the rest of the world. He thought of the rope they had used to lower themselves into Lhakrinor; in all likelihood it was still hanging frozen from the piton.

He shivered, glad he was not up there.

North of Trang, toward Tibet, was the dark, foreboding gorge which led to Narling. Its walls, increasingly sheer as the river disappeared into its gloomy depths, were dotted with a number of solitary meditation cells, each perched in a more improbable fold of the gorge than the one before.

To the west, behind the high wrinkle of mountains at his back, lay the rest of Lhakrinor. This remote land was perhaps the highest inhabited region on earth, and yet the mountains, ranging above twenty thousand feet, did not seem as high as they might, because the valleys—at a full fourteen thousand feet—were so high themselves. More than once the landscape had made him feel as if he were somewhere in the north of Scotland; that is, until he spotted a *chorten's* thin spire protruding above a ridge. The villagers of Lhakrinor were scattered across this bleak expanse, primarily in the narrow valley bottoms where there was flat land to cultivate crops; there were less than a thousand people, distributed among a half-dozen small villages.

They would move to one of these villages, Jaramar, once he had completed his work around Trang.

Directly across the river from where he stood, dominating his field of vision, rose the solitary, weathered bulk of Torma Mountain, soaring through an intensely blue sky. On its lower slopes he was able to make out three separate herds of bharal. He set up his scope and brought the nearest herd into focus, feeling happy. He was exactly where he wanted to be: alone with the animals, the data, the landscape. Alone with the mystery of the world and of being in its starkest, most noncomplicated form. No airplanes crossed these mountains; there was no sound of distant motors. In one of the loneliest places on earth, he was, by a quirk of temperament, perfectly, and finally, at home.

The afternoon light swept up the canyon walls as he worked his way back down toward Trang. The river caught a late reflection from the peaks high above. Tattered prayer flags snapped in the wind, a lonely sound, as he walked through the monastery compound. Atop the monastery was a stained iron trident; in the thin evening light it looked like the coldest thing in existence.

The hut welcomed him with gratifying smells of smoke and dinner. True to his word, Dorje had created a stew of potatoes, turnips and green nettles. Little was said until they had devoured the meal and moved closer to the fire, enjoying the last of its warmth and a final cup of tea.

Dorje belched amiably, and said, "David *sahib*, I think I have figured out why Lhakrinor seems like such a strange place. At first I did not understand it. I am used to wild places with few people. I am used to high mountains, and cold rivers, and wild animals. But this is a different sort of wild place."

"How?"

"There are no *trees* here."

Trowbridge gestured at the small stack of firewood in the corner of the hut. They had purchased the wood from the old woman at considerable expense; in Lhakrinor firewood was a precious commodity, husbanded for years, and passed on to one's children as an important inheritance.

Dorje said, "But why don't the trees grow back?"

"Thin topsoil and extreme weather conditions. You get long periods of drought, then heavy storms in which the topsoil washes away. Once the trees are cut down, the slopes erode before they can grow back."

"Can something be done?"

"It's possible. Be a big job."

Dorje thought this over. "Did you see any of the animals you were looking for today?"

Trowbridge shook his head. "Only bharal, which I've seen every day, and some wolf sign, but it was pretty old. Tomorrow I'll cross the river and visit the area around Gelingdo lamasery. I may have better luck there."

Dorje yawned. "Will you visit the lama?"

"Yes. Although I'm not sure he'll talk to me."

Trowbridge set down his cup, bade Dorje good night, and carried a flickering lump of candle across the dark slope toward his tent. Climbing into his sleeping bag, he pulled it up to his armpits, leaned back against his pack, and began transcribing the day's observations into a notebook. From time to time he held the tip of his ballpoint pen in the yellow candle flame to keep it from freezing, and listened to the sound of the monastery wind chime, a tiny bell whose delicate tones echoed with extreme clarity in the night.

A white face appeared at the flap of his tent. Trowbridge made a clicking noise with his tongue. The goat came in, folded itself downward, and settled against his sleeping bag with a sigh. Trowbridge propped his notebook against the goat's back and went on writing.

22

Trowbridge's knees, as he knelt on the cold stone floor of the lama's study, hurt fiercely. At various heights around him yak-butter lamps flickered on dusty shelves, casting an eerie, uneven light, filling the room with a peculiar smell. Loosely bound religious books with leather buckles sat in heaps on the shelves. Ancient *thankas*—religious paintings—were illuminated by shafts of light entering through slits in the thick stone walls.

Staring straight ahead, Trowbridge had little choice but to study the *thanka* directly before him.

The central image was a pair of wide-eyed, copulating skeletons. The female nestled in the lap of the larger male, skeletal legs wrapped around his pelvis; their arms were outflung, their heads tipped back in macabre ecstasy. Around them at crazy angles floated mountains, dragons, clouds, an ocean filled with strange fish; in their hands were skulls filled with smoking liquid; around their necks hung garlands of tiny skulls. Beneath their feet were seashells, a reminder of a time when the Tibetan plateau was under water.

On a shelf beneath this riotous *thanka*, as if to provide contrast, sat a simple bronze Buddha with serene, bulging eyes. Nearby hung the blackened beak and claws of a pelican, an ancient suit of Tibetan armor, and what looked like a shriveled human hand.

The lama, hobbling in a circle around him, had not said a word. The strong features of his lined brown face, shaped compactly on high Mongolian cheekbones, were impossible to read. His upper torso looked powerful, but his left leg was shrunken, and he moved with obvious difficulty. He was younger than Trowbridge had expected, perhaps in his early forties. Moving to one of the shelves, he took a butter lamp in his hand and hobbled close to Trowbridge. He held the flame close to Trowbridge's face, studying his eyes. Then he stepped back. A look of satisfaction came over his face. When he smiled his white teeth shone in the gloomy interior.

"You are not a *gyami-khoum-teng!*" he said with evident pleasure.

"*Gyami-khoum-teng?*"

"A stranger who comes from the north. You do not have the eyes of a *gyami-khoum-teng*. Your eyes are round, and pale in color."

What was "*khoum-teng*"? Trowbridge searched through his barely adequate Tibetan, then realized with astonishment that it must be a corruption of "Kuomin-tang"—the soldiers of Chiang Kai Shek, who'd been chased out of China by Mao at the end of the Chinese Revolution. It made sense; lying on the north side of the Himalayas—in a region which had once been a part of China—and having been inundated by Tibetan refugees when the Chinese appropriated Tibet, it was *China* the inhabitants of Lhakrinor feared, not India.

This was not the sort of modern lama who wore eyeglasses, traveled to a clinic to receive inoculations, and had regular conversations with mountaineers and trekkers. Evidently, Trowbridge was one of the first Westerners he had ever seen.

The lama was looking at him doubtfully, as if another concern had occurred to him.

"You are not blind, are you?"

"No," Trowbridge said, "I am not blind."

"Good! If you were blind, then you would have been a very holy lama—or indeed, a demon!—to have climbed this difficult trail to visit me. Surely we do not need another demon or holy man in Lhakrinor!"

The lama paused, studying him with his head tipped to one side. "Yes! You may laugh! It was intended as a joke! An excess of seriousness is a great sin."

Smiling, Trowbridge bowed his head and presented the lama with a white *kata*—prayer scarf—which he had brought for the purpose. The lama received the scarf good-naturedly, hobbling over to place it on a pile of similar gifts.

"It is a pleasure to be able to speak with you, lama. I was told I would find you in silent meditation."

"The old woman at Trang? Ah, yes . . . she is like an old potato, that woman, which has been roasted too long in the fire. Very hard on the outside! But her desire was a worthy one: to protect me from intruders."

"'If a valley is reached by a high pass, only the best friends or worst enemies are visitors.' "

The lama looked at him, visibly impressed. "Not only do you speak Tibetan, you can quote our proverbs! Are you quite certain you are not Tibetan, and simply have some disease which has caused your eyes and skin to be so pale?"

"Quite certain, lama."

The lama pondered this.

"If you are not a man from the north, and not a Tibetan, then you must be a man from the southern valleys."

Trowbridge considered how best to explain. Lhakrinor was almost precisely on the other side of the world from New York. "In fact, lama, I am from the east, or the west. But at a great distance."

"The east . . . *or* the west. I shall probably have to understand that idea in another lifetime. In this lifetime, however, I do not believe you are my enemy. Are you hungry?"

The lama led him past a pair of small rooms filled with rice and barley, heaps of radishes and small potatoes, goatskin bags of yak butter, strings of red peppers, and rounds of cheese. Seeing his inquiring glance, the lama explained.

"My people are concerned that if one day I begin a solitary meditation, I will starve to death. Dry up and blow away for lack of nourishment."

"The villagers must love you to bring you so much food."

The lines around the lama's eyes crinkled slightly, and he smiled. "Yes, they love me. But also they worry about having no lama to protect them from the demons and spirits which stalk the passes. No lama to consecrate their new houses, or bless their crops. No lama of whom to ask forgiveness when they have slaughtered a defenseless animal. The villagers bring me food out of love and selfishness in equal parts. This is as it should be. By a mixture of the sacred and the selfish, we make our way toward enlightenment."

They sat on a small stone terrace in the sun, eating sun-dried curd and handfuls of barley, gazing at the mountains. The lama drank black tea, swimming with salt and yak butter, from a cup made of a human skull; upside down, jaw removed, the skull served as a reminder of mortality. Trowbridge was given a mug made of chipped green porcelain. Beneath the terrace a sheer drop of several hundred feet ended in a jagged explosion of rock.

"It is good to live on such a holy mountain," the lama said contentedly. "Even though I can no longer walk its circumference. When I was younger I walked around it many times. Once on my knees! I can tell you that on one's knees, the trail seems much longer. Do you know how this became a holy mountain?"

"I would like to hear the story. Especially from the mouth of a lama who lives on the mountain."

The lama leaned back in satisfaction, and sipped his tea.

"A thousand years ago a great Tibetan teacher came to this mountain, riding through the sky on the back of a magic snow lion. The people, in those days, were wild and confused; they slaughtered animals without remorse, and did not know the way to enlightenment. The original god of the mountain—a very old and wicked god—welcomed the great lama and pretended to go along with his enlightened teachings, then attacked him treacherously with an army of *naga* demons. The magic snow lion, however, was brave and resourceful. He recreated himself one hundred and eight times, and flew around the mountain at great speed. The mountain was enveloped in a wondrous whiteness, a shining storm. The *nagas* lost their way in this storm of enlightenment and fell to their deaths, and the mountain god was vanquished. When the mountain reappeared, it was larger and more beautiful than before."

The lama pointed calmly up toward the invisible peak of Torma Mountain, perhaps four thousand feet above them.

"At that moment a white conch shell fell from the sky, and the great teacher, riding the faithful lion, rose into the sky. Above the peak of the mountain the sky was filled with rainbows, and the people were content, because now they had been shown the true path."

Trowbridge nodded in fascination, sipping the salty tea. Reduced to prosaic history, this legend probably represented the story of a charismatic Buddhist teacher who had come to this area many centuries ago—as part of the wave of Buddhism which had swept through the mountains—and done religious battle with the existing Bon-po lamas. Something like the story Nima had told him sitting above Dre-Mo Lake.

More important, for his purposes at least, the lama seemed to have a good feeling about snow leopards, and the protection of animals in general.

"The white conch was never found," the lama mused, "even though men of good reputation saw it fall. Personally I believe that when it touched the earth it was transformed into a *gter-ma*, a holy book. It is written that a wandering lama found this book and fell in love with its wisdom, so much so that he could not share it with others. This lama is said to have built a *chorten* around the holy book, and to have died there because he could not leave its sweetness—not even to obtain food."

The lama paused a little wistfully. "I would like very much to see that book. When I was younger I searched the mountain every day. Now such a thing is no longer possible."

The lama gestured at his leg.

"Still, it is not important. In spirit, one can fly through the sky on the back of a magic snow lion. Surely that is more important than being able merely to walk around a mountain!"

"Has anyone ever climbed the mountain, lama?"

Yesterday, from a place high on a slope across the river, he'd studied Torma Mountain. A strong technical climber, he had decided, could probably reach the peak in less than a day.

The lama looked at him critically. "Climb the mountain? To the top? Why would anyone want to do such a thing? To stand atop a holy mountain, brushing one's head against the sky which is itself holy. . . . No, it would be a worse foolishness than falling in love with a book. It is not the thing itself that matters—but the *essence* of the thing! To think that one has conquered a mountain simply by tramping to the top . . ."

The lama shook his head dismissively.

Above the terrace on which they sat, in the turquoise sky, a pair of Himalayan griffons described slow circles on wings which looked to be made of stiff paper. Across the river, Trang monastery was just visible beyond a high stone buttress.

"You have a very good view of the slopes, lama. Do you watch the animals that live here?"

"Of course! Every day! It is one of my responsibilities."

How closely do you watch, Trowbridge wondered. Closely enough that you can tell me about population trends, and predators?

As if reading his mind, the lama declared, "There are three herds of bharal which live on the slopes of this mountain, and two smaller herds above Trang monastery. The villagers know that these animals graze on holy slopes—and they know that I can count—so they do not dare harm them."

This explained the relative fearlessness of the bharal in the area. The slopes were sacred, and kept so by the sharp eye—and sharp tongue, he imagined—of the lama.

"And what of *sao*—the snow leopard?"

"Yes," the lama nodded vigorously, "I have seen *sao* many times. They feed on the bharal, usually those which are old or sick. Rarely do they kill a healthy bharal."

"Have you seen *sao* recently?"

To Trowbridge's disappointment, the lama shook his head.

"Since I last saw a *sao* it has been at least . . . twenty-five days."

Only that long! This was good news. Pleased, Trowbridge said, "You would make a very good biologist, lama."

He used the English word, since he had no idea how to say it in Tibetan.

"I have eyes which see," the lama admitted, "but what is a 'biologist'?"

"A scholar who studies animals."

The lama studied him for a long moment.

"That is perhaps a *second* idea I will comprehend in another lifetime. A scholar is one who studies the religious texts, and commits them to memory. It has always been so."

"And yet, according to Buddhist doctrine, animals have souls. In the same way a book contains spiritual meaning, an animal contains a soul. Since both are sacred vessels, the study of both should be of benefit to a true scholar."

The lama shot him a shrewd look. "*You* would have been a good lama! Very clever in the dialectic training. However, unless I am mistaken, it is not the *souls* of animals which interest you. It is their habits."

"I would not dispute a lama as wise as yourself."

"Ah! You are more flattering than a villager who fears he has a demon in his barley field! Nonetheless, I admire your technique of putting words into my mouth, then complimenting me for speaking them!"

The lama looked pleased at this sally. Then his face grew more serious. "Since you are interested in the habits of the bharal, I will tell you that there are fewer and fewer each year. The young are less numerous, and smaller. Perhaps because they must compete for grass with the yaks and goats. When I was a young man the villagers took their animals north to the great plains, where there was plenty of grass. Now there are soldiers on the border, and there is not enough here for the animals to eat. Lhakrinor is a poorer place than before."

"I have seen evidence of that."

The lama nodded slowly. "Then you also have eyes which see."

"Lama, do you know the set of horns over the door to Trang monastery?"

"Have I seen my own prayer wheel in the morning? Of course I know these horns."

"Have you ever seen such an animal alive? In my country it is called a 'shou.' "

The lama looked doubtful. "Such an animal was described to me once, but I have never seen one here in Lhakrinor. However, anything is possible. The world is filled with miracles at every turn."

They fell silent. Across from them the sun shimmered madly on blinding snow slopes. Eventually the lama spoke.

"You are not my enemy, of that I am certain. And yet I sense that you want something from me. Some kind of help. Do you wish to tell me what it is?"

"Not yet, lama. It is not yet clear in my mind."

"Is it help of a spiritual nature?"

"In a sense, yes. But also of a practical nature."

The lama nodded, and sat a moment in meditative silence. Then he clapped his hands together, as if he had reached some sort of conclusion.

"Well," he declared, "when you are able to tell me what sort of help you require, I will be able to decide if I can render it! In the meantime perhaps you could help *me*."

"How, lama?"

"As you study your four-legged 'sacred vessels,'" the lama said with dry emphasis, "perhaps you could watch for a hidden *chorten* somewhere on the mountain. If you found such a thing, it might contain the holy book I described."

"It would give me great pleasure, lama. But you said that you have searched the mountain many times already."

"That is so. But it is possible that your eyes might see more clearly than mine, which have been dulled by familiarity."

Trowbridge nodded agreement.

"There is one other thing, my *gyami* scholar. As I sit sipping my tea, I find I am still curious about this 'east or west' idea of yours. How can your home lie in both directions?"

Trowbridge thought a minute. "Imagine the world to be the same shape as this mountain, lama. The place from which I come is on the mountain's farthest side."

The lama made a globe shape with his hands, and studied it a moment before speaking. "Tibet, then, would be the peak of the mountain, and the place beyond the southern valleys, known as India, the base?"

"Something like that."

"It is your feeling, then, that the world on which we live is round."

"Yes."

The lama shrugged, as if the idea were not particularly momentous. "That is quite possible. The earth, finally, is nothing but *samsara*—illusion—and there is no more reason an illusion should be flat than it should be round. A bubble is round, after all—as is the eye which perceives it. You are staying at Trang?"

"Yes."

"Then you have visitors."

Trowbridge stood and peered toward the monastery. A pony and three figures were coming into the compound.

"You are surprised," the lama observed. "Is it at seeing them? Or at how happy it makes you to see them?"

"Perhaps both."

"Then you must go and make them welcome. Return another day to visit me. I would like to hear more about your oddly-shaped world."

In this high, lonely place, so far from any of their homes, the small reunion which took place at the hut was a very real pleasure. Dorje was animated and happy to have Jeet, Nima, and Chandra crowding into the small shelter. Jeet set his hand to dinner as if he had been gone only a few minutes, while Nima tethered and fed Seto outside the hut. Trowbridge noticed immediately that her face was clean, and that beneath her baggy clothing was the shape he remembered seeing by the river, unencumbered, now, by the elaborate padding. Chandra, seeing Trowbridge's glance, launched into a lengthy speech about what a bewitching creature Nima had become since she began washing her face, and admonished her, in fatherly tones, that she ought to have performed this miracle long ago. Trowbridge wondered if Jeet, more quietly perceptive than Chandra, realized that there was more to Nima's transformation than a bath and clean clothes.

As the fire burned low, he and Dorje explained what had happened atop the Krimshi La, when Norbu had refused to enter Lhakrinor.

Chandra shook his head. "Norbu was always a mysterious fellow. Still, I do not understand it. Most men *wish* to return to their homeland. I, for one, will be glad to return to my village."

Jeet nodded agreement. "It is the same for me. I am late for my stay at Rongbuk Monastery already—although it has been worth it to see Torma Mountain once in my lifetime."

Dorje looked glum at this reminder that their newly regained friends would be departing so soon for the lowlands.

Chandra sighed, stretched, and said with evident pride, "With the help of Nima's pony, Trowbridge *sahib*, we have brought you a good deal of food. You will certainly need it in this barren place."

Chandra paused, then added, "But Trowbridge *sahib*, if Norbu is not here, who is helping you with your study?"

"No one," Dorje said. "I can cook, and visit the other villages to find food and firewood, but I am not any good with animals."

It was true. Dorje was an excellent *sirdar*, but he had been fidgety, bored, and noisy on the one day Trowbridge had taken him up onto the slopes.

"Perhaps Nima could stay," Jeet suggested.

"I do not know enough about animals," Nima said immediately. "I could never take Norbu's place."

"But it was you, Nima, who spotted the blue sheep near the top of the second pass. You have the best eyesight of any of us."

"It is true," Dorje affirmed.

Chandra, studying her with a sly face, said, "Ah, I understand. You prefer to leave with Jeet and me so you can see that young man once again in the village we passed through—where was it? Ah, yes, Poldad."

Nima flashed a scornful look at Chandra. Ignoring her, Chandra grinned knowingly at Trowbridge.

"This young farmer fell in love with Nima the moment he saw her—and truthfully, I do not blame him. Ever since she began washing her face, she has grown more beautiful. I would say, now, that Nima is even more beautiful than the *kumari* herself!"

Trowbridge looked from Chandra to Nima in amusement, and saw that Nima had gone perfectly still.

No, he thought.

The others did not appear to have noticed her reaction; Dorje had leaned forward to take the teakettle off the fire, blocking Jeet's view of Nima, and Chandra was still looking at him expectantly.

Nima glanced up, saw from the expression on his face that he'd seen her give herself away, and widened her eyes in a brief plea that said, quite unmistakably: *Do not tell them.*

Whatever doubts he'd had about her identity were erased by the intensity of that look.

Casually, he said, "It's true, Chandra—Nima looks much prettier with her face clean."

Chandra nodded vigorous agreement, extending his teacup for Dorje to fill.

Dorje said, "What do you think, David *sahib*? Do you wish Nima to stay and help you study animals?"

Trowbridge knew that it might be wiser, in some ways, to send her away immediately, given what he had just discovered; the last thing he needed was a scandal of some kind. On the other hand, she learned quickly, moved with quiet confidence in the presence of animals, and was tough enough not to complain at the end of what would be long, hard, and frequently boring days. He couldn't count on finding the same qualities in any of the local villagers—and he could probably rely on her help for as long as he required it; she'd made it clear that she had no pressing desire to return to the lowlands.

And in truth, he had to admit that she intrigued him, more so now than ever. He deliberated a moment longer, then came to a decision.

"If you're willing to stay, Nima," he said, "I could use the help."

23

The light was cool and gray as they crunched across the gravel island beneath Trang monastery, then hopped from rock to rock across a shallow channel on its far side. Shallow pools at the river's edge were sheathed in ice. Upstream, stone conduits channeled a small part of the river's flow through a set of prayer water-wheels. Only two of the wheels turned, with an ancient creaking; the others were frozen in place.

A plank bridge carried them over a final tributary channel, and they began climbing the slope. After a few minutes the silence was disturbed by a short, harsh croaking. They stopped, breathing hard in the thin air, and looked upward.

"Good morning, crows," Nima said cheerfully, blowing on her fingers.

"Tibetan ravens," he said.

"Yes?"

Three of the glossy black birds tilted through the sky above them, feathers ruffling slightly as they banked off invisible mountains of wind.

"How does one know the difference?"

"A full-grown raven is nearly twice the size of a crow. Ravens have shorter call notes, and powerful-looking beaks. And they like high altitudes."

"Ah," she said.

They resumed climbing. After a few minutes the sound of the river receded; there was only the crush of their upward footsteps on the narrow, eroded trail, and one another's breathing. High above, the sun moved slowly down the dome of Torma Mountain.

"You know who I am," Nima said in a matter-of-fact voice.

"I didn't mean to. But yes, I know."

"I am sorry."

"My knowing is not a problem."

"But now I must ask you to keep a secret for me."

He snorted in amusement.

"What is funny?" she asked.

"I didn't mean to laugh. It's just that I have no intention of giving you away. If it became known that the recently retired Virgin Goddess of Nepal had run away from her husband to join the expedition of an unmarried Western scientist . . . well, it would generate the kind of controversy I do my best to avoid."

She was silent a moment. Then she said, "I did not mean to be a risk to your project. I will leave if you like, Trowbridge *sahib*."

"Unless you want to be addressed as the Living Goddess, perhaps you'd better start calling me David."

They climbed without speaking a while longer. Then he asked, "Does anyone else have a suspicion of who you are?"

She shook her head. "The only person, perhaps, was the Indian fellow who traveled with us. One day he walked with me and asked me too many questions."

"Lord," Trowbridge said, "him again."

"But we have not seen him in a long time. And he was on his way to Mt. Kailas, was he not?"

"That's what he said."

Although with any luck, Trowbridge thought, Vikram's arrested him and he's languishing in a jail cell in Jorkhang.

The ravens banked away, disappearing up the canyon toward Narling, leaving the sky to a single Himalayan griffon. The bird's wings turned slowly against the morning sky.

"I have arranged for Chandra to take Seto with him when he goes," Nima said. "There is not enough food for him here, and we do not need him to continue the study."

He looked at her, somewhat surprised that she could sever this tie so quickly.

She saw the look. "I am not giving him up altogether. Chandra will keep him for me in return for the work he can do. After the expedition is over I will go to Chandra's village and collect him. It is a much better arrangement for everyone."

He considered this, then said, "You've come a long way from an arranged marriage to a Brahman Hindu, and a life in a small village."

She looked at him sharply. "How do you know these things?"

"You told me you lived in a village. The *kumari* would not have been allowed to marry someone of a lower caste than a Brahman, and most Nepali marriages are arranged."

"It seems that you study more than animals in my country."

"Given the circumstances, I'd say it was rather brave on your part to have run away."

"Bravery would have been to stay in the village. Like the other women."

"Maybe. For what it's worth, I'm not that kind of brave either."

They reached the top of a narrow ridge, then followed it north toward the lamasery at Gelingdo. A hundred yards ahead of them a lock-step series of steep cliffs soared directly upward; falling away beneath the cliffs was a barren, mile-long slope.

"There," he said with satisfaction.

A small herd of bharal grazed on the slope. At his and Nima's appearance a number of heads lifted; the bharal regarded them with curious, unfrightened stares.

"Their horns are like the wings of birds," she said.

He'd never seen it that way, but it was true. The horns curved out and down in graceful, wing-like, flaring motions.

"Is there a way to get closer?"

"Gather dung."

"Please?"

"Did you see the old woman gathering yak dung yesterday?'

She nodded curiously.

"That's how we get closer. They're accustomed to the motion, and don't perceive it as a threat."

Stooping, moving slowly, they traversed the slope until they were barely fifty yards from the herd. There, a small clump of rocks and a scrubby thorn bush formed a natural blind just large enough for two people to squeeze into. They leaned back against a rock which was only mildly uncomfortable; Trowbridge opened his pack and pulled out the altimeter, binoculars, spotting scope and tripod.

"The binoculars are for scanning a large area," he explained quietly. "The scope gives you better magnification once you've found something. Ever used a telescope?"

She nodded. "In the *che* in Kathmandu, I made the *kumarima*—in English you would call her a nanny—give me a telescope so that I could look at the mountains."

She raised the scope to her eye, focused, and breathed in sharply. "They are beautiful! We are so much closer than the last time."

Trowbridge raised the binoculars to his eyes, focusing on the largest member of the herd. The bharal male stared back with golden, eerie eyes. His massive horns framed an expressive face with slight upward turns at the corners of the mouth. His neck and chest were powerful; his flanks solid, and rimmed with dark markings; his belly white.

"They are much nicer to look at than the goats I tended in the village," she said. "And much larger."

"You tended goats?"

"I tended goats, and carried water, and cooked and cleaned. I worked very hard in the village. But why are they called blue sheep? They are not blue."

"Good for you. Skepticism of provided information is an important trait in a biologist. Actually, in certain lights, their coats appear to be a sort of slate blue color. Tell me what else you see."

"There are eleven. Only one has large horns. I think he must be a male. Let me see…yes, he is definitely a male."

Good, he thought. A biologist—or a biologist's assistant—couldn't afford to be shy.

"There are three which look quite small. Each stays close to a particular female. Aiee! One is nursing. And there is one who is larger than the babies, but not full grown—perhaps this one is a year older than the little ones?"

"Right. That's a yearling. The others were born only a couple of months ago."

"Why is there only one male for this many females?"

"Until the rut begins in November, males generally—although not always—form their own herds. This fellow is unusually sociable. He's dropped in for a visit almost every day I've been up here. He'll probably wander back to the bachelor herd later this afternoon."

She put down the scope and looked at him.

"You like these bharal."

"It's not a matter of liking them or not liking them. I study them."

"But do you like them?"

"Yes. Now, look at the carpal joints of their front legs."

"Carpal joints?"

"Knees."

Obediently, she raised the scope.

"I don't see anything special."

"Most true mountain-dwelling goats have knee calluses which help them scramble up steep slopes and cliffs. For some reason the bharal doesn't, and it's one of the curious things about them. You'll wish you had calluses, by the way, after you've scrambled up and down this slope a few times—assuming it's still something you want to do. I won't hold you to it."

"Of course," she said, intent on the bharal. "What else would I want to do?"

They observed the animals grazing a while longer. Then he pulled out a small pad of paper and a pen and jotted some notes: 0915, 6 ♀, 3 nb, 1 yrl, 1 ♂, 15,600 ft, E-fcg slp, fdg avlch path, 100 yds cliff. He handed her the pad.

"With cold fingers, you don't want to spend any more time writing than necessary. See if you can read this back to me."

"Nine-fifteen," she read, "six females, three newborn, one yearling, one male. Elevation 15,600 feet, east-facing slope, feeding on avalanche path—how do you know it is an avalanche path?"

"See the scree—the loose stones at the bottom of the slope? The slope forms a kind of chute."

"—one hundred yards from the cliff," she finished. "Why is it important how close they are to the cliff?"

"You tell me."

Her dark eyes moved back and forth between the bharal and the craggy cliffs above them. With a slight shock, he realized it must have been her, at the balcony window, that he'd seen five years ago on the earlier expedition to Nepal. It seemed impossibly strange, and yet somehow perfectly normal, that this young woman who'd been raised in luxury and isolation, with the King himself bowing before her in the confines of her Kathmandu dwelling, was now sitting beside him on an uncomfortable mountain slope, three weeks' walk from the nearest trappings of civilization, taking an intense interest in the grazing patterns and knee calluses—or lack thereof—of an obscure species of goat antelope.

"Can they climb on the cliffs?" she asked.

He nodded. "Their hooves are soft and spongy in the center, with a harder rim. Ideal for cliff climbing."

"But there's nothing to eat on the cliffs." She scanned the rocky fastness above them. "Nothing that I can see. It must be a way for them to escape from enemies."

"The trick to survival for a bharal—as for most animals—is to get enough to eat without getting eaten in the process. Snow leopards and wolves can't follow them up those rock walls."

"Snow leopard and wolves are their great enemies?"

"They think so, and most people would assume that to be the case.

In fact, predators rarely reduce a herd population by much, and they rarely pull down healthy animals. It's mostly the old and sick which don't reach the cliff in time to avoid becoming a predator's dinner. The bharal ought to be more afraid of the domestic yaks and goats in the area."

"Yaks and goats?"

"Look at what the bharal are eating."

She focused the scope carefully.

"It is a small bush, with thorns and little pink flowers. This bush!" she said, putting down the scope, reaching out and touching the thorn bush which formed their blind. "They eat the tips of the leaves."

She broke off a leaf and sniffed it curiously.

"Taste it."

She chewed gingerly on the leaf, then made a face and spat it out.

"They feel the same way," he said. "They would prefer some of this . . ." He brought his fingers together carefully on a non-thorny portion of branch, and lifted, revealing a few tousled, pale-green strands of grass.

"The slopes should be covered with this grass at this time of year. And the bharal should be filling up on it so they have energy to get through the rut, and survive the winter. But the grass has been cropped right down to the ground by the domestic animals. There's nothing left but thorn bushes, and juniper, both of which—because they're filled with nasty oils and chemicals—can only be digested very slowly."

"Where are the yaks and goats now?"

"According to the old woman, they've been taken over to one of the next valleys. They'll be back, no doubt, when they've stripped the slopes there."

"And yet these bharal do not seem unhealthy. Or unhappy."

"Do the math. How many females?"

"Six."

"How many babies?"

"Three," she said.

"Out of a group of six bharal females, there's a fair chance of a set of twins. That means there should be six or seven newborns on that slope."

"And there are only three."

"Right. Now, how many yearlings?"

She was silent a moment.

"Only one. The first winter must be very hard, then."

"And there's no guarantee this yearling will make it to adult-hood."

Nima looked troubled. "And yet the people here are poor. I am sure they need their yaks and goats if they are to have enough to eat ."

"You're learning fast. Unfortunately, in this line of work there always seems to be a group of human beings whose needs take prece-dence over those of the animals. The result is that I spend most of my time recording not how animals live, but how they disappear."

"But there must be a solution. A way for both the animals and peo-ple to live together. Surely you have an idea, David, or you would not be here. Oh look!" she said. "One of the little ones is playing!"

One of the newborns, on spindly legs, was tearing up the slope as if possessed. Reaching a little outcropping of rock, it whirled, then raced at breakneck speed back down the slope past its mother, who grazed placidly, head down, ignoring these antics. Skidding to a stop in a clatter of stones, the newborn spun in a circle, chased its tail in three tight revolutions, then headed back toward its mother. At the last minute it made a tremendous leap into the air and landed squarely on its mother's back, teetering there on elegantly skinny legs, looking around with triumphant curiosity.

The mother raised her head and looked skeptically over her shoul-der. Then she casually twitched her rump, forcing her newborn into a heroic bound down onto the slope. Immediately he trotted back to her, angled his head low, and began to nurse.

Trowbridge was scribbling happily in his notebook.

"That's a first," he said. "I've never seen a bharal play in that fash-ion before. I've never even heard of it in the literature."

Nima was still watching the little bharal.

"I hope this one, at least, survives the winter," she said.

24

On the following morning Jeet and Dorje went to pay their respects to the lama. Trowbridge watched them as they returned, walking together up the trail from the river. A few minutes later they all stood in the late afternoon in a small group outside the door of the hut, stamping their feet and hugging themselves to keep warm as they said their good-byes.

Chandra wished them luck, and assured Nima that he would take good care of Seto until she came to collect him. Then he exacted a promise from the others to visit him in his village as well, and added that he would have liked them to attend his daughter's wedding. Nima put her arms around Seto's neck, then stepped back and cuffed him once, with rough affection, as a form of good-bye. Her face was surprisingly free of conflict. Jeet and Dorje arranged to meet at Rongbuk Monastery in the Solu Khumbu late in the fall. Then Jeet wished each of them peace and good luck, and turned, a look of contentment on his strong, scarred face—contentment that he would soon rejoin his lama—and hefted his pack. He and Chandra, followed by the pony, set out along the river which led west toward Jaramar. As their figures dwindled into the distance, Dorje cried unashamedly, standing with his feet close together and his hands atop his head.

The next day Trowbridge and Nima went back up onto the slopes. To his satisfaction, she'd forgotten nothing he told her on that first day of study; she was already able to identify many of the animals on Torma Mountain by their individual physical and behavioral characteristics, and was proving adept at compiling data tables on what the bharal ate, how the females cared for their young, and types and incidences of aggressive behavior in males. As they sat in the same small blind she began asking the more difficult questions. He had expected it; she was too intelligent not to.

"I think I understand, now, what you want me to do," she said. "But I do not understand why you need me to do it. You already know how many bharal there are on this mountain. And you know the condition of their grazing. What do you need me for?"

"Someone has to keep an eye on the herds while I go farther afield to look for predators. I've been here over a week without seeing a wolf or a snow leopard."

"So it is not only the bharal you are interested in."

He shook his head. "This is an interactive, not a single-species study. I need to find out how many wolves and snow leopards live in the area. How widely they range. How stable their populations are—that is, are they reproducing efficiently enough to maintain their numbers, or are they dying out."

"Why would the predators die out? They have bharal to eat, and you told me the lama protects the animals on this mountain from human hunters."

"The number of bharal around Trang—when you consider accidents, disease, and their poor reproduction rate—could barely support a single wolf pack, or a handful of snow leopard. In territory this barren, predators need hundreds of square kilometers of range to support themselves."

"So even if they are protected here, they may be killed when they travel to the next valley."

"That's right."

"And that is why you are here. To protect them, somehow, over a large area."

"If possible."

"Your idea is to make a national park, then."

He nodded.

"But if the people who live here need their yaks and goats to survive—and if those yaks and goats are ruining the land—how will you make a national park?"

"It's a good question. The people and the park may be incompatible."

"I am sure that the people would like to help save their land."

"They might. On the other hand, setting up a park around them would require some substantial changes in their way of life. Try explaining to a villager that a national park is a good idea when it means he can no longer graze his animals where there's grass, and isn't allowed to destroy a wolf or snow leopard when it kills the domestic animal which represents his only wealth. My guess, at this point, is that we'd have to relocate the villagers."

"Move them away from their homes?"

"Yes."

"Do you have a right to do that?"

"Legally, it could be done. Ethically, I'm not sure. If the situation goes on as it is, though, this area will become an arctic desert in a few years—at which point the people will move away on their own to keep from starving. If they're going to leave anyway, maybe it's better they do it now."

She said nothing, and he wondered if he'd made a mistake by telling her this.

"How will you make your decision, finally?" she asked.

"It'll depend on the data we gather over the next three months."

She meditated on this a moment.

"It seems I am not the only one with a secret to keep."

"I guess not," he said.

The sun, spilling down the slope, finally reached the blind where they were sitting. As the temperature rose they removed their heavy outer clothing. The hillside shimmered with heat waves. Far below them the river, mournfully dark when they had crossed it in the early morning, was a bright, cheerful blue, cut with clean-looking white water. Above their heads the broad dome of sky was flecked with small white clouds; cloud shadows moved in a gentle procession across the rounded hilltops, the snowy slopes, the yellow and red out-croppings of rock. One by one the bharal grew lazy in the noon sun, pawed shallow beds in the slope, and settled in to chew cud. Trow-bridge brought out *chapatis* and peanut butter and began making lunch.

"If I were a wolf," Nima said, "this is when I would try to catch a bharal, when they are taking naps."

Without looking up, he said, "See the one on the rock outcropping above the herd? She's the designated sentinel. They take turns."

"Ah," she said.

After hours of sitting in the cramped, chilly blind, the warmth of the sun was immensely welcome.

"It is nice to be warm again," Nima said, stretching with pleasure. "I could almost imagine myself back in Kathmandu."

"I saw you once, you know," he said. "Five years ago, when I was leaving Kathmandu for Manang. I ducked in behind a group of tourists. It's odd, because it's not the sort of thing I do very often. But I remember watching for you to appear at the balcony, and getting impatient, and nearly leaving. Then you appeared, for just a few sec-onds."

"And what did you see?"

He thought for a moment. "A composed, beautiful, and apparently fearless young girl. But I'm not sure I saw a goddess."

"Do you know the beginnings of the legend?"

He tried to remember what he'd read. "It has something to do with the king's wife being jealous of the goddess, doesn't it?"

She nodded. "Centuries ago, the goddess of the Kathmandu Valley would visit the king to give him advice on ruling the kingdom. When his wife grew jealous the king asked the goddess to visit him in the body of an unapproachable young girl—a 'perfect vessel'—and live in her own palace, the *che*, separate from that of the king."

The list of perfections required of a *kumari*, Trowbridge recalled, was formidable, and included perfect health, unblemished skin, black hair, no loss of teeth, beautiful features, and a personality which was calm and fearless. And all *kumaris* came from among the best families of the Kathmandu Newars.

"I remember wondering what they would do if none of the candidates for *kumari* measured up," he said, handing her a *chapati*.

"They simply choose the best one and hope the goddess accepts her."

"Did you fulfill all the perfections?"

"They said I was the first candidate who had done so in generations, which helped protect me later, when it became known that I was wilder and more willful than some *kumaris*. My behavior was attributed to the strong power of the goddess within me."

"You weren't startled when the priests jumped out at you in the temple?" he asked.

"It was more than priests! It is called the 'black night,' the eighth day of Dasain, and hundreds of animals are sacrificed. You can hear them screaming and smell the blood in the air. Eight buffaloes are tied to long poles in one of the palace courtyards. One after another their throats are slit so that the blood spouts in the air toward the holy shrine of Bhagwati. I was made to walk between their severed heads, which had candles set between their horns. Of course, I am not sure what is real memory, and what I learned later. But it is very clear in my mind."

"How old were you?"

He noticed the sentinel bharal shift uneasily for a moment, then relax again.

"Three years old. On the following morning I was installed as the living incarnation of the goddess, and from then on I lived in the *che*, and did not see my parents, except on rare occasions, for many years. I was dressed with great ceremony every morning in beautiful clothes, and the sacred *tika* mark—the fire eye—was painted on my forehead. I sat on my throne to receive visitors, and stood on the balcony looking out at crowds of people who had come to see me."

"And even the king visited you."

"Once a year." She looked thoughtful. "When he visited I would sit very straight on my throne, the attendants fanning me with peacock fans. The King would come in, looking serious and handsome—well, a little fat, but handsome nonetheless—and he would bow, and put his forehead close to my feet, and slip a gold coin between my toes. And I would place the sacred *tika* mark on his forehead to bestow the protection of the goddess."

In the warm, cramped blind, Trowbridge suddenly became acutely aware of Nima's physical presence. In spite of himself, he noticed her smell, a pleasing blend of warm skin and sweat.

Nima, looking out at the slope, shrugged. "Beyond that I wasn't terribly different from other children, simply more indulged. My lessons were informal, because a goddess wasn't supposed to require an education, and when I played with the *kumarima's* grandchildren, I am afraid I tormented them horribly."

She glanced over at him to add something, then stopped. She seemed suddenly conscious as well that their thighs and shoulders were pressed unavoidably against each other. Trowbridge knew that he should probably stand up, but if he did he would spook the herd.

A strange whistle echoed across the mountainside.

"David!" Nima said urgently.

He grabbed the binoculars and scanned the animals on the slope. The sentinel bharal stood with her neck arched and tail vertical. She stamped her foreleg twice, then blew the air out her nose, once again, in an unmistakable sound of warning. The bharal bunched quickly and began streaming upward to the safety of the cliffs.

"What are they running from?" Nima asked.

"Look! There!"

The wolves spilled out of a crack in the mountainside. There were five, fanning out across the steep slope, moving at what appeared to be little more than a steady lope. Their deceptive pace, however, ate up the barren ground. They gained steadily on the bharal.

"They will catch them!" she said.

"I don't think so."

The lead pair of wolves were barely fifty feet behind a fleeing female when she turned straight upward, bounding toward a precipice which seemed to grow straight up from the slope. The two leading wolves veered after her, quickening their pace. They were only a few body lengths behind when she made a tremendous, apparently off-balance leap directly at the cliff face, alighting on a tiny ledge. She teetered a moment, then launched herself, in two more zigzag bounds, up beyond the wolves' reach.

A rock, dislodged by her hooves, skittered down the nearly sheer wall of rock, landing at the feet of her frustrated pursuers.

The other three wolves, redoubling their efforts, raced after the rest of the herd, attempting to get between them and the cliffs. The bharal were forced into an ever-lengthening arc to reach safety. Finally, like pale bits of yarn, they scattered up onto the cliff face where the wolves could not follow. In a powerful, surging line, the wolves continued along the base of the cliff—as if it had all been a game, and they had intended to go in that direction anyway. Rounding a wind-eroded precipice, their gray gold coats gleaming in the sun, they disappeared from sight.

Later, in the dying light, he and Nima tramped happily back down the trail toward the river.

"The best day yet!" he said. "By a long shot!" He stopped to pick up a bit of wolf scat and slipped it contentedly into his pocket.

"Perhaps tomorrow we will see snow leopard," she said.

He grinned skeptically. "That would be something."

"Have you seen many snow leopard?"

"I've seen five, in twelve years of looking, and it seems to be getting more difficult all the time. Last year I tried to census the snow leopard population in a remote part of the Altai Mountains, a region that had a sizable population a few years ago. In an entire summer I saw only one leopard—unless you want to count the furs in the bazaars."

"Why do you care so much about snow leopard?"

He was about to say something about reduced habitats, shrinking populations, and depleted gene pools, when he realized that was not what she was asking. Instead, he said, "The snow leopard—for me, at least—is the most beautiful animal on earth. I admire its ability to walk alone, seemingly without loneliness or regrets."

"Do they always live alone?"

He shrugged. "Some biologists think they get together only to mate. Others think that they travel together on occasion to hunt, or for companionship. No one really knows. I certainly don't, and I'm supposed to be an expert."

Above the Krimshi La, in a sky the color of a bruise, a tiny, rising moon shone like a silver trinket.

"It seems that you—like the snow leopard—work alone a good deal," she said.

He nodded. "That's part of it."

Across the river a tendril of smoke indicated dinner was being cooked in the stone hut. At a great height above Trang monastery, dimly, in the dying light, he saw movement. He stopped, swung the binoculars to his eyes, then handed them to her, pointing wordlessly.

"Ah," she said. "I see them. Another herd of bharal. You have sharp eyes."

"Comes with the profession."

She gazed through the binoculars, focusing on the herd.

"See it?"

"You are right," she said. "In the evening light, they are blue after all."

25

He stepped out into the darkness, and walked away from the hut toward a low, crumbling wall. It was icy cold once the sun went down; his urine, splashing against the stones of the wall, steamed in the chilly air.

He stood a moment before heading back inside. Torma Mountain loomed mysteriously to the east, blocking out the stars, and a half-moon, partially obscured by clouds, soared above him. He felt, once again, the sense of being perfectly at home here, perfectly in balance.

Then he became aware of someone in the darkness, standing only a few feet away.

He felt a split-second of startled panic, then caught something familiar in the stance and realized he knew only one person who could slip up on him so silently.

The figure flashed a grin, and said, in a lazy voice, "So—you did not get lost without me to guide you?"

"No," Trowbridge said. "We didn't."

Norbu shrugged out of the straps of his pack, lowering it, with a weary groan, to the ground.

"Aiee," he said, hunching his shoulders. "This pack is heavy, and it is a long walk from the Krimshi La."

"Longer when you do it five times."

He and Dorje, after Norbu had turned back at the pass, had been left with ten full loads; they'd spent their first three days in Lhakrinor ferrying those loads from the base of the Krimshi La.

"I would think so," Norbu said quietly.

In the ensuing silence, Trowbridge noted two distinct feelings within himself: First, that he was, in a personal sense, completely and unabashedly happy to see Norbu. Second, that he had absolutely no intention of accepting him back—assuming that was what he was here for—without a good explanation for what had happened atop the Krimshi La.

"What about your vow never to come back to Lhakrinor?" he asked.

"It wasn't a vow," Norbu said. "It was more a decision. A knowledge that coming back to my homeland was wrong."

"I'm not sure I see the distinction. If you knew from the beginning you wouldn't help me cross the Krimshi La, you could have said so."

The moon moved from behind the clouds and illuminated their faces; Trowbridge saw that Norbu's expression was troubled.

"I was not sure. Not until the moment I looked out on Lhakrinor. And even after I turned back I was not sure. I spent five days in Choko, David, battling with myself. Every night I resolved to leave for the lowlands, and every morning I was unable to do so. I could not live with the look I had seen on your face."

Trowbridge considered this a moment, then said, "I'll be honest with you, Norbu. I've missed you over the last ten days—missed your help and your company. On the other hand, I've had ten good days gathering data without a hint of outside complications or trouble."

He paused, marshalling his thoughts. "I have no idea why you left me on the pass. I also have no idea what was the source of all the problems we had getting up here, and to be honest, I don't care—I don't even want to think about it. But I have to be certain this secret of yours has nothing to do with those problems—and that your return is not going to start them back up again."

"I do not know about these other things," Norbu said simply. "As for the demons which kept me away from Lhakrinor, they have only to do with me."

Trowbridge studied him, looking for signs of reticence or duplicity, but Norbu's face was clear. Saddened, but clear, and in that moment, Trowbridge was convinced.

"All right," Trowbridge said. "I believe you. And I know you must be hungry. Let's go in. The others will be glad to see you."

Norbu, to his surprise, did not move.

"I will tell you why I left you on the pass," he said, after a moment's hesitation. "So you can be certain in your belief. It was because of a vow I made seventeen years ago. A vow to kill the man responsible for my father's death."

"The Gorchok bandit."

"Not the man who pulled the trigger, but the man who sent him to meet the bullet—the man who was truly responsible. My father died when I was seventeen, David. He was the only family I had. I believed there was more to his death than the rifle of a Gorchok bandit, and I vowed to find proof, and to kill the person behind it. I was young, and I was filled with grief and rage, but I never felt truer to anything than I felt to this vow."

"Did you kill the person? Is that why you left?"

Norbu shook his head. "The lama at Gelingdo convinced me to leave. He did not ask me to go back on my vow, but he said that my only choice—if I were to avoid the terrible sin of killing another human being—was to leave Lhakrinor. I knew he was right—and that my father would have felt the same way."

"And this is the first you've been back?"

Norbu nodded, then grinned suddenly. "So now you know my story, and we can go into the hut. I have missed Dorje's cooking. In fact, the real reason I came back was because I missed Dorje's cooking."

Trowbridge lifted Norbu's pack and slung it over his own shoulder. "It's good to have you back, whatever the reason."

Dorje learned from the old woman, who had gradually become more accepting of their presence, that the village of Jaramar was holding a festival. It struck Trowbridge that this would be a good time to meet the villagers—since they would be moving their operation there in a week or two—and they decided to attend, locking the hut and following the trail which led east along the river toward Jaramar. As they climbed, Trowbridge glanced back at the foreboding canyon to the north, in the direction of Narling. It was time to extend the range of the study; tomorrow, before first light, he planned to cross the river with enough provisions to stay out for two or three days, hoping to spot snow leopard in that labyrinth of narrow trails, ledges, and solitary caves.

"She told me it is held in a place near the river," Dorje was saying, "perhaps two-thirds of the way to Jaramar, and that it is the most pleasant place for a festival in all of Lhakrinor."

They were wearing their best clothes, which—excepting Nima, who had purchased a new outfit on the way into Lhakrinor, and now carried it carefully wrapped in newspaper—was not saying a great deal. The old woman had left for the festival the day before, so they had no sure way of knowing they would even find it, but the track toward Jaramar was clear and the morning beautiful. Trowbridge felt his pulse quicken and his soul expand as he surveyed the new territory. The rugged hills around them seemed to tumble on forever in wild rolling motions; in the distance, in every direction but north toward Tibet, were lordly, snow-topped mountains. For vastness and sheer geographical splendor, Lhakrinor was even more impressive than he had expected. If it were not for the cropped and eroded hillsides on either side of the track, he would have felt himself to be walking through an outlying region of heaven itself.

As they walked, he reviewed the map of Lhakrinor which he carried in his head. The region was divided, for all practical purposes, into two long valleys; the valleys ran diagonally, roughly parallel to one another, and were separated by high rocky ridges. Trang, where they were staying now—along with Gelingdo, where the lama lived, and the tangled canyon to the north toward Narling—were all contained in the easternmost valley, the more isolated and least populated of the two. The festival would be held in the western valley, known as the Robshi.

Three hours later, after crossing a high ridge, they came down into the Robshi Valley. On a rounded hilltop they paused, looking down on the hospitable river basin half a mile beneath them. At a point where the river widened, embracing a flat grassy area, prayer flags had been erected on long poles, fluttering in a soft breeze, sending their edifying messages toward the four corners of the universe. Beside the slow-flowing water stood a pair of large tents; spread out along the river's banks were the inhabitants of Jaramar and neighboring villages, dressed in bright holiday colors. Children splashed in the shallows. Even the air seemed warmer and more hospitable, less dry and austere, than that in the valley at Trang.

Beyond the festival, at a bend in the river, was a stand of green willows.

"I see two miracles," Dorje said. "People, and living trees."

26

The people of Jaramar welcomed them as graciously as if they'd been expected, pressing food and drink on them, offering them blankets on which to sit. He and Norbu were sitting on a soft blanket of brightly colored goat's wool near the river bank. Around them families were spread out on the grass; babies cried, and were nursed by their mothers; older children tumbled, shrieking with laughter, among thickets of wild rose. Nima had slipped off somewhere to have a bath; Dorje was deep in conversation with a Lhakrinor trader who had traveled through his home district, the Solu Khumbu.

"*Sahib*! What would you like? More *chang*? You must make yourself at home! Or do you prefer *rakshi*?"

A jaunty figure in a bright vest stood before them, holding a jar in each hand. Trowbridge recognized him as the fellow who had been playing a slender-necked lute a few moments before.

"*Chang*!" Trowbridge said cheerfully, speaking what would be, to this fellow's ears, heavily accented Tibetan, and extending his cup. "*Rakshi* gives me a headache."

"*Rakshi* gives me a headache as well!" the lute-player laughed, filling Trowbridge's cup with the light, milky *chang*. "But it is my favorite kind of headache. And well worth it on a festival day!"

After filling Norbu's cup as well—then peering at Norbu with a curious expression—he complimented Trowbridge on his command of Tibetan, and insisted once more that they make themselves at home here in Lhakrinor. With another glance at Norbu, he wandered off.

"They do not recognize you," Trowbridge said.

Norbu shook his head. "Jigme was a friend of mine. But it has been seventeen years—and I was only seventeen when I went away."

Trowbridge felt a light touch on his shoulder. Beside him a plump little girl, perhaps four years old, was holding out a lacquered tray covered with tidbits of roast goat cut into crescent shapes. Trowbridge partook, nodding his thanks with a smile. The girl offered the tray to Norbu courteously, but continued to stare at Trowbridge.

"*Sahib*, are you blind?" she blurted out at last.

"No," Trowbridge said.

"Are you certain?"

"If I were blind, would I know that your *lhams* are red?" he asked.

The little girl looked down at her cloth slippers.

"They *are* red!" she said, looking up. Then she looked at him a little suspiciously. "If you are not blind, why are your eyes the color of the sky?"

"Because I come from far away."

The explanation seemed to satisfy her, and she wandered on to the next group of people.

Norbu took a deep breath, closed his eyes, and turned his face for a moment to the sun. Then he opened his eyes and looked over at Trowbridge and flashed a contented smile. "It is very good to be here," he said. "I feel that I have healed a wound by returning."

"But you've opened another wound?"

"Yes," Norbu said. "And I do not know what will come of it."

A great commotion arose from the direction of the river, and they walked over to see what was going on.

A number of the girls had pulled off their *lhams* and waded out into the water. Lifting their garments to their thighs as the water grew deeper, they paddled and splashed each other with their free hands. Several of the older men protested, not very seriously, that this was unseemly behavior. The girls ignored them and began singing at the top of their voices. One, who seemed by virtue of her audacity to be their leader, fell completely under water, and was hauled out onto the bank, soaked through. Amid increasing laughter, she took off her vest and stood naked from the waist up in the warm sunlight.

"She is a beauty, that one," Norbu said.

"Her name is Pema," volunteered a boy standing beside them. "Her mother died of a fever. She has three yaks and lives with her father. My father says she is a good businesswoman, but my mother says she is a little wild because she has no one to discipline her."

Trowbridge's attention was caught by movement in the valley to the north.

"It looks like we're not the only ones to arrive late," he said.

A dark spot on the valley floor was growing larger, taking shape in the crystalline corridor between mountains. They walked back to their place on the grass; Trowbridge pulled the binoculars from his pack and trained them on the latecomer. It was an older man, hunched over, riding a donkey. He handed the binoculars to Norbu. Norbu studied the figure a moment, then lowered the binoculars.

"Someone you know?" Trowbridge asked.

"Yes," Norbu said. "Someone I know. Do you have the permit?"

Trowbridge nodded. "I have the permit. And I can handle this, whoever it is. Slip away down by the river somewhere."

Norbu shook his head. "For seventeen years I have slipped away. Now I think I will remain."

When the individual on the donkey entered the encampment, a certain self-consciousness arrived with him. The noise level did not lower appreciably, and no individual conversation ceased, but Trowbridge had the feeling that every villager was aware of the newcomer's presence. The openness and joy were gone; there was a feeling of constraint in the air.

"He is even less popular now than when I left," Norbu said quietly.

The newcomer reached an open grassy area between several blankets, nudged his donkey to a stop, and sat slumped imperiously, making no move to dismount. He wore a thick sheepskin *chuba*, even though it was warm, and a round fur hat. He was stocky, with small feet. His eyes squinted unsmilingly as he looked around. Trowbridge noticed that his saddle was very fine, and that he wore a great deal of turquoise around his neck.

"Will no one welcome the headman of the two valleys of Lhakri-nor?" he asked.

Various half-hearted greetings echoed around him.

"That is much better," the headman said sardonically. "Now I know that I am well-loved once again."

His gaze lighted upon Trowbridge. With a touch of his knees, he guided the donkey closer.

"Here is a figure that stands out," he said. "A *gyami* man, accompanied by other strangers."

"*Tashi delai,*" Trowbridge greeted him politely in Tibetan.

The headman looked mildly—if sarcastically—impressed. "The *gyami* man speaks our language!" he said. Then his voice hardened quickly. "I wonder if you have a permit to be in Lhakrinor."

Wordlessly, Trowbridge pulled the permit from inside his shirt and handed it over. The headman studied it a moment, then tossed it to the ground at Trowbridge's feet.

"You should have checked in with me at Tingri when you arrived in Lhakrinor," he said coldly.

Trowbridge made no move to pick up the document. "Actually, no," he said. "The permit states that I must check in if I am within fifteen kilometers of Tingri. I have been staying at Trang, which is twice that distance."

The headman looked around himself in mock wonderment. "This *gyami* scholar is giving me—me, a man who has lived here all his life!—a lesson in the geography of Lhakrinor. He must be a very great scholar indeed! Next he will be telling you when to water your barley crop, and how to mate a yak with a *bri*."

If the headman had expected laughter at this sally, he was disappointed; Tibetan politeness required the villagers to smile, but the smiles were little more than courteous, and no one met his eyes. Somewhat bitterly, he turned his attention once again to Trowbridge.

"So you did not feel it was necessary to inform me of your arrival."

"You don't seem surprised to see me."

"I am surprised by little that happens in Lhakrinor."

"That is very impressive, Drokma," Norbu said quietly.

The headman shifted his gaze to Norbu. He stared a moment, then leaned back in the saddle, leather creaking beneath him, and addressed the crowd around them once more.

"A porter," he said contemptuously. "A man without a home or property, who, for small amounts of money, bears heavy loads for this great scholar. Does it make you feel important, porter, that these good people have told you my name?"

"A name is a sound a man makes with his voice, nothing more," Norbu said evenly. "And it is true that I am homeless. But I do not need anyone to tell me your name. It would be easier to forget my own."

A child cried, and its mother shushed it urgently; the silence around them deepened.

"Who are you?" the headman said, his voice suddenly wary.

"It is a good question. Perhaps I am a ghost. Many times, since the death of my father, I have felt like a ghost."

"It is Norbu," someone said wonderingly behind them. "The lama's child."

"Norbu has been dead many years," another voice said. "Like the lama himself."

"It is him," the first voice insisted. "I am sure of it."

Recognition dawned slowly on Drokma's face; his expression showed a flicker of fear, mingled with a desire to be seen as fearless. In a gravelly voice he said, "Are you accusing me of a crime? If so, then say it out loud, so all can hear."

"Is there a crime I should accuse you of?"

Drokma stared silently at Norbu. Then he spat contemptuously, jerked on his donkey's reins, and turned to leave.

"You may be sorry for having returned, *gyami* Norbu," he said over his shoulder. "For you *are gyami* now. You are no longer of this place."

The headman rode out of the encampment without meeting anyone's eyes.

For a long moment there was absolute silence. Then, with a wild whoop, Jigme came running across the encampment and leaped into Norbu's arms. A moment later he stepped back, and said in a sorrowful voice, "I did not recognize you. For a man to forget the one with whom he spent his boyhood running the hills is unforgivable."

"There is nothing to forgive," Norbu said. "It is good to see you again."

Jigme flung his arms around Norbu once again and called out, "Hai! Someone bring more *chang*! My friend Norbu, the lama's son, is returned to Lhakrinor!"

The sun had sunk below the spiky mountain horizon; the air remained warm, the light gentle and soft. Above Torma Mountain, ten miles to the east, the leading edge of a full moon lofted slowly into the evening sky. Trowbridge, watching the relaxed merrymaking of this festival, knew that the daily life these people led was—at least by Western standards—poverty-stricken, difficult, and filled with terrifically hard work. The average life span in a mountain community like this was probably nearer forty than fifty; no one here, in all likelihood, had ever seen a Western-style doctor, and many of them would suffer from chronic health problems which might be cured simply in the lowlands. They were tied to a failing subsistence economy, to a way of life which was being slowly destroyed by a combination of political and environmental changes. And yet there was no sign of any of this in the faces around him, which were generous and relaxed. The long hard winter had been survived, and it was June, the time of renewal and planting. Wildflowers covered the hills around them, there would be dancing tonight, and there was enough food—last year's harvest, it seemed, had been reasonably successful. For the moment, at least, life in Lhakrinor was adequate unto itself.

The dance seemed to be signalled by the rising moon. Only the young women participated at first, very slowly and seriously, holding hands in the long twilight while the men watched. Then a few of the younger men joined in, and two lines formed. The dancers faced each other, moving forward gradually until the lines nearly met, then parting once again. They sang of love which was unreturned, and called on the gods to participate helpfully in human affairs.

Norbu stood watching on the sidelines. Pema—the girl who had gone swimming—broke out of the line and danced up to him, making fun of him a little. Norbu watched her a moment, then slipped into the dance opposite her, mirroring her steps perfectly. She stopped, stared at him open-mouthed, then laughed, and moved back to the line. Norbu took his place in the line of men.

"After all this time," Nima said, "he remembers the steps."

She had returned from her bath shortly after the headman's departure, dressed Tibetan style, in an undergarment of light wool and wide trousers drawn in with tapes just below the knees. Over this she wore a short cotton shirt and a sleeveless gown. Her dark skin shone in the firelight, and a pair of gold earrings dangled from her ears.

"It is different from the way we dance in the Solu Khumbu," Dorje said thoughtfully. "But not so *very* different. What about you, Nima— are you going to dance?"

"I do not know," she said reluctantly. "I do not wish to be the only one who does not know the steps."

"In that case," Dorje said, "David *sahib* must also dance."

Trowbridge found himself rising to his feet. The three of them walked toward the flat grassy area which served as the dance floor. Yellow flames from a pair of fires leaped in the purple twilight, as young mothers left their infants in the arms of grandmothers, rose, and joined the dance. Jigme sat on a three-legged stool, fingers flying over the five strings of his instrument. The music made a plaintive, pleasing counterpoint to the soft shuffle of the mukluk-like *lhams* on the grassy riverbank. Soon the dance quickened; laughter and encouragement came from those who sat around them on blankets. Trowbridge, dancing forward with the men toward a line of smiling women, felt himself caught up in an unearthly sweetness.

"We are not very good at this, I am afraid," Nima called out to him, speaking Tibetan.

"You dance very well for one who has never danced."

The lines swept them apart. The fellow to Trowbridge's right slapped him enthusiastically on the shoulder; Trowbridge grinned back, pleased. When he and Nima were face to face again she said, speaking English, "You look very happy here, David—do you still think these people should be transplanted to lower climates?"

He made no reply as the lines of dancers drew them apart.

Soon the dancing grew faster and wilder, allowing no more chance for conversation. The moon cast a silvery light over the scene; the sound of the singing seemed to drift away from the festival toward the high darkness around them, toward the snowy slopes which hung like vast distant drapes. To be contained within this small circle of warmth and singing and humanity seemed a kind of miracle.

Eventually he grew tired and stepped out of the dance. Nima followed him, breathing hard from the exertion. Only the most dedicated—among them Dorje, Norbu, and Pema—carried on. They walked back to the blanket spread out on the grass.

"I would like to dance this way every night," Nima said.

"There was no dancing in the village?"

"Ho!" she exclaimed, a quiet bitterness in her voice. "The bride of a high caste Hindu does not dance. And there was certainly no dancing in the *che*. But I no longer regret it. If I had danced before tonight, perhaps tonight would not have been the same."

Nima looked at him with sudden curiosity.

"Do you dance like this in your country?"

"Every night."

"I am jealous!" she cried. Then she checked herself, and said, "You are teasing me."

"I'm afraid so."

"Tell me the truth."

"I don't dance very often in my country. It would ruin my image as a scientist."

"Ah, your image as a scientist! You looked very scientific, I will tell you, dancing by moonlight on the riverbank. Your face was glowing in a most scientific manner as you looked at these lovely Tibetan women."

It was *you* I was looking at, he thought. Not the others. It was on the tip of his tongue to tell her this, but somehow he remained silent, unable to ignore the tiny warning voice: In the frank light of dawn he would be a Western scientist with a job to do, and she would be . . . well, whatever she was. A sacred princess with a pension from the Royal Palace. A runaway bride from some tiny, forgotten village in the hills. Or just a stubborn, bright young woman, good with animals, good with a pair of binoculars, tough when it came to walking uphill all day, confused when it came to who she was, to what she was doing on the face of the earth.

Nima was looking happily at the dancers. "I am very glad I joined your expedition and came to Lhakrinor. I am learning a great deal about studying animals, and now I have learned to dance as well. I like both things very much."

"You're as good a biologist as you are a dancer."

"Am I really?"

She turned her face to his, amusement in her eyes, and he nodded, because he suddenly didn't trust himself to speak. His heart was pounding. This is getting very unscientific, he thought. Very unprofessional.

He looked away, reminding himself that Nima was married, and barely eighteen years old. That an involvement with any Nepali woman would mean something far different to her than it would to him. And that an involvement with this particular Nepali woman represented a potential scandal, one that could ruin not only this study, but his prospects of ever working in Nepal again.

"David," she said quietly. "I know that tomorrow we will work together as if nothing happened tonight. And I know that I am a married woman. But still, tonight I must tell you that I like you very much."

His eyes moved to hers. The vulnerable clarity of her gaze, the stillness with which she held herself in the aftermath of this announcement, broke something inside him. He leaned over, and, for a brief moment, touched his lips to hers. When they pulled apart she looked at him with a mixture of pleasure and doubt.

"Is that a wrong thing for us to have done?" she asked.

"I don't know," he said.

The witch of Narling entered the encampment and stopped unobtrusively in the firelight. She wore a thick, ankle-length *chuba*, felt boots, rosary beads at her belt, and rested her weight on an intractly carved wooden cane. Her hair was cropped quite short. Like the lama, her face was lined but not wrinkled; her skin was burnt quite dark by the sun. Her features were a mask, but her head was tipped slightly to one side, as if to demonstrate infinite amusement at—and independence from—the life which swirled around her. Trowbridge, watching her, had the feeling that the rest of her might disappear at any moment and leave her face floating precisely where it was, with precisely the same expression.

The villagers acknowledged her presence without particular fuss, as if she had been expected. Clearly, they did not dislike her the way they did the headman. There was a certain care they seemed to take in their movements, however; if not fear, then certainly a respectful awareness, as if she were a force not to be provoked by any sudden movement.

Food was brought to her, and a three-legged stool with a seat made of yak leather. She sat a little ways away from the others, ate lightly, then set the plate of food down and looked around.

"Is she a real witch?" Nima asked in a low voice.

Norbu nodded. "Some call her a nun. Others a witch."

"Which is the truth?" Dorje asked.

"I believe that depends on her mood."

At that moment, as if she knew she were being discussed, the witch looked directly at them. She rose, picked up her stool, and moved deliberately across the encampment in their direction. Trowbridge noticed children being gently restrained by parents from crossing her path. The witch set the stool down in front of their group and sat down, regarding them as if they were an exhibit in a museum.

"*Tashi delai*," Norbu greeted her with deferential politeness.

She studied him a long moment. "You are a stranger. And yet you speak with the tongue of one who is from Lhakrinor."

Norbu nodded. "Both of those things are true."

She studied him a moment longer. Then, in an otherwise motionless face, one eyebrow lifted dramatically.

"You are the lama's son, called Norbu."

"And you are the first to recognize me without my help."

The witch smiled, a not entirely unthreatening event. "That is because I believe sentient beings may return from the dead, and the others, in their hearts, do not. But you are as crafty as your father when it comes to dispensing compliments. Is it because you want something from me?"

Norbu shook his head. "No. But it is good to be recognized by you."

"Not everyone dares to flatter the witch of Narling. And not everyone is so pleased to be singled out by my attention. You, for example," she said, swiveling her bright stare toward Dorje. "What is your name? And why are you afraid of me?"

"My name is Dorje Thondup, and I am afraid of you because you are a witch."

"Are you afraid of all witches?"

"No."

"Then why are you afraid of me, in particular?"

Dorje opened his mouth to speak, then closed it, looking to Trowbridge for assistance.

"In Chitragong," Trowbridge said, "Dorje was told that you were in the habit of eating young men for breakfast."

"Ah," the witch said. "I have heard that story as well."

Her attention shifted to Trowbridge.

"You are not afraid of me," she said.

"No."

"And yet you sense something in me that you do not understand."

"That is true," he said. "But there are many things in this world I don't understand. You are only one."

The witch smiled, as if pleased at this response. Then she turned her gaze on Dorje once again, observing him with a playful look.

"Were you told, Dorje Thondup, that I built my bed with the whitened bones of young men?"

Dorje swallowed uneasily, then nodded.

"Would you like to see that bed?"

Dorje shook his head.

"What if I told you that my bed is built of wood, not bones?"

Dorje considered this. "Then I would think that the others had been lying. But I would *still* not ask to see your bed."

"No? There was a time when handsome young men would have given their lives to see that bed. And perhaps, if you blinked very quickly, you might see the bones of young men scattered beneath it. But the bones would be from many years ago. And when you blinked again the bed would be wooden, and the floor beneath it quite clean."

The witch shifted her gaze past Dorje and stared into the night behind him. Dorje looked behind himself nervously, following her gaze. When he looked back she had leaned forward, resting her weight on her cane. Her face was close to Dorje's. Her eyes glittered in the firelight; her mouth made a dark hole as she spoke.

"If you *must* be frightened of a witch, Dorje Thondup," she said slowly, "then it is my sister you ought to fear."

"You have a sister?" Dorje said uneasily.

"Many years ago the lamas buried her in the ground near Lhasa, far to the north. But their spells were not powerful enough to kill her. She still lives. Only the top of her head shows. You can see the fleas playing in her hair."

"I do not believe it," Nima declared.

"Do you not?" the witch said, looking at her for the first time.

"No," Nima said. "First, because the border with Tibet has been closed since twice my own lifetime, so how would you know such a thing, even if it were true? And second, I believe you are only playing with Dorje because you sense he is frightened of you. You are like a cat choosing to climb onto the lap of someone who is afraid of cats."

The witch ignored Nima's words, peering at her—and through her—as if ghosts danced in the darkness behind her silhouette.

"And who are you?" the witch asked quietly.

Nima seemed suddenly to have run out of words.

"The others I understand. But something about you remains concealed. You are from the lowlands, are you not?"

Nima said nothing.

The witch addressed Trowbridge. "You, I believe, know what is concealed."

Trowbridge nodded slowly.

"What are you going to do about it?"

"It's not my place to do anything about it."

"No?" The witch looked at him skeptically, then turned her attention to Nima once again. Nima's gaze faltered and she looked down, avoiding the witch's eyes. At that moment, to Trowbridge's surprise, a look of compassion flickered across the witch's ageless face.

"You have much to let go of, little one," she said quietly to Nima. "And much to learn. But you have already journeyed farther in this lifetime than many souls do in a thousand. There is a rare light in you which will help show you the way further."

The witch leaned back on the stool, tipped her head back, and began a low chant. Around them the villagers grew quiet. The sound of the witch's voice thrummed in the night. Trowbridge, in spite of himself, felt a prickling at his neck.

A few moments later the witch finished her chant, glanced once more at Nima, stood up, and walked off unceremoniously into the darkness.

27

"Even from the age of eight or nine I was different from other *kumaris*," she said, "very interested in life outside the palace. My tutor at that time was young, not much older than I, and I insisted she come often because she made me laugh. She liked giving me English lessons, because she didn't have to work very hard—she could just chatter on about her family in Kathmandu, or the school she'd been to in India. I was fascinated by these things."

They reached the top of the hill and stopped for a moment, looking back down on the festival, a bright ember in the darkness. Dorje and Norbu had stayed for the dancing, which would go on all night; Trowbridge, who would be taking off again before first light, wanted to get home to Trang, and Nima had decided to walk back with him.

As they turned to go on through the moonlight toward Trang, Nima continued, "One afternoon when I was twelve I was standing at the highest window of the *che*, looking at the mountains, which I had loved to do since I was little. I noticed a group of porters walking through the streets. There were women among them, independent, tough-looking Sherpa women, carrying loads. It was mid-winter, and the air was clear, and mountains filled the horizon. Something happened inside me, and for the first time I understood what it meant not to be allowed to leave the *che*.

"If I had been interested in things outside the *che* before, I was now obsessed, and asked questions constantly of anyone who would listen. To bribe me to behave, the *kumarima* allowed me to learn Tibetan— although she was horrified I would want to learn the language of what she called a barbaric and filthy people, the poorest and most backward in our country."

"Why Tibetan?"

"Because I knew Tibetan was the language spoken in the mountains."

The sky above them was cloudless, milky with stars and moonlight; the only sound was of their steps crushing the soil.

"You said you learned to handle horses in Kathmandu. Certainly the *kumarima* didn't let you ride."

"Of course not—I was only allowed to leave the *che* once a year, and on that day I was drawn through the street in a carriage. One of my earliest memories is looking out from the carriage, and wanting to touch the horses. By the time I was six, I had already begun making the *kumarima* take me to the stables of the *che* to see the horses. She was not supposed to, but she humored me, as she did in most things."

She shrugged. "As a child I was headstrong, and as a teenager I was restless and badly behaved. Then, when I was fourteen and a half, the expected 'imperfection' occurred to end my tenure as *kumari*."

"You had your first period."

She looked at him curiously.

"I have never heard a man speak of it so calmly. In the *che*, of course, it was a subject that could be discussed naturally among the women. It was not shocking, or taboo. Still, even in this matter I was different from other people—for me, the monthly blood signified I was no longer a fit vessel for the goddess.

"The *kumarima* kept my secret for more than a year. And the search takes a long time, so I was almost seventeen by the time the new *kumari* was installed in the *che*. I then spent six months in the house of my parents—whom I hardly knew—while they searched for a high-caste Brahman for me to marry. When they found one they told me that my life would be very different, but that they were sure I would be good and submissive, and bring the same honor upon the family as a wife that I had as *kumari*. On the day of my wedding my mother was crying. She gave me a sum of money and told me to keep it secret, not even to tell my husband of its existence. I left my parents' home in Kathmandu and moved to a little village in the eastern hills."

"I've traveled through the Nepali midlands. The dirtiest and poorest villages are those where the inhabitants are mostly Brahman."

"That is the sort of place I had gone to be married."

"Did the others in the village know you'd been the *kumari*?"

Nima nodded. "Everyone in the village knew."

"I don't imagine that made your life any easier."

"It didn't. And beyond that, I discovered my status was very low."

"But you're of the Sakya caste. The goldsmith caste."

She nodded. "Among Newars and Buddhists, and even among the Hindus in Kathmandu, the Sakya caste ranks very high. But according to orthodox Hindu doctrine—and the beliefs in small villages are very conservative—those who disturb the elements by melting gold and separating it from copper are polluted by such behavior. Thus I found that on the day of my marriage ceremony I had gone from being a goddess to one who was practically an untouchable.

"I believe my mother-in-law decided not to like me even before the marriage. The final ritual of the wedding day is called the *mukh herne,* 'seeing the face.' The bride sits slumped over with downcast eyes while the women of the groom's family lift the veil to look at her. My mother-in-law placed a coin in my lap—a custom which buys her the right to be critical—lifted the veil, and pronounced me ugly and affected."

Nima was silent a moment as they walked along the moonlit trail.

"It is normal to be critical, but this brought gasps from those who were watching. Nevertheless, I touched her feet with my forehead, as was proper. I am sure she feared I would be dangerous or unlucky for her son; she told me openly that she had only agreed to the match because of my dowry and pension from the government. She was also convinced, I'm sure, that I would be soft and lazy after my life as *kumari.*

"I was determined to prove her wrong. My husband, like most Brahmans, viewed physical labor as undignified, so I did all the work for the three of us—all the work she had done before I came, and more."

She fell silent. After a few moments he said, "You had an American friend. A Peace Corps worker."

"Ah," she said, her face lightening somewhat. "I had forgotten I told you about him. We were good friends, partly because I was the only one there who spoke English—and his Nepali was very bad—but also because we were the two loneliest people in the village. He gave me books to read to improve my English, and I helped him with his Nepali.

"At first, I was treated well by the villagers. I was complimented for being *laj manne*—modest and shy—and for being *cup lagera basne*— one who sits and says nothing. I was pointed to as an example of a good wife. But it was not long before I would stand in line at the well, and one of the women behind me would say, '*je pani bhanchi, jaha pani hirchi,*' which means 'she says what she likes, and goes where she pleases.'

"I began going to a different well, a long way from the village; fortunately, my mother-in-law could not complain, since the water was from a purer source, and was beneficial to my husband's spiritual state. My only happiness was in making this long walk, and I grew stronger physically than I had ever been. On days when the haze lifted, there was a hilltop from which I could see mountains in the distance—the same mountains I had seen from the window of the *che* in Kathmandu. I was closer to the mountains, now, but in reality I knew I was farther away than ever."

She stopped speaking. The only sound came from their footsteps. Nima looked up at the sky, then around them at the high moonlit slopes.

"And now you're here," he said.

"And now I am here."

They descended the final slope toward Trang. The monastery compound, after the liveliness of the festival, seemed a somewhat lonely place; only a wisp of smoke emerging from the roof of the hut made Trang seem like a place where people might live.

The goat, having apparently given up on Trowbridge's return, was curled up against one of the abandoned monastery buildings. Trowbridge and Nima went into the hut, stoked the fire, and drank tea thirstily after the long walk. Briefly, they discussed which herds she should observe during his three-day absence, and the possibility of tracking the wolf pack. Then, because he was not sure what else to do, he said good night and went to his tent.

She slipped in with him a few minutes later, carrying her sleeping bag. Without a word, she unzipped it, pulling it over both of them. Awkwardly, he unzipped his own sleeping bag, and she came into his arms. Her body, still clothed, was cold against his. For a moment they lay like that, utterly still. Was she here to make love, he wondered, or simply for companionship, and because she felt lonely?

As if in answer, she pulled out of his arms, sat up, and tugged her heavy wool shirt, then a soft undershirt, over her head.

This is crazy, he thought, as she helped him take off his sweater, then lay back down against him. Her skin was astonishingly warm against his. His arms went around her and he felt the muscles of her back, solid and delicate at once, and he realized he didn't care whether this made sense or not. They were a long way from anywhere, she was making her own decision, and he wanted her more than he could remember wanting any woman ever.

She didn't know how to kiss him back, exactly, at least not the way a Western woman would, but he found this naiveté—and her obvious willingness at what they were doing—to be intoxicating, and her body to be equally intoxicating, and it kept him from realizing that things weren't going as well for her as for him. Suddenly she was struggling away.

"What's wrong?" he said. "What happened?"

She sat with her back to him, shoulders tense.

"Nima," he said.

She neither answered nor moved. Her breathing was quick, catching slightly, and then she was crying, the painful sobbing of someone who didn't cry often. It was the first time he had ever seen her break down.

He touched her shoulder and she pulled away.

"Nima, tell me what's wrong."

"There was only one other time for me," she blurted out, "and I was forced."

He was astounded. How could that be possible, if she'd been married for almost a year? Then he remembered that Nepali brides—because they often married so young—were free to choose when sex would begin, within reasonable limits. Nima might have invoked this freedom and refused to sleep with her husband altogether.

He asked quietly, "Forced by whom?"

She was still crying. "By my husband," she said bitterly. "My husband who could have only the purest well water so he would not become soiled like the rest of us, but who drank *rakshi* every day until he was stupid and fell down in the street. Who cursed me in the evenings for withholding myself, then cursed me again in the morning for being a temptress, for seducing him away from his spiritual path."

She was sobbing violently now, arms crossed, holding herself tightly. He saw gooseflesh on her arms, and took her shirt and wrapped it across her chest. Then he put his arms around her and pulled her back down next to him. She struggled a moment, misunderstanding, then let him hold her.

She cried for a long time. When her breathing was finally calm, and her body relaxed, she said, in a voice so quiet he could barely hear it, "I wanted to, David. I did." Then she fell asleep, and he fell asleep himself, and was only wakened by her leaving the tent.

28

An hour before sunrise, with the moon down and the valley lit by brittle and insufficient starlight, Trowbridge crossed the river. In his pack was the comforting presence of a sleeping bag and the weight of three days' provisions. He had a slight headache; the fact that he'd slept only two hours added an edge to the simple actions of climbing, of breathing, of stopping to survey the familiar trail and carrying on.

He walked steadily. The headache went away, and he stopped thinking about what had happened last night, and began, instead, to feel the excitement of being *out*—out and moving, a spot of warmth and purpose sifting quietly through the darkness.

At a place where the narrow track divided, one fork turning up toward Gelingdo, he stopped. The increasingly faint trail was an unknown quantity from here on, and tricky: crumbling slopes, icy ledges, smooth sections of rock where the way disappeared altogether, and false spurs which dead-ended at partially walled-in caves—once the abodes of Buddhist monks living in holy isolation, now abandoned to the sky and wind.

Beneath all this, a lengthy drop to the rocks beside the river. He dropped his pack on the trail and hunkered down beside it to wait for daylight, pulling his jacket close around his neck. The first hints of pale green and pink entered the sky to the west, in the direction of Jaramar. Closing his eyes, he dozed.

Half an hour later he was moving again. In the pale gray light the trail beneath his boots was now legible. He began watching for snow leopard prints in the occasional patch of crusted snow. The terrain was perfect: a maze of ledges and caves where a leopard could hole up for protection, or lie in the sun when it was fine. And the trail was so taxing it would only rarely be used by human beings.

If I were a snow leopard, he thought, I'd be very comfortable here.

Across a deep ravine, above a sheer drop of at least a thousand feet, was an abandoned hermitage, its prayer flags long since torn to insubstantial shreds. A few minutes beyond the hermitage, as the sun lofted into the sky and dusted the canyon wall with warmth and yellow light, he came across the first trace of leopard he had seen in Lhakrinor.

In the clear, slanting light of morning the pug was as clear as anything he'd ever seen. He stood above it a moment, exulting not only in its existence, but in its freshness—its edges were sufficiently distinct, unsoftened as yet by breeze and rain, that it could be no more than a day or two old. The pug was large, that of a full-sized animal, and had a curious scar across the pad; the leopard, at some point in its life, had slit its paw on a sharp outcropping of rock or ice.

He crouched, sifting the soil between his fingers, and began to feel a mounting excitement. The soil was peculiarly fine, almost pumice-like—the dust of melting glaciers—and it held an imprint extraordinarily well. He might actually be able to follow this leopard over a substantial distance, something he had never been able to do in the Altai.

Farther ahead, at a bend in the trail, he found a distinct scrape in the soil—one of the calling cards which leopards deliberately left to keep track of one another as they moved. At a place where the trail rose a little before turning hard to the left and dropping down into a dark ravine, he found another calling card—a neat pile of frozen leopard scat.

"I knew it," he heard himself muttering excitedly. "I could have told you it would be there."

He pried the scat apart, studying its makeup, then slipped it into a plastic bag. The partially digested hairs in the scat indicated that this animal had been dining on both bharal and domestic goats. With the diminished wildlife in the area, it was no surprise that the snow leopard was forced to raid the villagers' animals to survive. And yet it was worrisome, because it would expose the leopard to the villagers' wrath.

Still, the scat could not be more than twelve hours old, probably much less. He was on a fresh trail—and there, by that rock, only ten feet away, he could see another pair of prints in the fine soil.

He lifted his head and scanned the intricately formed, nearly perpendicular terrain ahead. There was nothing. No movement. No haze of pale frosted fur drifting from rock to rock. No burn of suspicious eyes. And yet it was more than possible that the snow leopard he was following was, at this precise moment, studying him.

Late in the morning he came across a sunny ledge where the leopard had rested a while. He saw a number of pale hairs caught in a spiny shrub, and a pair of distinct scrapes. The leopard, he'd decided, was following a regular circuit between hunting grounds. One of the hunting areas encompassed the slopes around Gelingdo; another was somewhere up ahead. The longer he could stay on the leopard's trail, the more he would know about where and how widely it ranged, and the requirements of a national park to protect it.

This is what I came for, he realized with a quiet certainty. This. He felt strong, capable, and relaxed; his senses were sharp and his movements efficient. For a moment he understood the thrill of the hunt. And yet it wasn't necessary to kill the animal to feel this way. Only to follow it.

The trail turned up, out of the high-walled canyon, leading him for the first time in hours onto relatively level ground. The tracking job grew simpler, with pug marks standing out clearly in patches of shaded snow. After each pug or scrape he scanned the area ahead, looking for prominent points and likely routes, then struck out, scanning the ground as he went, hoping he'd guessed correctly.

In a particularly rocky stretch, the trail disappeared. Trowbridge moved forward on instinct alone, worried that the leopard might have turned off somewhere among the rocks. When he emerged onto soil again his fears were confirmed; there was no sign of the animal's passage. He stopped, scanning the area ahead, letting the way come to him.

There, to the left. By that sharp outcropping of rocks. That had to be the direction. He set out swiftly, scrambling over rocks which the leopard had probably cleared in a single bound. To his intense satisfaction, he found that he had guessed right: a scuff of tracks marked the place where the leopard had landed after its fifteen-foot leap, and carried on.

Then, beneath a scraggly juniper, a second set of leopard tracks—smaller, and unscarred—angled in and joined the first.

He stopped, dumbfounded, and studied the mingled pug marks. The second animal was smaller, but unquestionably an adult. Was it following the first leopard, the one with the scarred paw? Or were they actually traveling together?

He looked up the slope, in the direction from which the new prints had come, and saw a sunny ledge fifty yards above him—a place where the newcomer might have lain waiting for the first leopard to come by. Then he moved forward again, following two animals now, instead of one.

A hundred yards farther on, his question was answered. In a small clearing, amid heaps of high dark stones and patches of snow, the two leopards had rolled together in the dust, making a confusion of swept-out tracks and swirling body shapes. Quickly he eliminated the possibility of a genuine struggle; there was no evidence of blood, and the tracks, on the far side of the clearing, moved off in regular company once again. The second leopard had caught up to the first, and the pair had been *playing*, like a pair of house cats on a living room rug.

He would have given a great deal to see that. Pulling out his camera, he took some quick photos, although he wasn't sure they'd show much.

All right, he thought, moving through the clearing and into the rocks on the far side. One more question, the most crucial of all: What are these leopards to one another? A mother with a grown cub? A pair of grown litter mates? Or a male and female who had paired earlier for mating, and had joined back up for some reason?

Was it possible that a pair of leopards might simply meet up and travel together for no other reason than companionability?

He found another pile of scat. Dropping into a crouch, he examined it quickly. To his surprise, there were no domestic goat hairs. Only those of bharal, and something that looked like marmot.

The smaller leopard, he thought. For one reason or another, it hasn't preyed recently on domestic animals. Only the larger one, the one with the scarred paw.

It was late morning. Against the sun, which was high in the sky, a lammergeier turned in smooth spirals. He stopped long enough to strip off his jacket and sweater, and moved on.

On a low promontory, only fifty feet above the soft shush of the river, he crouched and pulled out the map.

A mile farther up the canyon, Narling—its earthen walls a lurid red—squatted on a barren hillside. A whisper of smoke went up into the sky; prayer flags moved slowly, as if they were waving in water.

The leopards, after traveling more than a mile together in relatively open country, had split up, the smaller one climbing up into high, broken boulders, and the larger animal slipping down over the edge into the canyon. After a brief hesitation, he had decided to follow the larger animal, which he guessed had made its way down the rocky canyon wall and crossed the river. A sand bar rose in the center of the river with a series of protruding rocks which would allow an animal with substantial leaping abilities like the snow leopard to cross without getting wet.

Why had it decided to cross the river? Was it to avoid coming any closer to the settlement at Narling?

"Fine by me," he said. "Let's keep it between the two of us."

At the river's edge he stripped off his clothes and boots, stuffed them into his pack, and waded out into the icy flow with the pack above his head. The water was fiercely cold, the gravel beneath his feet small and sharp. The water rose to his waist, and then his shoulders. In a narrow channel the flow swept him off his feet. His head went under. He kicked hard, holding his things above the water, as the cold struck his ears like a physical blow.

Painfully, he kicked the sloping gravel bottom once again.

On the far side he slicked the water off his body with his hands, his skin drying quickly in the arid atmosphere. He dressed quickly and began climbing a nearly imperceptible trail. Two hundred yards along he came to a fork. One path led into a northern canyon, which meandered, according to the map, in a direction generally away from civilization. The second canyon led to the southwest, in the direction of Jaramar. The slope was stony and trackless. No clues this time. He had to guess—one way or the other. He hesitated a moment. Then, remembering the domestic goat hair in the leopard's scat, he chose the southwestern fork.

Above the canyon a snowy peak turned purplish scarlet in the encroaching sunset. There were no flowers here, nor any grass; the slopes around him were as empty as if they had never been graced by life, unsoftened, in their severity, by the failing light. At a point when he had nearly lost all hope, he found the trail once again: a distinct, scarred pug. He was exhausted, and it was nearly dark, but he felt a quiet exultation. He hadn't lost the animal entirely. There was still a chance of spotting it tomorrow.

"Norbu," he said quietly, not taking his eyes off the trail as he moved forward, "you would have been proud of me today."

Eventually, dusk forced him to halt. If he carried on any longer he was likely to overshoot the trail and lose it entirely. A lot depended now on whether the leopard would continue through the night, or stop and rest. Either was possible; leopards slept when they wanted to, hunted in darkness or daylight as they pleased. Was it moving through the darkness right now, placing too much distance between them for him to catch up tomorrow?

He wouldn't know until morning. For a few minutes he sat on his sleeping bag, too exhausted to unroll it and climb in. It occurred to him that he should eat something. He'd had nothing but water all day, and little enough of that. He undid the flaps of his backpack, pulling out a couple of hard buckwheat disks and a handful of dry *tsampa*. He ate one of the parched, hard disks, washed it down with what was left in his first water bottle, then opened the second and drank half of that. He put the rest of the food away, spread out his sleeping bag, pulled off his boots and pants, and climbed in.

A hundred yards away a lonely prayer flag flapped in the last light, the last breeze.

Twelve hours, he thought. His head, pillowed on his folded jacket as he stared up at the rapidly appearing stars, was spinning slightly. I followed a snow leopard for twelve straight hours today. Has anyone ever done such a thing?

He watched the constellations prickling the sky. In the darkness, and in his exhaustion, he became vulnerable to his own doubts. The leopard was heading directly toward Jaramar. The canyon he was in now—a barren corner of the universe if ever there was one—had been grazed, at times, by the villagers' domestic animals, and it was part of the leopard's range. He would have been happier if the leopard had gone into the northern canyon. Once again, he doubted the viability of the national park unless the villagers were moved out of Lhakrinor completely. Would they consent to being barred from this grazing area in order to preserve a species of animal they considered vermin?

One day at a time, he reminded himself. There's nothing more to be done tonight. The decision will be made when you have enough information. Now sleep. You may have to run the soles off your boots tomorrow to catch this leopard.

But he couldn't sleep. His head was still spinning, as if the earth's great whirling passage through the universe had suddenly accelerated. He felt peculiarly lonely. When, some distance off, in the silence of the lifeless valley, a stone clattered down a slope, the sound was so distinct and startling it was nearly painful.

You're borderline dehydrated, he told himself, which is bad for judgment. And you're a little dazed by the intensity of the day's efforts. You need to sleep.

His nerves remained vulnerable, on edge. In spite of himself he listened tensely for another sound from the darkness. There was only the gentle flapping of the prayer flag. He thought about the fact that a living human being had raised this flag, in this lonely place. Had worked to pile the stones about the base. Finally he got up, draped his sleeping bag over his shoulder, and—walking carefully in the darkness—carried his things over to the prayer flag. He laid out his sleeping bag in a reasonably smooth patch of dirt beside it, and slept.

In the cool light of dawn he studied the pug mark. The leopard had lain up during the night. The trail was so fresh he almost expected it to be warm.

He scanned the ridges on either side of the valley. No movement. But at least he hadn't fallen behind while he slept. There was a chance of seeing the leopard still. Feeling refreshed and strong, he set out.

A few minutes later he saw movement high on the north-facing slope of the valley. Streaming out of deep shadow came a disorganized group of bharal. An alarmed whistle echoed distinctly across the valley. Something was hunting them. He moved forward at a dead run, trying to improve his angle of sight. There was no reason for surreptitiousness on his part; predator and prey would be too involved in this life-and-death struggle to be looking anywhere else. The fleeing forms of the bharal were just visible beyond a promontory; whatever was hunting them, lower down on the slope, was hidden from view. He stumbled over a hump of dirt, kept running. If he could just manage to reach that high spot fifty yards ahead he had a chance of seeing the predator.

Several of the bharal reached the safety of the cliffs. One, lower on the slope, was sprinting frantically. Designated prey, and aware of it. He still couldn't see what was chasing the bharal, although it almost had to be the leopard. Twenty yards more to the high spot. Something caught his foot and he went sprawling onto the trail.

He scrambled to his feet and scanned the slope, seeing that the last bharal had reached the safety of the cliff. The hunt had failed. The predator remained invisible.

For a moment, he was so disappointed he could have cried. Then he realized that for the first time in the twenty-four hours since he'd come across the first pug mark, he knew exactly where the leopard was.

The bharal looked down at him curiously from their rocky perches as he moved across the slope, reconstructing the hunt: first the careful stalking, then the unsuccessful dash along the base of the cliff. If the leopard had been ten yards higher he might have witnessed the whole thing. He glanced up once more at the bharal—so close he could have flung a rock among them—and set out after the leopard with the slit paw.

When the sun grew noticeably lower in the sky, he ate a handful of *tsampa* and washed it down with the last of the water. The water situation would become critical if he didn't catch up to the leopard before darkness. Already his tongue felt swollen in his mouth, and his head felt thick.

But you can live with that, he told himself. You've done it before.

What was more worrisome was the leopard's unswerving progress toward Jaramar. The village couldn't be more than two hours away. For a moment he wished he'd attempted to follow the smaller leopard. He had no desire to encounter people, and would have been more than content to disappear after the smaller leopard—the one which ate only wild prey—into those inaccessible craggy heights.

Think clearly, he reminded himself. You would have lost the trail up there. You aren't built to follow leopards up sheer cliffs.

But I'm not built to follow them on long distance races either, he thought. His muscles were not responding as precisely as he would have liked as he moved across the barren landscape. More than once he had to make a conscious effort not to stumble over obstacles in his path.

As if in counterpoint to his exhaustion, and to his increasing sense that the animal he was following was in danger if it strayed any nearer Jaramar, the afternoon around him was beautiful. The sky was fresh and blue; neat bursts of white cloud paraded above him on a gentle breeze; the air felt filled with life and warmth. Around him, in occasional sprays of color, wildflowers made the stony slopes cheerful.

But what about the leopard? Why is it going straight toward the village?

Because it's hungry. There was no other answer. Because there were goats in the village. Goats in small enclosures. Because it was a predator, and if it were to live, it had to eat.

Trowbridge had studied tigers in India. Once he'd watched a nine-foot tiger bound into a village enclosure, kill a full-grown goat with a single swipe of its enormous paw, then take the animal in its mouth and leap back over an eight-foot wall to safety. The tiger's massively strong jaws, and its powerfully built shoulders and neck, allowed it to escape with its prey to a place of safety in which to eat. The largest snow leopards, by contrast, were barely six feet long, and half of that was tail; they were lithe, more delicate through the chest, smaller of head and jaws—perfectly suited to stalking animals in the heights in which they lived, but not well suited to stealing goats from villages. After a successful hunt a snow leopard generally left its prey where it had fallen and lingered nearby, during a several-day period, to feed. From all reports, it was surprisingly timid in the face of human attack—as if it were baffled by the vehemence with which villagers objected to its behavior.

He spurred himself on, forcing his tired muscles, one more time, to pick up the pace. The sun seemed to be plummeting toward the horizon, taking with it his chances of spotting the leopard before darkness. He wasn't sure how much good he'd be if he had to get up tomorrow and do this again.

Beside the trail, he saw a pile of human excrement. The sight depressed and alarmed him. With increased urgency, he moved toward the top of yet another bleak ridge. There he stopped, gazing downward.

Jaramar, spread out beneath him in a gentle valley cut by a deep gorge. The first houses were perhaps a quarter mile away. There was a prayer flag on a rise above the village, and trees scattered among the houses; the village was well kept, neatly laid out, and clean.

But where was the leopard? The trail led directly down the slope.

He started downward, hoping the leopard would skirt the village, shy away from the smells of smoke and the noises of human activity. If that happened, he would be able to refill his water bottles and set out after it once again. Perhaps sometime tomorrow he would catch up with it. See it alive and well, moving through the high mountains, turning to glare back at him, alone and intact in the lonely place it was born to inhabit.

He had a moment of hope that this would be the case.

In the crystal air of early evening, he heard a sudden hue and cry. Figures were streaming from a number of houses toward a structure which looked like a large shed, perhaps a barn, at the near end of the village. He began to run down the slope. His pack came off and he ran faster. His feet pounded on the trail and the blood rushed in his ears. The yelling from the village grew louder. He was running as fast as he could now, but it was taking too long. There was a knot of people outside the low shed. As he grew closer he heard a squealing of goats. Goats burst outward through the knot of people in a panic. One or two villagers peeled off to chase them; the rest crowded closer, blocking the entrance. When he arrived he was yelling. He forced his way through the crowd. He burst past the clutch of onlookers and in through a low door.

The darkened interior smelled of hay and goat. Light from a torch flickered across the scene. He was yelling. The group of men at the far end of the stable turned and looked at him with open mouths. Their faces were filled with a kind of excitement that was nearly madness. Several had wooden pitchforks in their hands. Beyond them the slim body of the snow leopard lay quiescent against the rough-hewn wood of the shed wall. Its pale fur was marked, not with the darker rosettes he remembered from the leopards he'd seen in Mongolia, but with irregular openings, either red, or black, according to the flicker of torchlight.

In the sudden, deafening silence, he felt himself about to be sick. He turned and staggered out of the stable, oblivious to the stares, and walked out of the village into an empty dusk.

29

"Excuse me, Trowbridge *sahib*."

The voice was kindly, familiar and at the same time unfamiliar. He lifted his head. Moonlight illuminated the face before him.

"How do you know my name?"

"We met two nights ago. At the festival beside the river."

Trowbridge nodded. Now he remembered.

"I have been watching you for some time," Jigme said. "I did not know if it was right to disturb you. But it is growing cold, and you did not have the proper clothing."

He paused. "It seemed that a blindness was upon you."

For a minute Trowbridge said nothing. Then he remembered running down the hillside toward the village.

"My pack," he said.

"I have retrieved your things from where you dropped them. They are at my house. My wife and I would be pleased if you would stay with us tonight."

Trowbridge looked back in the direction of the village. A loathing for its inhabitants rose in him like a sickness. A loathing for all people everywhere. Then he looked at Jigme's concerned face, and the feeling subsided.

"Yes," he said. "I would like to stay with you. If you'll have me."

He woke to the sound, and then the smell, of barley on a hot iron grill. Sonam, Jigme's wife, was making *tsampa*, filling the house with the satisfying smell of warm grain. Seeing he was awake, she brushed the hair from her eyes, brought him a cup of tea, then looked away politely while he got up and dressed.

After breakfast he and Jigme stood outside the low front door of the house, which was set up the slope, a little ways out of the village. The sound of singing birds came from the few trees scattered between the houses. In almost any other place, the trees would have looked pathetic and scraggly; here they were a kind of miracle.

"You have trees," he said simply.

Jigme nodded. "Almost the only trees in all of Lhakrinor, except

for the sacred willows near the river. We have arranged among our-
selves not to chop them down. Only to harvest certain branches as we
need them. The other villages think this is crazy, and yet they would
like to have the wood. One time we even defended our trees against
bandits."

"Was it your idea, to conserve trees like this?"

"The idea was Norbu's father's—this was years ago, when I was a
young man. He reminded the villagers that in their parents' day it had
been easy to gather wood for fire and to build houses. He said that if
we could raise barley for *tsampa*, we could raise trees for fuel. It was a
practical suggestion and the people saw sense in it."

Trowbridge looked around the village. Above it, on a rise, a prayer
flag fluttered on a high slender pole. A quarter mile away was a dark
slash resonant with the sound of moving water—the deep gorge he'd
seen last night.

"Norbu and his father lived here in Jaramar," he said, "is that
right?"

Jigme nodded. "But I am afraid Norbu's father was wasted here.
He was a great scholar in a very small place."

Shading his eyes, Jigme looked up and studied the sky, which—to
Trowbridge's eyes—was clear, warm, and unthreatening. "It will be a
cold afternoon," he said. "Perhaps you should stay with us another
day, and leave tomorrow morning."

"They'll worry," Trowbridge said. "I told them I would only stay
out two nights."

"Then you still have tonight."

Trowbridge shook his head.

Jigme looked at him doubtfully. "You followed the *sao* for two full
days?"

He nodded.

Jigme said, "That is something to be proud of—although I understand that you do not feel proud at this moment. In any case, the
weather will be cold, but I do not think it will rain."

In vain, Trowbridge searched the sky for signs of worsening
weather.

"Whatever you're seeing when you look up there, I'm not seeing
it," he said.

Jigme smiled. "I have lived here all my life. This sky is like the ceiling in my own house."

* * *

Walking down the slope into Jaramar they met Pema, the girl who had gone swimming at the festival. She was carrying a bucket of water up from the narrow tributary which emptied into the gorge and served as Jaramar's water supply. She set the bucket down, wiped her forehead, on which beads of sweat glistened, and greeted Trowbridge pleasantly.

"I am sorry they killed the *sao* that you were following," she said forthrightly. "Although if it had eaten one of my yaks I might have done the same. How are your friends?"

"They are fine."

"I was pleased, at the dance, to see you and this fellow Norbu stand up to Drokma. Everyone hates Drokma, and yet they are afraid to tell him so. It was good to see fear in his eyes for a change."

"It may have been easier because we're strangers."

"Even so, it was a pleasure. I wish you luck—and I hope to see you and your friends again. Now I must take this water back to the house so that my father can have his cup of tea. It is a great deal of work being an only daughter! Remember that, Mr. Trowbridge, and have many children!"

She laughed, picked up her bucket, and set off up the slope. The younger people in Lhakrinor, he realized, were the ones to call him "Mr." instead of "*sahib*." Even in this remote place, certain English-isms had penetrated.

The other villagers greeted him with a careful friendliness, as if he were a fragile being. At the far end of the village several men sat spinning yak's wool in the sun. One of them got up and spoke quietly to Jigme, who turned to Trowbridge.

"I do not know if you wish to see the skin of the *sao*," he said. "But it is there, drying in the sun." He motioned past a low shed.

Trowbridge nodded and followed Jigme to the far side of the shed. The pelt, scraped clean and pegged flat to a wooden door, made a pale, spread-eagle shape against the dark wood. He touched the thick fur of the ruff. It was stiff with blood. In the distance, beyond a sharp sunny ridge, scavenger birds—individual specks against the sky—whirled in a slow funnel.

"Who will keep the skin?"

"The man who lost the goat. He may sell the skin to a trader, if he wishes, but it does not bring a high price. Do you wish to have it?"

"No."

"I did not think you would."

"Did the men who butchered it notice what sex the leopard was?"

"The men told me that it was a male."

He looked to the northeast. Somewhere out there was the other snow leopard. He wondered if it would return to that sunny ledge above the river, waiting for this one to appear as it had before—this one whose guts had now been dumped on a hillside for vultures and lammergeiers.

There's no use thinking like that, he reminded himself. The point is not to mourn an individual leopard, but to remake the situation so this doesn't happen to them all.

But *how*?

He touched the pelt once more, and glanced at the cloud of scavenger birds. Then he and Jigme returned to the house for lunch.

"The animal had a scar across the pad of one paw," Jigme said, as they finished their soup. "You must have seen that when following it."

Trowbridge nodded.

"It was not the first time this *sao* had eaten goats from the village."

"I knew that too," Trowbridge said.

Jigme said slowly, as if to make certain Trowbridge understood, "We care for our goats and yaks as if they were our children. It is unfortunate that the snow leopard cannot be cared for in the same way, but it is a practical matter—do you understand? It is not in the villagers' interest to care for a wild snow leopard."

There was a long silence, broken only by the soft crackling of the fire. Trowbridge was considering what he had seen today: a prosperous village, a place whose people cared for their land and protected their trees. He knew that the appearance of prosperity was somewhat misleading; in a bad year, these people would go hungry; two bad years in succession and they might starve. Still, this was not the marginal existence that he'd expected to find.

Not the sort of marginal existence which would justify moving a population away from its homeland.

When he looked up, Jigme was studying him with some amusement. Trowbridge realized that he must have been staring absently into the fire for some time.

"Something occurred to me," Trowbridge said apologetically, "which might solve a problem I've been thinking about."

"Keep it, for the moment, to yourself. You must come back and visit us another day, and we will talk about it then. Now you had better start back to Trang, unless you wish to walk in the dark."

"I'm grateful you let me stay with you."

"There is no need to be grateful," Jigme said. "We are all travelers."

30

Nima set down her plate and looked at him thoughtfully. "So the people could continue to live on their land?"

Trowbridge nodded. "It's already been done at Sagarmatha, near Everest. They've had some problems, mostly because the locals make money selling wood to trekkers and don't like restrictions on cutting down trees. But Lhakrinor is so isolated that wouldn't be an issue. If the villagers have a way to make a living besides raising domestic goats—and if they understand it's in their interest to leave the wild animals alone—it could work. It'll certainly be easier here, say, than in Pakistan, where the tradition of hunting is so ingrained. These people believe in their hearts—and are reminded by the lama—that it's wrong to kill animals. If they have an alternative I think they'll take it."

"But how?" Dorje asked. "You have just told us that a leopard was killed in Jaramar for eating a villager's goat."

"The first thing is for the villagers to be financially involved in the park. That means jobs as rangers and guards, and on the few occasions when some scientist like myself is willing to walk this far, as guides. Every villager who makes his living working for the park is one less villager with a herd of goats. Then we work on agricultural productivity, get some trees planted so the soil stops washing away, and get the grass growing again. Handled properly, Lhakrinor could support more trees, more farming, and several times its current population of wildlife."

Nima said, "But you had two doubts about a national park in Lhakrinor, David. The people were only one problem. What about the wild animals? Have you decided there are enough to justify the effort of making a park?"

"That's still an open question," he said.

When Trowbridge left for his tent Nima followed him out into the darkness, as he'd hoped she would.

He intended to tell her he was sorry that things had not gone well. That if he had known, he would have been more careful—and that he was sure they could work it out. Nima, however, did not give him a chance to make this speech.

"David, what happened the night of the festival . . . we should not let it happen again."

"Why not?" he said immediately.

When she spoke, she chose her words carefully. "While you were gone, I thought about you a great deal. I worried that you might be hurt. That you would not come back for some reason. I found myself hoping you would think about me as you searched for your leopards—"

"Nima—"

"David, let me finish. I came a long way to escape being a wife, the one who was once a *kumari*. To escape being the child of my parents, who wished me to be a good daughter and do as I was told. I gave up a great deal to gain this freedom—I caused pain not only to myself, but to others. All so that I could be free and walk to the mountains. When I found myself standing in front of the hut, scanning the slopes with the binoculars, wanting you to come back . . . it was as if the freedom I had paid so much for had suddenly been lost."

"It doesn't have to be that way. You don't have to lose anything."

She shook her head. "I'm afraid I don't believe that. And I believe we should not let what happened happen again."

He was silent a moment. Then he said, "Okay. I don't like it, but okay."

He was hurt—and more than a little angry—to see a look of relief cross her face.

She said, "And I can still help with the study?"

"Nothing's changed there. I can still use your help. We'll go on like before."

He heard the coldness in his own voice. She heard it too; when she spoke, she sounded unsure of herself, and, for the first time, regretful.

"Thank you," she said, "for letting me stay. And I'm sorry."

"It's cold," he told her. "You should go back inside."

"Yes."

She hesitated, then said, "Sleep well."

He said, "You too, Nima," and turned toward his tent.

31

The headman of Lhakrinor wasted little time getting to his point.

"You are forbidden to remain in the area around Torma Mountain. This includes Trang monastery, Gelingdo, and the canyon toward Narling."

"May I ask why?"

Drokma leaned back in the saddle, regarding Trowbridge with steady, indifferent eyes. "I am not required to tell you why. But if you would like an explanation, try this one: The area you are in is holy to the Buddhist faith. Torma Mountain itself is holy. It is not permissible to have *gyami* strangers who pretend to be scholars disturbing our most holy places."

Norbu, emerging from the hut, said, "I did not remember the headman of Lhakrinor being so devout. It warms the heart to hear you speak in such a fashion."

Drokma leaned forward, his face terrible.

"You are penniless, Norbu, and landless. You have no animals and no family. You are *no one* in this land. The stones themselves do not hear what you say. Before long you will disappear from Lhakrinor, like you did before, and Lhakrinor will forget that you ever existed."

Drokma looked back at Trowbridge, his voice steady and cynical once again.

"You will be out of this area tomorrow."

"But it is not legal!" Dorje declared indignantly. "You would not dare do this if we were nearer the authorities! David *sahib's* papers are perfectly in order!"

Drokma regarded him contemptuously. "Squeal like a wolf pup,

Sherpa, if it gives you pleasure. But remember that you are a long way from the rest of the pack. My word is law here. Now, Mr. Trowbridge, do I have your cooperation?"

There was one more area he'd planned to explore while based at Trang, a blank space on the map just north of Torma Mountain. It could wait, however; they might even be able to survey it on their way out of Lhakrinor in September.

"Yes," Trowbridge said.

A look of surprise flickered across Drokma's face.

"I expected you to make difficulties. Where will you go?"

"Considering that the permit is in order, and that I'm cooperating with your request, isn't that my affair?"

"Not when you are in Lhakrinor. At any rate, I will find out where you are staying without your having to tell me."

Drokma wrenched hard on the reins and turned away. As he did so his donkey flung its nose in the air and stepped nervously to one side. Drokma clutched at the pommel, missed, and lurched out of the saddle, landing awkwardly on the ground.

Norbu was the first to reach him. Drokma, grimacing at the pain of the fall, allowed himself to be helped to his feet. Then he saw who had helped him and pulled violently away. Without the stature he had when mounted on his donkey, he looked suddenly small.

"You should not have helped me," Drokma said, his voice shaken but contemptuous.

Norbu said nothing, but Trowbridge could see the tension in his body.

"The vow is to kill me, is it not?" Drokma taunted. "It would have been easy to do so while I was on the ground. I am an old man whose body is no longer strong."

"If I kill you, Drokma," Norbu said, an edge in his voice, "it will not be because it is easy, or because you are old."

Drokma motioned recklessly at his donkey. "There is a pistol in my saddlebag, lama's son. Fulfill your vow and be done with it. I am sure your friends will tell no one."

Trowbridge tensed, not knowing what he would do if Norbu reached for the saddlebag. Norbu, however, made no move; Drokma, after a moment, seemed to regain his mocking confidence.

"You never obeyed your father," he said, a sneer in his voice, "and now you will not even adhere to your own vow."

"The vow was to kill you—but only if I could prove your guilt."

"Ah! Not only violent, but scrupulously just."

Drokma turned toward his donkey, boosted himself stiffly into the saddle, and looked down at Norbu.

"You must be careful, lama's son. If you give up hating me, your father will be lost to you forever. I am all you have left."

He clicked his tongue, turned his donkey, and rode up the slope.

The following morning they divided as much as could be carried of their food and possessions into four heavy loads—Trowbridge would hire someone in Jaramar to come back for the balance—and made a little procession up the long trail past the *mani* walls. Fresh wolf scat was scattered on the flat stones; the snow, in the shadow of the wall, was stained yellow where the wolves had marked their passing. They stopped a moment, breathing hard, and looked back across the canyon at the slopes of Torma Mountain.

"Should we have wished the lama good-bye?" Nima asked.

"I think we'll see him again."

"But you are forbidden to return to Trang," Dorje said.

He said nothing. They started on up the slope. To their right, on the high, rounded, barren slope, the figure of the old woman straightened a moment from gathering yak dung and stood motionless, without waving, watching them go.

32

With Jigme's help they located an abandoned house twenty minutes from Jaramar, on a hillside near the deep gorge above which the village was built. After haggling for a respectable time with the owner over the rent, they blew away the heavy clouds of fine, high-mountain dust, repaired a broken doorway, and scrubbed the floors; then Jigme burned sprigs of juniper throughout the ancient, two-story wooden structure, ritually fumigating it with the fragrant smoke. "It would be preferable if the lama were here to lend his protection against spirits," he said. "But it is a good house. You will be safe here, and comfortable."

Dorje stocked the kitchen with the relatively wide variety of food available in Jaramar, and purchased dried yak dung for fuel. Norbu negotiated with Pema for a few pieces of furniture—she dealt on the side, it appeared, in used household articles—and they settled into a substantially more comfortable way of life.

It was July. Flowers bloomed in tiny, riotous profusion on the slopes around them. The few carefully tended trees in and around the village made a gentle, distant whoosh in the wind. Barley fields sprouted pale green, the deep gorge beneath the village roared with rushing snow melt, and in the distance there was always the bleating of domestic goats, a noise which—even if it did signify the progressive destruction of the slopes around Jaramar—seemed cheerful and pleasant after the austere silence of Trang. It was hard to believe that only a hundred miles to the south, on the far side of the Himalayas, the heavy fury of the monsoon washed down from perpetually leaden skies, and leeches crawled by the millions in the mud.

With Norbu and Nima's help, Trowbridge began a systematic wildlife census of the Robshi Valley, which ran a full thirty miles northwest and southeast of Jaramar. Nima proved skillful not only at gathering data but analyzing it, and Trowbridge—somewhat to his surprise—was almost entirely comfortable working with her.

He also hired two young men from the village to help them locate bharal, and to search out the likely haunts of wolf and snow leopard. From the villagers' expertise at the task it was clear that at one time or another they had hunted the animals. They proved adaptable, however, to the idea of simply studying them; if the underlying concept left them slightly puzzled, the pay was good, and the work pleasant. Trowbridge saw this as a hopeful sign. If the park were set up properly, the villagers might come to regard healthy herds of bharal in the same way that they now regarded healthy herds of domestic goat: as a measure of wealth.

Casually, he inquired whether any of the villagers had ever seen a live shou—even going so far as to draw and circulate sketches of the deer-like creature–but no one had. The animal might still be alive somewhere, he was told. Perhaps to the north, in Tibet, or to the east. But not in the Robshi Valley.

He often ranged far from Jaramar, up into the mountainous areas which surrounded the Robshi. The land there was wild, craggy, and uninhabited; much of it, above the tree line, remained locked in snow year-round. Twice he came across solitary snow leopard tracks; another time he found the jumbled tracks of a mother with two young cubs. An actual sighting continued to elude him, but Trowbridge was encouraged by the fact that he was dealing with what seemed to be a living population of snow leopards, not a dying one.

Jigme sat alone at the *mani* wall a mile outside Jaramar, engrossed in the slow, exacting work of carving inch-high characters on a piece of gray-blue slate perhaps three feet across. He looked up calmly at Trowbridge's approach, smiled, and continued to work.

"Did you find many animals today, David?" he asked.

"A few. How's the carving going?"

"It is going well."

Jigme had been working for six days carving *Om Mane Padme Hum* onto a rectangular piece of slate. This *mani* wall—and there were dozens like it scattered throughout Lhakrinor—was forty feet long, waist high, and covered with hundreds of the stones. To Western eyes the wall might look broken down, messy, and repetitive; in fact, created over a period of centuries, by artists who felt no individualistic compulsion to sign their work, it represented an astounding record of spiritual devotion.

Jigme's contentment at what he was doing, as he sat cross-legged, concentrating deeply, was infectious. Trowbridge sat down next to him, watching in a silence broken only by the clink and tap of Jigme's hammer, realizing that something was changing in him. As he lived in this village and spent more time with the people, he increasingly *wanted* the park to come off—both for the people's sake, and for the animals'—in a way he hadn't before.

It would depend, still, on a cold-hearted analysis of the possibilities for successful regeneration of the land and the animals. And the scientist in him would not skew the data to arrive at a conclusion which might be personally preferable. Still, he hoped he would find enough vitality left in the animal population to justify a positive recommendation. Representing, as the park did, a more sensible way for these people to manage their land—as well as a critical infusion of outside money—it might be their only hope.

After five or ten minutes of work Jigme set down his tools and looked at Trowbridge. "You want to ask me something."

"Actually, I want to tell you about something—and then to ask for your help."

Briefly, he sketched out the idea of the park. He explained how the terrain would be improved and the wild animals protected. How the villagers would keep fewer yaks and goats, and would lose the right to graze them where they pleased, but would gain jobs, and a permanent livelihood. He explained how outside money from the Nepali government and some Western donors would improve the economy. Eventually there would be trees in many places throughout Lhakrinor, not just in Jaramar.

When he had finished, Jigme stared thoughtfully out across the pale, stony landscape, marked, in places, by dark irregular patches of dwarf juniper.

"It is a very new idea," he said slowly. "No one, of course, would disagree with the idea of more trees and grass. And the lama has been telling us for a long time not to kill the wild animals. But fewer goats and yaks?" He shook his head. "That is very different. The men, especially, would not like it, because it is their job to watch over the animals."

"You told me there hasn't been enough grass in years to feed the animals properly."

"It is true. Ever since the *gyami khoum-teng* closed the northern border and we could no longer send the animals into Tibet for the winter. Still, I do not know if the people of Lhakrinor will be open to this. It would require accepting many new ideas all at once."

"The most respected people in the community must lead the way. In the long run, Jigme, your children would grow up in a more prosperous and happier place."

Jigme nodded. "I understand," he said noncommittally, "and I am not necessarily against your idea. But it is the *lama*, above all, whom you must persuade. If he is against the project—or even if he takes no position—it will surely fail."

"And if he agrees?"

"If he agrees," Jigme said, "then you still have Drokma to consider. He will be a serious problem, since your plan would take away from his power. And if you take away from his power, you take away from his wealth—which is all he cares about."

Trowbridge said, "Was Drokma really responsible for the death of Norbu's father, as Norbu seems to believe?"

Jigme looked at him appraisingly.

"The answer to that question, if anyone knows it, is a dangerous thing. Norbu has vowed to kill Drokma—or whoever was responsible—if he finds real proof."

"Norbu has told me that much. I'd like to know the rest of the story." He paused a moment, then added, "Norbu is my friend as well."

"I have seen that. And I know that he trusts you, so I will trust you also, since it may be good for you to know these things. But you must be careful with what I tell you."

Jigme picked his carving tools back up. He seemed to want something to do with his hands while he spoke; his words were punctuated by the tiny tap of hammer on chisel.

"Norbu's father was a brilliant scholar, even as a young man," he began. "More than a scholar; he also worked hard in the fields, and was funny and well liked—as was Drokma, although it is difficult to believe now. He and Drokma were good friends.

"When Norbu's father was eighteen he went to study at one of the great lamaseries in central Tibet. He was taken on as a student by a famous lama, and married, and Norbu was born. They would probably have lived out their lives there, but Norbu's mother died of cholera, and then the Chinese came. At first they left the monasteries alone, but it was clear such forbearance would not last, and Norbu's father decided—or perhaps was instructed by his lama, who by this time was very old—to return to Lhakrinor. The lama entrusted him with a religious treasure—a small golden dragon with eyes of lapis lazuli and turquoise-encrusted wings.

"Norbu's father told only Drokma and my father—and of course Norbu—about the dragon. He hoped Norbu would become a lama as well and take on the sacred trust of possessing it. As the years went by, however, it became clear that Norbu would not become a lama—and Drokma, who had always been ambitious, became increasingly greedy and ruthless. He became involved with Gorchok bandits, and he began, I am afraid, to lust after the sacred dragon. One day, when Norbu and I were out hunting and Norbu's father was away from the house, the dragon disappeared.

"Norbu's father, I think, still believed there was good left in Drokma, for he went to him and asked him outright if he knew anything. Drokma must have been shaken by this directness in his old friend. He claimed he had seen a Gorchok bandit with the sacred treasure, and even said he had tried to talk the bandit into returning it. I think now that Drokma intended only to discourage Norbu's father, but it didn't work. He went looking for this Gorchok bandit, and when he found him—or when he found some bandit, who can say it was the same one?—the bandit killed him."

"That was when Norbu made his vow."

Jigme nodded. "Norbu swore that if he could prove Drokma had lied—had taken the dragon himself and sent Norbu's father to his death—he would kill him. Shortly afterward, Norbu disappeared. Many people believed he had been killed by the same bandit who killed his father. I chose to believe that he went away to escape the labyrinth of anger and illusion in which he had become trapped."

"It was the lama of Gelingdo who convinced him to leave."

"Ah! So you know some of the story I do not."

"Does Norbu still want to know the truth?"

"I think he is torn, as before. He wants to know the truth, and doesn't. In his place that is how I would feel."

Trowbridge considered this, watching silently as Jigme—who sat perfectly straight, his face clear and calm—worked on the *mani* stone. He looked beyond the *mani* wall at the cloud shadows moving across the landscape. Then something else occurred to him, something he ought probably to have asked sooner.

"Jigme, was there a foreigner here in Lhakrinor last year? A man from India?"

Jigme looked mildly surprised. "Yes. He came with a number of porters, and stayed for several weeks near Torma Mountain. Evidently his visit was of a religious nature. The only people he spoke to, so far as I know, were the lama, and of course Drokma, who talks to every-one who comes to Lhakrinor."

"That's all?"

Jigme shrugged. "That is all I know. He never came to Jaramar."

"Simply *participate* in your breathing, David. Do not force it, and do not follow its progress as if it were a thing different from yourself."

He closed his eyes once again, concentrating on his breathing.

He and Jigme were sitting on the flat roof of Jigme's house. To their left was the ridge which dominated the village's skyline, topped by the solitary prayer flag. Straight ahead of him, down the open valley in which the village was situated, there was nothing but clear air for twenty miles, then mountains, looming clean and distant.

He concentrated for a long time. Finally he opened his eyes, shaking his head.

"It doesn't feel any different. I want this to work, Jigme—but the truth is I'm just sitting here with my eyes closed."

Jigme had instructed him to visualize himself someplace complete-ly different from the place he considered to be "real"; he was supposed to create a forest, to surround himself with trees and thickets, and then to walk through that forest, feeling the sensations and seeing the sights of a thickly wooded place.

Jigme studied him with amusement.

"In fact, I think you are getting closer. Your problem is that you are impatient—you wish to take the Thong-Lam, the direct path to the top of the mountain. But we will keep trying. Think about your breathing. And David, your back is crooked again. You must make your backbone—"

"I know, like a pile of coins."

He sighed, and closed his eyes.

"Jigme," he said after a moment, "help me—give me a different challenge. I can't make the forest come to life."

Jigme thought a moment, then said, "This time, do not try to visualize anything special. I think you must stop *trying* to do anything at all. Remember that at this moment you do not need to defend or prove yourself."

Jigme continued to speak for several minutes. He explained how certain lamas practiced a form of meditation similar to this called *tummo*, or inner heat; how *tummo* allowed such lamas to sit out all night beside a freezing lake, as their disciples dipped sheets in the water, wrapped them about their masters, then a short time later removed the sheets, now dry from the internally generated heat. Trowbridge, released from the task of visualizing a specific set of images, simply sat, and listened. An agreeable calm came over him; at one point he noticed his heartbeat had slowed significantly.

Later he became aware that Jigme had fallen silent.

This time, when he opened his eyes he opened them to a changed landscape. This was the same high ridge, the same mountains at the far end of the horizon, the same white clouds moving above him, in a steady procession, through a high blue cauldron of sky. But it all rang with a suppressed vibration, as if it might whirl apart at any moment.

The sensation was terrifying.

Fighting a sense of vertigo, he squeezed his eyes shut, and said, "If I'm supposed to make it all come to a halt, Jigme, I've failed. The more I look the more it seems to move."

"At least you have perceived the motion," Jigme said calmly. "It is the first step toward achieving stillness, and an open way of being."

33

The morning sun had just cleared the mountains. The warmth of its first rays was welcome as he stooped above his pack on the stone porch before the house, wrapping a sleeping bag carefully around the camera, packing the other equipment for the trip-wire system into side pouches.

Nima appeared in the doorway. Blinking, fresh from sleep, her dark hair tousled, she stood with one hand on the rough wood of the doorway, watching him as he worked.

"You are trying the camera again?"

He nodded. "I may have better luck near Ngong. It's ideal snow leopard terrain."

"How long will you be gone?"

"Two days, maybe three. Any sign of the wolves?"

Nima had come in late last night, long after he'd gone to sleep; she'd been scouting the southern area of the valley in the hopes of spotting the wolf pack they'd seen at Trang.

"Not yet."

"I'm positive this valley must be part of their circuit."

"If they come through, I will see them."

"Norbu may spot them on the western slopes. He should be back tonight."

Nima was silent a moment. "Ngong," she said. "That is where Norbu says there are often Gorchok bandits. You must be careful."

He looked up at her and grinned. He was in a good mood, excited that soon he would be walking toward the high mountains to the northeast.

"If you start worrying about me, Nima, you haven't accomplished much by sleeping alone."

As soon as he said it he wondered if he'd gone too far, breaching the easy comfort they'd developed over the last few weeks, but she smiled in amusement.

He zipped the last zipper and shouldered his pack.

"Watch for the wolves?"

She said, "I will watch carefully for my wolves."

He brought his hands together before his chest and dipped his head in the traditional Buddhist salutation. Nima did the same. He turned, walked to the corner of the house, and came face to face with the witch of Narling.

Despite the fact that the witch had, no doubt, simply reached the corner of the house at the same time as he had, he couldn't escape the uncanny feeling that she'd materialized out of the thin mountain air. She studied him quizzically a moment, then stepped past him onto the porch, glancing past Nima into the interior of the house.

"You have installed yourselves very comfortably," she said in an approving tone. Then she turned back to Trowbridge. "I suppose you know this is not a good house in winter when the snow is deep?"

"We'll be leaving in October."

"Ah," she said. "And where is Norbu, the wandering son of my old friend the lama?"

"He's gone to see Pema."

A look of amusement crossed the witch's intelligent face. "Perhaps it was to be expected. The wild girl of Jaramar, for whom no man in the village is good enough, and the lama's son who left for so many years. Many interesting things are happening this year in Lhakrinor."

"What else?" he asked.

"Your presence, of course. And perhaps the smoke I have seen rising, more than once, from a place high on the slopes of Torma Mountain above Gelingdo."

The witch lifted her arms, examining her solid body with a wry, surprised look. "Even *I* have done something unusual, leaving my home in Narling to journey to Jaramar."

She fixed her gaze back on Trowbridge. "You are wondering why I have made this journey. The answer is simple: I came to see how this one was doing."

She gestured at Nima.

"And if you wonder why am I interested, perhaps it is because she reminds me of myself when I was a young woman."

With that the witch turned and walked through the doorway. Nima met Trowbridge's eyes, her expression a combination of curiosity and alarm, then followed the witch into the house.

It was a rough, dirty, ugly glacier, and it lay at an altitude where there was half the oxygen at sea level. Pitted with earth, deformed by slag heaps of filthy snow, the glacier sloped upward for a full mile above the ice cave in which he would spend the night. Splinters of sunset light glanced spectacularly off the summit above him as he worked. The warm colors were deceptive; it would be a cold night.

He anchored the far end of the trip wire to a small ice screw, then piled loose snow atop the screw until it disappeared. Carefully, he led the slender wire across the trail, then attached it to the tripping mechanism on his flash. This too he buried in snow. He stood and inspected his work, blowing on numb fingers. Then he walked quickly up the narrow trail, over a crest.

In the distance, Tibet: a cold and windy plain, darkening rapidly. By a geographical oddity, Lhakrinor was walled off from Nepal—its own country—by high mountains to the east, south, and west, but to the north it was wide open to China.

He stood watching a moment, then turned and retraced his steps, letting his eyes wander easily, watching for anything out of place. The snow leopards' eyesight was keen, their sense of what was normal and what was not, acute. Even by faint starlight a leopard might sense something had been altered.

It looked all right. If he hadn't known precisely where the wire was he would have blundered into it himself. Even the cave looked invisible, little more than another dark opening among many on the slope. He stopped, crouched above the trip wire, closed his eyes, and placed a finger on it. There was a faint electronic click, a bright, feathery pressure against his eyelids, and a quick whir of film winding forward.

Perfect.

"Apologies for the surprise, leopard," he said quietly to the ice and snow around him.

He'd piled rocks and snow at the cave's entrance, making a low wall. Carefully he eased in over the wall's top. The frigid air inside the cave struck him immediately. The cave was small, however, and he knew that in a few minutes his own body heat would make it relatively comfortable. He slipped off his boots and wriggled into his sleeping bag, then rolled over onto his belly. Lying propped on his elbows, he lit the stove, chipped some snow into the large metal cup which served as a pot, and heated some dried soup. The blue light of the gas illuminated the fossil-studded ceiling of the cave barely a foot above his head.

When the cup began to steam he turned off the stove and sipped the soup slowly, one eye to the chink in the wall which allowed him to observe the trail. It was fully dark now. The trail, only a few feet away, had disappeared. He placed the cup onto a little ledge of ice, set his watch for an hour before dawn—to allow him an early start down out of the mountains—then crawled deeper into his bag and went to sleep.

He woke before his watch went off. The moon was up; his senses were alert and straining. Something was coming down the trail, making a steady, heavy crunching in the snow. He put his eye to the chink in the wall, realizing as he did so that no leopard would make a noise like that. Whatever was coming down the trail was walking on two feet.

At night? On a forgotten trail that led from a windswept Tibetan waste? The only night travelers on this trail should be snow leopard, or perhaps wolves, although he'd seen no sign of wolf in the area.

He realized suddenly that a human being, with a higher center of gravity and only two legs, might be sufficiently startled by the bright flash to lose his footing on the icy trail. He raised his head above the wall of the cave and opened his mouth to shout a warning. Then something stopped him. A voice in his head—Nima's—reminding him to be careful.

Think, he told himself. Who would be walking this trail at night? A smuggler coming in from Tibet? A Gorchok bandit returning from the other side of the border? Either would be armed and jumpy; neither would take kindly to being yelled at, on a dark night, from a place of concealment.

Slowly, he lowered his eye back to the chink. The squeak and crunch of boots in snow grew louder. By faint moonlight, a substantial, heavily bundled figure appeared, carrying a pack.

Nearly to the trip wire. Trowbridge narrowed his eyes to slits. Any second now.

A flash of light, impossibly intense in the darkness. An enraged, shocked curse. Then the heavy thud of a body hitting the snow. For a moment, there was no sound. Had the person been knocked unconscious?

As if in answer, there came an abrupt slithering noise. Then the unmistakable click of a rifle being cocked.

Whoever it was, Trowbridge thought grimly, had quick reflexes. Blinded by the flash, he would now be scanning the area, rifle at ready, waiting for his night vision to return. For the moment, Trowbridge had the upper hand, but the slightest movement would telegraph his position to the man with the rifle as surely as if he had stood up and announced it. He made himself very still, his breathing infinitesimal.

There's no one here.

He filled his mind with the thought.

No one. No one at all.

As the silence deepened, he became intensely aware of the presence of another human being only a few feet away in the darkness. He could hear, faintly, the sound of breathing; could almost feel the wary personality of the stranger reaching out, trying to gauge if there was someone nearby.

Then he heard a surreptitious rustling, a noise as if someone were crawling across the snow. A sound of snow being scraped away. He realized that either the camera, or the snow screw, was about to be discovered. He put his eye to the chink in time to be stunned by a second flash of light.

Terrific, he thought. Now we're both blind.

There came a muffled, enraged curse, and a steady smashing noise which suggested that he now owned one less camera. If he's making this much noise, Trowbridge realized, he must have decided he's alone. In a few moments he'll move on.

Trowbridge took a careful, slow breath, and began to relax, and in that moment something occurred to him. Carefully, he brought his arm up out of the sleeping bag and looked at the luminous face of his watch. The alarm was set to go off in just over two minutes. He could press a button to turn it off, but that itself would cause a single, clear, unmistakable beep.

He placed a finger on the alarm-deactivating button, and studied the watch face carefully.

Smash!

The camera would be in electronic shreds by now. Still, the person out there kept flailing away at it. The trick would be to time the beep with the next—

There was a grunt, and a silence, and then he heard what was left of his camera go flinging down the slope. Less than a minute now before the alarm sounded. Heart pounding, he put his eye back to the chink. Dimly, as his eyesight recovered, he saw a dark figure raise itself into a crouch and look around warily, holding the rifle in a loose, practiced grip.

He felt the regular pulsing of the seconds go by, one after the other, and wondered if he was about to lose his life in the mountains of

Nepal because of a digital watch for which he'd paid twenty dollars in a New York discount store.

With another grunt, the figure hefted his pack and began moving slowly down the trail.

Ten steps away. Twenty.

Less than twelve seconds remained on his watch. He brought his wrist slowly down into the sleeping bag and buried it between his legs. This wouldn't cover the sound entirely, but it would help. He counted off the seconds in his head.

Four, three, two...

He pressed the button. From inside the sleeping bag came a muffled, but very audible, beep.

He held himself utterly still. The artificial noise had seemed to pierce the night. Heart thudding heavily, he put his eye back to the wall. The figure continued to grow smaller down the rounded rim of trail. Slowly it disappeared into the darkness, the sound of footsteps trailing off into silence.

Trowbridge rolled over onto his back and stared upward, his elbows aching. He took a deep breath and let it out very slowly.

He'd had a lucky escape, of sorts. But he was presented with a new problem. He'd only seen the face of the individual outside the cave for a split second, during the second flash of light, but it was not a face he would forget. The last time he had seen it had been above a rifle barrel, in the hot lowlands, in Pokhara.

34

"Are you sure?" Norbu asked.

"It's not a face I'd forget. Or a rifle, for that matter."

"No," Norbu admitted.

Jigme said, "I have heard of the presence of this Indian hunter of yours, this *shikari*."

Trowbridge and Norbu looked at him in surprise.

Jigme said, "Sonam's brother brought news a few days ago from Trang. It seems that since you left Trang this *shikari* has been seen there several times. The old woman was worried about the lama, and so my cousin visited him to be sure all was well."

"And?"

"The lama was fine. But he had received a visit by another Indian, a very lean man, my cousin said, with eyes which are intense. Do you know this one also?"

Trowbridge nodded slowly. Krishna, it appeared, had come to Lhakrinor for the second year in a row.

"I saw the wolves!" she said excitedly.

Nima had burst through the door, flung her pack down, and collapsed next to him where he sat working on the map. Barely able to contain herself, she pointed out where she'd been.

"It is the same group we saw at Trang!" she said. "Only this time there were two cubs with them. They look very fat and very healthy."

She looked around the empty house. "Where are the others?"

"Norbu went to the southern end of the valley to finish the bharal survey. Dorje's gone to Serkha—he heard a rumor there were fresh strawberries there."

She paused a moment, then turned back to the map. "I found the wolves right here—exactly where you said they might be. I watched them playing for hours. I wish you had been there to see! They were teaching the little ones to hunt by playing games with them."

"And then?"

"After they finished playing they took a nap, and headed in this direction."

She traced their course on the map.

"I followed them until sundown. Then I made camp. That was yesterday. This morning I followed their trail backward for several miles—it leads here, in the direction of Trang—and then I returned home."

Trowbridge penciled in the path taken by the wolves.

"This is good—it matches up with what we learned at Trang. We've got the whole circuit now."

He looked at her with approval. "How did I ever get along without you?"

"I do not know," she said, "but I am sure your work was not nearly so good. Did you find a place in Ngong for your camera?"

Some of the pleasure he felt at her return dissolved as he told her about the encounter with the *shikari*, and of the fact that Krishna had appeared in Lhakrinor.

"David, why are these men here?"

"I have no idea."

"What will you do?"

There wasn't much he *could* do, short of going to Torma Mountain, finding Krishna, and asking him point blank what he was up to— something he had no intention of doing. He didn't owe Vikram that much.

He shrugged. "We'll keep our eyes and ears open, but the main thing is to get on with the study and stay out of their way. There was a government official in Jorkhang interested in what Krishna was up to. On our way out of Lhakrinor I'll tell him that Krishna turned up again, this time with a rather nasty friend."

"What about the park?"

"Nothing's changed, in terms of the park."

"You still have not decided?"

"I still need more information."

"Will you visit the lama soon?"

He nodded. "I wanted to get a clearer idea of what the boundaries of the park would be before I bothered him. We're closer to that goal because of what you've done today. You're a first-rate field biologist."

"Is that why you like me?"

The question took him aback. "Yes, partly." He thought for a moment. "Also because you're tough and intelligent and independent, the qualities I admire most in the world. And because, for whatever reason, I'm more at ease in the same room with you than I am with most people."

She considered this a moment, then said lightly, "Ah! I am filthy! I must wash before it becomes dark. It is very dirty work, being a biologist."

She jumped up, took a kettle filled with hot water from over the fire, and replaced it with another. Then she carried the first kettle out the back door to where they'd rigged a bathing porch—a simple arrangement with canvas sides, a slat floor to let the water run through, and a shelf on which to set soap and a bucket of water. Soon she was splashing at her bath.

Trowbridge sat by the window, working on his notes in the after- noon light. One significant area remained to be surveyed in the Robshi

Valley, a wild corner of the mountains at the valley's extreme northeast end. He planned to explore it with Norbu later in the week.

The water in the second kettle began to bubble. He poured a small amount of cooler water into it and carried it to the back door.

"Hello," he said, extending it outward past the threshold.

"Thank you."

Her arm appeared in his field of view—slender and brown, her skin lustrous with water drops—and took the kettle. He was tempted to ask her if she wanted her back washed, but resisted. He turned, and was about to go back to his notes, when the splashing stopped, and there was only the sound of water dripping through the bathing area onto the ground, and she said, "David, I think perhaps you need a bath as well."

They made love on the bathing area floor, lying side by side on the slats, their bodies warm from the bath water and from each other, cool air coming up between the boards. At first he was the more nervous and careful of the two of them, worried that something would go wrong. Then he realized that this time there was no hesitation in her, only a touch of curiosity and a great deal of passion. He pulled her on top of him, and felt her weight, her lips against his. He wondered momentarily how much the witch of Narling had to do with this, then lost himself in the miracle of Nima's body, mysterious and familiar at once.

35

He and Norbu left early, following the Robshi Valley northward for the best part of the day. In the late afternoon they reached the Robshi's northern end and began climbing a game trail up into rougher country; in blue twilight, beside a stream vigorous with snow melt, they made camp.

Above them, a hazy film of stars portended a possible change in the weather. He hoped it wouldn't rain, because rain would wash away tracks and lessen their chances of a sighting. Unable to sleep, he turned his attention to tomorrow's job.

The Latin classification was *panthera uncia*; the common name, snow leopard. In Tibetan, *sao*; sometimes called, in archaic English naturalist literature, the "ounce"; in India, *bhural he*, or bharal killer. Graceful and stealthy, with huge paws and smoke-gray fur marked by dark rosettes, the snow leopard was found in Central Asia at remote elevations between ten thousand and eighteen thousand feet. It was not distinguished from its better known counterpart, the lowland leopard, until 1770. Recognition did it little good; it was classified as vermin, and hunted relentlessly in every place it lived for its fur, for sport, or for the sheer pleasure, peculiar to humans, of seeking out and destroying that which is shy, difficult to approach, beautiful, and keeps to itself.

Like most big cats, a snow leopard could subdue prey three times its size; this meant, in theory, that a one-hundred-eighty-pound human being ought to be eligible prey for a sixty-pound cat. Given the relentless efforts made to exterminate it, the snow leopard might be forgiven for striking back on occasion, but reports of a snow leopard killing a human being were unknown. The animal had retreated steadily before human encroachment, making itself scarce in the shrinking handful of habitats left to it.

It was an unequal relationship, and *panthera uncia* was losing.

The following morning, after a Spartan breakfast, he and Norbu began climbing due north, directly into a crooked, narrow range of mountains—the Thongsa Himal, which formed Lhakrinor's northeastern border with Tibet.

"This is the wildest part of Lhakrinor we've seen yet," Trowbridge said, surveying the land around them.

Norbu said, "When I was a boy the old men of the village always said that it was faster to go around this place than to go through it."

It was not hard to figure out why. In contrast to the rolling hills and vast slopes which filled much of Lhakrinor, the land about them was chopped, maze-like, and filled with rushing streams. Several times they followed a rising gully for a substantial distance only to find themselves brought up short at the base of an unclimbable cliff. Ridges which started out in a promising manner ended abruptly in dizzying precipices. The terrain was unforgiving, almost surly in its nature; the going was extremely tough, requiring a great deal of skill and patience, and with every step Trowbridge felt happier. The area might look barren to the casual eye, but there was plenty of evidence that wildlife was thriving here. Mice made intricate burrows in sandy hillsides. Smooth, shiny-bodied skink lizards did pushups on flat rocks, tilting their blunt heads toward the sun. Tiny wildflowers bloomed in bright spurts: white cuckooflower, yellow potentilla, edelweiss, and wild parsley. Prickly, mauve-colored poppies, seemingly impractical in their size and audacious color, wobbled in the slight breeze.

On a number of the slopes were stunted, bonsai-like junipers; within the undergrowth, an occasional rustle and a staccato call indicated the presence of long-tailed marmots, each busily stuffing itself for its upcoming winter hibernation. During the summer months, when snow leopards could catch them, marmots were a dietary staple. Like the area around Narling, this was ideal snow leopard country.

And there were no villages nearby.

Above their heads, drifting silently, a golden eagle patrolled the hazy blue sky. The backpack was heavy; Trowbridge could taste the sweat in his mouth as he climbed, and his shoulders ached. When the sun was high they stopped for lunch. Around them a number of shallow bharal beds had been pawed into the slope. Again, Trowbridge was encouraged. An area which supported healthy populations of marmot and bharal should, at least theoretically, support snow leopard. Increasingly, he began to feel that he'd discovered what he'd been looking for ever since he entered Lhakrinor.

"Forty-eight hours?" he said, crouching, studying the bharal hoof marks in the soil.

The tracks were less than distinct, slightly softened, edges crumbled by the wind.

"About that," Norbu said.

After lunch and a brief rest, they pushed on. The sky clouded over and grew dark, and the wind began to pick up. They kicked steps into the soft dirt of a winding slope, then descended to the edge of a noisy, silt-thick river. Norbu said he could smell rain and suggested that they begin looking for shelter. Trowbridge agreed, content, finally, that they had walked deep enough into this high, remote corner of Lhakrinor.

They continued up the eastern bank of the river. A few minutes later drops of rain began falling from the darkened sky, making wet spots in the dirt. Norbu spotted an opening in the slope above them; they scrambled up a series of rounded rocks and ducked into a low cave. The cave was not deep, but its floor was dry and more or less flat. From this vantage point they looked down on the yellow, swollen torrent below, which rushed down from a great chaotic mass of boulders. The rain came down solidly and the wind intensified, driving the drops nearly sideways in noisy sweeps. Small rocks began skittering down the slope above them.

"Bharal?" Norbu asked. "Or just the wind?"

"Could be either."

They sat looking out at the weather. It was a pleasure to be dry amidst this summer storm; a luxury, after having walked for most of the day, to rest.

Norbu said, "Always bharal. When I was young, there were argali sheep, and tahr as well."

Trowbridge nodded. "It's not a good situation. If some virus came through to which bharal were particularly susceptible and they died off, the wolves and snow leopard would die off with them. Most areas I've studied have a less vulnerable network of predator-prey relationships."

"Could you bring back some of the other animals?"

Trowbridge shrugged. "Nima suggested the same thing. We might be able to get hold of some troop helicopters from the Nepali government. My guess is that it wouldn't be worth bringing in argali sheep; the winters are fiercer now, according to Jigme, and the argali probably died off because they couldn't survive the deep snow. But I think tahr would do just fine. That is, if they had reasonable protection from the villagers, and enough grass to eat."

"Helicopters," Norbu grinned, looking out at the wild scene before them.

Trowbridge found himself smiling as well; the idea of helicopters setting down in Lhakrinor, filled with rows of bundled, bewildered tahr, was comical.

As the last few drops of rain sparkled down, Trowbridge fixed a telephoto lens to his remaining camera. He and Norbu stepped out of the cave and began working their way down the muddy slope. They had barely taken ten steps when a sustained rattling of rocks came from above them. They looked upward and saw nothing; above the noise of the river, however, they could hear a hoarse, terrified blatting.

Up the river bank, perhaps two hundred yards away, they spotted a group of bharal surging skittishly along the slope. Trowbridge recognized instantly the behavior of prey made uneasy by the presence of a predator. At that moment, in desperate plunges, down from the base of an overhanging cliff, came a full-grown male bharal. Clinging to its back in a wild, life-or-death flight was a snow leopard. The terrified bharal negotiated the steep slope with extraordinary strength and balance, humping and bucking in an attempt to shake its attacker. The cat, which must have missed its initial grip on the bharal's throat, had only a superficial hold on the bharal's neck with its teeth, and was being carried a full hundred and fifty yards down toward the river.

With his heart in his throat, shooting photos steadily, Trowbridge watched the two animals hurtle toward the rushing water. If the bharal reached the water, they would, in all probability, both drown.

In an area of soft sand barely ten yards from the river's edge, the bharal stumbled suddenly, and dropped its head. In that moment it almost escaped; the snow leopard, its wild flight abruptly checked, was nearly flung over the bharal's horns. With a desperate raking of its claws, it maintained its hold on the shoulders and flanks of the bharal, which struggled to regain its footing, surging and kicking through the flat basin of dry sand. Seeing its opportunity, the leopard, in a move too quick to follow with the eye, lunged forward and down. Its powerful jaws achieved a purchase on the bharal's throat. The hoarse bleating stopped abruptly and the bharal went down, only a few feet from the rushing water.

The wild scene before them was suddenly still.

Trowbridge and Norbu had dropped into a sitting position on the slope; Trowbridge, camera to his eye, continued to focus and shoot steadily. The bharal and the snow leopard had come to a halt barely thirty yards beneath them.

The leopard crouched beside its prey, victorious but still careful, teeth sunk deeply into the bharal's throat, one paw protectively on its shoulder. For a full eight minutes—Trowbridge timed it—the leopard held that position. Then it eased its hold, and looked around with the wary curiosity of a wild animal which knows it hasn't been keeping an eye on its surroundings. Almost immediately, it spotted Trowbridge and Norbu on the slope. With a surprised snarl, it stalked uneasily to the far side of the bharal and stood appraising them with a frosty, suspicious stare.

Don't run away, Trowbridge prayed. We mean you no harm.

The snow leopard had no intention, it appeared, of being frightened off its prey. Emitting a low, threatening rumble, then a coughing roar, it sent a clear challenge in their direction. Slowly, Trowbridge lowered the camera, content, at this moment, simply to observe.

The snow leopard rumbled doubtfully at this movement on his part, its long tail twitching uneasily in the sand. A moment later its attention was distracted by the arrival of the first scavengers. A pair of lammergeiers—great bearded vultures, with heavy bodies, scraggly necks, and lurid red eyes shining in dark heads—banked down close to the river. One swooped in a tight circle and landed, with a kick of sand, a few yards away. Folding its enormous wings awkwardly, it strained its neck forward, studying the bharal greedily. The snow leopard made a fierce rush in the lammergeier's direction; with a guttural hiss, and a hasty and ungainly working of its wings, the great bird took off and rejoined its more patient companion, circling a few yards above the kill.

In the distance, Trowbridge heard a hoarse "cawk" as the ravens began to arrive. From this moment on, until it finished—or was chased away from—the carcass, the snow leopard would have no shortage of volunteers to share its meal.

The snow leopard cast one more long look at him and Norbu, then took the bharal by the throat and began the difficult task of dragging it up the slope.

He raised the camera slowly and began shooting again. The snow leopard appeared to be heading for a place among the rocks more or less level with where he and Norbu were sitting. Trowbridge could hardly believe their luck; if they'd known ahead of time, they couldn't have chosen a better observation site. Faintly, above the roar of the river, he heard an occasional knock of horn against rock as the snow leopard dragged the heavy bharal upward.

"Do you think it's the one you followed?" Norbu asked quietly.

"It could be. It's about the right size."

The answer came a moment later. Reaching an area of flat rocks, the snow leopard, clearly winded after its climb, turned and made a chuffing noise through its nostrils. Out of a dark cleft in the rocks emerged a ball of white and black fur. This was followed immediately by a second, slightly smaller. As the cubs rushed to her, Trowbridge could hear, faintly, their high-pitched, hungry meows.

"Not the same animal," Trowbridge said happily. "Six weeks ago this leopard was giving birth to cubs, not leading me on a wild chase across half of Lhakrinor."

"Then there is another snow leopard about somewhere," Norbu said.

"At least one," Trowbridge said.

* * *

For two hours they watched the family of snow leopards feed, play, and sleep in the sun. The leopardess nursed the cubs and encouraged them to try feeding from the kill; at the same time she kept a careful eye on the greedy gallery of birds, and on Trowbridge and Norbu. In the late afternoon, so as not to disturb the family any further, and to avoid disturbing any other potential prey in the area—with two small cubs, the leopardess dared not range far, and had to hope her prey would come to her—they left.

A good deal of what he had learned was new information. Most accounts in the professional literature suggested that a snow leopard killed its prey by breaking its neck with a massive swipe of its paw, or—after the fashion of wolves—by slashing its jugular. This kill had followed neither pattern. From the relatively superficial marks in its neck, and from the length of time the leopard had crouched beside the bharal, Trowbridge was certain the animal had died of strangulation.

In addition, the snow leopard had hardly shown itself to be the murderously efficient killer it was often portrayed to be. Only luck, and a grim ability to hang on, had prevented it from being dashed onto the rocks or taking a suicidal plunge into the river on the back of its panicked prey. One possible explanation was that the leopardess, compelled by the need to acquire food for her family, had risked an attack of doubtful outcome; the bharal she had eventually pulled down was at least three times her own weight.

A dangerous and difficult world, Trowbridge thought. Even for snow leopards in the wild.

His last view of the leopardess was that of a frosty gray shape reclining on a rock, her head moving slightly, observing them as they moved away. He took with him nine rolls of exposed film, a notebook filled with observations, and the certainty that he had finally found what he was looking for: the wild, untouched core of Lhakrinor, a place where animal life went on as it had for centuries. A place around which to build the park.

36

" 'Many evil-doers took vows not to take life and gave up such evils as hunting, and we made reserves where animals might not be killed in the mountains around. In short up to this present day the very name of hunting and the like is unknown in the district.' "

The lama looked up keenly at Trowbridge from the block-printed page. "So you see, your idea is not new. We have tried for centuries to stop the people from killing animals."

He closed the book carefully, and buckled it shut with its ancient, frail straps. "However, I am afraid your plan would require more change among the people in a single generation than we have seen in a hundred. I admire your idea, but we have been doing things in Lhakri-nor in the same way for a very long time."

"Lama, I have been doing some reading among the religious texts which Jigme has at his house. Would you object if I recited a few lines?"

"Of course not! All recitation of religious texts brings enlightenment to he who recites, and virtue to those who listen."

Trowbridge began: " 'At dusk a strong wind arose, and at dawn a man appeared to me showing a respectful manner. He was dressed in pure white clothes, with a turban of white silk and wearing jewelry. "If you go round the mountains today," he said, "no harm will come from snow and rain." Then he disappeared. It was the time of the heavy summer rains, and in accordance with the morning's prophecy, the sky was clear and we saw sights unseen before. . . .' "

"This is from the Biography of Lama Religious Protector Glorious and Good!" the lama exclaimed. "Written by Lama Merit Intellect in the Year of the Male Wood Horse, over four hundred years ago! Did you read this yourself?"

"With Jigme's help."

"You are a scholar after all! And now I must discover your purpose in reciting this to me."

The lama, bringing his hands together before his face and narrowing his eyes, was silent for several moments. "'It was the time of the heavy summer rains . . .'" he said finally. "You recited this passage to remind me that there have been no heavy rains this summer, or for many summers past. Your point is that things have changed in Lhakrinor since the Year of the Male Wood Horse. That we must change also."

The lama stood abruptly and moved, leaning on his wooden cane, out onto the balcony. Trowbridge followed him. With his crippled knee pressed against the low parapet of stone at the balcony edge, the lama stood looking out at the treeless, shimmering slopes.

Meditatively, he said, "I remember my grandfather telling me a story I could hardly believe. When he was a young man, and was required to go out and round up the yaks, it was difficult to find them because they hid in the forests. The land was filled with so many trees, then, that trees were a nuisance."

The lama turned to face Trowbridge. "You are right, of course. And yet I feel a powerful reluctance. Is it simply an old lama's fear of change? A fear that he will wake up one day and not recognize the place in which he finds himself?"

"There will be change, lama. But there will also be preservation of what exists. Without some change, and soon, all that you value will disappear. I've seen it happen other places."

The lama no longer appeared to be listening. Once again he stared across the void which separated Gelingdo from the slopes above Trang.

" '. . . the sky was clear,' " he repeated, " 'and we saw sights unseen before.' "

There was a lengthy silence. Trowbridge could hear the sound of dripping water somewhere. The success or failure of the park depended, very probably, on what the lama said next.

The lama brought his hands together with a sudden clap, and blew a breath of air vigorously from his lungs, as if expelling bad spirits. This time, when he turned, his expression was serene.

"Perhaps it is time, in Lhakrinor, for sights unseen before. Very well, your project has my blessings. Now, since you seem to have accomplished what you came for, will you make the tea?"

Feeling a quiet elation, Trowbridge went inside and prepared two cups of salty yak-butter tea; one in the chipped ceramic cup, the other in the lama's skull cup. He brought the tea to the lama, who was sitting now on the stone parapet. The lama sipped it gingerly. Trowbridge sat near him on a stool and asked, "Lama, have you had another visitor recently? One who wasn't from Lhakrinor?"

The lama nodded. "I have," he said. "A pilgrim from India, who came last year as well. It seems he is drawn irresistibly to the holiness of Torma Mountain."

There was more than a hint of sarcasm in the lama's voice.

"Last year he merely paid his respects, as was proper. Since then he has clearly gained greatly in wisdom—he now wishes to instruct me in a lama's proper behavior! He suggested I should concern myself solely with my little monastery, and ignore whatever else I might see."

"That almost sounds like a threat."

The lama tipped his head, and looked at Trowbridge. "A threat? Why would anyone wish to harm an old lama who lives on parched barley, air, and tea, and who can hardly move from one small room of his lonely monastery to another? In truth, Mr. Trowbridge, I am more interested in whether you have come across any sign of the lost *chorten* I told you about, and the sacred text."

"I kept a close eye out when I moved about the mountain, but I saw nothing," Trowbridge said. "My friends also looked."

The lama shook his head. "Perhaps it does not exist," he said. Then he set down his skull cup, stood with difficulty, and moved slowly along the balcony's low edge to the place where it disappeared into rough stone. "And yet," he said, looking up at the mountain, "the notation in the text is quite specific: 'High on the slopes of the mountain, in a hidden valley, he built a *chorten*, and within it he placed the sacred text. . . .'"

"Is it possible, lama, that this *chorten* is higher on the mountain than any of the trails lead?"

"Anything is possible," the lama said, turning impassively back to Trowbridge. "Now, what about your search for this animal whose horns are atop Trang monastery, this shou you told me about? Has it been more fruitful than mine for this foolish *chorten*?"

"No."

The lama sighed. "The lot of true scholars, it seems, is to do more searching than discovering."

He placed his hands on the stone balcony, leaned forward, cleared his throat enthusiastically and spit out into empty space.

"Yak-butter tea," he explained. "I always have to spit afterward."

37

He swung happily down the steep trail. With the lama behind the project, and with Jigme and the others behind the idea as well, he should be able to convince the villagers to cooperate. Of course there was still Drokma to deal with—and this business with Krishna hanging in the air—but he felt convinced, for the first time, that the park was going to happen.

Within a couple of weeks the field study would be completed and he would be on his way to the lowlands. There would be a winter's work in Kathmandu and New York, drawing up a formal proposal, arranging finances, and enlisting the support of the University and the various government bureaucracies; next spring, when the snow melted and the passes were clear, he would return and set up the park. And only a few weeks ago he'd sat on these slopes explaining to Nima why the idea of a park probably wouldn't work.

He wondered, briefly and not for the first time, what would happen to him and Nima when they left Lhakrinor.

Across the valley and below him, on the slopes above Trang, he saw movement. A small herd of bharal. He dropped to one knee, pulled out the binoculars, and focused on the animals. Two females and two yearlings, looking decidedly skittish; preliminary evidence, perhaps, of the approaching rut, a time when the herds became more fluid, when the male bachelor herd began to break up and associate with the females.

He continued to stare intently through the lenses, through the crystalline air of Trang, watching the animals scatter on a diagonal across the slope, stopping briefly to graze, raising their heads, moving along again. They looked itchy, oddly spooked. Something about the way they moved inspired a distinct feeling of uneasiness in him. It wasn't precisely rut behavior. What did it remind him of?

They were moving like animals accustomed to being hunted. Hunted not by natural predators, but by man.

Something reared abruptly into his field of vision. Great blurry shapes, practically on top of him. Startled, he lowered the binoculars. Standing in the trail before him was a pair of familiar figures, looking as shocked as he no doubt did himself.

Slowly, he rose to his feet.

Krishna Sanwal was first to recover his composure.

"Mr. Trowbridge!"

Krishna's elegantly accented English rang strangely in these sur-roundings. His tone was as smooth, self-deprecating, and unreadable as ever, although physically he looked a bit the worse for wear.

"Krishna," he said slowly.

"Naraka, this is the gentleman whose company brightened my lonely travels for a few days on the way to Lhakrinor. Mr. Trowbridge, you know my compatriot already, do you not? I'm afraid the two of you met under less than ideal circumstances in Pokhara. A terrible misunderstanding, that."

Naraka bared his teeth in an insolent greeting. Slung over his shoulders was the body of a recently killed bharal. Fresh blood ran down his collarbone and onto his dingy white clothing. The bharal's tongue lolled, and its eyes were milky.

"I've seen your friend more recently than that," Trowbridge said coldly. "Sprawled on his face at midnight on an icy trail, looking frightened enough to shit his pants."

Naraka's eyes widened slightly, gleaming with surprise and hatred.

"You were there. I wish I had known."

"I see that you two still do not get along," Krishna said regretfully. "Perhaps that is not surprising, since you, Mr. Trowbridge, have gotten the better of my assistant here on two occasions now. Naraka, perhaps you should leave us for a few minutes."

Naraka shrugged—no mean feat, with a hundred-and-twenty-pound bharal over his shoulders—and moved up the trail past Trow-bridge, deliberately shoving the carcass into him, forcing him to step aside. The animal's ears had been cut off; they hung on a bloody string, with a number of others, from Naraka's belt.

Naraka disappeared around a switchback in the trail. There was a muffled "thump" as the carcass was dropped beside the trail, and he found himself alone with Krishna.

"He's not a bad fellow, really," Krishna said, his tone wry, as if they were standing at a cocktail party discussing a colleague. "And he's very useful."

"I suppose, if one requires the services of a butcher. Listen, Krish-na, are you aware that these slopes are considered sacred? That the lama, and the people who live here, have chosen to leave these animals in peace?"

"Small sacrifices, Mr. Trowbridge, must sometimes be made in the name of a greater expediency."

Trowbridge studied him evenly. "Why don't you tell me about that greater expediency."

"I suppose I do owe you an explanation."

"Considering that your assistant tried to kill me, I'd say that's an understatement."

"To kill you? No, Mr. Trowbridge, he didn't try to kill you, exactly. He did undertake to delay, and perhaps to *discourage* you from leaving Pokhara. But it was at my instruction, with the goal of saving you wasted time and effort. There was some concern that you might unwittingly damage . . . well, a delicate operation. An operation being conducted jointly by the Nepali and Indian governments."

Trowbridge said skeptically, "You're here with the blessings of the Nepali government?"

"If I were not," Krishna said, "I would risk damaging India-Nepali relations, wouldn't I, Mr. Trowbridge?"

Trowbridge considered this. If it were true, why hadn't Vikram known about it?

"I hate to be rude, Krishna, but I don't believe you."

"Skepticism, especially in a scientist, is a virtue. But so is an open mind. Allow me to explain. As far as my own person is concerned, you were quite right when you guessed that I was a soldier. And of course I am not retired, but on active duty. A lieutenant colonel in the Air Force, detached—obviously—from my regular duties."

"And this 'delicate operation'?"

"I am here, Mr. Trowbridge, to do the preliminary work toward establishing a small garrison of soldiers. A trip-wire garrison, if you will."

"In *Lhakrinor*?"

"Lhakrinor is a sensitive border region, Mr. Trowbridge, and China's expansionary aims are well known. We were attacked once before, if you recall your history. Thirty years ago the Chinese defeated us quite badly in our northwestern mountains, the Aksai Chin. The People's Liberation Army slaughtered a large number of ill-prepared Indian soldiers and appropriated hundreds of square miles of Indian soil. They still have this territory today! This happened because the Indian military forces were taken by surprise. We are determined never to let the same thing happen here."

"Krishna, that's idiotic—the Chinese don't want Lhakrinor. There's nothing here in a political sense worth conquering. And they're still having trouble digesting Tibet. The last thing they need is another restive population to manage."

Krishna said serenely, "More highly placed individuals than myself have concluded that Chinese aggression is a clear and present danger. Individuals, I remind you, in both the Indian and Nepali governments."

"Sorry, but it doesn't wash. The Nepali government threw your soldiers out years ago. They would hardly invite them back now."

"Naturally, the Nepali government cannot *publicly* support Indian soldiers on its soil. That is why the operation is going forward under such secrecy."

Krishna paused. "If you have any doubts about the Nepali government's cooperation, you may refer yourself to the difficulties you had with the police chief in Jorkhang. He is one of us. It is only because you are so capable and persistent—and lucky—that he failed. The fact that this meddlesome government official—Vikram was his name, I believe—intervened and allowed you to continue simply demonstrates that not everyone can be privy to all government operations! Unfortunately, he did not really do you a favor—you have wasted a good deal of time here."

"How do you know about Vikram?"

"Because I passed through Jorkhang behind you, of course."

"And you passed through Bragamo ahead of us, and arranged for a police escort to Jorkhang. Which you knew would be necessary because you'd been eavesdropping on me and my English friend."

Krishna shrugged. "This sort of thing is my business."

Trowbridge felt his impatience rise. "Make it simple, Krishna. What's the real purpose of the garrison?"

"The Nepalis do not wish to let the roof collapse and have Chinese soldiers falling into the house. An Indian garrison here in Lhakrinor would discourage adventurousness on the part of the Chinese, because they know that if Indian soldiers were fired upon, it would be full-scale war. Quite soon now there will be Indian soldiers stationed here, for the protection of the Nepalis—in precisely the fashion your country has soldiers in Europe."

"You're performing a public service, then."

"You are cynical. Naturally we are also concerned about Chinese soldiers achieving a closer proximity to our own border."

Trowbridge looked across the valley, remembering what the Soviet soldiers garrisoned in Mongolia had done to the wildlife there.

"You're aware of what I'm doing here in Lhakrinor," he said. "There's no way a garrison of soldiers and a wildlife park can exist side by side."

"Regrettably, no. But Nepal is a large country, Mr. Trowbridge. A park could be put any number of places! And, while I am not a biological expert, it seems to me that this area is rather depleted anyway."

Trowbridge said nothing. With bitter irony he realized that the two of them had come to Lhakrinor for essentially the same purpose—to do a feasibility study for their respective projects. Assuming, that is, that Krishna was telling the truth.

Krishna continued, "No, I am afraid that Lhakrinor has a higher destiny than becoming a park for wild animals. Look at these barren slopes, Mr. Trowbridge . . . Lhakrinor is *dying*. Surely you can see that more clearly than anyone! It has no reason for existence except as a political—and military—outpost."

"And the people who live here?"

Krishna shrugged. "Once again, small sacrifices must sometimes be made. At any rate, they will have jobs working for the soldiers, so they can hardly complain."

Trowbridge thought of the peaceful rhythms of village life in Jaramar, and considered what would happen if a couple of thousand Hindu soldiers were garrisoned here—soldiers who would loathe the climate and the elevation, shoot the animals for target practice and for meat, and despise the "godless" Buddhists. Lhakrinor, for all intents and purposes, would cease to exist.

Krishna continued. "You must realize that I have compromised security to reveal this to you, Mr. Trowbridge. But I felt you were owed a complete explanation. Surely, under the circumstances, you will understand and cooperate."

"Explain 'cooperate.' "

"It is quite simple. First, you say absolutely *nothing* to anyone—including this Vikram fellow—about having seen or talked to me. Beyond that, you finish your study, return to Kathmandu, report that the area is unsuitable for a national park, and go on your way."

"And if I choose not to cooperate?"

"I would rather not state the case in threatening terms. But if you oppose us, Mr. Trowbridge, you will never work in the developing world again. India is the largest member of the nonaligned movement, and the most influential. We will 'expose' you as a CIA operative—and

I promise you, we know how to generate very convincing evidence for that sort of charge. Your career will effectively be finished, unless you wish to study the ducks in Central Park."

Krishna paused, then said, "I implore you to weigh carefully the worth of an entire career—a career of doing good for a cause in which we both believe—against a foolish gesture. Do not let the loss of a single battle destroy your ability to carry on the war."

Krishna bent down and picked up what looked like a white stone. He studied it for a moment, then looked up.

"I have lost a few battles of my own, Mr. Trowbridge, during the course of my career. I have found that one must take the long view."

Casually, Krishna tossed the stone in Trowbridge's direction. He caught it and held it in the palm of his hand. It was a fossil; the delicate white whorls of a prehistoric trilobite swirled amid the fine veins of an ancient leaf. The fossil had a fine, satisfying weight in his hand.

"As I am sure you know, these mountains were once under water," Krishna said. "Then the Indian subcontinent crashed up into the belly of Asia, and pushed them up into the sunlight. I take a great risk, I realize, in lecturing a scholar like yourself. But my point is simple: Certain forces are simply too great to be resisted. This is one."

"It looks to me as if the Indian subcontinent is still crashing into Asia," Trowbridge said, unable to keep the bitterness out of his voice.

A voice came from above them, where Naraka had reappeared at a bend in the trail. "Krishna—" he began.

"I have told you before that you will address me as 'Colonel,' " Krishna interrupted coldly.

Sullenly, Naraka muttered, "I am not a soldier."

"That is painfully obvious. But for the moment you are being paid as a soldier. To the extent of your abilities, you will behave as one."

In a lowered voice, Krishna said to Trowbridge, "Unorthodox operations sometimes call for unorthodox operatives. Well, Mr. Trowbridge, can I count on you to behave as a professional in this matter? There is one more issue I forgot to mention—a 'sweetener,' if you will. Once you have abandoned the idea of a national park in Lhakrinor, we will exert our considerable influence to help you establish a similar park somewhere else in Nepal. Or, for that matter, in India."

"And you may build a big house," Naraka called out in a salacious voice, "and install the Palace whore, and visit her when you are not watching your filthy animals."

Trowbridge threw the fossil with instinctive aim. It clipped Naraka square in the forehead and dropped him in the trail. With a bellow of rage Naraka sat up, blood running into his eyes, and pointed his rifle at Trowbridge.

"Naraka!"

The barrel of Krishna's pistol was pointed at his assistant's belly.

"Put the gun down."

Naraka looked malevolently at Krishna, as if he were considering shooting him instead. Then, slowly lowering the rifle, he looked at Trowbridge.

"I am forbidden to kill you. But I will find *her*, and make her wish she had never been born. That will be my gift to both of you."

"That's enough," Krishna said sharply. Then he said to Trowbridge, his voice apologetic, "I'm afraid my assistant carries a grudge from the incident in Pokhara. In addition, he seems to feel that this young woman has erred in her actions, and deserves punishment. His idea of an appropriate punishment for her is, I am afraid, mixed up rather morbidly with his own satisfaction."

Krishna let that pleasant thought sink in, then added casually, "Perhaps this is a reason for you to finish your study and leave Lhakrinor somewhat sooner than planned. Do I have an answer?"

"Yes. The hell with you, and your butcher assistant, and your tripwire garrison."

Krishna's jaw tightened.

"I choose not to take that as your final answer, Mr. Trowbridge. You would do well to reconsider when your head is clearer."

They stared at each other a moment. Then Trowbridge stepped around Krishna and walked down the trail, feeling an itch in the small of his back, the place where he would receive a bullet if Naraka changed his mind and pulled the trigger.

Silence, however, reigned behind him. It was not until he reached the river that it occurred to him to wonder where Krishna and Naraka had been going. They had been traveling *up* the trail. There was nothing in that direction but cliffs.

PART 3

38

Trowbridge stood in the doorway of the house, looking out at the high white horizon, the pristine, brutal ring of mountains which surrounded Lhakrinor. A cold, late-afternoon wind had come up and was whining quietly around the corners of the house. Little eddies of air moved through the room, shifting the pages of notes and hand-drawn maps spread out on the table.

"So what do we do?" Dorje asked.

Trowbridge turned back to Dorje and Nima, who sat by the fire, looking at him with concerned faces. Norbu had disappeared sometime during the morning without telling them where he was going. It was not unusual for Norbu to go off alone; still, Trowbridge felt uneasy at the unexplained absence.

"We wind up the study as quickly as we can. Beyond that, I don't know."

"What about the place north of Torma Mountain?" Nima asked.

This was the last blank spot on the map—and extremely promising snow leopard terrain. The two of them had planned to explore it together just before leaving, when it wouldn't matter any more that Drokma had forbidden it.

"We can't risk it," he said. "Not with Krishna and Naraka there."

Nima kept her expression even, but he could read her disappointment, and it only intensified his own. He longed, one more time, to experience the solitude and silence of the wildest reaches of Lhakrinor. And he'd been telling himself that somehow, alone with Nima on the north side of Torma Mountain, the two of them might work out what they would be to each other once they were flung back into civilization.

Now everything was happening too fast. He needed more time in Lhakrinor, and he needed more time alone with Nima, and it didn't look as if he would have either one.

Especially not with the *shikari's* sadistic threat against Nima still ringing in his ears.

He turned and looked out the doorway again. The wind was rising, and chilly; he felt his eyes tear slightly in the cold. He wondered, as he had a dozen times since talking with Krishna, whether Vikram would be able to put a stop to the trip-wire garrison if he learned about it in time. This was far from certain; Trowbridge had no way of judging how influential Vikram might be within the government—or of how much momentum the plan had already developed.

The only thing he could be reasonably certain of—if he spoke to Vikram—was that Krishna would follow through on his threat to make sure Trowbridge never worked in the developing world again.

On the other hand, if he cooperated with Krishna—kept his mouth shut and recommended against the establishment of the park—he would be assisting in the destruction of one of the most fragile and yet still preservable habitats he'd ever seen, and destroying the lives of people he had come to like and admire.

There were no good answers, and, at the moment, nothing to be done. They would wrap up the study and get ready to leave. And then, somewhere between here and Jorkhang, he would choose between helping Lhakrinor—in all likelihood, a lost cause anyway—and his ability to go on working.

It was well after midnight when Norbu returned to the house. He moved straight to the dwindling fire, saying nothing, and crouched beside it, warming his hands. Trowbridge, who'd been sitting up working on notes, handed him a cup of tea and said, "Well?"

"I went to Drokma's," Norbu said.

Trowbridge's heart sank. The last thing he needed now was for Norbu to have done something reckless.

Norbu, reading the expression on his face, shook his head.

"I never even spoke to him. There were three bandits at his house. Gorchoks—I could tell from the saddles and the rifle scabbards of their horses tied up out front. I hid, and waited all afternoon for them to leave. Instead, at dusk, two more rode up, tying their horses next to the others, and went into the house carrying their red-barreled rifles.

When it grew dark I slipped up beneath the window to listen. Drokma was paying the Gorchoks in gold—quite a bit of gold, from the clink of coins. Then Drokma asked, quite clearly, how long it would be before the others arrived.

"I realized that if more bandits rode up out of the darkness I would be in trouble, so I left. But I saw something interesting when I turned in the darkness, fifty feet from the house, for a final look in Drokma's window. There was a radio transceiver there. A modern one, on a table against the wall."

"Jesus," Trowbridge said.

Quickly, he told Norbu about meeting Krishna, and the plan for the garrison.

"The strange thing," he said, "is that Krishna brought a radio—maybe two radios—up here last year. It looks as if Drokma's either stealing from Krishna or working for him."

"Knowing Drokma," Norbu said, "it could be both."

The following morning a messenger arrived. A villager from north of Narling, who had been passing through Trang on his way south. The villager said that a *gyami* man named Krishna Sanwal had paid him to deliver a message to Trowbridge in exactly these words: That he, Krishna, and his assistant were leaving Lhakrinor. That he thanked Trowbridge once again for his enjoyable company in the foothills of the Himalayas. And that he wished Trowbridge wisdom, prudence, and a long and productive career.

39

Two days later, in the earliest pink light of sunrise, he and Nima closed the door of the house behind them and set out toward Torma Mountain. They went north from Jaramar, making roughly the same circle, in reverse, that he'd made when he followed the two snow leopards seven weeks earlier.

At sunset they crossed the river, stripping naked and holding their packs above their heads; the water, as before, was icy cold, but it served as a much-needed bath after a hard day of walking. On the far beach they shivered themselves dry, then dressed in clean clothing and made camp.

After dinner, sitting beside a small fire before the tent, Trowbridge unlaced Nima's boots, pulled them off, and began rubbing her feet. He found this curiously relaxing, almost as if he were rubbing the soreness out of his own feet rather than hers. He glanced up at her, and saw to his surprise that she looked puzzled, almost upset.

"This ought to feel good," he said.

"It does," Nima said. "But it is not something I would expect a man to do for a woman. And it makes me think of something. Something about my husband."

"Want to tell me about it?"

"I'm not sure. It seems so far away from here."

"I could stop."

She shook her head. He finished rubbing her feet, then put her boots back on for her, leaving the laces loose, and went to his pack for the last small bottle of rum. They sat close to each other in silence, watching the fire, listening to the river go by in the darkness.

"I will tell you what I was thinking about," she said after several minutes. "One of the duties of a Hindu wife is to wash her husband's feet and legs in the evening, and to rub them with oil. When I knelt before my husband to do this I could hear his breathing, and smell the *rakshi* on his breath. At these times I remembered the yearly visit of the King. His grave, dignified face. The moment when he placed his head above my feet so I could not see them. Then the cool strange feeling of a gold coin sliding between my toes."

She paused. "When I was thirteen or fourteen," she said, "in the *che*, I came across some books of Tantrism."

She looked at him to see if he knew what she meant.

"The branch of Hinduism that views sexuality as a path to enlightenment."

She nodded. "In the books, there were pictures of gods and goddesses together. I was aroused by these books. Then, in another book, I found a picture of the goddess of Kathmandu—the goddess who was said to inhabit my body—as the Vajra *yogini*. It was different from other pictures I had seen of her, and I remember it very clearly: The goddess stands on one leg, a smoking skull in one hand and a white conch shell in the other. She looks confident and calm. Her breasts are round and very beautiful, and the cleft between her legs is displayed without shame.

"By the time I was twelve I had become skeptical that I was really inhabited by a goddess. But when I saw this picture I *wanted* it to be true—the thought of her within me gave me a feeling of strength. And I began to think about marriage. I saw it as an escape from the *che*, and I imagined, I suppose, that I would be married to someone like the King, someone who would be gentle, and handsome, and teach me of the things in the pictures."

She paused, gathering her thoughts. "As I said, it is a Hindu wife's duty to wash her husband's feet. It is also her duty to splash some of the water into her mouth. The idea is that a husband is so high above a wife that what is pollution for him is purification for her. To make this custom more pleasant, a wife usually brushes away most of the dirt before immersing her husband's feet, and takes only a small sip of the water.

"To punish me for not lying with him at night, my husband refused to let me brush away any dirt, and he made me drink all the water, which was very muddy. Then, in the morning, he would accuse me of polluting him with my seductive behavior, telling me I was worse than a whore."

In the darkness, deep in the bottom of this canyon, the sound of the river echoed quietly around them.

"In the village, I began to hear jokes that I was submissive to my husband in public, but not in private. He had complained to his friends, who were telling their wives. It was a very difficult time for me. The other women had told me—before they had come to dislike me—that when I had children my life would improve. But I could not bring myself to lie with my husband, and I was terrified of being tied to him forever because of a child."

"Could you have gone back to your parents?"

Nima shook her head. "If a marriage does not succeed it is considered the wife's fault, which reflects badly on the parents. And in truth, I had little to complain about. One woman in the village was beaten to death by her husband because her family had been poor and her dowry small. The husband told the police she had died falling down the stairs. The police said that young wives were careless and stupid, and that falling down stairs was a common occurrence. Soon afterward, the man married a younger wife, with a larger dowry."

The fire had burned down; he could no longer see her face.

"Perhaps I am lucky, the way it all ended. One day my mother-in-law told me to fetch some things from the *bhandar*—the locked store-room—to which only she had a key. I refused, knowing she would accuse me of stealing something. She flew into a rage and left the house, leaving the key in an obvious place by the door. When darkness fell she had not returned, and I was alone with my husband, who was very drunk, and pressuring me more than usual because of his moth-er's absence. I was almost glad to hear her come home—until she burst into the house cursing me, accusing me loudly of having stolen a brass pot, saying she had told the whole village of the theft.

"For the first time I spoke back to her. I told her she was lying, that if the pot was gone *she* had taken it. She began screaming at my hus-band that I was a worthless wife. I began screaming at them both that my husband was a weakling, that he was worse than a Jumla Brah-man—these are Brahmans who suck their mother's breast at their mar-riage ceremony. The two of them fell upon me and beat me, and then my husband dragged me to our sleeping area, and I knew nothing would stop him from having his revenge."

Nima shrugged. "He felt righteous in what he was doing, and fell asleep immediately afterward. When I pushed him off me he did not even wake up. I felt like a dead person, but at least things were clear to me. If I were going to have a child from what had happened, then my fate was to stay in the village. If I were *not* going to have a child, then my fate lay elsewhere.

"Months before, my friend the Peace Corps worker had slipped a pamphlet into a book he loaned me—he was not like you, he was embarrassed to talk about such things—explaining on which days the marriage bed is likely to make a child. My husband had forced me on the last of those days. In the two weeks that followed my husband avoided me, and my mother-in-law said nothing more about the brass pot; I think it frightened them to see a *kumari* so badly bruised. When my monthly blood came, I dug up the money I had hidden—the money my mother had given me on the day of my marriage—and ran away."

Lying on his belly, he lit a candle and set it into the sand before the open tent flaps. They'd helped each other out of their clothes before climbing in; he wasn't sure if she would want to make love, after the story she had just told him, but in some fashion he didn't care. It was enough to be here.

He watched the candle flicker for a moment, listening to the river, then rolled over onto his back. Without a word she moved on top of him, a knee on either side, bending forward so that her forehead rested on his chest. He kissed the top of her head, and she raised her face to his, her expression intent and peaceful in the flickering candlelight.

Afterward, as they lay shoulder to shoulder in the small tent, he asked her, "What did you learn from the witch that day?"

"I learned," she said quietly, "that I can choose what goddess I want to inhabit me."

They spent most of the morning working their way up a series of frighteningly difficult ledges. Trowbridge was discouraged by the terrain, which was so steep and rocky that even bharal would have a hard time finding sustenance. He said nothing to Nima, but realized if this endless, ledge-cut slope didn't open out soon they would have difficulty even finding a place to camp.

Finally, two hours after lunch, they crested a steep ridge, dipping down into a valley which had been invisible from below. They were above the snow line now; at the lowest point of the valley was a small lake half-covered in pale green ice. They set up camp in a flat space not far from the lake. Trowbridge was ready to call it a day, but Nima insisted they make use of the remaining few hours of light, and they continued climbing.

An hour before dusk, sitting on a frozen ledge, Trowbridge exclaimed in quiet exultation.

"There!"

He handed Nima the scope, pointing out the place where the leopard lay atop a large snow-dusted boulder, surveying the valley with a calm stare.

"Where?" she asked intently, scanning the far side of the valley with her naked eyes.

"There. You'll need the scope."

"Is it the one you saw before?"

"I'm not sure yet."

Nima handed the scope back to him.

"Decide," she said firmly. "If it disappears while I am watching we will not know whether to count it as another animal or not."

He grinned. "You're getting even more professional than I am."

He focused carefully, studying the animal's markings, comparing them, mentally, with the sketches he had made earlier in the summer.

Then, as the leopard turned its head, he saw that it had a torn ear.

"No," he said. "This is a new one. Looks like a young male."

"Now let me look," Nima said.

She peered through the scope.

"I still cannot see anything."

"On top of that boulder, above the diagonal cut in the slope."

A moment later she exclaimed softly.

"His fur is so thick and beautiful! But his ear is torn. How did that happen?"

"Hard to say. Maybe in a fight, or a hunt."

Or maybe, thought Trowbridge, playing a bit too roughly with a larger leopard, one with a slit paw.

"If you look about a hundred yards down the slope," he said, "you'll see rather less than half a bharal, slightly frozen. This leopard made a kill a couple of days ago."

He took his camera from his daypack, fastened on the telephoto, and began shooting, although the valley was too deeply in shadow for good shots. The leopard looked calm and healthy aside from his torn ear, and glanced at them only occasionally. Eventually it stood, stretched, and began descending, a pale shape against the dark slope, toward his kill.

"We need to get moving," Trowbridge said reluctantly, putting away the camera, "or we won't make it back to camp before dark."

They stood up stiffly on the ledge. Trowbridge breathed the thin air deep into his lungs, looking out across a high ridge. There were more leopards out there, he told himself as they started down. He was sure of it.

In the last light, in a little valley lying parallel to the one in which they were camped, they came across a pair of antlers, jammed by some unknown hand into a crevice in an ice-covered rock.

Nima looked at the antlers, then at Trowbridge.

"Shou?" she asked.

Trowbridge nodded. He reached up, grasped the antlers, and pulled them from the rock. They came out with a grating sound and a trickle of dusty ice crystals.

"How old are they?" Nima asked.

He examined them silently, then opened his pocket knife and cut a notch in the base.

"I don't know," he said finally. "They're not exactly fresh—but I'd say they've been here for years, not decades."

"And how long is the shou supposed to have been extinct?"

"Decades."

This shou had lived and died sometime in the recent past. Maybe in this valley—or maybe in Tibet, or in the coniferous forests of Bhutan, where the animal had last been seen alive. Had someone carried these antlers hundreds of miles, only to jam them into a crack in a rock?

The stillness around them was formidable, and provided no answers. Twenty miles to the northeast, the high peaks of the Thongsa Himal shattered the horizon in a black-and-white scrawl. Could there be shou up there right now? Could they have adapted, somehow, to an existence in this relatively barren landscape? Biologically, it was not impossible. Forced out of its native habitat, an animal species could slowly transform its habits and even its physical makeup to enhance its survival. The ancestors of bharal—an animal which now lived in sizable groupings on the open slopes, depending on herd behavior and fleetness of foot to survive—had once lived in small family units in the primeval forest, surviving by stealth and stillness.

He studied the antlers a moment longer. Then he reached up, set the base of the antlers against the crevice, and shoved them back into place.

If he'd needed any more evidence that Lhakrinor was worth saving, he had it now.

"Aren't you taking them?" Nima asked.

"No," he said, hearing the conviction in his own voice. "I'm coming back for them."

In the thin light of morning, before the sun came over the mountains, they pulled their mats and sleeping bags out of the tent and made love with an intensity that bordered on desperation. Afterward they flung the bags away and lay in silence under the immensity of the sky, covered with a sheen of sweat as the icy morning air played across their bodies. To the south the sky was clear and vast; to the north, in the direction of Tibet, it was impenetrable with dark clouds.

"We'll be leaving in less than a week," he said.

She said nothing.

He sat up on one elbow. "I want you to stay with me," he said. "When we get out of the mountains."

There was a long silence. Then she took a deep breath, and said, "We should not talk about it."

"Why not?"

"I am married."

"You can get a divorce."

"I have decided to try. But I do not want to depend on anyone else again in my life—not even you. And we do not know how we will feel about each other once we are out of the mountains."

He was about to say all he was asking was that they give it a try, when he heard something. At first he couldn't place the sound, which was distant and strangely regular. Nima heard it too; she sat up straight on their bed of sleeping bags, listening. It had been months since either of them had heard anything but people's voices, the sounds of wind and water moving over the earth, the crush of footsteps and the crackle of a fire—sounds which rose and fell in natural and familiar rhythms.

What they were hearing now was the sound of an engine.

He listened in disbelief as the sound grew louder. It was the regular hissing drone of a small plane. He scanned the sky. There was nothing to the south, where the atmosphere was clear, and he doubted an airplane could come from that direction, anyway—the mountains were too high, and the distances too great.

It had to be from the north, from Tibet. Which meant that he was hearing the sound of a light plane of the Chinese military. A plane which was violating a forbidden border.

The sound became nearer, more specific. Still, he saw nothing in the opaque northern sky.

There's no place in Lhakrinor for a plane to land, he reasoned. Which leaves two possibilities: reconnaissance, and the dropping of supplies. But reconnaissance in Lhakrinor, in weather like this? And if dropping supplies, to whom?

The hissing drone slowed to a putter. There was a sudden flash in the heavy sky to the north: a plane's underbelly, high above the upper reaches of Torma Mountain. As they watched, a white shape fluttered away from the plane, filled, swayed unnaturally in the sky. Then the cloud cover shifted, the plane altered course, and both shapes were gone. The lowered sky yielded nothing more; the sound of the engine grew harsh and high and dwindled slowly into silence.

40

Trowbridge paused at the top of the ridge and looked back down at the house. A wisp of smoke from the breakfast fire curled up from a hole in the roof. Nima would be sitting before that fire, finishing a second cup of tea, working on her notes; later she would begin packing in preparation for their departure.

A pang of loneliness struck him hard, and he looked at Norbu.

"Four hours each way?"

Norbu nodded. Their plan was to try to reach Tingri by noon, speak to Drokma, and be back before dark. Trowbridge still had doubts about Norbu coming along—but he knew it might be dangerous to go alone, and figured he might be able to diffuse a confrontation between Norbu and Drokma if one developed.

They set off quickly along the ridge. There was no longer any question in his mind that when they passed through Jorkhang he would tell Vikram what he knew. And then help Vikram, if possible, try to stop the garrison. He would take the consequences, whatever they turned out to be.

At the moment, however, none of what was happening in Lhakrinor made sense—not Krishna's trip-wire garrison, Drokma and his Gorchok bandits, or a plane flying in from Chinese-occupied Tibet. It was possible that Vikram could put these contradictions and mysteries together into a sensible whole, but Trowbridge needed to provide as many puzzle pieces as he could.

Drokma was the only person in Lhakrinor who might be able to help. Whether he could be persuaded to do so, of course, was a different matter.

They walked hard for nearly three hours, each preoccupied with his own thoughts. At the crossroads where the main Robshi trail joined the track leading southwest to the passes they met a villager from Tingri, sitting on his *doka* beside a *mani* wall, having an early lunch of cold *tsampa* and barley cakes.

"You will not find Drokma in Tingri," he told them. "He left this morning on his donkey. I saw him pass through the village with full saddlebags."

"Going where?" Norbu asked.

The villager looked amused and somewhat bitter. "Our headman rarely explains his comings and goings. But he was traveling ahead of me on this trail," he said, motioning the way he had come, "and I did not pass him along the way. So if you did not see him either. . ."

He gestured at the narrow track, the route Nima and the others had taken when they entered Lhakrinor in the spring. Norbu took a few steps along it, knelt, studied the fine dust, then looked up at Trowbridge and nodded.

Half an hour along the trail they came across Drokma's donkey lying beside the track. Its eyes were open, its expression oddly peaceful. It had been killed by a single bullet which had entered its head just behind the ear. Their first thought was that the animal had broken a leg and been shot by Drokma to put it out of its misery.

"The bullet was fired from a good distance away, and from off to one side," Norbu said, examining the edges of the wound. He sat back on his heels and looked meaningfully at Trowbridge. "And there are no other injuries."

"The donkey was shot out from under him."

"It would seem so."

Trowbridge noticed that the saddlebags were gone, then looked more closely at Drokma's saddle. The intricate turquoise ornaments had been sliced cleanly, almost surgically, from the leather.

Someone, he thought, used a very sharp knife to do that.

Norbu was studying the ground a few meters off the trail. "I think Drokma planned to flee Lhakrinor," he said. "He is carrying the saddlebags now, and they are heavy."

"And someone is following him," Trowbridge said.

The two sets of tracks led them steadily upward into the mountains which loomed over the western side of the Robshi Valley. The twin trail was not difficult to follow, and became even easier once they reached the snow line.

Drokma was tiring; in one place they saw a depression in the snow where he had fallen, struggled to his feet, and carried on. Beside these irregular tracks those of the pursuer continued with an ominous consistency. Trowbridge began to sense some of the desperation Drokma must have felt at that inexorable progress behind him.

A half mile farther along it looked as if the pursuer had stopped and crouched. Norbu scanned the area, then stepped off the trail. He found a tiny opening at an angle in the smooth snow, something like the burrow of a large insect. Lying down, he buried his arm up to the shoulder. Trowbridge could see his shoulder muscles working as he felt around in the snow.

"It must be here," he grunted.

A moment later a triumphant look crossed his face. He worked a little longer, pulled his arm out, stood, brushed the snow off himself, and dropped something cold and hard into Trowbridge's hand.

Trowbridge rubbed the dirt from a small-caliber bullet, examining it closely.

"Drokma's pistol?"

"I think so," Norbu said.

"If he's close enough to fire at his pursuer with a handgun, why isn't that person firing back with his rifle?"

"I do not know," Norbu said. He looked at the tracks of the pursuer, which continued steadily onward, and shook his head. "An hour ago, I was tracking my father's enemy, possibly to kill him. Now I wonder if I am tracking my father's friend—a man who is being pursued like an animal—in order to help him."

They crossed a snow bridge over a deep crevasse and continued up into a gravel-and-ice moraine. There, at the base of a small glacier, they found the saddlebags.

The bags lay open, surrounded by an odd profusion of belongings: a set of blackened cooking utensils, a heavy woolen sweater, a bag of dried lentils, some yak butter in a leather bladder, a twist of small brown onions. The sharp smell of the onions struck their nostrils in the crisp air.

"Drokma's getting desperate," Trowbridge said. "He must have taken out what he thought was most important and left the rest."

"I don't think so," Norbu said, indicating the marks in the snow around the saddlebags. "He dropped the bags without stopping. It is the pursuer who looked through the contents, not Drokma."

Trowbridge squatted for a closer look at the items on the ground. In the folds of a dingy blanket was a small bundle—hardly larger than his fist—wrapped in an old striped cloth. He moved it aside, and heard a sharp intake of breath from Norbu, who knelt beside him, picked up the bundle, and held it a moment before he began to unwrap it.

Trowbridge saw first a glint of tarnished gold, then the unmistakable blue of lapis lazuli. A moment later Norbu held in both hands a small, perfect dragon, glaring fiercely out at the snowy world. Proof, after seventeen years, that Drokma was responsible for his father's death.

"Maybe we shouldn't go on," Trowbridge said quietly.

Norbu looked up at him quickly.

"I know the story," Trowbridge said. "Jigme told me."

Norbu looked back down at the dragon, then picked up the cloth, rewrapped it, and tucked it in his shirt.

"We should go on," he said.

Beyond the moraine, in the lowest part of a silent, snow-filled depression between two ridges, they came across something in the snow. They moved toward it in a slow, wary silence, then stopped. Trowbridge's stomach rebelled at the sight and he looked away.

There was no sound. No movement or life in the valley. Except for what lay before them, he and Norbu could have been alone on another planet. He took a deep breath and forced himself to look back at the thing in the snow that passed for a human being.

A handgun and a pile of clothing lay beside the corpse, which was naked not only of clothing, but of skin. Whoever had removed the life from this body had also gone to great efforts to remove, carefully and professionally, most of the epidermis. Raw expanses of bright flesh were exposed, and strings of whitish tendon. Bone protruded at the elbows and at the rib cage where the belly widened. One knee was a nauseating mess of splintered bone and cartilage, shattered by a single bullet. A bullet intended, no doubt, to bring the victim down but leave him alive for what would follow.

The only skin remaining on the body was on the face—unquestionably Drokma's—and on his hands and feet, where the ropes bound his wrists, behind his back, to his ankles. Drokma's head was arched backward, his mouth etched open in a scream.

He would have done better to shoot himself with his own pistol, Trowbridge thought. But one could never really imagine the worst; even at the last, as he lay with his knee destroyed, with his pursuer tramping toward him down the slope, Drokma must have hoped he could bargain his way out of his fate.

He saw something else. Drokma's ears had been neatly sliced off close to his skull.

"Would a Gorchok do this?" he asked.

Norbu shook his head.

"Then it's Naraka. He takes the ears as a trophy."

Uneasily, Trowbridge realized that if Naraka were still in Lhakrinor, Krishna was probably here as well.

Looking up at the sky, Norbu said, "This is a lonely place to die—not even the vultures have found him. Drokma was responsible for the death of my father, and he took from me a life, in the place I grew up. But this..."

His voice trailed off. Then he said, "It would have been better, at least for Drokma, if I had killed him that day in Trang. I nearly did."

"Do you think Drokma was alive?"

"When he was skinned? I would think so."

"This looks like more than a simple killing," Trowbridge said. "It looks like punishment of some kind."

"It does," Norbu said. "And it brings us to another mystery. What did Naraka want out of Drokma's saddlebag?" He touched the bundle in his shirt. "He must have been looking for something else and found it—or he would have continued looking and found this."

At the head of the little valley they stopped for a moment, looking back at the spot of scarlet behind them.

Norbu had performed an abbreviated version of the Tibetan practice of sky burial, carving up Drokma's body with a knife so it would be eaten by vultures, crushing his skull with a rock so that Drokma's spirit would not be tempted to reenter its former vehicle and become a vampire.

They lingered, looking at the fierce, broken highlands around them.

"At least he died in Lhakrinor," Norbu said. "Within this ring of mountains, in the place where he was born."

"I doubt it was much comfort to him."

"No. But it is some comfort to me."

They turned and moved down the slope. The sun was sinking quickly; Norbu knew of a yak-herder's hut below the snow line where they planned to spend the night. They had no desire to encounter Naraka, but for now they followed his tracks, which traced the only logical route down out of the mountains.

A few minutes later the trail led them into a narrow cut between a pair of steep slopes. At the cut's far end was a peculiarly shaped boulder which hung over the trail. Beneath the overhang, in the blue evening shadow, the snow was scuffed and packed in an unnatural fashion; beyond this place, Naraka's tracks continued again steadily.

Norbu looked at Trowbridge, then dropped to his knees and began digging. Three feet below the surface, digging together, their gloved hands rasped on a large flat stone.

They widened the hole. Beneath the stone, in the bottom of a dirty shaft, they found a small cylinder, about the size of a flashlight, wrapped in black electrical tape. Trowbridge lifted it out, surprised at its weight. Norbu unsheathed his knife, slit the tape on one end, and peeled it back. There was a warm flicker; several slender disks fell out, making individual slots in the snow. Carefully, Norbu fished one out.

"I should have guessed that Drokma would die for gold," he said.

He handed the coin to Trowbridge, who studied it curiously. "I've never seen a coin like this."

"I would be surprised if you had. I have only seen one or two in my life. It is from Tibet."

"But—"

"From the old Tibet, David. When it was an independent kingdom, and rich. Before the Chinese invaded and brought their paper money."

"Where would Drokma get a fortune in Tibetan coins?"

Norbu looked at the roll of coins and shook his head. "I do not know. But I cannot believe that Naraka will put it to good use. Perhaps we should move it."

"Who would have had that kind of wealth?" Trowbridge asked, huddling close to the yak-dung fire. "In Tibet, I mean. Before the Chinese invasion."

The hut was small, filthy, and smoky, but it was stocked with a pair of goat hair blankets and enough fuel to keep them from freezing. Naraka's tracks, to their relief, had branched away from their route a mile past his cache.

"The monks," Norbu said, "and the wealthy landholders."

"Both of those classes were stripped of their possessions after the invasion. Most were killed."

"Not immediately," Norbu said. "For a while the Chinese left the monks alone, hoping they could persuade the Dalai Lama to cooperate. It was only after he fled that the soldiers began looting the monasteries."

Trowbridge thought for a moment. "What if the People's Liberation Army didn't send all the gold it took from the monasteries to Beijing? They were a long way from home, the Tibetans hated them, and it wasn't even clear, at that point, if Mao would maintain control of the country. With all that uncertainty they might have hung on to some of the gold."

"Certainly this is possible," Norbu admitted. "But it does not explain how such gold would cross the border and end up in Drokma's hands."

For the hundredth time, Trowbridge saw a parachute drifting down toward the slopes of Torma Mountain.

"I'd be willing to bet it crossed the border by airplane," Trowbridge said, "and landed in Krishna's hands before it ended up in Drokma's."

"Krishna is an Indian soldier, David—and India and China are bitter enemies."

"Wouldn't it be possible for soldiers—even from countries who believe themselves to be enemies—to have more in common with one another than with their own governments? Maybe Krishna is in league with the Chinese military, somehow. And maybe Drokma was working for him when he hired the Gorchoks. It would explain why Drokma had the radio."

Norbu said, "It is possible, in theory. But if Krishna is hiring Gorchok bandits—men who have spent their lives blowing up Chinese trucks and assassinating Chinese soldiers—I cannot imagine why the Chinese Army would give him gold for that."

Trowbridge looked at the strange trio of items laid out beside the fire—a turquoise-winged dragon, Drokma's pistol, and a roll of Tibetan coins. He shook his head. "None of this makes sense, does it?"

"At the moment," Norbu said, "the only thing I am sure of is that trouble is coming to my homeland—and that we are a long way from anyone who might help us."

41

It was an uncomfortable night; breakfast, in near darkness, was a handful of dried barley and a mouthful of icy water. They moved quickly down out of the mountains, the sunrise in their eyes, and then along the trail toward home. Trowbridge was intensely conscious that Naraka was still in Lhakrinor; he felt a knot of worry in his stomach which grew steadily worse as the morning wore on.

In Jaramar they were told by one of the villagers that Dorje, the afternoon before, had gone to pay a farewell visit to friends he'd made in Nyi-tar. The villager was not sure if Dorje had stayed the night there, or returned late.

Fifteen minutes later, breathing hard, they crested the ridge behind the house. A thin feather of smoke rose as always from the roof, but the front door sagged open strangely on its leather hinges, and an article of what looked like Nima's clothing—her woolen shawl—lay crumpled in the open space before the stone porch.

"David, wait!" Norbu called out, but Trowbridge was already tearing down the slope.

He reached the front door and ran through the house. There had been a struggle. One of the benches in the kitchen was knocked over; rice had been spilled on the floor. He raced upstairs, but there was no sign of either Dorje or Nima. Bursting out onto the roof, he scanned the area desperately. From this vantage point he saw Norbu scouting the area, unsuccessfully, for signs of life.

A dark-robed figure appeared on the ridgeline, and the witch of Narling walked quickly down the slope in the sunlight.

"I came an hour ago," she said, "to warn you. But I was not in time."

"Warn us of what?" Trowbridge asked.

"Of seeing this Indian fellow and his ugly assistant on the slopes of Torma Mountain. Of seeing an airplane circle the mountain every day for the last week, and drop boxes beneath great parachutes."

Trowbridge forced himself to think—and speak—calmly. "Do you know what they're planning?"

"No. But when Indian spies and Chinese airplanes come to Lhakri-nor, it is not because they are concerned that we have enough to eat."

The witch fixed Trowbridge with haunting, motionless eyes. "I have no love for the Chinese. My older sister was a nun in Tibet. The Chinese forced the monks to violate her in public. Then she was buried alive because she would not repudiate her religion. If I had not been studying here in Lhakrinor I would have suffered the same fate."

Norbu came up to them breathlessly.

"I do not think Dorje returned from Nyi-tar. Nima was dragged from the house. There was a struggle here—" he indicated a wide scuffed spot in the dirt—"and then her tracks disappear, and the other set of tracks becomes deeper."

"He tied her up," Trowbridge said, "and he's carrying her."

He didn't voice the other possibility: that Nima had been killed. But why kidnap a body? She had to be alive.

Norbu said, "From the tracks, I would say he has a head start of at least two hours. We must hurry. I will get the things we need."

Norbu disappeared into the house.

The witch looked at Trowbridge impassively. "What will you do when you reach Torma Mountain?"

"Begin looking for them."

"Where? It is a big mountain, and there is little snow on the slopes. You will not have an easy time following them."

He said nothing. If Naraka reached the mountain ahead of them, and achieved the heights with his high-powered rifle, scouting the exposed slopes beneath him would be not merely difficult, but suici-dal. Still, what choice did they have?

The witch said, "Do you know the great overhanging rock? Beyond the north end of the slope, directly across from Trang monastery?"

"Above the trail which leads to Gelingdo."

She nodded. "Five days ago I watched them retrieve one of the boxes dropped by the Chinese planes, and carry it up that trail. I was curious, and stayed where I was, and watched to see them come down."

"And?"

"They did not come down. All that day and night they did not come down."

"But there's nothing up there. Just cliffs. I've been there myself. Even the lama agreed."

"Simply because you do not see a thing, my *gyami* scholar, does not mean it does not exist. Open your eyes! And go carefully. I do not wish anything to happen to this young woman. Nor do I wish Chinese soldiers falling onto our heads here in Lhakrinor."

Norbu emerged from the house carrying a light pack. Drokma's pistol was tucked into his belt. In one hand he carried a bow; over his shoulder was a stained leather quiver packed tight with arrows.

Trowbridge slipped into the pack, and looked at the witch.

"Thank you," he said.

42

They stood at the place where Trowbridge had talked to Krishna a week before; high above them the weathered profile of Torma Mountain loomed massively. They'd had the advantage for the first four hours of the chase, gaining steadily on Naraka, but it hadn't been enough. By now he'd reached his stronghold—wherever it was—and the advantage had reverted to him.

With only the two of them, a thorough search of the mountain could take days. And they'd be in constant danger of being picked off from the heights above.

"Perhaps we should have gotten help," Norbu said.

"There wasn't time."

"No," Norbu agreed, looking up at the steepening trail. "I confess, David, that I am not too happy about our position. From here on, we have the low ground."

He took the pistol from his belt and handed it to Trowbridge.

Trowbridge hesitated. "You're better with this than I am," he said.

"That is true." Norbu indicated the bow over his shoulder. "But I am also better with this, and I cannot use both at once."

Trowbridge slipped the pistol into his own belt.

"To the overhanging rock?" Norbu said.

Trowbridge nodded.

The trail grew steeper and narrower; in many places, it eroded away entirely. Norbu found the faint edge of a footprint.

"Someone passed by here not long ago," he said.

"Naraka?" Trowbridge asked.

"Impossible to tell. Whoever it was, he was trying not to leave tracks."

They moved steadily—keeping a few yards between them so as not to present a clustered target—to the place where the trail petered out on the highest slopes, and the overhanging rock loomed outward from the crumbling facade of the cliff. In its shadow they studied the ground carefully, finding nothing but the narrow hoof prints made by bharal.

Trowbridge had fought back images of rape and torture as they raced from Jaramar to Trang, telling himself that Naraka would wait until he reached his stronghold before doing anything to Nima. But now they were wasting valuable minutes scouting up and down an empty slope, and he felt increasingly desperate.

Out of the corner of his eye, at a distance along the slope, he saw movement. Instinctively, he crouched and froze.

"Bharal," Norbu said disgustedly, his voice carrying across the slope from where he stood a few yards away. The small herd had blended amazingly into the sere mountain flank.

"Dammit!" Trowbridge said, overwhelmed by tension and frustration. He kicked savagely at a rock and slipped, his feet going out from under him in the loose soil of the slope. He twisted in the air, managing to land on his side; the slope was steep enough that he slid a full ten feet downward before he was able to pull himself onto his belly and self-arrest.

Spitting dirt from his mouth, he sat up slowly.

"Are you all right?" Norbu called, coming down the slope toward him in great sliding leaps.

"I'm OK," he said, blinking to clear the dust from his eyes as he got to his feet. His unexpected and fairly spectacular performance had spooked the bharal; they scattered away in great excited bounds, angling toward the cliffs.

Exactly like when Nima and I watched them flee from the wolves, he thought.

A moment later a yearling bharal separated from the herd, for no obvious reason, and began racing directly down the slope. Sitting back suddenly on its haunches, it slid to a halt, turned, and began charging upward again until it reached the base of the cliff. From there it leaped, with a clearly audible clatter of hooves, onto a tiny pedestal outcropping perhaps eight feet up. It teetered for a moment, gathered itself, leaped upward again, and disappeared.

He and Norbu studied the apparently impenetrable cliff, expecting the yearling to tumble back down into sight. But the cliff face gave up nothing: no sound, no movement. If the two of them had not watched the bharal disappear only seconds ago, it would have seemed impossible.

They looked at each other.

"Yes," Trowbridge said suddenly.

"Keep your eye on the place," Norbu said, and they set out swiftly toward where the yearling had disappeared.

"That was a hell of a leap," Trowbridge said, looking up at the pedestal outcropping of rock which had been the yearling's first perch.

Except for this pedestal, the cliff presented a rough, but nearly sheer face; there was no indication that once the outcropping was reached there would be any place farther to go.

"We could have walked past this place a hundred times," Trowbridge said.

Norbu studied the cliff face. "Boost me up on your shoulders," he said.

"Then what?"

"Then I will let down the rope, and pull you up."

"You brought rope?"

"Of course," Norbu said. "I used to be a mountain climber."

Trowbridge squatted at the base of the cliff and Norbu stepped up onto his shoulders. Slowly, Trowbridge straightened, bracing his hands between his chest and the rock.

"Enough?" Trowbridge grunted.

A moment later Norbu's weight lifted from his shoulders. Trowbridge stepped backward and looked up. Norbu was sitting on the small outcropping, passing a loop of rope around his waist. He let the rest of the rope down the rock face, then braced himself, leaning back into the cliff, as Trowbridge walked his way up hand over hand.

There was barely enough room on the outcropping for both of them. Norbu stood, balanced himself coolly, and studied the way up.

"You may not like this, David. Have you ever climbed a rock chimney?"

"No."

"It is exactly what it sounds like. Walls that are straight up and down, with rock on three sides. To climb it, you must brace your feet and hands against the two facing sides, and inch your way up."

Norbu paused reflectively. "In fact, we have another small problem. Getting to where the chimney begins."

"It can't be worse than clinging to this bloody rock."

Norbu looked down at him and chuckled. Then he turned his attention to the rock face, and started up while Trowbridge watched in wonder.

Norbu clung above him from a vertical—and apparently featureless—rock face. He searched out and discovered cracks Trowbridge could barely see; more amazingly, he was able to suspend his weight from those places. He moved steadily upward across the rock, his movements at once fluid and precise, until he reached what was, in relative terms, a luxuriously wide ledge, perhaps all of ten inches.

The whole thing had taken three or four minutes. Above Norbu, and slightly to the left, Trowbridge could see the bottom of the chimney—a vertical column of air.

"It was easier than I thought," Norbu called encouragingly. "You should have no problem—I will tell you the moves as you go along. I would help you with the rope, but there is no way to brace myself. Now, do you see the crack above your head?"

"No."

"Raise your hand—no, your left hand. Yes, you have it."

"That's it?"

"It is one of the larger ones you will encounter. Now, your right foot—good, you have it. Now, push yourself up."

Flattening himself close to the rock, he pushed upward, as Norbu had suggested, and promptly began going over backward. Panic-stricken, he slid back down to the safety of the outcropping.

"A good lesson!" Norbu called. "Did you see how I kept my body *away* from the cliff? The mountain does not give itself up easily—if you cling too tightly, it throws you off. You must push yourself out from the rock, and up at the same time."

"Out and up," Trowbridge muttered, glancing at the drop behind him before starting up again. This time, keeping his body away from the rock—something that went against all his instincts—he had better luck, and held the position.

"Now the left foot—good! You are learning fast. Now your right hand, as high as you can stretch it. To the left a little. There, you have it."

"It's a vertical crevice. There's nothing to hang on to."

"You will not use your fingers here. Place your whole hand into the crevice, make a fist, and hang from it."

"Hang from my fist?"

"Yes. And listen carefully: Aside from that crack, it is very smooth there. There is nothing else to hang on to. Once you are hanging from your fist, you will have to swing to your left to get another hold."

Standing on his tiptoes on an irregularity of rock, he put his hand into the narrow crevice, slid it down an inch or two, and made a ball of his fist. Slowly, he put his full weight on it.

"See?" Norbu said. "It is easy."

"It's not easy. It hurts like hell."

"Swing," Norbu commanded.

He launched himself across, scrabbled for a finger hold, and missed. A moment later he found himself hanging by one fist straight down from the crevice. The outcropping of rock was no longer beneath him.

"That is bad," Norbu said cheerfully. "What you must do now is swing your legs from side to side to get yourself moving again. And you must keep your fist in a ball, and not miss the handhold this time."

The last thing he felt like doing, in his precarious position, was to swing from side to side, but there was no alternative. He moved his left foot, then his right, then his left again, until he had a pendulum motion going. He reached out, and missed. He started over, and swung again. This time his fingers achieved a purchase. Still suspended from his fist, he found a toehold for his left foot, and boosted himself a few inches upward. Moving his left hand higher, ranging blindly over the rock above him, he found another niche. He pulled himself up farther, taking the weight from his right fist.

"Very good!" Norbu said. "You are almost here."

Several painful moments later he sat beside Norbu on the narrow ledge, catching his breath.

Norbu studied the chimney above them, and pointed to a tiny ledge eight feet off to the side. "The yearling jumped from the first outcropping to that ledge. Then back up at an angle, to the top of the chimney, where we will come out. Since we cannot make eight-foot leaps, we will have to take the direct route."

"Krishna and Naraka could never have climbed this on a regular basis," Trowbridge said.

Norbu gestured at a number of shiny places on the inside walls of the chimney, where rock and lichen had been rubbed away. "A rope was let down from above," he said. "Which is what I hope to be able to do for you, once I get to the top of the chimney."

He tucked one end of the rope loosely through his belt. "Please feed this rope out gently," he said. "And David, I do not expect to fall. But if I do, you must not interfere. There is no sense in us going down together."

Norbu took a deep breath and started up the chimney.

It was a slow, painstaking process. Sitting uncomfortably on the narrow ledge, Trowbridge watched Norbu move upward. If Norbu fell, he would plummet past him, almost within reaching distance, down onto a jagged collection of rock. At one point where the chimney narrowed, Norbu was forced to shift his spread-eagled stance to a more cramped posture, his back wedged against one wall of the chimney, his feet braced against the other. As he completed this rather complicated-looking maneuver, he began to slip. The movement was slight, a split-second scraping of one foot, but Trowbridge saw Norbu's eyes widen slightly. Norbu froze and held his position. Then a slight smile came over his face.

"I am out of practice," he said, in a voice which struck Trowbridge as impossibly relaxed, before continuing upward. Eventually Trowbridge could see only his legs and feet. Then, as the chimney doubled back upon its original angle, Norbu disappeared entirely. For Trowbridge, this was worse; he could only imagine the difficulties Norbu might be facing.

It occurred to him that he would never be able to duplicate Norbu's feat. He didn't have the training, and his right hand—the one he had jammed into a crack and hung from—was oozing blood, and swelling fast.

Above him, in the chimney, came a sudden snicking sound. To his horror, he heard something coming downward. A moment later the end of a rope ladder tumbled down into view, skittering past him all the way to the base of the cliff. A quiet hoot of triumph echoed down the chimney.

"David," Norbu called softly, amusement in his voice, "you could have waited on the ground!"

Three minutes later he joined Norbu at the top of the chimney. The rope ladder was secured by a substantial-looking pair of ringbolts hammered deep into solid rock. Beside the ladder was a third ringbolt; from it hung a block and tackle, and a coil of sturdy line.

"For pulling up supplies," Norbu said. "Or gold."

Or people, Trowbridge thought, grimly imagining Nima being dragged up through the chimney.

"I am almost sorry there was a ladder," Norbu said, pulling up the ladder with professional movements, hanging it neatly over the ringbolt. "You were learning very fast."

Trowbridge looked at the narrow gully, flanked by precipitous walls, which led upward at a steep angle. Clear footprints stood out in a patch of snow.

"They're not trying to hide their tracks any longer."

"No," Norbu said. "They won't expect us to have found our way up here."

43

The shadowy passage led them steadily upward. At one point it grew so narrow—V-shaped and deep, like the gouge of a giant ax-head—that they had to wedge themselves through sideways. They moved as quietly as possible, placing their feet with care to avoid slipping on the fist-sized stones which littered the floor of the gully, but speed was their main objective; they knew, without having to say it, that every moment that passed increased the danger to Nima.

In spite of the danger, there was a dream-like quality to their progress into the high heart of the mountain.

A hundred yards ahead the gully began to widen into a basin shape. Trowbridge stopped and sniffed the air.

"Smell it?"

Norbu nodded. They dropped into a crouch, and moved forward

cautiously. The close, damp air of the gully had changed; there was a fresher, breezier feel to what they breathed, as if the air contained more oxygen.

There was also a faint tang of wood smoke.

The mouth of the gully was half-filled with scree from the high slope to the left. Crawling to the top of the loose heap of stones, they peered over the top. Before them was a gentle, pebble-strewn rise. Beyond that, they could see nothing but two high walls of stone, opening like great wings on either side.

"There is a small valley beyond that rise," Norbu said quietly.

Trowbridge nodded. They scanned the slopes carefully for movement, then separated around opposite sides of the heap of stone, moving slowly, ten feet apart, up the gradual incline. He felt an uncomfortable prickling in his spine. If Naraka were hidden on one of these slopes, he or Norbu might be in the cross hairs of his rifle sight right now.

Slowly, they raised their heads over the top of the rise and studied the scene which lay before them. The first thing which drew their attention was a spectacular ice fall, perhaps a hundred feet high, at the far end of the valley. Spilling out of a channel in the mountain above, it cascaded downward in sinuous, frozen sheets, ending in an explosion of blocks and splinters at its base.

Across the central depression of the little valley—it was no more than two hundred yards long, and fifty yards across—was a crudely constructed hut, roofed with corrugated metal and topped by a makeshift chimney constructed out of an aluminum jerry can. A tiny trickle of smoke came from the chimney. Beyond the hut, atop a little knoll, was a head-high, bulbous orange *chorten*, daubed with white. The *chorten* appeared to have been broken into; a wooden door lay torn from its hinges before the shadowed interior.

Down the center of the valley, in stark contrast to the tumbledown look of the hut and the dilapidated *chorten*, ran a neat set of parallel lines. Head high, covered by dark green tarpaulins pegged firmly into the grass, the two long stacks appeared to consist primarily of wooden boxes.

"Where could all that have come from?" Norbu said. "If it is food, it could feed a hundred men for a month."

"Air lift. Dropped onto the slopes near Gelingdo. And I'll bet there's more than just food in those boxes."

They studied the scene warily. There was a good chance that Nima was inside the hut, or in the *chorten*. There was also a good chance that Naraka was either with her or not far away.

Something occurred to Trowbridge. "Norbu. Have you ever used a single sideband radio?"

Norbu looked at him quizzically. "Like Drokma had in his house? Yes. On mountain-climbing expeditions."

"If anything happens to me," Trowbridge said, "get out of here, go to Drokma's radio, and call Vikram, the official in Jorkhang. Tell him about Krishna, and about all these supplies." He closed his eyes, thinking hard. What had Vikram told him? "Use fifteen two-fifty megahertz."

"I will do that," Norbu said. "But before you go knocking on the door of that hut, let us see if anyone is home." He took the bow from his shoulder, notched an arrow, rose quickly, and shot. The arrow flew through the valley and lodged, with a quiet *thunk*, in the wall of the hut.

They waited a long moment, but there was no reaction.

Taking a deep breath, Trowbridge moved over the rise in a crouch and headed for the hut, staying out of the line of sight of its single window. He slipped up close and peered in. There was nothing inside but a pair of disheveled bunks, a stove, and some personal belongings.

Norbu joined him at the window. "I know that smell," he said quietly, sniffing the air. "Curry."

"There's another smell," Trowbridge said. "They're not very good housekeepers."

"Let's check the boxes," Norbu said.

Keeping a wary eye on the slopes above them, they moved across the open space to the two lines of provisions and slipped between them. Norbu pulled a box out from under a tarp, then found a crowbar and pried off the lid. The box was filled to the top with flat metal tins, each covered in Chinese script. One of the tins had ruptured, probably when it hit the slope; rice in some kind of sauce had spilled out of its interior.

They moved down the line a few feet, and dragged another box—heavier this time—out from under the tarp.

"Any guesses?" Norbu said.

The box was about four feet long, and two feet wide.

"Rifles?"

Norbu wrenched the top to one side; there was a squeal of protest as nails withdrew from wood.

"Rifles," he confirmed.

The guns were individually wrapped and slathered in grease. Norbu lifted one out and peeled back its covering.

"Not a very *good* rifle," he said, holding it gingerly because of the grease. "But a rifle nonetheless. As soon as I clean it and find a box of shells, we will be at something less of a disadvantage."

"I'll check the *chorten*," Trowbridge said.

He moved cautiously across the grass. Atop the small dome was a multitiered cone which culminated in a truncated white spire. Someone had used the *chorten* for target practice; the dome was riddled with chinks and grooves, and most of the spire—the closest part of the *chorten*, in a Buddhist's eyes, to God—had been shot off and replaced with a whip antenna.

He crouched, put his head into the small open door, and saw a pair of eyes peering back at him from the gloom of the *chorten* interior.

He backed out so quickly that he nearly lost his footing. Then he paused for a moment, and looked in again. The milky eyes regarded him unblinkingly. A mummified lama, shrouded in dark robes, sat slumped on a wooden throne. A tall black conical cap was perched on his head; one side of his nut-brown face was contorted strangely, as if he'd had a stroke before dying. Trowbridge realized that the mummification process must have taken effect unevenly; the leftward slump of the body seemed to take its cue from the asymmetry of the face.

He ducked inside. This was the *chorten* for which the lama of Gelingdo had spent his life searching. Which meant that the mummified corpse before him was the lama who'd found the *gter-ma*, the sacred text. If the lama of Gelingdo was right about his dates, this mummy had been sitting like this for three hundred years.

Unfortunately, Trowbridge thought, those eyes won't stare much longer. With the *chorten* broken open, with light and air reaching the corpse—even the thin dry air of Lhakrinor—a rapid process of decay would have set in. This mummified body would soon be little more than dust and feathery bones.

He looked around the interior of the *chorten*. There was no sign of the sacred book. But atop an intricately carved wooden altar, beside a broken conch shell and a stained bronze lamp, was a very serious-looking radio in a hardened, olive-green case. On the floor in the corner was a small portable generator, and a pair of what looked like car batteries.

Krishna had brought the two radios to Lhakrinor. And Drokma obviously was—or had been—working with Krishna.

Should he try to reach Vikram by radio, before continuing the search for Nima? Would he even be able to get through from this valley?

He stepped out into the light, intending to call Norbu, and noticed a faint, pale irregularity on the grass. A scrap of parchment. He bent down to pick it up and it came apart in his hands. He studied the largest fragment; except for the faintest hint of lettering, the text had been bleached away.

Slipping the scrap into his pocket, he looked around. Other pages lay in the grass around his feet. The lama's book, which had lasted hundreds of years in the sealed sanctity of the *chorten*, had been scattered about, and had deteriorated, in the course of a single year, into pulp. He reached down to pick up another bit of parchment from the bright grass, and saw it explode before his eyes.

44

He dropped to one knee, reaching into his belt for Drokma's gun as the scene before him opened with painful clarity. Krishna, who'd appeared over a low rise on the far side of the valley, ran toward him with a pistol in his hand. Norbu was racing in a low crouch between the long rows of boxes toward the valley entrance. A moment later Naraka appeared behind Krishna, rifle in hand, moving at a dead run after Norbu. Trowbridge watched in horror as Naraka stopped, dropped to one knee, and brought the rifle to his shoulder.

"Norbu!" he yelled desperately.

Naraka squeezed off two shots a split second after Norbu dropped and rolled. The ground beyond him erupted sickeningly. Norbu glanced back over his shoulder at Naraka—who was calmly adjusting his aim—and flung himself up onto the pile of boxes, rolling over the top, dropping out of sight on the far side. As he disappeared, three more shots stitched the boxes beneath him.

Krishna was still running in Trowbridge's direction.

"Mr. Trowbridge," Krishna yelled breathlessly, and with a somewhat comic formality, "do not move, or I will shoot!"

Trowbridge ignored him, calculating Norbu's chances. Norbu was safe for the moment, but he had only a bow and arrow against Naraka's rifle, and he was trapped; there was a good fifty yards of open space between where the boxes ended and the entrance to the valley. Naraka, realizing the same thing, stood confidently, looked over his shoulder at Krishna, and began berating him, in extremely insulting terms, for having fired too soon and given them away. Krishna, even as he continued to trot toward Trowbridge—the pistol aimed in the general direction of Trowbridge's chest—began yelling back at Naraka, looking over his shoulder in a rage.

They've gotten a little sick of each other, he thought, as he sat calmly, rested his right elbow on his knee, and drew a bead on Naraka. There's no way I'm going to get out of this valley, he told himself, but I might be able to bust Norbu loose.

"Norbu, go!" he yelled, then squeezed off a shot. Naraka looked to his left, where a bullet had dug into the grass. Then he stared at Trowbridge with a shocked expression, as if he could not believe that a scholar, of all people, would be shooting at him. A moment later he dropped, rolled onto his belly, and began squirming for cover.

Krishna, with an inarticulate cry of rage, was forced to do the same. Trowbridge took careful aim and sent a bullet in Krishna's direction.

Drokma's pistol, unfortunately, was old, and he was not a marksman; his chances of hitting something at a distance of better than forty yards were not good. He squeezed off one more shot at Naraka, then dived behind the *chorten*. A moment later, as he had expected, the edge of the *chorten* dome began chipping away in lethal, steady explosions. Naraka was blasting away with what sounded like a semi-automatic rifle. Trowbridge leaned back against the rounded clay surface, breathing hard, shading his eyes from the clay fragments, watching with grim satisfaction as Norbu sprinted across the open ground. Krishna, seeing the same thing, cried out a sudden warning. The firing stopped instantly. Trowbridge rolled quickly out from the other side of the *chorten*, yelled to draw attention to himself, and fired at Naraka, who had risen again and was aiming his rifle at Norbu. Naraka was forced to flatten himself and return his attention to Trowbridge, who dived back behind the *chorten*.

Chips of clay exploded into the air, inches from his head. A moment later he saw Norbu disappear over the rise.

How many shots do I have left? he wondered. He couldn't remember how many times he'd fired; he didn't even know, in fact, how many bullets the bloody pistol contained.

The point now—with whatever ammunition he had left—was to try to give Norbu as much of a head start as possible.

He waited until the hailstorm of shots abated, then took a deep breath and flung himself out from the protection of the *chorten*. Rolling several times across the grass, he came up onto his elbows, aimed carefully, and squeezed the trigger. There was a satisfying explosion which caused Krishna and Naraka to lay their heads flat. Then a series of clicks—metal on metal—clearly audible throughout the valley. He slammed the pistol down on the grass in frustration.

Naraka wasted no time. He leaped up and began running toward the valley entrance, jamming a fresh clip into his rifle. For a big man, he moved with frightening speed.

How much of a head start had he been able to purchase for Norbu? A minute and a half? Maybe a little more? He closed his eyes and prayed it would be enough. He'd done everything he could, at any rate.

When he opened his eyes Krishna stood ten feet away. The pistol was pointed at his face; Krishna held it firmly in a no-nonsense, "once burned" grip. It was a powerful, efficient-looking gun, an officer's gun.

With a pistol like that, Trowbridge thought as he sat up slowly, I might have been able to hit one of these bastards.

"My congratulations on having found our little hideout, Mr. Trowbridge," Krishna said, attempting a jocular tone. "Rather amusing, don't you think? The way this has all turned out? Set a hunter to catch a hunter. A scholar to catch a scholar."

Trowbridge studied him. Krishna's nerves had to be raw. He'd been cooped up for months in a one-room shack with Naraka, he was in the middle of organizing some illegal and no doubt dangerous military adventure, and he'd just made a rather stupid mistake in front of his rebellious assistant.

I need to keep him on edge, Trowbridge thought. See if I can get him to make a second mistake.

"A scholar?" he said, putting an icily polite skepticism into his voice.

"Ah, Mr. Trowbridge, be generous in your defeat! I do, in fact, have a doctorate in military history. From Cambridge, no less."

"But you weren't happy to watch history. You wanted to make some yourself."

"Like you, Mr. Trowbridge."

Krishna smiled triumphantly at this sally, then moved slowly to his right, toward the chorten. Reaching inside he retrieved a folding canvas stool and sat down, drawing a deep contented breath, keeping the pistol trained carefully on Trowbridge's belly. Some of Trowbridge's hope ebbed; Krishna was a soldier, after all. He knew the value of a cool head, and was rapidly regaining it.

In a conversational tone, Krishna said, "Given your dislike for my assistant, you may be pleased to know that your arrival here caused him to lose a small bet. Naraka swore to me, barely an hour ago, that you would never find this valley. I pointed out that the two of you were expert trackers—but he insisted you could not possibly follow his trail, even carrying the woman, as he was."

"Where is she?"

Krishna ignored the question.

"When Naraka showed up, as a matter of fact, I nearly put a bullet in his head for this foolish kidnapping stunt. His obsession with your female friend might have placed our entire project at risk."

"What's he done with Nima?"

Krishna waved his hand dismissively. "Why not call her by her real name? The *kumari*—the Living Goddess of Nepal!"

Krishna laughed. "A barbaric and childish custom, really—although my assistant takes it quite seriously. It seems to bother him on a personal level that a religious figure of her importance broke tradition and ran away from her husband. He believes that if you allow a woman like this to get away with an exhibition of independence, all sorts of terrible disruptions will ensue. Millions of good Hindu women will leave their husbands, and society will fall apart. I find it all rather foolish—nevertheless, things have turned out in a satisfactory manner."

Krishna shrugged coolly. "And perhaps Naraka, in spite of his obvious shortcomings, deserves some sort of . . . well, I suppose you could call it a reward after this long and rather difficult project."

Trowbridge swallowed. He was suddenly in danger of losing his own composure.

"All I asked you is where she was."

"Come now, Mr. Trowbridge, do you really think I would gain anything by telling you that? Not that it makes a good deal of difference any more. For your peace of mind, though, I will tell you that

Naraka has not yet had a chance to, ah, pay attention to her. When he arrived with her slung over his shoulder, and I realized what he had done, we left immediately for the cliffs so that we might intercept you when you appeared on the slopes below. You appeared more quickly than we expected."

Krishna's breezy tone outraged him; still, something in him relaxed. Nima was alive, and unmolested. Norbu had at least a fighting chance. As for himself, he wasn't dead yet.

Krishna continued expansively, "And so it has turned out like this. With you sitting on the ground, and me on a camp stool, here in this high and unpleasant valley—would you like a stool, Mr. Trowbridge? We have dozens. There is no need for you to be uncomfortable."

Trowbridge shook his head.

Krishna went on in a tone which was solicitous, almost confidential; the pleasure of a conversation with someone beside Naraka seemed to be making him positively garrulous. "I confess I take an extra pleasure in this stool because of the irony that it is the Chinese—our enemies—who have supplied us with it. You have noticed, I am sure, that there is enough food and equipment here for a small army."

Trowbridge said nothing.

"Do not be dull, Mr. Trowbridge! Please, ask me what I could possibly have in mind to do with all of these Chinese supplies and weapons."

"All right. What do you plan to do with all this?"

"Attack the Chinese who gave it to me!" Krishna burst out gleefully. "What better use could I put it to? As soon as I organize my pathetic group of Tibetan irregulars into a semblance of an army—and it will not take long; they begin arriving tomorrow, and I must simply arm them, and fire within their naive hearts the hope that this time, at last, they have a real chance of freeing their homeland from the Chinese oppressors—we will cross the border. And then I will create a stir the entire world will hear about."

"Won't the Tibetans be suspicious at the fact that you're arming them with Chinese weaponry?"

"They believe I have a spy within the Chinese army. One who has smuggled these things over the border, and who will give us information on Chinese troop movements. All of which is true!"

Krishna took a deep breath, nodding with the pleasure of what he was saying. "In a few days, our bellies filled with Chinese rations, we will cross the border and shoot Chinese bullets at our benefactors.

Now, you are probably wondering why the Chinese would be so generous in their support of such a project. Well, it is a paradox, I admit—and I am glad to be able to explain it to someone intelligent enough to understand its beautiful simplicity. Let me sketch in the background. Perhaps you are aware, Mr. Trowbridge, that since Mao died and China has been ruled by Deng and his less warlike successors, the People's Liberation Army has faded somewhat from its former glory? That when Deng proclaimed the Four Modernizations, the military came in fourth—and began receiving a rather small share of the available power and wealth?"

"I'm aware of that."

"Many of the older generation—some of whom actually fought with Mao on the Long March, lived in caves and saw their comrades die barefoot in the snow—found themselves being unceremoniously retired in favor of younger men who had never fired a shot; who had spent their time, instead, at a university. I will not bore you with further details, Mr. Trowbridge; suffice it to say that there are those within the Chinese military—both young and old—who would like to see it restored to its former standing."

"Which would require a conflict of some kind."

"Very good, Mr. Trowbridge! When else but in wartime do nations really appreciate their soldiers? When else are soldiers looked upon as heroes, instead of being ignored, or spat upon? And when else does a government provide its soldiers with enough money for them to do their job properly?"

"I still don't see what you have in mind."

"In precisely three days I and my little army of a hundred and fifty Tibetans will attack China. We will do so with great fanfare. The Chinese general who has jurisdiction over this border region will, to put it in non-military terms, overreact. He will exaggerate the magnitude of the attack in his reports to Beijing; then he will be 'forced' to counterattack over the border, citing immediate military necessity."

"And your little army of Tibetans?"

"They will be slaughtered, of course. But they are soldiers. They know they run that risk."

"They know they're taking a risk. Not that they're going to certain death."

"You could describe them as having a certain amount of bad luck, I suppose."

"And the people of Lhakrinor?"

"A detail. As I said once before, this place is fit for nothing but yaks, demons, and crows. Now, once Chinese soldiers begin pouring over the Nepali border—crying self-defense with every step, of course—Kathmandu will become understandably frantic and beg India to come to its aid. Which, of course, we are prepared to do."

"You're out of your mind. The Chinese can drive trucks and tanks here in a matter of hours. You'd have to bring your forces over the Himalayas, which would take weeks. There's no possible way you can defend Lhakrinor from the Chinese."

Krishna's eyes fairly gleamed with satisfaction. "As I said, Mr. Trowbridge . . . yaks, demons, and crows."

Trowbridge experienced a quiet shock of comprehension.

"You intend to let the Chinese have Lhakrinor."

"Lhakrinor, and Dolpo, to the east—while we will occupy the rest of Nepal! Everything south of the Himalayas, which happens to be the great majority of the country. During this conflict both the Indian and Chinese armies will justify their actions in the name of self-defense. There will be a few mountaintop skirmishes and some dramatic dog-fights between our two air forces over Everest. Then we will allow a well-intentioned team of negotiators from the United Nations to arrive and beg us, in the name of humanity, to halt this frightening conflict involving the two most populous nations on earth.

"China and India, as civilized and peace-loving countries, will agree to a temporary cease-fire arranged on existing lines of occupation—that is, the Himalayas themselves, give or take an unimportant valley. Then the diplomacy will begin. China will be enjoined by the nations of the world to disgorge Lhakrinor and Dolpo, and we will be similarly implored to remove our troops from the rest of Nepal."

"And it will never happen."

Krishna gave a worldly shrug. "You know as well as I do, Mr. Trowbridge, how these sorts of things drag along. As long as Chinese troops are poised along the Himalayas, we can hardly leave Nepal open to another treacherous attack by withdrawing to our borders. And the Chinese, loudly proclaiming themselves the injured party, will not withdraw either."

"What if the Nepalis are intelligent enough to see through this, and not ask you for help?"

Krishna smiled delicately. "We will help them anyway. Imagine your government's reaction, Mr. Trowbridge, if Mexico or Canada were invaded by a hostile power. No, your objection is an intelligent one, but we have anticipated it. Now, if only for my own satisfaction, may I summarize the situation as I have laid it out? The Chinese military can claim a minor victory for itself in Lhakrinor; at the same time, with the greatly increased military tension along the border, the government in Beijing will be forced to provide significant increases in money and political power to its generals. Which, of course, is what they really want. As for us—"

"What if the Chinese betray this little agreement you have? What if they keep coming over the Himalayas?"

"A calculated risk, Mr. Trowbridge. But I assure you they will not. To begin with, as you have pointed out yourself, it is not possible to conduct a modern war across a mountain range such as the Himalayas. These are not the Alps, to be crossed by elephant. And of course China wants to appear the international kindly uncle these days—it cannot afford to be perceived as the aggressor, which would be the case if it refused to accept a U.N. cease-fire. As long as China swallows no more than Lhakrinor and Dolpo it will be able to look very much the injured and reasonable party in all of this."

"And India?"

"My country will have achieved Mahabharat—Greater India, Mr. Trowbridge. An empire stretching from the southern tip of the continent to the ramparts of the Himalayas. India will have fulfilled her manifest destiny."

"What about the destiny of the Nepalis?"

"Geography, in this case, is destiny," Krishna said serenely. "And I am afraid it is the destiny of the Nepalis to have new masters."

Krishna glanced around himself absently. "I rather wish I had a cup of tea. It is bothersome to have to keep this pistol aimed at you in this fashion. Well, what do you think of my plan, Mr. Trowbridge? It is mine, by the way, from start to finish. I have the support of some key elements in the military, but the glory will be mine alone."

"I think you're out of your mind. You'll never create a convincing invasion with a hundred and fifty Tibetan irregulars and a handful of grenade launchers."

"My little army may surprise you, Mr. Trowbridge. War zones are places of great confusion. It is easy to overestimate the magnitude of a threat—honest and well-intentioned men have done so since the beginning of time when they saw other men running toward them with hostile intent. For the Chinese to exaggerate a threat deliberately will be a matter of the utmost simplicity."

"And you think your government—and the Chinese government—won't figure out what's going on?"

Krishna shrugged eloquently. "Even if they do, it will not make a difference. Once my plan is in motion they will not be able to stop it. The Indian government cannot afford to slap its own army's hand when the newspapers are screaming that only the army stands between Mother India and the godless yellow hordes to the north! A conflict of this sort generates its own momentum, Mr. Trowbridge, and creates its own laws. The politicians will have to obey those laws as a matter of their own survival."

"And afterward?"

"Afterward we will have what we set out to gain. My country will be united against an outside aggressor. Nepal will have been assimilated and carved up into two or three docile Indian states. And both the Chinese and Indian military will have enhanced their prestige immensely. If I might offer one final lesson in military history—a brief one, I promise you—it is this: The reason armies have hesitated to start wars in the past—as a means of justifying their own existence—is the knowledge that they would be required to expend a good deal of expensive weaponry, and to place their well-trained soldiers at risk. Worst of all, they might lose the conflict! This, by contrast, will be the first intelligently managed war in history. Few will die, small amounts of munitions will be expended—and yet the goal will be accomplished. With a deftness and surgical skill not usually associated with open conflict."

"And you, Krishna?"

"I will be 'captured' early in the battle, and released secretly over the border shortly afterward to take up my duties—greatly enhanced duties, I might add—in the upper echelons of the Air Force."

"No personal risk, then."

"As little as possible. I may look like a soiled lieutenant colonel, but there is a great future for me in Mahabharat."

In the distance, they heard shots. Two of them. The high, cracking sound of Naraka's rifle was unmistakable.

"Ah," Krishna said meditatively, "it appears that the hunter, at last, has caught the hunter."

In the silence, they listened. A few moments later they heard a third, and final, shot. The sound echoed upward with a washy, distant ping from the far-off slopes of the mountain.

"That will be the one from up close. The one behind the ear to make absolutely certain."

Trowbridge swallowed hard, willing himself to believe it wasn't true.

Krishna glanced down at his pistol—resting lazily, now, on his thigh—then looked up at Trowbridge. There was a slight impatience in his voice.

"You have not told me what you think of my plan, Mr. Trowbridge. Now that I have dealt with your objections, will you relent, and admit that it will be one of the great strokes of history?"

Trowbridge said quietly, "No doubt it will. Too bad you won't be around to see it."

"Excuse me?"

"Once this thing is over you'll not only have outlived your usefulness, you'll be a dangerous man. Perhaps the most dangerous in India. Think of the powerful people you'd be able to destroy with a single word."

"I will be *among* the powerful people, Mr. Trowbridge. They have promised me that. They know I have made tremendous sacrifices and taken great personal risks. They will be grateful for what I have done."

"I see. In the same way you're grateful to Naraka."

Krishna frowned. For a moment his eyes grew distant. Suddenly his mouth curled contemptuously, and he glared at Trowbridge.

"Do you expect me to faint at this prospect, Mr. Trowbridge? So that you may escape with your life? I assure you that will not happen."

Trowbridge said nothing.

"I should put a bullet in you right now."

Trowbridge studied the mud and gravel beside his right hand, then looked up.

"How important was Drokma to your plan?"

Krishna looked at him suspiciously. "Not particularly important—but exceedingly useful. In fact, you might say that hiring him was one of my early strokes of genius. He has authority in the area, and close ties with a particularly fierce band of Tibetans which will form the core of my army."

"What was Naraka doing yesterday in the Robshi?"

"Meeting with Drokma," Krishna said impatiently.

"And what can you tell me about a roll of gold coins? Tibetan, very old."

Krishna's face had gone still. He seemed to weigh, for a moment, what he might gain by responding, and to decide he had nothing to lose. "The coins were given to Drokma for distribution to the Gorchoks, but stolen by a renegade member of the group."

This was virtually the same lie Drokma had told Norbu's father, seventeen years ago; the second time around it had gotten him killed.

"And you believe that," Trowbridge said.

"What are you getting at?" Krishna snapped.

"The gold wasn't stolen by a Gorchok. It was kept by Drokma, who was on his way to the lowlands when he was intercepted by Naraka. Naraka killed him and took the gold for himself."

Krishna took a deep breath, digesting this information. "If what you say is true," he said, "I confess that it doesn't please me. Still, in the end, it will make no difference. The plan will go forward. Naraka will pay heavily for his little intrigue, and Drokma was always expendable."

"Expendable," Trowbridge repeated slowly. "Think about this plan of yours, Krishna. You're supposed to be 'captured,' then released secretly over the border. How happy is your Chinese general going to be about that, I wonder? Setting free the man who could reveal his part in this little drama? Beijing might not be able to stop your filthy little war once it's up and rolling, but if they discover how it came about, they'll exact a price later. Think hard, Krishna. Put yourself in the place of *any one* of the people with whom you'll soon be entrusting your life. What would you do in their position?"

A muscle in Krishna's neck was working.

Trowbridge said, "At a guess, I'd say you'll take an accidental bullet sometime during the attack. Your Chinese general will apologize, in some secret communication, to your Indian generals. Then everyone will breathe a huge sigh of relief and get on with their phony war. It's not just Naraka and Drokma—you've been betrayed by everyone around you."

Krishna's eyes were flat and contemplative.

"First rule of politics, Krishna. Put yourself in the shoes of the people in power. What would you do with a dangerous—and expendable—lieutenant colonel?"

"In that position," Krishna said softly, "I would eliminate the lieutenant colonel in question."

He looked up with a grim light in his eyes. "You are even more intelligent than I realized, Mr. Trowbridge. I confess I had not explored this idea. No doubt it was my own ambition—perhaps my own vanity—that blinded me."

He paused, then continued stubbornly, a mixture of pain and pride in his voice. "Nevertheless, it is still a good plan. And I am a patriot. If

I am to die in the cause of my country—if I have to be betrayed—I will do so."

Trowbridge started to speak, but Krishna held up his hand. "You are about to tell me that I could call it all off. Destroy the supplies, disband my army of guerrillas, and let the woman go free. Well, that is certainly possible. But what then, Mr. Trowbridge? I could never return to India—I am at least as dangerous if the plan is called off as I am if it goes forward. Perhaps I could move to your country and serve curry in a New York restaurant? No, I am afraid the thing is in motion, and we are in motion with it."

Krishna took a deep breath and stared hard at Trowbridge. He was nervous, and far from happy, but his eyes were clear. Trowbridge realized he had lost. He had lost, and he was about to die.

Krishna added, "Perhaps I should say *I* am in motion with it."

From the corner of his eye, Trowbridge saw a pale shape move somewhere near the ice fall.

Krishna sighed. "Well, Mr. Trowbridge, I take this next step with great reluctance. I had planned to ask if there were any message you wished me to transmit after this was all over, but I'm afraid you have shown me that I am unlikely to carry any messages farther than the Chinese border. What a place to die, eh, Mr. Trowbridge? We are a pair of unsung heroes, after all, dying far from home in the service of our respective causes. It hardly seems fair."

Krishna shrugged. Then, with an apologetic look, he raised the pistol.

Behind Krishna, the pale shape was moving more quickly. A lateral movement, across the slope.

"To murdered heroes, Mr. Trowbridge," Krishna said ruefully. "And all that sort of thing."

The pistol was pointed at his forehead.

A clatter came from the slope behind Krishna. The kicking sound of a rock making its way down toward the valley floor. Trowbridge made his eyes wide and yelled, "Norbu! Look out! He's got a gun!"

Krishna whirled, stumbling over his camp stool, and fired several wild shots in the direction of the yearling bharal, which had been trying to work its way surreptitiously along the slope. The bharal kicked up its hind legs, skittering in panic-stricken flight toward the valley entrance. Trowbridge dug his hand deep into the valley floor; Krishna, realizing he had been tricked, turned back to Trowbridge and took the handful of mud and pebbles full in the face. He staggered backward, cursing, clawing at his eyes with his free hand, waving the pistol. Trowbridge set himself to rush forward; Krishna, however, began firing blindly in his direction.

He was forced to turn and run, not what he'd had in mind. Worse, he found himself running *away* from the valley entrance toward the ice fall.

Once committed to this direction there was no turning back. Krishna was already clearing the mud from his eyes, blinking and peering around. Trowbridge sprinted to the base of the ice fall and began scrambling desperately over the rough frozen blocks, working his way to its far side, expecting a bullet in his back at any moment. He risked a glance behind him. Krishna must have emptied his gun; he was reloading with shaking hands.

Briefly thanking the yearling bharal for the fact that he was alive, Trowbridge looked upward, traced an ascent route in his mind, and began scrambling up the series of four-foot stone benches beside the ice fall. He had to get out of Krishna's line of fire before he finished reloading, or it would be a short climb.

45

He climbed quickly, moving from bench to bench, making his way upward with all the speed he could manage. It was not difficult climbing, but he wasn't sure how far this route would carry him.

Eighty feet up from the base of the ice fall he came to a high, rounded boulder; from its top he felt sure he could jump to the next bench. It would be an exposed scramble up the boulder's face, however. If Krishna had managed to jam another clip into his pistol, and was in place beneath him, he would be an easy target.

He looked beneath him, but could see nothing. He jammed one foot into a small opening and started up.

The crumbling rock was made treacherous by a fine coating of silt, and his right hand—the one he'd jammed into the crack while climbing with Norbu—was swollen and painful. He was forced to use his left hand for most of the difficult work of finding handholds and dragging himself upward.

He heard the pistol fire beneath him. Rock fragments exploded against his leg and a sudden heat creased his ribs. Releasing his grip, he slid down the boulder face, back into the protection of the ledge. Two more shots echoed above his head, drawing dimples in the rock face. Gasping with the pain, lying on his side on the uneven stone, he unzipped his parka and ripped his shirt open. There was blood on his belly and chest. He swallowed, then ran his fingers through the blood until he felt a narrow groove. The bullet had ricocheted off the rock, losing much of its velocity, and had not penetrated deeply; he was lucky it wasn't worse.

He heard a scuffling sound beneath him as Krishna began making his way upward. Trowbridge, on his hands and knees, moved to the far end of the bench. It tapered off, ending in a fifty-foot drop. He crawled to the other extremity, which disappeared into the suspended sheets of the ice flow, lit a ferocious red now by the lowering sun. Moving close to the ice, he lay back against the cliff face, and paused a moment. He was breathing too hard. The panicky, trapped feeling would not go away. He turned on his side and opened his parka to the radiant chill of the ice, letting it cool the fiery track made by the bullet.

Think, he told himself. Clear your head. There has to be a way out of this.

He studied the boulder above him more closely and saw that it was split down its interior. There was a possible way up, a kind of diagonal envelope running up the inside of the boulder, exiting directly onto the bench above. He crawled to the opening and peered upward. In the declining light the passage was already dark; from this vantage point it was difficult to tell if it actually grew narrower near the top—as it seemed to—or if the gloom simply caused it to appear that way.

The idea of wedging himself into a lightless, narrow pocket of air beneath countless tons of boulder was far from appealing, but he had little choice. Removing his parka to make himself smaller, he slipped into the opening and began working his way upward, pushing the parka ahead of him with his left hand.

The first body-length was a relatively simple crawl. Then, as he'd feared, the rock ceiling began pressing downward. He felt its rough touch on his shoulders, then against the back of his head. He was forced to turn his head sideways to continue. His movements became necessarily smaller, and his progress slowed. Eventually, as the rock passageway grew narrower still, closing in around him, his movements became almost infinitesimal. He brought his arms, which had been out ahead of him, down to his sides. It was more difficult, now, to get a purchase on the rock, but his shoulder blades were slightly lower, and he was able to keep worming his way deeper and higher into the narrow crack.

How close? It couldn't be much farther. He felt drafts playing around his neck and shoulders; it seemed as if there were more light coming from up ahead.

Then he realized his tiny snake-like movements were taking him nowhere. He was stuck. Panic rose in him, which was dangerous in itself; with his heart pounding like a hammer, and fear forcing him to breathe great gulps of air, he was wedged even more tightly than before.

He forced himself to slow his breathing. Then, against his instincts, he eased all the air from his lungs, found a tiny irregularity of rock on which to lodge his toes, and pushed upward, realizing as he did so that if the passage continued to narrow he was finished, because he would never be able to go back.

There was space above his shoulder blades. He brought his arms in front of him, gripped a rocky knob, and pulled himself upward. A moment later he was lying on his back on a wide stone ledge, staring up at the sky, breathing great luxurious gulps of air, and feeling the tears pour from his eyes.

Never again, he told himself. Next time I'll let him shoot me.

He sat up, looked around the ledge, which was partly covered in snow, and threaded his arms through the sleeves of his parka, trying to ignore a shirt front sticky with blood.

The valley beneath him was sunk in shadow, although he'd climbed high enough to be in the last rays of the sun. Once again, he heard scrambling beneath him. Could he throw a rock down on Krishna without presenting himself as a target? It was worth a try.

He selected a fair-sized stone, the largest he felt he could throw with any degree of accuracy, crawled nearer the outside edge of the ledge, and flung the stone in the direction of the noise. There was a moment of silence, then a thump, and a muffled cry, and a sound as if a body had collapsed onto stone. In disbelief and exultation, he put his head out over the edge.

The pistol spat, and the bullet sang past his ear. He pulled his head in; a split-second later, another bullet clipped the stone inches in front of him.

That bullet would have taken me in the throat, he thought, rolling back away from the edge, feeling extremely foolish.

"A very old trick, that one," Krishna called out coolly. "I am surprised that it worked on a man of your intelligence."

He said nothing, angry at his own stupidity.

"Naturally, you must be a little bit upset, which tends to make one more likely to make mistakes. One of your friends is dead, the other is captive, and you are weaponless—and, I think from the stains I see on that boulder above me, wounded. Are you sure you wish to continue this foolish game of cat-and-mouse, Mr. Trowbridge? By climbing higher on this godforsaken mountain,"—here a trace of irritation showed in Krishna's voice—"you merely postpone the inevitable. There is not a hospital up there, I assure you. Nor, I am afraid, an American embassy."

Trowbridge got to his feet, flung a pair of rocks in the direction of Krishna's voice, and set out upward.

The series of benches died out. He stepped from rock into deep snow and began making his way up a slope toward a high ridge line, plunging his arms into the snow to keep his balance. Occasionally, his way was blocked by a cornice which he had to scale on his hands and knees. Eventually he reached the ridge—which was as sheer and perfect as a white roof line—and began trudging upward. On one side the ridge fell away in sheer rock; on the other, in steep, snowy folds. Far below, to his left, was a gaping crevasse.

He was being forced, whether he liked it or not, toward the peak of Torma Mountain. Above his head, perhaps two thousand feet up, its rounded dome loomed in the last of the light.

If I were a mountain climber, he thought grimly, I might appreciate this. A first ascent of Torma Mountain, in all likelihood. The only problem is that I have no climbing equipment, no tent or sleeping bag, and the sun has gone down.

And I never wanted to be a mountain climber anyway.

He climbed for what seemed like a long time before Krishna appeared, two hundred yards below him, well beyond pistol range. He'd evidently had more trouble scrambling up the outside of the boulder than Trowbridge had experienced squeezing up the middle of it. They stood staring at one another. It was an oddly calm moment;

Trowbridge had a fleeting impulse to wave. Then Krishna put his head down and began climbing doggedly upward.

Trowbridge turned and did the same.

The ridge petered out, eventually, against the base of a great formation of black stone—something like a roughly squared four-story tower—which rose before him, blocking his way. The tower's rugged face was frosted, on either side, with wickedly unstable ice formations. From where he stood, it was not a promising prospect. He looked back at Krishna, who was coming along steadily.

He had two alternatives: to go back down the ridge, into the sights of Krishna's pistol, or to go up the tower. For the first time it occurred to him—as the sky merged from orange to deep blue over a sea of jagged, shadowy peaks to the southwest—that even if he were able to beat Krishna at this game of cat-and-mouse, it would be a Pyrrhic victory, celebrated as darkness gripped the mountain and the temperature plunged below freezing.

Could he make it back down in the dark?

At the moment, the question was academic. Even to have a chance at a nighttime descent, he had to get away from Krishna. He studied the formidable rock face before him, took a deep breath, and started up.

Norbu's impromptu training session earlier this afternoon helped him in the first pitch, fifteen feet of steep rock chipped with small but abundant hand- and footholds. At the top of this pitch he faced his first real difficulty. He would have to crab sideways across a smoother section, with little to hold onto, before he could start up again. He took a deep breath, shook the tension from his arms, and set out, moving as Norbu had taught him, weight outward from the rock. With painful slowness, checking and double-checking every purchase, he worked his way toward the handhold he'd placed in his mind as his immediate goal. Halfway across he felt his balance go bad; one moment he was in control, gauging his next toehold, and the next he began drifting away from the mountain. He brought one shoulder closer to the rock, and pushed upward slightly with his toes, as if he were arching himself over a ball, willing his weight back to center. For a long second he seemed to be standing directly out from the mountain. His heart skipped a beat; the world spun deliriously away from him. Then he knew he'd regained his balance and would not fall. Slowly he brought himself closer to the rock, held himself in that position for several seconds—not daring to look down, fighting the sense of vertigo which threatened to throw him from his perch—and continued up.

A minute later he grasped the fist-sized outcropping that was his goal; no piece of rock had ever felt so good. He turned and looked back at Krishna, toiling slowly up the ridge. He looked above his head, pressed his foot into an indentation, and started up the next section.

Twenty feet up, at the bottom of an open chimney, he reached an impasse. The chimney was short, perhaps eight or ten feet high. He felt he could negotiate it once he got inside; getting there, however, would be a problem. He studied the rock face, realizing reluctantly that the only way to wedge himself up into the chimney would be a hand jam similar to the one he'd done with Norbu. And it would have to be the right hand, in order to allow him to reach out with his left and push off against the far wall of the chimney.

He brought his right hand close to his face. It was so swollen the knuckles had nearly disappeared; the skin was mottled and discolored. He blew on it gently, then reached above his head and found the niche. Jamming his hand into the narrow opening, he hung his weight from it—releasing a long breath as he did so—and began wedging his way carefully upward.

Negotiating the chimney proved to be less difficult than he'd expected. Part way up he found a jagged splinter of rock angled like a narrow blade up from the wall; he was able to place a foot on its point, rest a moment, and look back down at Krishna, who had seen him climbing the tower and was struggling more quickly up through the deep snow of the ridge, holding the pistol before him.

He doesn't want to have to follow me up, Trowbridge thought with a certain satisfaction. Bracing himself once again with his arms, he removed his right foot from the safety of the splinter foothold, and worked his way up the chimney out of Krishna's line of sight.

At the top, he pushed off lightly with his right hand and foot, stepping onto the safety of a three-foot-wide ledge. As he did so Krishna fired a blind shot up at him; the spent bullet ricocheted harmlessly up through the chimney.

The ledge on which he stood slanted upward, disappearing around the tower in a promising fashion. He felt heartened; if this ledge continued to the top of the tower, he would emerge into deep snow, where he could build a snow cave and spend the night. Krishna, he felt, would never make it up the tower. If he—Trowbridge—were able to survive the night, he could find another way down in the morning.

His footsteps crunched audibly as he moved around the ledge, which narrowed, suddenly, to a matter of inches. He kept himself from looking down as he worked his way higher, feeling that he must be near the top of the tower. Then he stopped, shaken and disbelieving.

The ledge ended. The stone simply fell away from the structure of the tower, leaving it sheer and smooth. He looked up. The crown of the tower was only ten feet above him, but the rock was smooth as a mirror. Worse, it sloped outward. If he were equipped with pitons and ropes, it might have been possible; without equipment it was not.

Slowly, he backed away from the narrow part of the ledge, and looked down. Eighty feet of empty space beneath him ended in a steep, slick slope, at the bottom of which was the broad crevasse he'd seen from the ridge.

He might—just possibly—survive the jump. But he would never be able to self-arrest on that slope, not without an ice ax. He would slide straight down into the crevasse.

There was no way up. And as long as Krishna was at the base of the rock tower, no way down. He was trapped on the ledge.

He heard a sound echo softly from the direction of the chimney. Krishna. Fighting back a feeling of despair, he forced himself to think clearly. All Krishna knows, he told himself, is that you went up the tower, and that you didn't come back down. He has to assume that you came out on top and were able to continue up the mountain—that you might get away from him, and find another way down. He doesn't know you're trapped here—that your only chance of getting off this mountain is to go back down the way you came.

Use it, he told himself. It's the only advantage you've got.

Another surreptitious sound floated upward. It sounded as if Krishna were standing at the base of the tower, deciding whether or not to attempt the climb. Trowbridge took two slow, careful steps along the ledge back toward the chimney, then stopped and listened. Had Krishna heard his footsteps crunching in the snow?

"Mr. Trowbridge," came Krishna's polite, mocking voice, "how is the view up there?"

Krishna had heard him. He nearly replied, then remembered how he'd been suckered into putting his head out over the ledge, and kept silent.

"You know, Mr. Trowbridge," Krishna continued conversationally, "neither of us is a mountain animal. It is getting dark, and we will freeze to death. I confess I find that an extremely unpleasant prospect. Don't you?"

He made no sound. Eventually Krishna spoke again. "I dislike reproaching you, Mr. Trowbridge, but it would be polite on your part, at the very least, to hold up your end of the conversation. . . . Nothing to say? Well, perhaps I'll continue my monologue. By now, I suppose, my assistant has finished removing the ears of your hunter friend, and is enjoying himself with your friend the *kumari*."

Krishna paused. "What exactly was the nature of your relationship with her, Mr. Trowbridge? Or let me rephrase that: What exactly is it like to make love to a goddess? Wouldn't you like to talk about it? Since you are going to die so soon?"

He felt like killing Krishna; at the same time, a quiet exultation coursed through him. Krishna hadn't heard him move, or he wouldn't be going to so much trouble to provoke a response. In the ensuing silence, he heard Krishna swear softly. Then he heard him start up the face of the tower.

He's a brave bastard, Trowbridge thought wonderingly. He's actually going to try to come up. It's darker now than when I made the climb; worse, he has to deal with the uncertainty of whether I'm up here waiting to throw something down on him.

Yes, he's a brave bastard. And when he's halfway up, I'm going to throw something down on him that will make him hurt.

He looked around the ledge. At first glance, nothing. Then he saw something translucent protruding from the snow, a chunk of ice which must have fallen from above. Carefully, he got to his knees, and began brushing the snow, with little movements, away from the ice.

The work went slowly; he was hampered by the need for silence and by the failing light. Still, he was not in a hurry. He wouldn't even be able to see Krishna until he reached a point directly beneath him. And the higher Krishna climbed before he fell, the better. He dug gently through the snow with his left hand, feeling his way around the irregular contours of the ice.

Eventually he dislodged it. There was nothing else on the ledge; this would be his only chance to knock Krishna down. He hefted the piece of ice in his hand, then looked over at the dark well of the chimney.

Krishna, from the sound of things, had negotiated the smooth face where Trowbridge had nearly fallen, and was making his way up toward the base of the chimney. He was moving fairly quickly; it was clear he had some climbing experience.

Trowbridge heard a grunt, a whoosh of breath, and a slight scrambling sound. Krishna was in the chimney, wedging himself upward with small, carefully braced movements. Soon he would find the sharp splinter of rock; if he had any sense he would rest there, as Trowbridge had.

Krishna took what sounded like a deep breath, expelling it slowly. That would mean he'd found the splinter. Trowbridge could almost feel the sharp bit of rock pressing up into the bottom of his foot, could sense Krishna's doubt seeping upward through the darkened chimney.

Was Trowbridge waiting for him at the top?

Krishna started upward. Trowbridge counted off ten careful seconds, then rushed toward the lip of the chimney. Krishna, hearing him, would be bracing for the attack, cursing himself for being caught in such a vulnerable position. Trowbridge reached the edge, raised the block of ice above his head with both hands, and flung it down at the shape in the well of darkness beneath him. Krishna cried out, shifting his position, tipping his head to one side.

The blow caught him on the shoulder. The ice bounced off, then rattled down the face of the tower. Krishna had not fallen, but he was sliding, a semi-controlled movement back down the interior of the chimney. As he slipped down, Trowbridge saw a sudden spinning glint; Krishna's pistol, tumbling down into the snow.

The blow must have numbed Krishna's shoulder; his left hand didn't seem to be working well. As he slid downward his right foot groped for the splinter of rock.

Trowbridge felt his stomach turn as he watched what happened next. Instead of gaining a purchase on the rock, Krishna's boot slid into the tight, narrow space between it and the chimney wall, wedging there. With his right foot immobilized in the equivalent of a sharp stone boot, and his body still sliding, an irresistible force was exerted on his leg.

There was an audible snap, as if a green twig had broken under pressure.

A long silence. Then Krishna, who was hanging now, head down, from his own broken leg, gasped quietly. Trowbridge stood staring from above, unable to help or harm him further.

Slowly, Krishna bent at the waist and began pulling himself up the leg until he gripped the splinter of rock with both hands. Trowbridge could only imagine what that effort must have cost him. Krishna was doubled over entirely now. Gripping the rock with one hand, his breathing audible and unsteady, he began fumbling with the trapped boot.

He's undoing the laces, Trowbridge realized, feeling a helpless admiration for his courage.

With another quiet gasp, Krishna pulled his foot from the boot. His feet dropped out from underneath him; he dangled a moment, his broken leg making a wrong shape against the chimney wall.

With the leg, he couldn't climb up or down. And he couldn't hang there forever.

Would he survive the fall?

Krishna looked up. "Good-bye, Mr. Trowbridge," he said quietly. Then he relaxed his grip, plunging thirty-five feet down onto the snow at the base of the tower.

46

There was a lengthy silence. Krishna's motionless figure lay in a dark heap at the base of the rock tower, a bare two feet from the edge of the slope which led down toward the crevasse.

Was he dead?

Krishna stirred, then rolled onto his belly and pulled himself slowly toward the tower, his hands searching around him in the snow as he went. He found what he was looking for, and pulled himself into a sitting position, collapsing backward immediately against the base of the tower. He remained still for a long time, as if his efforts had been overwhelming.

Finally he looked up, the pistol resting in his lap.

"Well, Mr. Trowbridge," he croaked. "Will you talk to me now? The issue appears to have been resolved. I will not descend from the mountain, and neither will you."

Trowbridge studied him a minute, then looked out across the vast, deepening twilight. He looked back down.

"How's your leg?"

"Not what one might have hoped for," Krishna said, sounding pleased that Trowbridge had responded. His voice was stronger now. "The bone is not only broken, but has emerged from the skin in several places. There is a fair amount of blood. Have you ever had a compound fracture, Mr. Trowbridge?"

"No."

"This is my first. You may be wondering about the level of pain. I would say that it is considerable. Fortunately, as the night gets colder, the pain should lessen."

Krishna sighed. "That was a very clever trick, Mr. Trowbridge."

"Krishna, I could go down the mountain and bring up a sleeping bag from your camp. We could get help for you tomorrow."

Krishna laughed softly. "You are suggesting that I allow you to climb down from there and then walk away—so that you can come back and help me? You must be joking, Mr. Trowbridge."

"I'm not."

Krishna was silent a moment. Then he said, "Oddly enough, I believe you. One of the dangers of this profession is that you begin to assume everyone is as ruthless as yourself—it can lead to errors in judgment."

"It's worth a try, Krishna. Before it's completely dark. Anything's better than sitting here freezing to death."

"Not true, Mr. Trowbridge. I am putting the finishing touches on my plan."

"Your plan's finished. Without you to lead those men, it will never come off."

"In fact, the Tibetans know how to find the valley, and they know enough of the plan to carry it out on their own. All that's necessary, really, is that they cross the border and begin firing at the Chinese. And of course *you* need to be quite dead, and not telling tales to the curious."

The pale handle of the pistol flashed suddenly; Trowbridge pulled his head back hastily from the ledge.

"Not to worry, Mr. Trowbridge," Krishna said. "I suppose I should try to shoot you, but I confess it feels rather lonely up here. I never did like mountains, particularly."

"I never much liked climbing them."

"For someone who dislikes climbing mountains, you led me a merry chase. Why didn't you continue, by the way? Are you trapped up there?"

"Yes."

"Ah. Well, it seems we have each had our share of bad luck today. And yet perhaps it has all worked out for the best. As you pointed out, I would probably have been killed in some 'accident' in Tibet before being returned over the border."

Krishna paused meditatively, then continued. "I wonder if anyone will ever find us up here? I have heard that at this height—in air as dry and cold as this—a body may be preserved in reasonably good condition for decades. Perhaps a mountain-climbing expedition will come across us someday and attempt to puzzle out what happened. They will certainly wonder at the fact that we do not have ropes or climbing equipment of any kind. Will they realize, I wonder, that you were killed by a bullet that never left this gun?"

Trowbridge felt suddenly weary of Krishna's ramblings.

"Do you have family, Mr. Trowbridge? Are there those who will mourn you?"

"Not really."

"Nor I," Krishna sighed. "My profession, I am afraid, has discouraged the normal sort of intimacies. You are a bit of a loner yourself, aren't you?"

"I used to think so."

"Ah!" There was genuine regret in Krishna's voice. "I am sorry I was forced to break up your happy household. If it is any help, Naraka will find himself rather hurried along by the events I have set in motion. He will not have much leisure in which to torment your female friend before he puts a bullet in her. You may be interested to know that she was in the valley all the time. Tied up, gagged, and neatly stowed in a small cave near the ice fall. You passed within a few feet of her when you began climbing."

Trowbridge leaned back against the cold stone, closing his eyes, feeling the strength ebb from his body. Norbu, in all likelihood, was dead, skinned, left on a mountainside somewhere; Nima was being raped and probably tortured right now. And he was sitting on a ledge, slowly freezing to death, unable to do anything. Unable, in all likelihood, even to save his own life.

He heard a pained intake of breath from below as Krishna shifted his position slightly.

"Goodness," Krishna said. "The anesthetic effect of the cold has not yet set in. I rather wish it was colder. It was colder last night, I think."

Krishna was right. A haze had moved in, and the temperature was not dropping as rapidly as usual; by Lhakrinor standards, it would not be a terribly cold night.

As he sat with his back to the mountain and his legs dangling over empty space, an odd sense of well-being stole over him. Beneath him the snowy slope shone faintly; it looked clean, and inviting, as if there were a form of forgiveness there, of forgetfulness.

With a jolt he roused himself. He'd been about to doze off. He forced himself to stand on the ledge, and began pacing back and forth, beating his arms across his chest to get the blood moving. His feet and fingers were numb already. He couldn't afford to make that mistake a second time.

"Bravo, Mr. Trowbridge," Krishna called up from below. His voice was relaxed, almost sleepy. "I hear you pacing around up there. You are certainly a courageous fellow. I must tell you, though, that it is lovely just to relax. The pain in my leg has nearly stopped."

There was a silence. Then Krishna added, in a quieter voice, almost as if he were talking to himself, "If only I were not so thirsty..."

Mechanically, Trowbridge continued to pace the ledge. His own thirst had become a torment; he'd had nothing to drink since early this afternoon, when he and Norbu had crossed the river below Trang. He scooped a bit of snow into his mouth with his left hand, letting it melt slowly. The cool trickle was delicious, but dangerous; if he iced down his interior with enough snow to quench his thirst he would jeopardize his chances of survival.

And yet thirst led to dehydration, weakness, and impaired judgment. There was no good answer.

He walked back and forth with leaden steps, reminding himself to stay alert, not to misstep. It grew steadily colder. He looked at his watch. The luminous face mocked him cruelly. It was barely eight o'clock.

Krishna had been quiet for a long time now. Trowbridge called his name; the sound echoed strangely down the chimney. No response.

He crouched, intending to fashion a snowball and throw it down on Krishna, waking him so he would have someone to talk to—then wondered if this was evidence, already, of a slight delirium. With his left hand he scooped snow into the palm of his right, realizing as he did so that his right hand was not hurting for the first time in hours. When he tried to pack the snow into a ball, he found that his hands weren't working properly. He stood, and brought his left hand close to his face, attempting to bring his thumb and forefinger together. He couldn't do it. Discouraged, he let the loose snow drop from his right hand. With a soft hush, it skittered down the walls of the chimney toward Krishna.

There was no movement from the base of the tower.

Not that it made any difference whether Krishna was shamming, unconscious, or dead. It was too dark now to descend the chimney, especially with hands which no longer functioned.

He put his hands into his armpits. His fingers were like blocks of ice. He began pacing again, resisting the urge, which overcame him almost immediately, to check his watch. Slowly his hands grew warmer. Feeling returned painfully, as if hot needles were being jabbed into his fingertips. He couldn't afford to let his hands freeze again or he would never make it down in the morning. How much time had passed? An hour? Perhaps two? Hopefully, he pulled his sleeve back and checked the watch once again. He stared at the face unbelievingly. Then he fumbled at the watch with clumsy fingers, undoing it from his wrist, and flung it into the night.

Barely twenty-five minutes had passed since he last checked.

There was a story he'd been told about a man who'd taken a bet: that he would be able to stand in the town square, all through a winter's night, wearing only a thin robe for warmth. Just when the man thought that he could no longer stand the cold and would have to give up, he'd noticed a single candle in the window of a house on the far side of the square. Taking heart from the tiny point of light, drawing strength from its flame, he'd stared at it, seeing it as a promise of the dawn, and so doing had survived the night.

In the morning the man told his friends about the candle that had given him the courage to stand out all night in the cold. They loudly declared that he had cheated; that in point of fact he'd drawn some amount of warmth from the candle, however small, and thus lost the bet, and would have to make them dinner, as agreed. On the appointed day the friends arrived and sat down in the dining room, greedily awaiting their dinner. The man reassured them, over and over, that dinner was nearly ready. Finally, after hours of waiting, when they could no longer sustain their hunger, they burst into his kitchen. They found him sitting before a huge pot. Beneath the pot was a single candle.

"Surely, my friends, if a single candle could give me warmth across the square on a winter's night, it will not have a problem cooking this food."

The friends had burst out laughing, and taken the man away to dinner.

A crescent moon, softened by the haze, had risen above the mountain peaks in the east. He'd told himself this story, speaking out loud—even though his tongue was thick and swollen—three times. Oddly, there was someone beside him now on the ledge. Someone who required his help if they were not to fall, or freeze. The small, dim moon soared upward, and he drew strength from its steady passage, the graceful parabola it made across the moist night sky.

"Here's another way we're lucky," he informed his companion. "The air is not so dry as usual, so we aren't so thirsty as we might be."

He moved his arms back and forth, and began pacing again. Occasionally he noticed his outside foot come down perilously near the edge, and reprimanded himself. You must be careful, he told himself. Don't step off the ledge now. Not when the moon is floating higher in the sky, and you have a chance to live.

The moon was gone behind the rock tower. The cold was terrible. He felt it on his face, and in his hands, but worst of all in his feet. He was sitting on the ledge, no longer able to stand.

He thought about lying down. About how nice it would be simply to give up and go to sleep.

Instead, with the last scraps of his determination, he sat up straight. He made his backbone like a pile of coins, his breathing slow and regular. Then he visualized himself—slowly building the scene around him—in a clearing in a forest. There were trees of different kinds, the sound of a stream somewhere, sun coming through the trees. It was a warm and peaceful place, a place where a person could sit for hours, and not fall from any height, and not suffer for his friends, and not be cold.

47

For what seemed like the thousandth time, he woke with a hopeless jolt, vertigo coursing through his body as he remembered his situation.

He was lying on his side, hands tucked into his armpits, knees extended out over empty space. He must have rolled over while sleeping, something that could easily have been fatal. It was time to get up and start moving again. The effort, however, seemed beyond his capabilities. He'd done it once too often; there was nothing left.

Then he noticed a luminous orange glow softening the horizon. Above it, a band of pearl gray. He'd survived the night.

He lay for several minutes, racked by bouts of shivering, and watched the sky lighten. Then he rolled to a sitting position, stood slowly, and began pacing. He had a monstrous headache, his tongue felt like dry leather in his mouth, and his lips were cracked and bleeding, but he was alive. He scooped a bit of snow into his mouth, put his hands back in his armpits, and continued walking back and forth, reviving himself, eyes fixed on the lightening sky to the east.

Ten minutes later he crouched on the edge of the chimney, looking down. Krishna sat like a frozen sentinel, his back to the rock tower. His posture was perfectly natural, almost relaxed.

He took a deep breath, feeling his heart race erratically, then braced himself with clumsy, swollen hands, and began working his way down the chimney. When he reached the splinter of rock he stopped and rested. To this point he'd only needed his hands to push off on either side, but beneath the chimney he would need his fingers to find holds in the rock. He wasn't sure they'd be good for that. He looked for a moment at the slope beneath him and to the right, at the dark crevasse at the slope's bottom, then lowered himself awkwardly past the splinter. His right hand felt like a piece of wood against the rock. He tried to explore the rock below him with his left foot. Then he began sliding.

He scrabbled desperately for a hold, but it was too late. He was bumping downward, turning as he fell. The edge of the slope below—and the vast empty space beyond it—spun through his vision, moving toward him in a vertiginous rush. When he landed snow collapsed beneath him and he felt himself going down the slope. His feet scuffed against the slick surface. He made a desperate grab, clutching blindly for a handhold, and grabbed something. Took hold of it and hung from it, and didn't fall.

He had hold of Krishna's leg. When he looked up Krishna stared back at him with serene—and very dead—eyes.

For a moment he didn't move, frightened that Krishna's frozen body might pull away from the tower. Krishna, however, remained where he was; a few moments later Trowbridge lay next to him in the snow, his heart pounding horribly. There was a milky tinge beneath Krishna's brown skin. His body was as rigid as a mannequin, and his broken leg—the leg which had saved Trowbridge from going down the slope and into the crevasse—was a dark hieroglyph against the snow, marked in three places with a frozen froth of blood.

He died peacefully, Trowbridge thought. Secure in the belief that his damned scheme would be a success. Which it probably will be, unless I get down this mountain.

Trowbridge pulled the pistol from Krishna's frozen fingers; there was a cracking noise as it came free. He put it inside his shirt, wincing at the icy touch. That's right, he remembered. I was shot yesterday.

He heaved himself to his feet and started down, noticing that the scene around him seemed hallucinogenic and unreliable. Yesterday, climbing this ridge, he'd made a point of placing his feet quite carefully. It was difficult to remember exactly why.

He slipped and fell. Felt himself beginning to slide. Instinctively, he plunged his arms into the snow and stopped himself. Sat stupidly for a moment, shivering again, then stood with great effort, made his way back to the center of the ridge, and continued down.

A while later he woke up. Sitting again, in the snow, on a knife-edge at the top of the world.

Your judgment is pretty much gone, he told himself in a brief access of clarity. You're delirious, hypothermic, and frostbitten, and you're still a long way from where you need to go.

Get up, he told himself.

I would like to. But I don't seem to be able to.

He was walking, taking five or six steps, resting, walking again. There was something happening beneath him. A figure coming upward. Someone had come up the series of stone benches and was climbing the ridge. He experienced a moment of indecision. The figure, which carried something long and dark—a rifle—also stopped.

Trowbridge put his hand into his shirt, fumbling for Krishna's pistol. How many bullets did he have? The pistol was in his hand. He raised it.

The figure seemed to make an "O" with his mouth, and dropped to the snow.

At the very least, Trowbridge thought wearily, he'd forced Naraka to drop to his belly one more time. He felt himself weaving on his feet. Held the pistol before him and attempted to focus on the dark shape lying on the slope. Tried to fire, but there was no strength in his fingers. Then he heard a shout, and recognized Norbu's voice.

The pistol fell from his hand. He dropped to his knees, trying to focus, and then he fell forward on top of the pistol. It seemed like a long way down.

48

There was an arm around his shoulders and a hand behind his neck. He felt himself being lifted to a sitting position in the snow. "David," Norbu was saying, "you must wake up."

"You're alive." Did he say the words out loud or only think them? He noticed he was no longer shivering, which was pleasant, but worrisome.

"Drink," Norbu commanded, tipping a canteen to his lips.

"Nima—"

"Yes, she is all right. Now drink."

The cool liquid burned over his parched lips and ran down his throat. The feeling was blissful.

Norbu helped him to his feet, supporting him as they stumbled down through the deep snow. He was vaguely aware that Norbu was talking to him—probably as much to keep him conscious as for any other reason. There was something about being hit, and about Naraka coming along too fast once he smelled blood. It took a minute for this to sink in.

"You were shot," he said, his tongue still thick.

"He caught me, a little, yes," Norbu said, flexing his shoulder with a grimace. "But I had the bow and arrow, which surprised him."

It took all his concentration to keep walking and not lose consciousness. Norbu continued to speak. The sound of his voice was reassuring. There was something about showing Naraka his knife, and Naraka telling where Nima was hidden in order to die in peace with his skin attached to his body. Then something about a radio, and Kathmandu. And then just snow, and ice, and not being able to walk any more, and the pain worsening, then grass and soil. Intense pain in his hands and his feet, pain in his head he could hardly bear. He felt his eyes fill with hot tears, and felt ashamed.

Blinking, he felt a soft touch brush the tears from his cheeks.

"David," a voice said, "it's all right now."

It was someone else speaking. A quality in the voice made the tears come faster, and helplessly, as if he were a child hearing his mother.

Nima's face was blurry above him. Her calm, accepting presence took away his shame. After a moment the tears stopped, and her touch seemed to lessen the pain.

She said, "You are going to be fine. We are all going to be fine."

He closed his eyes, believing her.

He woke to the weird, unmistakable chanting of the Bardo Thodol, the ceremony performed for those who had died, or were about to.

He opened his eyes, and blinked. The lama of Gelingdo, who'd been reciting loudly from an open text not far from his face, stopped in mid-verse and stared down at him with a look of frank surprise.

"I thought you were dying," the lama commented, and closed the book with a satisfied snap. "The fat one said you were fine, that you would wake up soon, but I was not sure, so I decided to give your soul some advice concerning the next lifetime—just in case it was feeling indecisive about this one."

Trowbridge looked around. He was in the lamasery, with no idea how he had gotten here. Why did his hands and feet hurt so badly? Then it came back in a rush. Krishna, and the valley. The Tibetan guerrillas, who might at this moment be cracking open cases of Chinese rifles. He struggled onto an elbow. "Where's Norbu?"

The lama looked at him sternly. "No wonder your spirit decided to return to your body—it is so highly agitated!"

"I have to get to a radio. The Indian—the pilgrim—was bringing in weapons from the *gyami-khoum-teng*." He felt desperate, realizing how unintelligible this must sound to the lama.

"Lie down, my restless scholar," the lama said serenely. "We already know all this. You must rest. I will make you some barley soup."

With this the lama left him alone with his questions. He lay back baffled and exhausted, and closed his eyes.

The next time he woke it was to the sound of a strangely familiar voice, speaking a cheerful King's English.

"Ah, that lumpish thing we left snoring on the bed is alive after all! I shall have to send you a sizable bill for my medical treatment."

Trowbridge stared at the face above him in disbelief.

"Rotten idea to have spent the night *al fresco* like that, Trowbridge old man. Hypothermia at a minimum, possibly complicated by pneumonia. And best not to inquire about your toes—one or two may end up a bit shorter than what you've been accustomed to. Still, I should think you're through the worst of it."

"Mallory! How did you get up here?"

"Sheer genius on my part," Mallory said, pulling up a stool and sitting down amiably next to the bed. "Some chaps in the Foreign Ministry took quite an interest in me after my Lhakrinor problems last spring and again when I got back to Kathmandu two weeks ago. Last night they called in a panic, asking whether your man Norbu was reliable, and I insisted on knowing what was going on. When they told me, I convinced them I was your best friend in the world, the only person capable of locating you if you were alive—or identifying your body if you weren't—and they brought me along. Wonderful chance to get to Lhakrinor without having to walk."

Trowbridge's head was spinning. "If you didn't walk . . ."

"Sorry. I'm telling this story backward, aren't I?"

Mallory explained that Norbu had gotten through to Vikram last night on Krishna's radio, and told him about the valley filled with Chinese weapons. The message, although a bit garbled, had been enough to mobilize Vikram and his colleagues. A trio of helicopters had left Kathmandu at dawn, carrying Mallory and a detachment of Gurkha soldiers; they'd set down in Jorkhang to pick up Vikram, and arrived at Trang late in the morning.

"It turns out that no one's ever flown a bloody helicopter into Lhakrinor," Mallory said, "which Vikram didn't tell me until we were in the air and squeaking over some frightening passes. They would never have tried it unless it was absolutely necessary and the weather was good."

Trowbridge was having trouble absorbing all this. "Where's Vikram now?"

"Up in the valley, with most of the Gurkhas. I'll go up tomorrow myself if it's safe—I'm dying to see this *chorten* Norbu said you'd found."

"What about Norbu and Nima?"

"Norbu's in Trang being worked on by a Gurkha medic—I guess you know he took a bullet in the shoulder. Nima stayed until she knew you were out of danger, then went off with some extraordinary-looking holy woman toward Narling. Who is she, by the way? She wasn't with you last spring."

"She was. The only female porter."

"That was her? The filthy one? I must be blind. Hang on, I think that soup ought to be about finished. You need some kind of nourishment before you drop off again."

Mallory disappeared. The lama had come into the room a few moments before. From what must have been an otherwise unintelligible babble he'd caught the word "*chorten*," and was looking at Trowbridge intently.

Trowbridge fumbled at his shirt pocket with bandaged fingers. The lama, seeing what he was about, hobbled over, unbuttoned the pocket and pulled out the bit of parchment. He turned eagerly to where a shaft of light illuminated the room and stood scrutinizing it for a long moment. Then he turned it over and examined the other side. Finally he looked at Trowbridge.

"This is all?"

"There is more, lama. But it is all in the same condition."

"All destroyed?"

"I'm afraid so."

The lama was silent a moment. Then he looked upward, at the place where the bright column of sunlight entered the room, suddenly overcome by emotion. Tears streamed lightly down his face.

"No more desire for that thing!" he cried fervently. "If this *gyami* were alive, I would thank him! I have been released from the slavery of my desire for the *gter-ma*."

He took a deep breath. "And the *chorten*?"

"The great master is mummified within the *chorten*. But it has been open to the weather since last summer. His body will not last long."

The lama nodded slowly. "All things are impermanent. Did not the Buddha say that Buddhism itself must be left behind on the way to enlightenment?"

He examined the piece of parchment once more, then tucked it away carefully inside his robes.

Mallory reappeared with a bowl of soup, which Trowbridge drank, feeling weariness overcome him. As he slipped into sleep he heard the faint clacking of a helicopter from across the valley, and wondered why Nima had gone to Narling.

49

"Why didn't she come herself?" he asked, feeling disappointed, wounded, and more than a little angry at the witch. He sat in the sun on a stone porch outside the monastery at Trang. His feet were still bandaged; he needed help from Dorje or Mallory when he walked.

"She was not ready. But she wanted to be sure you were well."

"No other message?"

"No."

"Does she know that the last helicopter goes out in two days? And that I have to be on it because winter's coming and I'm not fit to walk?"

She made no reply, looking at him with something close to disapproval.

"Norbu said she wasn't badly hurt," he went on. "Does she plan to spend the entire winter here?"

The witch remained silent, allowing him to consider the bitter tone in his voice, then said, "I do not think she has decided. Forget about yourself for a moment, and remember that she spent an entire day in this man's company, fully believing she would be raped and then killed. There are wounds which heal more slowly than rope burns and bruises."

He felt taken aback, and more than a little ashamed. Watching him, the witch's face softened slightly.

"I understand what you are feeling," she said. "But she will have to come to her own decision."

"Will you take her a note?"

The witch dipped her head slightly in assent. Trowbridge, with fingers that were still painful and clumsy, found his pen, turned to the back of his notebook, and began writing. He told her that he had spoken with Vikram, and that the park would have the full support of the Nepali government. That he had told Vikram who she was—not as a breach of trust, but to help her decide what to do next. According to Vikram, there would be no problem receiving her pension. All she had to do was to return to Kathmandu—in secret, if she liked—and claim it. Additionally, he could help arrange for a fairly rapid divorce.

He stopped a moment, reread what he had written, and continued. He told her he knew she'd been through a great deal—that the idea of returning to Kathmandu so suddenly must be overwhelming—but that he wanted her at least to think about coming back with him on the helicopter. Nothing more than that for now, though he hoped she would also think about coming to New York to work on the funding, then returning to Lhakrinor next spring to help put in motion the project they'd started together.

He stopped again, uncomfortably aware that his handwriting—because of his damaged fingers—looked childlike and clumsy, and that what he had written sounded more like a business proposition than a love letter. Somehow, however, he was incapable of writing: "Nima, I love you, I want you, come with me."

There was nothing more to be done. He folded the letter and handed it to the witch.

She took it, looked into his eyes for a moment, then turned and left.

One of the Gurkhas slung Trowbridge's pack, and a canvas bag containing notebooks and samples, up into the open side of the helicopter. Another soldier secured these things against a wall. Trowbridge boosted himself, with a wince, up into the open hatch, then turned and sat, feet dangling, looking out across the valley at Torma Mountain. A few minutes later Norbu and Pema walked up to the helicopter.

"I'll miss you," Trowbridge said, gripping Norbu's hand. "And I'm jealous you'll be spending the winter."

"It is cold here in the winter," Norbu said reflectively. "But it is also very peaceful, and beautiful."

"Where will you live?"

"In the house outside Jaramar," Pema volunteered.

Norbu looked at her in some amusement, then looked at Trowbridge and shrugged. "She is right. It is a good house."

"Say good-bye to Jigme for me," Trowbridge said.

Norbu nodded, touched his arm, and said, "We will see you in the spring." Then he and Pema turned and walked away.

Vikram, who'd been supervising the loading, came and stood beside Trowbridge. "Many people in Kathmandu believe they live in the center of the universe," he said conversationally, gesturing at the low cluster of buildings that made up Trang. "They forget that Nepal is a nation of villages. Did you know that more than ninety percent of our people live in villages of five hundred inhabitants or less? After the little adventure in which we have been involved, I think Kathmandu will be shocked into paying more attention to places like Lhakrinor."

Vikram paused. "We have spoken a good deal these last days, Mr. Trowbridge, but I'm not sure I ever formally thanked you. You played an instrumental part in maintaining the independence of my country."

Recognizing Trowbridge's discomfort at this pronouncement, he added, "I suppose you realize that the real difficulties with your park lie ahead? That your true challenge will be to persuade the people of Lhakrinor toward a different way of life?"

Trowbridge nodded. "I may not be such a popular figure here in a year or two. Certainly not with everyone."

"Ah, well, popularity is not the most important thing."

One of the pilots came aft from the cockpit and asked Vikram how soon they would leave.

"Ten minutes," Vikram said. He scanned the compound, gave brisk orders to the remaining Gurkha soldiers, then boosted himself up beside Trowbridge and stepped into the cockpit.

Mallory was striding toward the helicopter, looking pleased with himself. "Extraordinary man, our friend the lama," he said, swinging his small canvas backpack up through the door. "He lent me a couple of manuscripts, which I promised to send back with you next year."

He peered into the interior of the helicopter. "Nima's not coming?"

"Doesn't look like it."

"She's a mysterious one. Why the disguise last spring, do you suppose? She looks like she could be from one of the better Newar families."

"One of the twelve Kathmandu *bahas,* to be exact."

Mallory whistled softly. "One of the *bahas*! Most young Newar girls from the *baha* families never leave Kathmandu, much less—"

He stopped and looked open-mouthed at Trowbridge. "Good lord, she isn't—"

"She is."

There was a lengthy silence.

"Oh my," Mallory said finally.

Trowbridge found himself laughing. "I've never seen you at a loss for words."

"Trowbridge, this is fascinating! If she shows up after all do you think I could interview her? Good lord, I could probably get into the *Times*!"

"Mallory!"

Mallory eyed Trowbridge closely. "You're not just concerned about a porter, are you."

"No."

"Gracious," Mallory said, shaking his head. "I *have* been bloody blind."

He patted Trowbridge awkwardly on the shoulder, then swung up into the helicopter and went to find a place on one of the metal seats.

The last of the Gurkha soldiers climbed in after him, carrying a clipboard, as the engines started up with a powerful whine. Trowbridge looked across the valley to where Torma Mountain dominated the skyline. It was hard to imagine that he'd been up there less than a week ago, standing close to death on a frozen ledge. The river sparkled like mercury in the valley bottom, and there were tiny shapes, bharal, drifting across one of the higher slopes. He was overcome suddenly with a tremendous sadness, and filled with doubts about landing, in a matter of hours, back in civilization.

Dorje came trotting across the monastery courtyard. The helicopter rotors were beginning to turn, and to kick up dust. Dorje jumped up next to Trowbridge, shielding his eyes.

"Did Nima come?"

Trowbridge shook his head.

"I will miss her," Dorje said simply, and moved inside. Vikram came aft from the cockpit and crouched beside Trowbridge in the open cargo door.

"We'd better close this," he said.

"If it's all right with you, I'd like to sit here for the first few minutes. We can close it up before we get to the passes."

Vikram agreed, telling him to hold on to the canvas webbing, and disappeared forward. The blades above their heads began turning faster, in a high roar; dust filled his eyes, and he blinked to clear his vision. The helicopter began to lift off the ground, and he finally believed that she wasn't coming. He wondered if she would still be here when he returned in the spring from New York—and if there would be anything left between them.

It won't work, he told himself. It didn't work.

The helicopter continued to rise, pivoting to the west. He looked out at the fierce sweep of mountains, ranged against a brilliant blue sky. Faintly, above the roar, he heard yelling from the cockpit. It sounded like Vikram's voice. The helicopter stopped lifting, seemed to hesitate, then settled slowly back down to the ground before the monastery.

Trowbridge looked to the north, and saw movement. A slender figure, carrying a pack, walking down the trail from Narling.

Mallory appeared at his shoulder.

"Is it her?"

"Yes," he said. "It's her."